The Ha'penny Steps

Part 2: Nancy's Story

By CR Spencer

Part 2 of the Ha'penny Steps Trilogy

Copyright notice.

This book remains the copyright of the author, CR Spencer. You may not republish or use the material contained therein for any purposes without the express permission of the author.
    July 2024

First Published August 2024

This edition November 2024

Prologue Part 1
December 1937
London
Nancy Keeling

It was late. Peter Porteous sat in a window seat of the small café on the corner of Wardour Street and Brewer Street in Soho. He was sipping a cup of lukewarm tea. His chest was bothering him; he wasn't sure if he was going to get a full-on asthma attack. He had been visiting Jimmy Ryan in Holborn, who had been trying to persuade him to take some illicit goods back up to Kensal Town. These goods had apparently fallen off the back of a lorry in docklands...

Porteous was not entirely convinced that the good residents of Kensal Town would be that interested in men's shirts, socks and trousers...Now, if Ryan was offering good-quality hosiery or lingerie, that would be an entirely different kettle of fish...Porteous was very hesitant but Dennis Elphicke, the man who controlled all the stolen and black market goods in East London, wanted a return on the clothing and Ryan and Porteous would just have to get on with it, wouldn't they?

He looked out at the garishly lit street. The pavements were busy with couples exiting from some show or single men seeking out female company, if they were lucky. Every ten yards or so, on Brewer Street, a lady stood offering her wares with impunity. The so-called King of Soho, Charlie Maitland, had the franchise and with it came the Metropolitan Police, at a suitable price, of course.

Porteous looked at the row of ladies. Some were barely out of their teenage years. Some were on the wrong side of forty, but they all had one thing in common, the desire to earn quick money, despite the drawbacks.

Porteous looked for the minders. He could see them standing in shop doorways sucking on cheap tobacco and looking very furtive. A punter would be given the once-over as he negotiated with his chosen lady. The female would look over as she pointed out her keeper. This let the client know that there would be consequences if there were any funny business. Porteous smiled to himself. There were several ladies of the night in Kensal Town who were good customers of his.

Some of these females came up to the West End to ply their trade. Some of them worked out of King's Cross, or the back of Paddington Station. His good friend, Edith Bell, the landlady of the White Horse Public House on Kensal Road, was not really a prostitute. It was just something she did from time to time when the takings in the pub were a little low. Porteous smiled at the thought. Edith could certainly handle herself when requested. Although the licence was in her husband's name, he hadn't been seen in Kensal Town for a number of years. Edith had a way of persuading her friendly magistrate to renew the licence; the rooms at the back of the courthouse were secluded enough for that purpose...

He sipped his tea and stared at the humanity spread out in front of him. He picked up the evening paper. The front page was full of doom and gloom about the impending chaos in Europe. Britain and France had signed away the Sudetenland to Hitler and his Germans. There were grumblings about the amount of appeasement being lavished on the dictator. He flicked over the pages and glanced at the stories. One in particular caught his attention, that of increasing shortages in the shops. Porteous raised his eyebrows. Shortages meant an upturn in trade for him and Jimmy Ryan... He smiled...

He was startled when the door burst open. He looked up to see a dark-haired female in her early twenties standing still and breathing heavily as though she had been running. A voice cried out from behind the counter,

"Oi! I don't want no trouble in 'ere. Do yer 'ear me?"

The female looked over at the proprietress and nodded, "It's okay; just a little misunderstanding, that's all."

"Well, take yer misunderstanding and bugger off..."

Porteous could see a commotion outside. One of the minders had crossed the street and was engaged in a conversation with one of the working girls; she pointed a finger at the café.

Porteous raised his eyebrows and pushed out the chair opposite him,

"You'd better sit down." He looked at the café proprietress, "Two more teas, Mable, please."

Mable sighed, "It's on you, Porteous. If there's any damage, you're payin' fer it..."

Porteous looked up at the young woman, "Sit down and take off your coat, quickly. What's your name?"

The female sat down, pulling off her coat, "Nancy, Nancy Keeling."

Porteous smiled, "Well, Nancy Keeling, you've been sat here with me for the last hour. Isn't that right, Mable?"

The proprietress swore loudly as she poured two more teas and brought them over to the table. Several other occupants looked up from their refreshments and then looked down...

The door opened noisily. Porteous looked up to see one of Charlie Maitland's minders.

Mable called out, "If yer comin' in, then shut the bloody door. Otherwise, bugger off. Yer disturbing me customers."

The minder sneered at the woman, "Shut up, Mable. Mind yer Ps and Qs. Did you see a tart come in here? She was wearin' a beige coat?"

Porteous pushed the coat further under the table.

Mable raised her voice, "Do yer see any tarts in ere? This is a respectable establishment. Ah pays me dues to Charlie like everybody else, so clear off!"

The minder walked slowly over to the counter, "A tom was plying her trade in Old Compton Street. She's not one of ours. If you see her, tell her she's gonna have her pretty little face smashed in."

He slapped his hand on the glass counter making the whole unit shake and wagged his finger in her face. "If I find she's been in 'ere, you're in deep shit."

Mable rolled her eyes, "Yeah, and if you or one of your thugs lays a hand on me or me place, Charlie will chop yer fingers off..."

The thug snorted and blew the proprietress a kiss. She swore loudly at him. As he turned, his eyes landed on Porteous and Nancy Keeling. He looked at the couple. He walked slowly up to the table. Porteous sipped at his tea. Nancy stared straight ahead...

The thug leaned into Porteous, "What are you doin' up here, Porteous?"

Porteous blew away some steam from the hot tea, "Just a bit of business, that's all."

The thug nodded his head at Nancy, "Who's yer lady friend?"

Porteous put down his cup, "That's my cousin, Nancy. I was showing her the sights."

The thug stared at Nancy, "You wasn't just in Old Compton Street, was yer?"

Nancy Keeling smiled sweetly, "No, I've been with Porteous all day. We may have walked down Old Compton Street, but that was hours ago."

The thug straightened up and looked at Porteous, "You'd better watch yerself, Porteous. Charlie's bin asking questions about yer business. If I were you, I'd stick to that shithole yer call Kensal Town. You aint grand enough to play with the big boys."

Porteous stared at him, "Be sure to give Charlie my best regards."

The door opened. A rough voice called out, "Mifty; she's been seen at the other end of Wardour Street..."

Michael 'Mifty' Mitchell smirked, at Porteous, "I'll catch up with you soon enough, Porteous and yer'll get what's comin' to you, wiv interest..."

Porteous sipped his tea and stared at the bald ex-fairground fighter.

Mifty Mitchell rushed out of the door, grabbing his mate as he pushed past.

The silenced café collectively breathed a sigh of relief.

Mable spoke loudly, "Porteous! Take yer friend out the back door, now! And yer owe me one and sixpence for the refreshments..."

Porteous gripped Nancy Keeling by the arm and pulled her up as she tried to retrieve her coat from under the table, "Come on, Nancy, let's not push our luck..."

Mable ushered them behind the counter and shoved them through a door into a rather grubby kitchen and out into a backyard. She slid across the bolts on the high gate at the end of the yard that led into a dark alley. She said,

"Follow the alley down to Berwick Street and then yer on yer own."

She looked at Porteous, "Yer a pain in the arse, Porteous. Take yer lady friend and put her right." She smiled at him as she closed the gate and slid the bolts back into place.

Porteous grabbed Nancy Keeling and hurried her along the alley that was littered with evidence of recent sexual activity and out into the throng in Berwick Street. He felt her pull him back.

"It's all right, Porteous, I'll find my own way home now."

"Look behind you, Nancy. Look over the road. Maitland's boys are everywhere." He paused and then asked, "Where's home? At least I can see you there."

"I'm staying in a hostel near Russell Square."

Porteous shrugged his shoulders, "Okay, let's go there, then."

"I'm perfectly capable of finding my own way, thank you."

She pulled away from him as he shrugged his shoulders.

He smiled at her, "Look, Nancy, I mean you no harm, but if you think you can just come down to Soho and stand on a street corner without Charlie Maitland's permission, you don't understand how things work here."

Nancy Keeling looked down, embarrassed.

Porteous continued, "Mifty Mitchell will give you a right slap when he catches up with you and if you encroach on his territory again, he will catch up with you."

Nancy pouted, "I'm just trying to earn a few bob to send home to my mum and sister, that's all."

She began to leave.

He said, "There are lots of easier ways of doing it."

She shrugged her shoulders, "What's it to do with you, anyway?"

"Absolutely nothing, Nancy...take care..." He began to walk away.

Nancy looked around her into the thronging crowds. She had no idea who was who. Men stared at her; one man licked his lips as he approached her. Her heart began to beat quickly. A woman pushed past her, muttering audibly,

"Out of the way, whore..."

A female out on her own at this time of night in Soho could only be one kind of woman...

Porteous was about ten yards away from her. She ran quickly. He turned as he felt her arm in his. He allowed himself a little smirk...

She gushed breathlessly, "Porteous, you can walk me home, if you like."

He nodded as he stared ahead. They began to chat as they walked.

"What are you doing here, Nancy?" he asked, more in hope than expectation

She answered quietly, "I told you; trying to earn some quick money to send home to my mum and sister."

Porteous looked at her as they reached a very crowded Oxford Street.

"As I said, there are plenty of ways to earn money; you don't have to do what you are trying to do."

She looked down and clutched at him even more tightly, "My mum's in trouble."

"What kind of trouble?"

"Money; what other kind can there be? If I don't get her some money by the end of the week, she's going to be evicted."

Porteous raised his eyebrows, "How much?"

"Over ten pounds."

"That's a lot of money, Nancy."

She stared ahead, "I know..."

They were almost at Tottenham Court Road. He pointed at the Crown Public House, "There's just enough time to get a drink, and you can tell me all about it."

She didn't object as he led her over the road. The public bar was crowded and very smoky. He led her into a quieter area where the beer was a penny dearer. He pushed past several servicemen still in their army uniforms, clearly enjoying a night out before King and country called upon them. A Royal Air Force sergeant leered at her; she flushed up.

He plonked two gin and tonics on the little table; she began to talk.

They were ushered out of the pub just after eleven-fifteen. By this time he had learned all he needed to know about Nancy Keeling, and that she certainly had no idea of what life was like as a working girl in central London.

They stood outside the imposing four-storey house on Bedford Way, just along from the British Museum. The gin had loosened her tongue.

He said, "Look, if you are determined to follow your chosen line of work, you are going to need help. There are a couple of girls where I live who work for Charlie Maitland. It might be better if you speak with them first instead of freelancing on the streets of Soho."

She nodded, "You might be right." She stared up at the building. "I'd better leave you here. I'm supposed to be home by midnight before they lock the door."

She reached up and pecked him on the cheek, "Thanks, Porteous. How do I contact you?"

"The White Horse on Kensal Road. Look up the telephone number and ask for the landlady, Edith Bell. She knows a little of your business. She will get a message to me." He looked at the tall, extremely good-looking woman.

"In the meantime, keep off the streets. There's plenty of other work to be had..."

She smiled at him and went up the stone steps. When she reached the top, she turned but, Porteous had already disappeared into the night.

The night bell sounded as she opened the heavy wooden door. She stood in the dimly lit grand entrance hall that had somehow lost its charm over the years. The mosaic floor tiles were cracked and showing signs of a hasty repair. A wooden booth with a glass window had been created to the right. A rather stern-looking woman with reading glasses perched on the end of her nose glared at her.

The woman rapped on the glass. Nancy looked up. The woman beckoned her over.

"Miss Keeling, you've been here for four days. You know the rules. Have you managed to secure employment yet?"

Nancy looked down, "Not yet Miss Ledston, but I've had a number of interviews. I'm just waiting to be contacted." She paused, "Have there been any messages for me?"

Ledston cleared her throat and turned to a numbered board behind her with little slots. "You are in 501; there's nothing for you. Your rent is due on Friday. Do you have the means to pay it?"

Nancy nodded, "I'm sure I'll have something sorted by the end of the week."

Ledston summoned her even closer, "I have to tell you that one of the other residents saw you on Old Compton Street; was that you?"

Nancy swallowed nervously, "It-it's possible, Miss. I met my cousin, and we walked all over the West End."

"Cousin? You didn't say you had a cousin living in London."

"Yes-yes. He lives in a place called Kensal Town over in West London."

Miss Ledston narrowed her eyes, "I hope you haven't been working on the streets, Miss Keeling. The trustees of this hostel take a very dim view of such behaviour. This establishment is for respectable working ladies seeking to establish themselves in London, and not a sleeping house for common prostitutes. Do you understand?"

Nancy nodded and looked down, "Of course, Miss Ledston. I'll have employment in the next few days."

Ledston opened the wooden door to her little cubicle rattling a bunch of keys, "Now, if you'll excuse me, Miss Keeling, it's time I locked the doors. Good night..."

Nancy Keeling trudged wearily up five flights of stairs. Her room, for what it was, was situated at the end of a dimly lit corridor. She inserted a key into the old lock and opened the door. She immediately felt the cold, with the heating having been turned off a few hours earlier. She closed the door behind her and slid across the bolt. The room was barely ten feet by six. A single bed was on one wall, with a sink and a battered wardrobe on the other. The bed linen was threadbare. She had taken to throwing her only coat over the bed to keep warm.

The toilet was back down the corridor. If the ladies wanted a bath, they had to seek a key from whoever was on duty in the entrance hall. Residents needed to purchase a token to insert into the slot meter to acquire hot water. Rooms had a supply of lukewarm water that was sufficient for guests to give themselves an all-over wash standing in a basin. For the privilege of residing in this establishment, Nancy paid nineteen shillings and six pence a week.

Nancy threw off her coat and sat on the end of her bed. She could hear two of the girls chatting in the room next door through the thinly-partitioned walls. Her neighbours hadn't spoken to her since she had moved in the previous weekend, not that she was bothered anyway. Her local vicar in Mulbarton on the outskirts of Norwich had arranged the accommodation for her.

She kicked off her shoes. Porteous was nice and didn't seem to want to take advantage of her, but that was for another day...

She woke about eight the next morning. Noise from the other residents would have wakened the dead as they busied themselves for a day in their 'regular' jobs. Nancy pulled the pillow over her head...

The cafeteria was virtually empty by the time she got down there. Two assistants were making desultory efforts to clean up. She stood over the tea urn and poured some tea. She sat down, picked up a battered newspaper and skimmed through the advertisements for the job vacancies. There was plenty of work to be had, ranging from shop assistants to typists and even switchboard operators in the local telephone exchange. Unfortunately, none of them would give her sufficient money to stop her mother and sister being evicted by the end of the week. There was only one thing to do...She made her way to the payphone in the reception area and made the call...

Prologue Part 2
December 1937
Nancy gets a job.

The White Horse public house on Kensal Road was crowded. It was as though the impending doom and gloom in Europe was irrelevant. Christmas was rapidly approaching, so, who cared? Punters had a few bob in their pockets, so why shouldn't they enjoy a few beers with their mates? The missus was at home with the noisy kids, and they've all put in a hard day's graft in some factory, warehouse or building site. Who would begrudge them a little relaxation? A few drinks, then home to remind the wife who is the boss and all is well with the world...

Nancy Keeling opened the door and was hit by the pungent smell of stale beer and dodgy tobacco. She wrinkled up her nose. She didn't reckon much of Porteous' choice of drinking establishments. Edith Bell, the landlady, looked up from behind the counter. She caught Nancy's eye and raised her eyebrows. This lass was too good-looking to be on a street corner...

Nancy pushed her way through a group of men. She felt a hand on her backside. She stopped and glared at the culprit. She felt Edith's arm in hers as the landlady raised her voice.

"Oi! Keep your feckin' hands to yourself and leave the lady alone. Finish your drink and then piss off."

The man laughed at Edith. He didn't see the swinging hand that caught him flush on the side of his face. He reeled back in surprise as the stinging slap reddened his skin. He felt a large pair of arms pin him.

The pub went quiet. "Sling him out, Tommy, and give him a little kicking. He's new to the area and doesn't know the rules yet."

Edith leaned into the man, "If you want to drink in here, you behave yourself, okay?"

The man nodded as he felt himself being lifted off his feet and dragged back out through the door.

Tommy gave the errant punter a few slaps and sent him on his way...

Edith smiled at Nancy, "Sorry about that, love. We normally don't get much trouble in here."

She pulled Nancy to the bar, "What are you drinking?"

Nancy smiled, "Gin and tonic, please," she paused and then asked, "Are you Edith Bell?"

"Who's asking?"

"Nancy Keeling. Porteous told me to come here and ask for him."

Edith smiled and nodded at one of the bar staff. She turned to Nancy, "Porteous will be in soon. Tommy will let him know you are here. He lives just around the corner."

Porteous made his way to the White Horse. He lived on Bosworth Road, almost opposite the church. His flat on the top floor suited his needs. The tenants in the converted house kept themselves to themselves. He liked it that way. He could carry on his business without prying eyes. Even the landlord's appointed gatekeeper, Martha Cunningham, kept out of his affairs. To keep her sweet, he would sometimes drop her the odd pair of nylons or a slightly suspect bottle of whisky.

He pushed open the door to the public house and almost immediately, he felt his chest tighten with the aroma of cigarette smoke. It stung his eyes. He acknowledged the nods of a few acquaintances as he made his way to the bar.

Edith Bell slapped a glass in front of him; he smiled at Nancy Keeling. She looked at him nervously. He sipped at the lukewarm beer.

Edith said, "Take her upstairs, Porteous, it's quieter there." She lifted a section of the bar counter and ushered them through.

They sat in Edith Bell's first floor living room. Nancy crossed her long legs. Porteous thought she was a good-looking woman; too good for her chosen occupation.

He spoke quietly; one could hear the hum of the busy bar downstairs.

"Okay, Nancy, how can I help you?"

She shrugged her shoulders, "I'm in desperate need of money."

He nodded, "Yeah, ten pounds to stave off your mother's eviction."

He paused and took in this rather beautiful twenty-two-year old. She was tall; he guessed at five feet ten inches or thereabouts. In heels, she could be well over six feet. Her long hair was a golden auburn with just a hint of curls at the end. She was tastefully made up and well presented in a knee-length skirt, white blouse and a tan coat. He noticed she was bare-legged. This was not to be advised in the week before Christmas…He could rectify that, as there were literally dozens of good quality nylons back in his flat.

A tear appeared in her eye. "Look, it's my mum. She's no good at picking her fellows. She threw the last one out after he started messing with my sister Charlotte. The problem is he took all her money with him."

Porteous raised his eyebrows and sipped his beer, "Hmm, I can see that's a problem. How old is Charlotte?"

"She's fifteen and doing well in school. I want her to have the chances I didn't have, but grammar schools don't come cheap in

Norwich. The uniform alone is over ten pounds a year, and then there's the rent, the electric light, coal and food."

Porteous nodded, "Times are not good, especially with war a distinct possibility. Is your mum not working?"

Nancy looked down, "She's taken to the drink. No employer in the area will touch her."

"So Charlotte looks after her?"

Nancy sighed, "There are many days when mum is sober, but she's not reliable. She'll have a few pennies in her pocket and go down to the local pub. There are always plenty of men happy to buy her a drink for what they can get out of her. I don't mind her doing that, but it becomes a problem when she brings them home. I managed to install locks on Charlotte's room before I left."

"So, you've come to London to seek your fortune?"

Nancy smiled, "If you put it like that, well, yes."

Porteous finished off his drink, walked over to a cabinet at the other end of the room and poured two more gin and tonics.

Nancy asked, "Won't Mrs Bell mind?"

Porteous passed her the glass; "I doubt it, seeing as I provided her with this gin in the first place." He paused, "So tell me about yourself."

She sipped at the drink and then looked at it, "This is much better than what is served downstairs."

Porteous laughed.

"There's not much to tell, really. I'm twenty-two; never had a real job, and I was pregnant at sixteen; one of my mother's men friends."

Porteous froze. She continued, "Oh, don't worry. A lady over the old blacksmith's soon sorted me out... The problem is that she kind of messed me up, and now I can't have any more children. Well, that's what they told me at the hospital. Anyway, this world is too horrible to bring up children."

"I should have gone to grammar school, but there was no money. I didn't fancy working in the fields, so I took a job in a factory. The foreman got me sacked when I wouldn't put out for him. So here I am."

"And you want to work the streets?"

She stared at Porteous, "I don't want to work the streets, but what choice do I have?" She shrugged her shoulders, "I have an asset. Anyway, I've been using it since I was fourteen to provide for my family. So what's the difference?"

Porteous was silent for a few minutes. Nancy stared at the blazing coal fire.

"I spoke to a friend who lives in West Hampstead. She works for Charlie Maitland in Soho. She says she can get you a meeting with him. You know what kind of work he expects you to do?"

She nodded, "Do I have a choice? I need to send back at least ten pounds by the weekend, otherwise we get evicted."

"If you are sure, I'll take you over to meet her tomorrow morning."

She whispered a thank-you.

He said, "Come back to my place, and I'll sort you out with a few essentials."

"Like what?"

He pointed to her bare legs, "A pair of decent stockings for a start. You can't go and see Charlie Maitland like that."

Porteous lit the gas fire in his living room. He poured some more drinks. They sat and chatted for an hour or so. Nancy was wondering what she would have to do for his help. It was late, and she fell asleep on the sofa. He placed a blanket over her and went off to bed.

He woke her just before eight the next morning. She could hear the bath running next door. He handed her a steaming cup of tea.

"Go next door and have a bath; I just put another sixpence in the meter. There's a robe behind the door. After you have finished, go into the bedroom, where I've laid out some clothes for you. Choose whatever you need whilst I make some breakfast."

Porteous busied himself in the kitchen. He fried up some eggs, bacon and mushrooms. Nancy appeared at the door wrapped in the thick, soft robe with a towel around her head like a turban.

She asked, "Where did all those ladies clothes come from?"

He shrugged his shoulders, "I'm a trader. I get what I can and sell it on."

She turned away, "I'll just help myself to a pair of stockings, if that is alright?"

He nodded, "Sure; whatever you want."

She dressed after breakfast, leaving the bedroom door open. Porteous glanced at this rather attractive lady as she sat on the bed and rolled the hosiery up her legs. She smiled at him; "I've taken some lingerie as well, if that's okay?"

She stood in front of a full-length mirror, "Are the seams straight, Porteous?"

He nodded, reached into his pocket and produced a plain brown envelope.

"Look Nancy. There's ten pounds here."

Her eyes opened wide, "Are you sure?"

"Yes, I know you'll pay me back. We'll send it to your mother from the post office on the way over to West Hampstead. If all goes well, you'll just need to pop back to your hostel, clear your rent, grab your things, and then you can live your life the way you want without any busybodies interfering."

She reached up to him, put her arms around his neck and hugged him tight. It was not often that a man would give something to her without demanding she repay him in some form or other. She kissed him on the cheek and whispered,

"Thank you, Porteous. You're a good man."

He patted the back of her head.

Nancy Keeling and Peter Porteous walked over to West Hampstead. The December day was cold but dry and sunny. He felt her arm in his as they walked along Harvist Road and past Queen's Park. She looked in the windows of a few shops on Kilburn High Road before they turned into Gascony Avenue and on to West End Lane. They stood at the door of the three-bed terraced house on Crediton Hill.

A dark-haired beauty with sleep all over her face opened the door; it was gone ten o'clock.

"Jesus, Porteous, I've only just gone to bed."

Porteous smiled, "And a very good morning to you, Helen."

He pushed past her; "I'll brew some tea whilst you make yourself decent. You've got a visitor, in case you haven't noticed."

Helen Shenton pulled the thin dressing gown tightly around her naked body, muttered a few choice swear words and skipped back upstairs. Porteous ushered Nancy into the kitchen.

He looked at Nancy; "I'll introduce you to Helen when she comes back down. I've known her for some time. She's one of Charlie's top girls. She doesn't work the streets any more, only call-outs and private events. I think that's where you'll end up."

Helen Shenton appeared at the door. She was still wearing the same dressing gown, but she had combed her hair and brushed her teeth. She went up to Porteous, threw her arms around him, and kissed him on the lips. "Did you bring me anything?" Her soft voice purred like a kitten. She was used to getting her own way with men.

Porteous pushed her off, "You still owe me for three pairs. They don't grow on trees, you know."

She feigned a pout, "Have you got any silk?"

Nancy looked on at this interaction. She was a little jealous...

He replied, "I might have when all your debts have been cleared..."

He poured the tea and motioned Helen to sit down, "Helen, this is Nancy."

Helen Shenton smiled at Nancy; she took her hand, "Hmm, you were right, Porteous, she is indeed a beauty."

Nancy looked down and blushed.

"Charlie will snap you up for his more discerning clients."

Porteous sipped his tea and sat back whilst the two of them chatted to each other. After about half an hour, he stood up to leave.

Nancy reached out, "Wait, Porteous."

He shook his head, "I have to go, Nancy. Helen will take care of you."

Nancy looked anxious, "I can't stay in the hostel."

Helen Shenton reached out, "You can stay here. My previous housemate fell in love with a punter and moved out."

Nancy looked at Porteous; he nodded, "I knew that you could stay here before we came...I'll leave you to it."

He turned to Helen Shenton, "What time are you seeing Charlie?"

"After four. I'll sort out Nancy with some decent clothes, and then we'll go over to the hotel and square that off. She'll be fine with me as long as she pays her share of the rent each week."

Nancy nodded vigorously. Porteous left them to it...

Carmelo Messina, otherwise known as Charlie Maitland, worked out of a cramped office above a seedy club on Greek Street in Soho. He and his four brothers had followed their father into the brothel and prostitution business when they arrived in London from their home in Malta. Although they mainly imported women from France, Belgium and Spain, there were a fair number of local British girls in the stable. Maitland and his brothers controlled prostitution across this part of Central London. They operated with impunity, as they had many of Scotland Yard's finest officers on their payroll.

By 1937, Charlie Maitland couldn't get enough women to satisfy the demands of pre-war Britain as it geared itself up for the expected coming conflict. There were always servicemen looking for a quick knee-trembler down some dark alley behind one of his clubs. In addition, Maitland and his brothers had cornered the market with providing ladies to private establishments for the rich and famous, not forgetting the infamous Georgian house in Maida Vale.

Maitland sat behind an oversized desk, smoking a fat cigar and reading a newspaper. His brother, Alfredo, otherwise known as Alfred Martin, sat on a worn-out leather sofa sipping a large whisky and fiddling with one of the cocktail waitresses from downstairs.

Nancy Keeling and Helen Shenton knocked on the door. Alfred Martin extracted his hand from under the hapless waitress' skirt. He pushed her up, rapped her on the backside, tucked a ten shilling note in the waistband of her outfit and told her to bugger off. She winked at Nancy as she squeezed past her in the narrow doorway, pushing a pair of ample breasts in her face. Nancy blushed.

The two women stood in front of the desk. Charlie Maitland put down his newspaper and smiled,

"Who have you brought us, Helen?"

"Charlie, this is Nancy. She's just arrived in London."

He looked her up and down. Helen Shenton had dressed Nancy well in a fitted, low-cut dark blue dress with a hem that was just above her knees. She was wearing a pair of black court shoes that raised her height even more. She was already tall enough for a female. Her hair was combed out nicely and held on one side of her head by a gold coloured clip.

Alfredo stood up, licking his lips. He spoke to his brother in Maltese. Maitland nodded.

He put his hands together and sat back on his chair.

"Right, Miss Nancy, you'll do. You're on the payroll from now. Have you done this work before?"

"Yes," she lied.

"Good, good. Then you know how it works. You'll do call-outs and parties, and occasionally on the streets if business is a bit slack. You hand over fifty per cent of what you make. If you hide anything, you'll get a slap from your minder, understand?"

Nancy nodded. Maitland's accent was strong. She said, "Helen's told me how you operate."

"Right, then there'll be no misunderstandings, will there? Mifty will be your minder. Just do as he says and we'll all make some money. Oh, and one last thing, don't steal from your clients. I've got my reputation to maintain. If you do, you'll get more than a slap. Understand?"

Nancy nodded vigorously.

He asked, "Where are you staying?"

"With Helen."

"Good, I'll tell Mifty to pick up both of you at eight tonight. There's a party down by the Embankment; a load of coppers celebrating something or other. Right, clear off the pair of you."

With that, the two women left the office, walked down the stairs and out onto an already busy Greek Street. Helen Shenton put her arm through Nancy's,

"Told you it would be okay. His bark is worse than his bite."

They strolled back up to Tottenham Court Road. Soho was getting busy with departing office workers looking for a quick drink and those seeking a more sensory experience, before they faced the wife at home.

Nancy asked, "Who's this Mifty?"

Helen stared ahead, "Michael Mitchell; ex fairground boxer with a nose that goes with it. Short, fat and with a chrome dome. Now his bite is a lot worse than his bark. Watch out for him. He'll take your money after you've finished with a punter. Most of the call-out clients will give you a tip. Just hand over the agreed fee and shove the rest down your knickers. Mifty will feel you up, but he won't go down there."

Nancy nodded, "What's this party tonight?"

"Oh, just a load of pissed-up coppers. Most just want to touch you up. If they want a personal service, agree a price and tell Mifty. Do the business and then move on. We should make ten or twelve pounds in tips."

Nancy raised her eyebrows, "As much as that?"

They turned into Bedford Way. "Much better than standing on a street corner freezing your tits off waiting for a sweaty punter. All they're looking for is a quick tug for ten bob. Not much in that game. Leave that to the foreign girls. They've all got the clap anyway."

Helen Shenton waited whilst Nancy Keeling cleared her few belongings, paid up for the rest of the week and departed from the hostel, much to the relief of the miserable receptionist, Miss Ledston.

Nancy Keeling sat in the back of the Wolsely Hornet and stared out of the window as Michael 'Mifty' Mitchell weaved his way down through the traffic.

He looked at her in the rear-view mirror, "Do ah know yer? Ah swear I've seen yer somewhere before." His accent was as coarse as his looks.

Nancy ignored him. She couldn't be sure, but maybe he was the bruiser who had come looking for her in the café in Soho when she was rescued by Porteous...

Helen Shenton patted him on the knee, "Come on, Mifty, concentrate on your driving and leave the poor girl alone."

Mitchell cleared his throat, gave one last glance in the mirror and drove on.

It was gone three in the morning when Mitchell dropped them back to West Hampstead. Three other working girls had squashed into the vehicle. The car smelled of cheap perfume and equally cheap gin and cigarettes. These girls decamped somewhere in Kilburn. One of them was virtually sitting on Nancy's lap. As she exited the car, she ran her hands over Nancy's breasts and winked at her...

Helen and Nancy shared a bath before they retired to bed; they didn't have any more sixpences for the meter. Both of them arrived home with more than ten pounds in their purses and in other places. They were slightly tipsy...

The work wasn't too demanding; just a few tugs in a cubicle in the men's toilet and a chief inspector with wandering hands whilst she sat on his lap. Nancy thought she'd soon be able to pay off Porteous and then keep her mother and sister happy back in Norwich, but she knew this was only the start of her new life.

She lay in bed and dreamed of Peter Porteous...

Prologue Part 3
Christmas 1937
Norwich

It was Friday, Christmas Eve, and approaching five in the afternoon. Nancy Keeling wrapped the long coat tightly around her as she descended from the train at Norwich Thorpe Station. The platform was crowded with passengers hurrying to get home to see their loved ones for the short Christmas break. The air was filled with smoke and steam from the trains. Porters stood around with their trolleys, eager to snap up a customer or two before the pub demanded their presence after the last train at ten o'clock.

Nancy had dozed off in the carriage. She had sat opposite a woman who seemed to turn her nose up at her as though she knew what Nancy really was. Nancy didn't give a toss. She had fifteen pounds in her purse; enough to ensure her small family could have a decent Christmas and not worry about the rent.

She crossed over the River Wensum onto Prince of Wales Road and headed for a small parade of shops on Rose Lane. There was a queue outside the butchers; local residents hoping to get a bargain before the shop closed for the next few days. Nancy pushed her way into the shop, ignoring the complaints behind her.

Three assistants and the master butcher were trying to deal with the last minute rush. She smiled at one young lad who had little beads of sweat on his forehead underneath his round, white hat. His apron was dirty with smears of blood and other assorted remains of some dead animal or other.

He looked up at her and blushed, "Miss, you'll have to wait your turn."

Nancy waved a piece of paper at him, "I've come to collect an order."

The master butcher looked up and nodded at the young lad, who reached over and took her paper. He squinted at the writing under the yellow glow of the lights.

"Ah, Miss Keeling; one medium-sized turkey, two pounds of best sausages and a pound of best back bacon, not forgetting a tub of lard for the roast potatoes. It's ready for you wrapped up in the back."

The master butcher sauntered over, "Wait a minute, lad. Has the young lady paid?"

Nancy dropped a pound note on the glass counter, "Will that cover it?"

He smiled, "Go on, lad, look lively."

The assistant scurried off. The butcher said,

"You've only just made it, Lass. Another ten minutes and I would have sold this lot to the hungry hordes out there. I don't know why they couldn't have telephoned in an order like you did."

The young lad appeared carrying a large brown package tied up with string. It looked heavy.

The butcher slapped a few coppers on the counter, "Don't forget your change, Miss."

Nancy swept up the money and dropped it into her purse. The parcel was indeed heavy.

She lugged it back to the station and hopped into a taxi.

"Cringleford; just off the Newmarket Road, and don't be taking the piss. I know exactly where I'm going."

The driver swallowed hard and touched his hat. "Sure thing, Miss. We'll be there in ten minutes."

She tipped him a couple of coppers and struggled up the short pathway. The house was in darkness. She was about to put her key in the door when it opened. The beaming face of her younger sister appeared in the gloom. She dropped the package on the tiles in the hallway as her sister wrapped her arms around her and hugged her tight.

Nancy said, "Why is there no light?"

"The meter's empty."

Nancy rolled her eyes.

They walked into the front room. Two solitary candles were on the mantelpiece. Charlotte was trying to read by the fire. She rummaged in her purse and took out a small drawstring bag.

"Here, there's ten sixpences. Put five in the electric and five in the gas. That'll be enough for the next few days."

She looked at the blazing fire, "How are we off for coal?"

"Mum managed to get two bags yesterday on tick. He's coming back on Monday for his money."

"Where is Mum?"

She gestured to the first floor, "Upstairs sleeping it off. She hasn't got up today."

Nancy looked at her, "Don't worry. We'll manage until she comes to her senses. Now squeeze that turkey into the meat safe and put the sausages and bacon in the larder. Did you manage to get some potatoes and other vegetables from the farm down the road?"

Charlotte nodded, "I flirted with the young lad. We have to pay him next week before his dad finds out."

Nancy didn't know if she approved or not, "I'll go and see him on Boxing Day. Keep away from him, okay? I don't want you messing with any boys. How are your studies?"

Charlotte pouted, "Sister Mary says I'm doing well."

"Good, keep it that way. I'm not killing myself in London for nothing."

Charlotte fed the two meters and the lights came back on. She looked at her big sister as she blew out the candles and thought she was looking particularly pretty that evening.

"Tell me about your job?"

Nancy looked at her, "Oh it's nothing really. Just office work."

"It pays well?"

"Enough. I borrowed some money to pay the landlord. Did you go with Mum when she paid it?"

"Of course. We can't trust Mum with that kind of money when she has to walk past at least three pubs. Don't worry; I got the rent book signed. He wanted to charge a late fee, but I told him you would see him and straighten things out."

Nancy sighed; thus as it ever was...

As Charlotte made a simple evening meal, Nancy pushed open the door to her mother's bedroom; it was stale and stuffy. The room was cold.

She opened the window and switched on the bedroom light. There were complaints from under the pile of bedclothes,

"Jesus, turn off that light. It's hurting my eyes."

Nancy sat down on the bed, "It's Nancy, Mum."

Hilda Keeling emerged from under the eiderdown. She looked at her eldest daughter and smiled, "Nancy, I knew you'd come home to mama."

She reached up and began to pull Nancy to her. Nancy resisted.

"Mum, you're none too fresh. Charlotte is boiling some water for you to have a bath."

Hilda Keeling groaned and tried to bury her head, "I don't feel too well, Nancy."

"That's because you've got an almighty hangover, and you haven't drunk any water all day." She pulled the eiderdown away from her mother.

"When was the last time you changed these sheets?"

They were grubby with sweat and God knows what.

Hilda Keeling tried to cover her nakedness. She sat up, knowing that she couldn't get one over her eldest daughter when she's in that kind of mood.

"Pass me my robe."

"Please?"

"Please..."

Nancy reached behind the door and plucked a worn and very thin bathrobe. She held it for her mother who gradually climbed out of bed. Nancy was shocked at the state of her forty-something parent. She was thin, almost emaciated. Her breasts sagged forlornly from her chest. Her hair was lank and straggly. If her mother looked like her two daughters when she was younger, she certainly did not now. Her calories appeared to be coming out of a bottle rather than from a plate.

Nancy slid over a pair of battered slippers as her mother sat on the bed trying to tie the robe around her waist. She pushed her feet into the soft shoes.

The kitchen was full of steam. Charlotte was dispensing lots of hot water into the tin bath. Nancy stood over the sink and insisted that her mother brush her teeth. The two daughters poured water over their mother as she sat in the bath. Nancy washed her mother's hair. She lay back in the bath. Hilda Keeling was gradually coming back to life. She looked at her eldest daughter,

"My, Nancy, looks like London agrees with you."

Nancy shrugged. She rubbed soap into her mother's body, "It's okay. I was lucky. I found a kind man who helped me, and before you ask, he wanted nothing in return." Nancy had raised her voice.

Charlotte looked over from her preparation work with the turkey.

Hilda Keeling shrugged, "Not my business, my girl. And don't you adopt that tone with me."

Nancy placed her hand on her mother's head and pushed her down under the water. She held her there for a few seconds. Charlotte burst out laughing. Water splashed over the side of the tin bath and onto the stone floor as she emerged gasping and spluttering.

"What the..."

"Sorry, Mum, just rinsing off your hair."

Charlotte turned back to her chores, giggling.

Hilda Keeling sulked.

Nancy helped her to get dressed. She sat Hilda in front of the dressing table and carefully brushed out her hair.

"Come on, Mum, you've got to do better. Charlotte needs you."

Hilda sighed, "I know, I know. I'll try, I promise."

"Look, stay off the gin for a few weeks, and you'll soon perk up. There's plenty of food downstairs and we'll cook the turkey tonight. I topped up the gas meter. We'll have a nice day tomorrow, okay?"

An hour or so later, the women of the household stood in the kitchen, prepared all the Christmas food and laughed together. The house was warm. After dinner, they sat in the parlour in front of the blazing coal fire and listened to some modern music on the National Programme from the BBC. Charlotte was reading.

Hilda sat in the old rocking chair that had been her mother's.

"Tell me about London, Nancy."

"Nothing to tell, really. I'm living in a place called West Hampstead with a really nice girl from Hampshire. We both work for an entertainment company based in the West End. The pay is good, and we don't exactly kill ourselves."

Hilda looked at her daughter, "Entertainment? What do you mean?"

Nancy brushed it aside; "We work in the office taking bookings from clients. I'm learning to type, and I do some filing." It was only a partial lie. Helen Shenton was actually a qualified typist and she had been teaching Nancy the basics on an old Olivetti when they had some spare time.

"You get good money?"

"Enough."

"Where did you get the ten pounds from?"

Nancy glared at her mother, "I told you I borrowed it, otherwise we wouldn't be here for Christmas." Charlotte looked up from her reading.

Hilda rocked on the chair, "Tell me about your man friend; the one who helped you out."

"Oh, Porteous. He's really kind."

"Porteous? That's a funny name."

"That's what everyone says. He's a trader. He buys and sells clothes and whatever he can get his hands on."

Hilda Keeling snorted, "He's a black marketeer, you mean. Most of the stuff will be stolen. You mark my words."

Nancy turned away, "He's a good man; that's all I know."

"Did you bring any gin, Nancy? I could do with a little pick-me-up."

"Nope. There's none in the house. If you want some, you'll have to use your own money to get some from the pub."

Hilda wrung her hands, "I haven't got any money, love. Lend me ten bob."

"No, Mum. We've already had this conversation."

Hilda Keeling shook her head and turned up the radio.

Just after midnight, the daughters got their mother undressed and into bed. Charlotte had changed the sheets, so the bed was fresh. They didn't want to leave their mother downstairs in case she slipped out to the pub. There would always be a few men there willing to buy her a drink in return for a kiss and cuddle round the back of the pub. Having had an alcohol-free day and a substantial meal in her belly, Hilda Keeling was soon snoring loudly...

The two sisters shared a room but in the middle of winter they also shared one of the single beds to keep warm. There was never enough coal to light the fires in the bedrooms. Charlotte snuggled up to her big sister,

"Tell me about this nice fellow you've met. What's his name, Porter something?"

Nancy turned away, "Porteous."

Charlotte reached her arm over her sister, "Go on...tell me about him. What's he like?"

"Hmm; tall, handsome and very good-looking."

"Is he attached?"

Nancy turned around, "Now that's a question. He has a group of women around him but he seems to be just friends with them all."

Charlotte leaned up on an elbow, "Go on, then; I'm waiting."

"Well, there's the landlady, Edith. She's a bit older but she's very close to Porteous. And then there's this Polish Jew from somewhere down in Paddington whose husband is a jeweller. She's called Shira. She's great fun especially after she's had a few drinks. She often stays with Porteous after she's had a fight with her husband, and she's drunk as much gin as she can get. I can't quite work her out."

Charlotte stared into the darkness.

"And then there's this rather attractive dark haired beauty from Liverpool called Alice. She's a bit funny."

"Charlotte asked, "What do you mean, funny?"

"She got a girlfriend called Phyllis who is about to join the navy. They are both really nice, but I've got a job to understand Alice. Her Liverpool accent is very strong when she wants it to be; you should hear her speak."

Charlotte said, "You mean she's one of those?"

She felt her sister nod, "Yup; one of those. They live together in some place called Golders Green. Alice is very close with Porteous. She sometimes works with him selling stuff. Anyway, we often sit together in his flat in this strange little place called Kensal Town. You get into it by way of a bridge called the Ha'penny Steps that crosses the canal. They say it's a rough area, but I've never had any problems because I'm friendly with Porteous."

Charlotte thought for a minute, "What about your job, Nancy?"

"It's fine; easy work and well paid. Porteous helped me set it up. I share a nice, clean and dry house with a girl called Helen. We also work together."

Charlotte asked, "What exactly do you do, Nancy?"

Nancy Keeling pretended to snore...

The smell of cooking woke Charlotte early on Christmas morning. She got up and shivered in the cold. There was frost on the inside of the window. She wrapped herself in a robe and padded down the stairs.

Nancy was already in the kitchen, busy preparing food. Charlotte put her arms around her sister and hugged her tight,

"Happy Christmas, Nancy."

"And to you, too, Charlie."

Charlotte playfully punched her; "I hate it when you call me that."

"Go upstairs and wake your mother. Tell her I'm doing a fry up. That should make her get up."

There were some early morning carols on the wireless radio. It smelled and felt like Christmas. Nancy wondered what Porteous was doing. Was there someone in his bed?

The Keeling household was a happy one that Christmas. Nancy insisted they all get dressed after breakfast before they opened the few gifts she had managed to bring home. Hilda, of course, hadn't thought about such niceties.

Nancy sat cross-legged in front of the fire. She handed Charlotte a little packet. It was a hardback edition of one of Charles Dickens' novels. It was wrapped in a silk scarf that she had obtained from Porteous. Charlotte squealed with delight and wore the scarf all day.

Hilda carefully opened her present. There were three pairs of stockings, one of which was silk. The cellophane packets were wrapped in a lovely deep blue blouse. Hilda hugged her daughter. There was nothing for Nancy.

They held hands and said a prayer before Hilda Keeling insisted upon carving the turkey as she was head of the household.

Boxing Day passed quietly. Hilda Keeling didn't have any man callers, which was just as well as they would have gotten short shrift from Nancy. Hilda, having now completely recovered from her drinking binge, stripped the turkey and made a pie. The bones were simmering in a large pot. There would be some nice soup for starters that evening.

On the Monday, despite it being a public holiday, Nancy got her mother up early. They had an appointment with the landlord, who was not one to waste a day on frivolities.

Hilda looked more like her old self. Some colour had come back into her cheeks. Her skin had lost its pale and waxy hue. Nancy had insisted that she dress correctly, and she actually looked quite smart and presentable, although her hair needed a trim, but Nancy pinned it up nicely.

The office of Hodges and Sons, Property Developers and Managers, was on Richmond Hill in the centre of Norwich. The town was quiet. Only a few shops had bothered to open, it being a holiday.

The bell above the doorway to the gloomy office sounded, as Nancy pushed her mother through the entrance. The little glass booth where tenants came to pay their rent was closed. Albert Hodges shuffled into the room from a doorway behind the old oak counter. His pin-striped three-piece suit had seen better days.

He cleared his throat, "Ah, Mrs Keeling. I'm so glad you could make our appointment."

Hilda Keeling shrank back. Nancy pushed in front of her,

"We've come to sort out all the arrears, Mr Hodges, and to agree a new payment plan."

He raised his eyebrows, "Hmm, it's a bit late for that..."

He reached underneath the counter and extracted a very old and heavy leather-bound ledger. It contained records from all his tenants going back to the turn of the century, when his father had come into some money and started the business. Now, in 1937, he had nearly sixty properties on his books and he was always looking for more. He had even started acquiring land in order to build new houses.

The one thing about Albert Hodges is that he knew every single one of his properties and who lived there. He didn't need to ask the Keelings where they lived.

Nancy slapped the rent book on the counter, just in case Hodges had any thoughts of 'making an error.'

He ran his finger down the ledger. And stopped at their address. He tapped the ledger with his finger and made a pretence of whistling some tune or other.

"Ah, I see that ten pounds was paid last week."

Nancy spoke up, "That's what it says on the rent book."

He peered over his horn-rimmed spectacles and thought that this young lady was indeed quite fetching. His mind went instinctively to his rather large and overbearing wife, which is why he spent an inordinate amount of time in his office...

He took out a piece of paper and began writing some figures. He made a show of adding up the numbers, "That means you are still three pounds, four shillings and sixpence in arrears including late fees, of course."

Nancy slowly dug into her purse and extracted some money, "I tell you what, Mr Hodges, let's call it an even three pounds, and we are all good?"

"Err, well, I'm not sure. You see, your mother signed a contract agreeing to late fees."

Nancy sighed, "Is that also the contract that you countersigned?"

He looked up, "Well, yes, of course."

She reached again into her bag and took out a folded piece of paper, "Would this be the document?"

She opened it up and thrust it in his face.

He quickly glanced at it, recognising one of his identical agreements.

"Well, yes, of course," he repeated.

"Good, then let's look at clause six. You know, the one in small print at the bottom of the page. The bit about you maintaining the property to a reasonable standard."

Hodges cleared his throat again. Spending too much money on basic repairs ate into the profit margins.

Nancy rattled off a long list of defects that she personally had reported to this office, ranging from loose roof tiles, sticking sash windows and a warped rear door to the toilet in the yard.

He interrupted her, "Ah, yes. I'm afraid there's been a delay in the maintenance department. These items will be dealt with as soon as possible, Miss Keeling."

Nancy pushed over the three pound notes, "Up to you, Mr Hodges, three pounds is all it is until you make good the repairs."

He looked at the money and then at Nancy. He sighed. It wasn't worth getting into a fight over four shillings and sixpence.

"Oh, very well. I'll make an exception this time." He moved over to the glass booth, took out his keys and opened the door, "Please come over to the paying in window and I'll take the payment.

Nancy rolled her eyes at this little pantomime. She stood there whilst he carefully entered the amount in the ledger, and then did the same on the rent book.

Nancy tucked the little book back into her bag, she asked,

"Mr Hodges, would it be alright with you if I sent you the rent by postal order?"

He smiled at her, "Of course. Just send it to this office. I'll tell the clerks to expect it in your name."

Nancy smiled at him, "How about I pay the next month up front now and then every month from then on?"

He rubbed his hands, "That would be acceptable to Hodges and Sons."

She placed some more money on the counter; "The rent is twelve shillings and sixpence a week, so for four weeks it's two pounds and ten shillings, agreed?"

She could hear her mother whispering in her ear.

Hodges shuffled back to the little glass booth and went through the same performance. Nancy made a thing of inspecting the rent book...

He made a little bow, "Thank you, Miss Keeling, I'll make sure the repairs are undertaken as soon as possible."

She pulled her mother to the door and then turned around, "Mr Hodges, I understand you are always looking for cleaners for your boarding houses?"

He sighed, "Yes, no one wants to do this work today."

"My mother's looking for a job."

Hilda Keeling pulled at her daughter's sleeve and hissed, "I don't want a job."

Nancy glared at her, "Oh yes you do, mum. I can't keep supporting you and your gin habit…"

Hilda flushed up.

Hodges spoke up, "Five mornings a week, seven till noon. One pound seventeen shillings and sixpence minus deductions."

"Good, she'll take it."

Hodges smiled; he rather liked this feisty young girl. He addressed Hilda,

"Seven sharp at the Pinkerton on Bar Street. Mrs Chatham will be expecting you. Oh, we have a strict rule about no alcohol on the premises. Is that acceptable?"

"Perfectly, Mr Hodges…"

Nancy pulled her mother out on to the street. Her mother's rage was plain to see, "I told you I don't want a job, especially working for him and that old bat Chatham."

Nancy pulled her mother into a shop doorway; she leaned into her.

"Look, Mum, it's not about you. It's about Charlotte. I've got my life to lead and I can't keep looking after you. You are supposed to take care of Charlotte and me, not the other way around." She raised her voice.

"You need to grow up and take some responsibility for your actions. I said I'd cover the rent. All you have to do is make sure you buy food, feed the meters and pay the coal man. How hard is that?"

Hilda began to sob. Nancy shook her head and gripped her mother tightly,

"I swear if you mess this up this time, I'll come and get Charlotte, and she can stay with me in London. There are plenty of good schools where I live that will be only to happy to take in Charlotte with her grades. At least she won't have to worry about studying in candlelight and whether you are sober enough to make some dinner. That is, of course, if there's any bloody food in the house."

With that, she flounced off down the road. Hilda had to run to keep up with her. Nancy turned to her, gave her sixpence and said,

"Go and get the bus. I want to spend some time on my own..."

Hilda stood there open-mouthed as her daughter walked away.

It was getting dark by the time Nancy opened the front door to the house in Cringleford. The smell of warm cooking assailed her nostrils. She kicked off her shoes and walked into the kitchen. Her mother smiled at her,

"Ah, Nancy; just in time. I've made a vegetable stew. Charlotte has set the table. Go and wash your hands..."

Nancy glanced at her sister and winked...

Nancy slept in her own bed that night. She pushed away her sister. She didn't want to talk. She turned her back and looked at the light seeping through the stuck sash window. The curtains never did fit properly. She was returning to London early the next day. Mifty Mitchell was due to pick her and Helen up for an engagement somewhere over in Mayfair...

When Nancy woke up, Charlotte was pressed against her, snoring loudly.

Chapter 1
February 1941
Fire-Watching

Peter Porteous was wary. Peter Porteous was very wary. The encounter with the parachute bomb near the BBC some time ago had left its mark in more ways than one. Never mind that he was nearly killed by the rather large German device, he was almost caught carrying a newly-liberated silk parachute. He didn't fancy a six-month stretch in one of His Majesty's Prisons any more than going off to meet his maker at his relatively early age.

Whilst his Air Raid Precautions uniform afforded him a measure of protection from the prying eyes of the Metropolitan Police, there was little to be done about the nightly threat from our Germanic cousins across the Channel.

As he cycled through Hyde Park, Nancy Keeling's words rang in his ears. She had told him once as he sat outside Oxford Circus Underground Station,

"You were always a lucky sod...anyone else would have been in bits in the morgue..."

He half-smiled as he came out of the park and rode down Exhibition Road on his way to fire-watching duties at St Luke's and Christ Church opposite the Royal Brompton Hospital. It was dark, but the nightly bombing had not yet started. He looked up; it was a clear night. The stars shone brightly, making it even easier for the bombers.

The church tower was cold. He sat in an old deck chair and stared through a dirty, glass window out at the hospital. When the bombing started, he would go out on to the open turrets. His job for the night was to keep an eye on any sporadic fires that might break out from the incendiary devices that seemed to rain down. At his feet lay stubbed out cigarettes; he kicked them away. The old wind up Bakelite telephone on an old bedside table was tucked under an arch. If there was a fire, his job was to turn the handle several times, wait for it to be answered and then report its approximate location.

He sat back in the worn chair and took a swig from the battered silver flask that was secreted inside his greatcoat. The decent brandy was smooth and warmed his throat as he swallowed. He nestled into the canvas and briefly closed his eyes. He was tired and still grieving the death of his lover, Maruska Bergman, a couple of months earlier. He had been up to the Jewish cemetery a number of times with Nancy Keeling, but it always made him sad. Nancy had told him to get on with his life and move in with her.

The phone in the eaves rang. He jumped up quickly. It was all too easy to fall asleep, especially after a long shift on the day job at Smiths in Cricklewood making cockpit instruments for Spitfires and Hurricanes.

"St Luke's and Christ Church," he answered quickly.

"Porteous? Is that you?" Porteous recognised the voice.

"It certainly is, Harry."

"I thought you weren't on until tomorrow?"

"That's what I thought, but I got a message earlier today at the factory."

"I wish they'd keep the rota up to date." There was a pause. "Just had a call from Kent. The early warning is about to go off."

Porteous held his watch up to the light; it was barely nine o'clock. This meant a particularly heavy night's bombing. Porteous sighed, "Thanks for the heads-up."

Harry Harris whispered down the phone, "I'll pop by later..."

The phone went dead. Porteous smiled. Harry Harris had a wife, three grown-up married daughters and a mistress half his age...

Porteous reached into his bag and flicked through several packets of stockings still in their cellophane packets...He smiled...The early warning siren began to wail...

There was a pause in the bombing just before one in the morning. He hadn't seen any enemy action, as the Luftwaffe was concentrating on the docks in the East End. If he craned his neck to the left when he looked out from the open south turret, he could just see the glow from the fires in the east.

He sighed, "The poor devils are getting a right pasting tonight..."

After a while, you don't hear the dull thuds of the exploding bombs anymore. He concentrated on the area around the hospital, which had already taken a few direct hits over the previous weeks, not that he believed even the most fanatical of Nazi bombers would deliberately target a hospital...or would they?

Porteous heard the old door to the winding stairway creak. A voice called up,

"It's alright, Porteous, just me..."

Harry Harris was breathing heavily by the time he managed to climb the never-ending stairs to the clock tower. It didn't help that a smouldering, hand- rolled cigarette, was stuck between his lips. Porteous stepped back as he entered, not wishing to inhale any tobacco smoke with his asthmatic chest.

Harris added to the collection of cigarette ends on the floor and ground the stub out with his boot. He dragged over another old deck chair and sat down.

"Bugger me, Porteous, that stairwell will be the death of me."

Porteous snorted, "Perhaps if you smoked a little less and lost a bit of weight, you might manage that climb a little better."

Harris ignored the jibe, "Any action tonight?"

Porteous sat down and picked up the binoculars, "Nah; all quiet. I should have stayed in bed..."

"I'm knocking off in a few hours; can't see our Jerry friends bothering with us this late."

"I bet you are. Got somewhere pressing to go?"

"Oh, just a little diversion in Fulham. Which reminds me, what have you got for me?"

Porteous reached down into the canvas holdall and fished out three cellophane packets, "Two bob a pair."

Harris whistled, "That's a bit steep."

Porteous shrugged his shoulders, "It costs what it costs. These are not cheap copies from some backstreet shop in Nottingham. Jimmy Ryan says they came from a South American ship."

Harris laughed, "I wouldn't believe a word that old scoundrel says."

Porteous smiled, "Do you want them or not?"

"Put them on my account..."

The stockings were soon stuffed inside Harris' tunic. It wouldn't do to be caught with black market goods while dressed in an Air Raid Precautions uniform...

Harris asked quietly, "How are you getting on, Porteous?"

Porteous stared out into the gloom, "Oh, not so bad, really. I'm too busy to spend my time grieving. There's people a lot worse off than me."

There was a large explosion somewhere down by the Albert Bridge across the River Thames. They both spun around quickly with their binoculars trained in the general direction. Then, the boom of the anti-aircraft guns started on Battersea Park.

Harris shook his head, "Looks like I spoke too soon..."

They looked up as a Junkers JU 88 was suddenly caught in the glare of two searchlights. The two watched as a couple of delayed-action bombs were ejected from the underneath of the plane; parachute bombs.

"Bastards..." muttered Harris.

The searchlights lost the bomb as it sailed serenely down through the darkened sky. There would be a short delay before the ordinance did its deadly work.

Harris and Porteous instinctively ducked down below the turret wall, even though the bomb was well out of range. The church tower shook when the two bombs went off. It wasn't long before fires lit up the area around the bridge. The anti-aircraft guns stopped booming. The sole plane made its escape over south London.

Porteous asked, "What on earth are they after down there? It's residential."

Harris tucked his binoculars into his tunic, "God knows, Porteous, and he probably won't tell us either..."

Harry Harris left an hour later, having finished off the remainder of Porteous' brandy. He had an urgent appointment with his young lady friend down in Fulham. That is if our German cousins hadn't demolished her house.

Porteous knocked off just before six. He had to get home to his new house on East Row, Kensal Town, have a wash and make his way up for a shift at Smiths in Cricklewood making cockpit instruments for the war effort. He wasn't on fire-watching duty that night, so he'd stay with Nancy in Golders Green. She might not have any appointments that night. Kensal Town was lonely without Maruska or Shira...

Alice Halpin smiled as she greeted Porteous. He made sure their precious bicycles were secured; no one could be trusted during these difficult times. Alice Halpin was of medium height; dark and very lovely, even dressed in a boiler suit with her auburn hair tucked under a turban. Most factory girls dressed like this. War is not a good time to worry about how one looks when bombs are falling nightly.

They walked together into the makeshift canteen of Building Number 3. There was still enough tea in the ancient urn for them to have their early morning brew. Back in the workshop, the girls were all sat about doing nothing when Porteous entered. He clapped his hands, and they scattered to their benches. Some dreary music came on the tannoy. They groaned.

The factory supervisor, one Cedric Walker, waddled into the workshop. Porteous looked up; Alice drifted off to one side.

Walker handed Porteous a piece of paper, "We need these done by the end of the shift."

Porteous glanced at the list and shook his head, "We'll do what we can, Mr Walker, but we can't do miracles."

Alice winked at Porteous. He did his best not to smile. Walker glared at him.

"As I said, we'll do our best. It all depends on the state of that pressing machine." He nodded over at an old and very worn-out contraption over by the far wall.

Walker cleared his throat and turned away, "Just get it done, Porteous..."

The girls stood and watched as the supervisor walked away.

By the end of the shift, most of the order on the docket was sitting in a rolling bin awaiting pick-up for the next phase of the manufacturing. The pressing machine behaved itself for once with a bit of love and attention from Alice. She was used to crawling underneath and squirting lashings of oil on any moving parts and her face.

The hooter sounded at three, much to the relief of the girls, who were out of the workshop in a flash. Porteous and Alice Halpin watched them leave. They were sitting on an empty bench, swinging their legs.

Alice said, "It's funny how Walker never comes to thank us when we make the docket. He only comes to tell us off."

Porteous shrugged his shoulders, "He would say we get paid for it; that's better than his thanks."

Alice slipped off the bench and tugged at her turban. She had little specks of oil on her face. Porteous reached over and wiped them off with his thumb.

"Go and wash up, Alice, you can't let Phyllis see you like this."

Alice smiled, "Oh, I don't know. She likes a bit of rough from time to time."

Porteous laughed, "I don't think so."

He rapped her on her shoulder as she walked by.

Cedric Walker came through as she went past him, glowering.

Porteous observed the man from his position. He was wearing the same old threadbare, brown suit and the shirt with the frayed cuffs together with a faded blue tie.

"What's up, Mr Walker?"

"Big order tomorrow. Can you get the girls to do a double shift?"

Porteous shook his head, "I don't know. I'm back on ARP duty tomorrow."

Walker glared, "Then Halpin will have to supervise."

Porteous raised his eyebrows, "I'll ask, but I'm fairly sure she's busy."

Porteous knew that Phyllis was due back at Devonport to finish her officer training.

"Just tell 'em it's double pay…"

Porteous nodded. He knew his girls wouldn't pass up the opportunity to make a little more money, care of King and country, of course. He also knew that if they worked flat out, they could be home with their loved ones in half the time. Cedric Walker would have been long gone to the pub by then. Porteous had some business to attend to with Jimmy Ryan.

Alice Halpin went off to spend the evening with soon-to-be Third Officer Phyllis Manley of the Women's Royal Naval Service.

Porteous pushed his bicycle up the short pathway of the house in Crediton Hill, West Hampstead, the home of Nancy Keeling and Helen Shenton, although Helen hadn't been seen for a while. Fortunately, the landlord had paved the small front garden. It just needed a quick sweep from time to time. He glanced at it. He put a key in the lock and wheeled the bike inside. If you left a valuable machine unattended and in full view of passers-by, it would be gone before you had a chance to remove your coat.

He thought about Maruska's precious Saxon bicycle.

Nancy Keeling was in the back kitchen. She was sitting at the table smoking. She stubbed out the cigarette as soon as she heard Porteous. She, too, was always wary of his asthma.

Porteous removed his coat and rubbed his hands; it was cold outside, perhaps cold enough for snow. Nancy got up and wrapped her arms around him.

"Oh, your face is cold."

He nodded, "I'm starving. What have we got?"

Nancy opened the vegetable cupboard, "Carrots, swede, turnips, onions and a few potatoes. I managed to get some beef stock off the butcher. It'll make a nice stew."

She pushed him out of the kitchen, "Go and clean yourself up and then come and talk to me." She pecked him on the cheek.

By the time he came down in clean clothes, Nancy had the stew well on the way. The old sash window was well and truly steamed up. He looked at the clock; it was gone seven-thirty. The bombers would soon be back, and he didn't fancy sitting in that damp, makeshift shelter for hours on an empty stomach.

Nancy was dressed in her boiler suit. It seemed that Maruska had supplied all of Porteous' ladies with the same outfit, adjusted to their particular size, of course. Indeed, Maruska had died in hers when the parachute bomb had taken out most of the houses on Bosworth Road.

They sat and chatted whilst they ate. The beef stock had made the stew taste as though it had real meat. Nancy had sent her ration books up to Norwich even though she was not supposed to. At least Charlotte would get some sustenance. She bought what she could on the black market and Porteous and whatever Mifty Mitchell managed to get for her.

She had been trying to stay out of the limelight. She had known the authorities would catch up with her sooner or later, and then they would send her off to do some dreary factory job at the other end of London. They could even recommend her for the services because by now she had learnt to type on the old Olivetti that her flatmate had left when she decamped back to Hampshire. She glanced over at the envelope on the mantelpiece.

Porteous had been given a medical discharge from the army, so his rations were safe, especially after he had volunteered for work at Smiths and as an Air Raid Precautions warden. But, he only undertook these tasks so he could continue his trading with Jimmy Ryan. The ladies of Kensal Town were fully supplied with clothing and other essential items without the need for the appropriate coupons...

Porteous asked, "Are you working tonight?"

Nancy looked up at the clock; "I doubt it now. Mifty would have been shouting for me long ago. There was supposed to be an engagement somewhere out West, but I suspect the toffs have got a little scared from the bombing."

Porteous raised his eyebrows, "How are things at home?"

Nancy was at the sink clearing away the plates, "Oh, okay, for now. My mother has kept her job. She only drinks on the odd occasion. Charlotte's doing well at college. I send her a few pounds from time to time but the company that sponsors her gives her an allowance, but we don't tell mum that."

Porteous said, "I didn't know they were training women to be engineers."

"Well, there aren't enough men left to do the jobs any more. She's very bright and good with mathematics. She could stand up to any man any time."

Porteous nodded, "Yup. I don't doubt it."

"Are you still paying the rent?"

Nancy nodded, "If I didn't there wouldn't be a home for Charlotte."

"It's time you stopped working for Maitland. There's plenty of work for typists now."

Nancy sat on Porteous' lap. She put her arms around his neck, "We've had this conversation. I'll keep doing what I do until there's enough in the bank to buy that wretched house."

Porteous shook his head.

She said quietly, "A letter came for me this morning."

She reached over and passed Porteous a brown, official envelope with OHMS on the top. He opened it carefully, as though it had been booby-trapped. People like Porteous did their best to avoid anything official...

He read it and smiled, "You've been summoned to the Ministry of Labour in Edgware Road. They are going to allocate you a job."

"I don't need their job."

"No choice, Nancy. You can do a 174. Everyone has to register. It doesn't matter if you are lord or lady, war doesn't discriminate."

She shook her head, "I don't want to do that. I might take a position in an office, so I can keep doing my evening job. I can't do a 174."

He pushed her off. They could hear the wailing of the early-warning siren way out to the east of London.

"174 is light entertainment. Nothing wrong with that."

"Yes, but it's mostly used for prostitutes."

Porteous was about to say something but changed his mind, "Fill up that flask, it could be a long night in the shelter..."

It was...

A bleary-eyed Porteous half carried Nancy back up to the house just before four in the morning after the all-clear had sounded. The makeshift shelter on the recreation ground was full, although Nancy managed to spend the night sleeping with her head in Porteous' lap.

They both sank onto her bed, fully clothed. Porteous was hoping to grab a couple of hours of sleep before he went off to Smiths. He put two sixpences in the meter before he left so that she could have a long, hot soak in the bath after she got up.

Chapter 2
February 1941
The Ministry of Labour

Nancy Keeling stood in front of the full-length mirror in the upstairs back bedroom of the terraced house in Crediton Hill, West Hampstead. The room overlooked the small recreation ground. She pulled aside the faded net curtains and gazed over the grass that the groundsman had done his best to maintain. She could see the makeshift air raid shelter where she seemed to spend so much of her time.

She craned her neck to see if her seams were straight. She was down to her last three packs of stockings, and she was damned if she would wear her expensive silk pair; God knows where Porteous was able to lay his hands upon these increasingly rare items of clothing.

Nancy and the rest of Charlie Maitland's stable of girls had forsaken the wearing of hosiery until the wretched so-called Stocking Strangler had been apprehended, which, given the general uselessness of the Metropolitan Police, seemed unlikely in the short term. Anyway, it was possibly a futile gesture, as he would strangle his victims using whatever item of lingerie he could lay his hands on. Poor Maple Churchyard had been strangled with her own French knickers...She sighed...

Her housemate, Helen Shenton, had gone home to Hampshire until the murderer was caught, but she was still paying her share of the rent. Nancy knew Helen had hopes of snagging a businessman down there who was besotted by her.

Tonight, she was going to warm the bed of a retired civil servant up in Wembley. She had been several times before. The job paid well and Fritz and his mates didn't go up there too often in their Heinkels, Dorniers and Focke-Wulfs, so it was safer than sitting in some damp make-shift shelter on a recreation ground in West Hampstead. Nancy just had to make sure she got up there before the bus service stopped at the start of the blackout. Even Nancy Keeling could find it difficult to persuade a reluctant taxi driver to make that journey.

She sat on the end of her bed and rummaged through her handbag, making sure she had all that she needed for the night. She flicked open a pack of CBC rubbers; there were still two left; she doubted she would require more than that... She much preferred the American Trojans, but even Porteous was having difficulty acquiring those. She reached into a drawer, extracted a pair of clean, white silk knickers, and stuffed them into her bag. She stood up close to the mirror, checked her make-up for the last time, locked up, and went off to the tube station at West Hampstead.

Reginald Barstow was enjoying his life. He particularly liked his garden and his precious allotment, upon which he grew most of his vegetables. He was so successful that he even managed to sell off his surplus stock to his neighbours. And then there was that shop on the High Street that would always purchase any fresh items via the back door. He lived up in north Wembley in one of those new semi-detached homes that had been built in the 1930s in what estate agents euphemistically labelled Metroland because of the development of affordable houses within easy commuting distance of Central London.

His only problem was that his beloved wife of forty years had caught the dreaded consumption and had passed away after a long and slow decline. In 1937, Barstow managed to get early retirement from his medium-level Civil Service position in some obscure department of government. Regrettably, the outbreak of war in 1939 meant that he was summoned to his office to backfill those able-bodied men and women who had been called up for active service.

He didn't really mind because it paid well on top of his modest pension and the hours were infinitely flexible. The only thing he resented was that his departmental manager was a woman; she clearly didn't know her place...

The other thing he regretted was that he now had to pay for sex. Reginald Barstow had been blessed with a high sex drive. His wife, almost up to the end of her life, willingly shared this; she always had time for her beloved Reggie...

Reginald Barstow had come across Charlie Maitland and his ladies quite by accident. He was in a reputable public house one evening after work on the Marylebone Road having a quick drink before he queued for the bus to take him up to Wembley. He could have taken the Metropolitan Line underground service from Baker Street to South Kenton, but being slightly claustrophobic, he preferred the upstairs of a bus where he could puff on his pipe and read the evening newspaper.

A petite blonde girl smiled at him as he was sitting next to the fire. She offered to service him in some first-floor mansion flat down the road, but he declined. Instead, she gave him a card with a telephone number, insisting that he could always book an out-call.

He did...and finally ended up with one Nancy Keeling. Now, it was a regular booking. He often refused an alternate lady if Nancy was 'indisposed.' He would normally save it up... Little did he know he was dealing with a notorious gangster...

Nancy walked along Norval Road and into Fairway. She liked looking into the tidy front gardens of the semi-detached houses. Local residents seemed to take pride in their little patch of land. The gate creaked slightly as she opened it. She walked up the tiled pathway and the brown front door opened as she approached.

Reginald Barstow smiled at her. He took her coat. He was delighted that Nancy always looked particularly attractive for their evenings.

The dining room table was set formally. Nancy sipped a sweet sherry. She much preferred his rather expensive whisky, but that was all that was offered.

She sat opposite him, making sure he had a good view of her long legs. She crossed and uncrossed them.

She ate slowly as he regaled her with his news. Not only did Reginald Barstow pay well, but he also was a half-decent cook. There were always some spare vegetables to take home in the morning and perhaps an expensive bottle of Scotch in the drinks' cupboard that could be liberated...

He was a kind and considerate lover and treated her well. There was never a discussion about wearing a condom. Porteous had drummed into her the need to protect herself despite offers of silly money to go without. She always refused, even though Mifty Mitchell would tell her off afterwards. Barstow didn't last long that evening and was soon asleep having had a few nightcaps.

Nancy closed the toilet seat cover and sat on it. She reached behind her and pushed open the small window. The house was dark. She lit a cigarette and stared down at her painted toenails. She didn't really enjoy this work, but she couldn't rely on her mother to provide for the family. She breathed out the smoke and mentally calculated how much she now had in the Midland Bank in Marylebone. Edith Bell had taken her down there to open an account, despite not having a regular job or any paperwork. Edith had a way with officials...

She now had almost five hundred pounds in the account, the proceeds of her work. If Mifty Mitchell hadn't taken half of what she earned, she would be nearly there by now. Alfred Hodges of Hodges and Sons, Property Developers and Managers of Norwich, had already agreed to sell her the family home for just under seven hundred pounds, but she needed to raise the money by the end of the summer. Yes, the house needed quite a bit of work, and it had no bathroom, but at least she could stop paying the bloody rent and maybe get a real job, and then perhaps Porteous would look upon her differently.

She flushed the cigarette end down the toilet, rinsed out her mouth and climbed back into Reginald Barstow's bed wearing just her camisole and French knickers.

It was gone ten o'clock by the time Nancy Keeling walked up to the front door of her house in West Hampstead. Reginald Barstow had woken early in order to get full value for his thirty shillings. Fortunately for Nancy, he didn't last too long. She was able to wash herself after about ten minutes. She left him shortly afterwards as he dozed upstairs and went out into the cold morning air clutching her coat around her.

She took a long soak in the bath until she began to feel the chill of the water as it cooled off. She slipped into bed in a pair of cotton pyjamas and slept for most of the day.

Mifty Mitchell came for her just before eight in the evening. The Wolseley Hornet was out on the road with its engine ticking over. Two other girls were in the back seat.

As she opened the front door, he held out his hand; she dropped fifteen shillings into his fat hand.

He asked, "Any tips?" The hand was still outstretched.

She shook her head, "You know he doesn't tip."

Mitchell pocketed the cash and leaned against the hallway wall. Whilst Nancy went to put on her coat and check her make-up, he took out a small notebook and the stub of a pencil. He licked the end of the pencil and made a note of his takings. His boss, Charlie Maitland, insisted on basic accounting...

She came down the stairs, ready for the evening's work. Mitchell looked at her,

"Where's Shenton? Charlie's asking fer 'er."

"Dunno, Mifty, she hasn't come back from Hampshire."

"Ah'll give her bloody 'ampshire. She's gonna get a gentle slap when she returns."

Nancy pushed him out, locked the door, and went and sat in the front seat of the Hornet. The girl that had touched her up the other night passed her a small hip flask...

Nancy Keeling managed to secrete just over twelve pounds that night, plus her share of what she had handed over to Mitchell. The party was held in honour of some minor aristocrat and his rich friends in the upstairs room of a public house in Knightsbridge. She had used the last three CBC rubbers in her handbag; she really should persuade Porteous to get some Trojans...

She had over twenty-five pounds to pay into the bank; she would do that on her way to the appointment at the Ministry of Labour...

Nancy Keeling dressed very modestly for her appointment. She was wearing a long calf-length pleated skirt and a plain, white blouse fastened right up to her neck. She was bare-legged with a pair of flat shoes. Her long, beige coat completed the outfit. She looked like one of the many office girls that crowded the streets of London. Nancy was a good timekeeper; there was no point in antagonising the clerks. They had the upper hand

The Ministry office was just on the corner of Seymour Street and Edgware Road, just up from Marble Arch. It was almost entirely staffed by women. Muriel Gardner had recently been transferred in from a countryside office to fill the ever-increasing vacancies as men folk were summoned into the military ranks to fight off the enemy. Muriel hadn't really wanted to take the assignment, but the offer of free accommodation and a generous subsistence package persuaded her and her husband to make the move. They were billeted in some run-down hotel in Bayswater, but they were able to return to their home each weekend, provided the trains were running; their official travel warrants smoothed away any problems...

The office served a mixed clientele. On the one hand, there were the rich and famous of Kensington and then there were the not-so-wealthy of the slums of Paddington, including Kensal Town. In theory, war does not discriminate but in practice, it certainly does...

Mrs Gardner had been doing the job for over six months, and it was her task to ensure that all clients were suitably placed in appropriate work for the war effort, either being directed to one of the services or to assist in some other vital occupation. She enjoyed the variety of the work. One day she could have a lady from Kensington coming in to complain that one of her maids had been identified for a more appropriate position, or one of the many women of somewhat dubious repute from the rough end of Paddington. The allocation of identity cards had greatly assisted the work. The Government now knew where almost the whole population was and what they were doing. One couldn't get ration coupons without the card and without coupons, one starved unless one was a dab hand at working the black market; think Peter Porteous...

Muriel Gardner looked at Nancy Keeling as she answered her name and walked slowly up to the little glass booth.

'Hmm, this doesn't look like a 174...' she thought.

Nancy sat down on the chair. Mrs Gardner slid open the glass window,

"Identity card, please."

Nancy slid across her card. The clerk took her time inspecting it. Periodically, she cast a furtive glance at Nancy to check it was the same person as the flimsy photograph stuck on the card. She placed the card on her desk and then ran a finger down the list of today's invitees. She found Nancy's name and ticked it off.

"Miss Keeling, we don't seem to have a record of your current employment situation."

Nancy paused, choosing her words carefully, "That's because I haven't been working, Ma'am."

Gardner cleared her throat and scratched something on her notepad,

"May I ask how you've been managing to support yourself?"

"My mother sends me money whilst I look for work."

The clerk rattled off Nancy's address, "Is this correct?"

Nancy nodded.

"How much is the rent?"

"I share the house with two other girls."

"How much is your share, then?"

"Fifteen shillings a week."

"Do you have a rent book?"

Nancy's landlord didn't bother with such niceties.

"One of the other girls has it."

There was more scratching of her pen...

There was a significant pause; Nancy looked at her shoes.

Mrs Gardner leaned into the window and spoke quietly, "Are you in the light entertainment business?"

Nancy blushed and shook her head vigorously.

"Because if you want a 174 you need evidence of a magistrate's fine or a police caution. We don't just hand these out willy-nilly."

Nancy feigned ignorance, "Sorry, Ma'am, what's a 174?"

Muriel Gardner snorted, "Okay then, do you have any skills?"

"I've just learned to type. I'm a beginner but I can manage."

"There's plenty of factory work."

"I'd prefer to work in an office."

"That may well be, but we need workers for the war effort, or perhaps you'd like to join one of the services. They are always in need of good clerks."

"I'm willing to work, Ma'am, but not the services. My mother's not too well and then there's my little sister."

Mrs Gardner eyed her suspiciously, "Hmm, let me look to see what's available. I'm not sure about a job in an office. You don't have any formal qualifications. Would you be prepared to take a short test? I can't just send you off for an interview without checking what you can do."

Nancy nodded; she had been expecting this. Helen Shenton had made her do several practice tests.

"Of course, Ma'am."

Nancy was taken to a small office, presented with one side of paper written badly in longhand, and told to type it on a fairly new machine.

She took her time, but she was pleased with the results; she had even corrected a couple of spelling mistakes on the original note.

Mrs Gardner cast her eyes over the piece, "Hmm, not bad but a little slow. Still, I expect you'll get quicker over time. Please go back to the waiting area whilst I see what's available."

One hour later, Nancy Keeling walked down Praed Street in Paddington. She was looking for the offices of Fitch and Sons, General Hauliers. She walked past the station and turned into Eastbourne Terrace. The station was piled up with sandbags placed at strategic points. Workmen were busy shoring up and repairing some light damage inflicted in a recent air raid. One of the workers called out to her; she ignored him.

She found the haulage yard on Bishop's Bridge Road. It was very congested. Lorries were queuing up to get in. There appeared to be a constant stream of vehicles coming and going, some fully loaded and some empty. Mrs Gardner had told her that the company had lots of Government contracts, so it was a very busy office.

A rather fierce-looking woman in her late fifties escorted Nancy to a small and poky office that didn't look like it had been cleaned for years. Nancy brushed away the dust on her chair before she sat down

The woman announced herself, "My name is Miss Hawthorn. I'm the office manager here. The Ministry telephoned to say they were sending up a typist, but you don't seem to have any formal qualifications."

Nancy stared at her.

Hawthorn sighed, "Alright, my dear, let's just take some details, and then I'll set you a little test. I need to check what the Ministry is saying. They sent a girl over last week with lightning speed, but she couldn't speak English. I mean, how do they expect us to do our jobs with these foreigners?"

Nancy shook her head; this was what Maruska faced when she first came to London...

Nancy answered all her questions in a monotone, not willing to engage. She deliberately messed up the typing and was summarily dismissed with a wave of the hand. Miss Hawthorn passed Nancy a reject form to take back to the Ministry. Nancy Keeling smiled to herself as she walked back down Praed Street. She would now have to go and ask Peter Porteous for a favour...

Two days later, Nancy was sitting next to Porteous in the front room of his house in East Row, Kensal Town. He had moved there when his long-time flat on Bosworth Road was destroyed in the bombing at the same time that his beloved Maruska Bergman was killed. The fire was blazing in the hearth; Porteous had a knack of acquiring coal...

Nancy rested her head on his shoulder; her arm was linked in with his. They had drunk a substantial amount of gin with Edith Bell and Alice Halpin. Edith had decided that she needed to get back to the White Horse to close up for the night. Alice was asleep in one of the upstairs bedrooms; it didn't matter which, as they all seemed to sleep with each other...

Porteous could feel his eyes closing. Nancy pressed herself even closer to him,

"Porteous, can you do me a favour?"

He grunted as his eyes closed firmly.

"Can you get me some headed notepaper from Smiths?"

Porteous' eyes opened wide, "What do you want that for?"

Nancy sat up. She leaned into Porteous, "I need something for the Ministry to say I'm working."

He snorted; he was fully awake now. "I thought you said they would get you an office job?"

"I have a job, Porteous."

"Then get yourself a 174 and the Ministry won't bother you again."

"They won't give me one unless I've already been arrested."

He sat up and pushed her away. Nancy had a way of getting what she wanted from the opposite sex.

"So," he went on, "What do you intend to do with this headed notepaper?"

"Write a letter to the Ministry to say I'm employed at Smiths."

He laughed, "Ahh, I see what you are up to. The trouble is that the stationery is kept locked up in the general office. And you have to go through Dot Jackson to get at it."

"But you know the girls in there; you provide half of them with the clothes they wear."

Porteous was no longer asleep, "I'll get sacked if I get caught, and you'll end up with a criminal record."

Nancy shrugged her shoulders; "They'll never check. You should see the amount of work in that Ministry office. People are queuing out of the door."

He stood up, "I don't know, Nancy. I like my job; it fits in with my other stuff, and the authorities leave me alone."

She wrapped her arms around him and looked at him with doe eyes, "Please?"

The following Monday, Nancy Keeling walked into the Ministry of Labour office on the Edgware Road clutching a brown envelope that had cost Peter Porteous three pairs of stockings and a bottle of cheap whisky. She waited over an hour to see Muriel Gardner.

Nancy sat down at the little glass partition. Mrs Gardner had a stack of papers on her cluttered desk.

The clerk spoke up, "You are?"

"Nancy Keeling, Ma'am. You sent me for a typing position at Fitch and Sons, but they rejected me."

Mrs Gardner sighed, and pulled out another clipboard. She ran a finger down the list until she found Nancy's name. She traced across the sheet and stopped, raising her eyebrows.

"Ah, I see you failed the typing test."

"Yes, Ma'am. I think I was a little nervous."

Gardner snorted, "Well. It looks like you'll have to go into a factory."

Nancy slid across the envelope; "I have a job, Ma'am, at Smiths in Cricklewood."

Muriel Gardner looked at her, picked up the envelope, slit it open with a tarnished letter opener and perused the contents. She smiled inwardly; one less client to worry about...

"Good, good, that's excellent. I thought you didn't want to work in a factory?"

Nancy looked down, "I don't, Ma'am, but my typing is not good enough at the moment."

Muriel Gardner wrote something against Nancy's name, "When do you start?"

"Later today at three o'clock. I've got the evening shift."

"Good, good," she repeated. "Don't be late. Smiths are doing a lot for the war effort. Now, off you go. I don't want to see you here again."

Nancy smiled sweetly at the woman and took her leave.

Muriel Gardner crossed out Nancy Keeling's name and never thought of her again...

Chapter 3
February 1941
An unpleasant encounter

Being 'indisposed' for the week, Nancy Keeling was sleeping late. The house was cold. She poked her head above the bed covers. The winter sunlight was bright. She blinked her eyes. The tea she had made a few hours earlier was cold in the cup on the little cupboard next to her bed.

She was wondering what Porteous was doing. It was just before midday; he would be cajoling his girls up at Smiths to make one final push before they clocked off for the day. Nancy was jealous; jealous of Alice Halpin. She got to spend so much time with Porteous, much more than she did. She was jealous of all the other women in his life.

Her thoughts went to Doctor Maruska Bergman. She had taken his heart so easily. When she was around, he only had eyes for her. Nancy had backed away from Porteous when he fell in love with the Czech woman. She felt she couldn't compete, but it was to her, he turned after that dreadful land mine killed Maruska. Edith Bell had too much baggage. Alice was not even on the agenda and as for Shira Adelman, who could tell? Speaking of her, where on earth was she? Someone had strangled her abusive old man with a stocking and robbed the jeweller's shop. Now the police suspected her, but as Porteous had often said, it wasn't Shira's style. She would have just stuck a knife in his heart, sat down with a bottle of gin and waited for the police to arrive.

Nancy smiled at the thought. Shira was good fun, especially when she had drunk too much, and she could take you down Church

Street market, flirt with the traders and get what she wanted at half price...

Nancy dozed off again, half-hoping that Porteous would stop by on his way back from the factory.

An hour later, she awoke to the sound of the front door being pushed open. In the winter, the wooden door swelled a little, just enough for it to stick in the frame; she really must get Porteous to ease it slightly, as the bloody landlord wouldn't.

She regained her senses quickly and sat up. She pulled off the pyjama top she was wearing and climbed out of the bed. She reached for the robe that hung on the door and threw it on. She slipped along the carpeted landing and stood at the top of the stairs. The robe hung loosely off her shoulders, exposing her full breasts. She called down,

"Porteous? Is that you?"

The beaming face of her housemate, Helen Shenton, looked up as she took off her coat.

"Nah, sorry, Nancy, you'll have to make do with me."

Nancy pouted, "You've decided to come home, then?"

Helen looked up, "It's bloody freezing in here. Why didn't you light the fire?"

"I couldn't be bothered and besides, the coal is running down and there won't be a delivery until next week at the earliest. Make some tea; I'm going back to bed."

Nancy sulked back into the bedroom, threw off the robe and put her pyjama jacket back on. She climbed back into bed; it was still warm under the covers.

Helen Shenton plonked a fresh cup of tea on the bedside table and sat down on the bed.

Nancy looked at her, "Mifty's been shouting for you. He says he's going to give you a slap when he finds you."

Helen snorted, "He'll be lucky. I'm not going back to work for him and his Maltese gangsters."

Nancy rolled her eyes; that's what they all say, "What are you going to do? Porteous says there's plenty of work up at Smiths."

Helen shook her head. Her idea of work didn't include working shifts with a load of clacking women on about how much they hate their husbands.

"No. I'm going freelance for a week or two until I can save some money."

"What do you need money for? I thought you had a load saved?" Nancy was intrigued.

Helen turned away, not wishing to look at Nancy, "James has struck a bad patch. He borrowed some money to tide him over, and now he can't pay it back."

Nancy shook her head, "Did you give him all your savings?"

Helen nodded.

"Jesus, girl. Are you mad or just in love? He's taking you for a great big ride, can't you see it?"

Helen sipped her tea, "I'm trying, Nancy. I told him I'd give him one last chance to get the business back on the straight and narrow."

Nancy sat up, "So the wretch has sent you back to London to earn a few pounds to clear up his mess?"

Helen nodded.

Nancy continued, "He does know what you do, doesn't he?" She shook her head. What kind of man sends his supposed lover to work as a prostitute?

There was a silence.

"How much does he need?" Nancy asked.

"Forty pounds, and then he's free of the money lenders."

Nancy swore again and pulled the covers back over her head; that was a lot of money when you just about get ten shillings for a tug or blowjob in a back alley...

Helen Shenton sighed and walked across the room. She sat down at the dressing table and looked at herself in the mirror. She picked up a brush and ran it through her long, blond hair. She looked at the prone body of Nancy Keeling,

"Nancy? Are you on red week?"

Nancy grunted from under the blankets. It wasn't strictly true. Nancy had stopped menstruating after the lady over the blacksmith's had solved her little problem, but Mifty Mitchell didn't need to know this. Besides, it gave her a break every four weeks.

Helen slipped out of her dress and hung it next to the robe, "I'm cold and

tired, Nancy."

Nancy sighed and lifted the covers. Helen Shenton quickly got under the blankets. She had on a camisole and pair of silk French knickers. She snuggled up to Nancy. Helen could smell her distinctive perfume.

Nancy pushed her away, "Your feet are cold."

Helen spoke softly, "Today's Wednesday. You should be up in Wembley tonight, correct?"

She felt Nancy nod. "Can I go?" she asked.

Nancy shrugged her shoulders, "You can try. Tell him I sent you, but he normally doesn't want anyone else."

"Don't worry, when he sees me he won't be able to resist. I'll be especially nice to him."

Nancy giggled, "You won't have to try hard and don't you take advantage of him, do you understand? The going rate for the night is thirty shillings and maybe some spare vegetables. He'll manage it twice so take two rubbers with you. Okay?"

There was no reply as Helen Shenton snored quietly...

It was going dark when Nancy was stirred by a loud banging on the door. Helen Shenton was still fast asleep. The door banged again.

Nancy stood at the top of the stairs. It wouldn't be Porteous; he had his own key.

She began to skip down the stairs wrapping the robe tightly around her lithe body.

She called out, "Who is it?"

"Father Christmas. Who do yer fink it is?"

Nancy rolled her eyes as she opened the door. Mifty Mitchell stood in front of her. She towered above the little man and folded her arms,

"What do you want, Mifty. You know I can't work this week."

"Just checkin' on yer, that's all. 'Ave you seen that bitch of a housemate yet?"

He was referring to Helen Shenton.

She shook her head, "I told you, Mifty, she's back in Hampshire. No doubt that when she's back she'll come and see you." Nancy paused and stepped to one side.

"You can check if you like?"

She knew that Michael 'Mifty' Mitchell would never dare to search the house on his own. Deep down, he was afraid of women. He only wanted them on his own terms and being in their own house was not part of his plan to discipline them.

She looked up at the Hornet with its engine ticking over. There were two girls in the back, "What's happening tonight?"

"Bookin' over in Aldwych. I'm short of a girl. Do you wanna come? You can do a few tugs and put that gobby mouth of yours to better use."

Nancy shook her head, disgusted by the idea. She moved back into the centre of the doorway. "I'll be back for Saturday night. I told Charlie already."

Mifty Mitchell moved away. He didn't want to mess with Nancy. She was up there with his boss's favourites.

"Tell that bitch she's gonna get what for when she comes back…"

Nancy spoke quietly, "I don't think she's coming back..."

Mitchell didn't bother to turn around. He just dismissed her with a wave of his hand. He got in the car, put it in gear and set off. Nancy stared at the car. One of the rear windows rolled down. The girl that was always touching her held up a small silver hip flask and smiled at Nancy. She blew her a kiss. Nancy held up five fingers of one hand and mouthed the words, "Five pounds..."

That was what she had told the woman it would cost to get her in bed...

The female pouted as the car drove away.

Helen Shenton was hiding in the little bathroom when Nancy returned to her bedroom. She said,

"Has he gone, Nancy?"

Nancy nodded, "Now get out of there, I'm going to take a bath..."

Just as Helen Shenton was smiling sweetly at Reginald Barstow up in Wembley in an attempt to persuade him to avail himself of her assets, Nancy Keeling walked into the White Horse public house on Kensal Road in Kensal Town. She had decided that she didn't want to spend the night in the damp air raid shelter on the recreation ground on her own.

Edith Bell acknowledged her from behind the bar. The pub was quiet. Nancy was dressed in a pair of high-waist trousers and a dark blue silk blouse that Porteous had purloined from some place or other. Her long, beige coat was open.

She walked up to the bar as Edith placed a large gin and tonic in front of her.

Nancy smiled at Edith Bell, "Where's Porteous?"

"Out with Jimmy Ryan, I believe. Alice is with them. They went to collect some stuff from Denis Elphicke."

Nancy must have looked crestfallen. Edith reached out and took her hand, "Don't worry, he'll be back soon. He's not fire-watching tonight."

Nancy sipped the bitter drink and frowned, "Jesus, Edith, what's this?"

Edith Bell raised her eyebrows, "That's all I've got, Nancy. Even Porteous can't get me some decent stuff. It'll be better after a couple of glasses."

Edith topped her glass up with more tonic water, "That'll make it taste better."

Nancy smiled. She dropped a shilling on the counter and knocked back the drink, "I'll wait for Porteous in his house. If he calls in, tell him I'm waiting for him."

Edith smiled, "Keep working on him, Nancy, you'll get him in the end."

Nancy raised her eyebrows and left the pub.

She lit the fire in Porteous' front room. She could tell Alice had been in, as there was a pan of one of her concoctions still warm on the stove. Nancy tasted it; it was good.

She sat in front of the fire and sipped a whisky she had found under the sink. It was palatable.

Just before nine, as the first sirens were sounding, Peter Porteous opened the front door. She reached up and kissed him on the side of the face.

"I thought you would pop by after work today."

He shook his head; she could feel the cold from him, "Had a rush job with Jimmy. Alice came to help out."

Nancy looked around, "Jimmy's dropping her home before the bombing starts," he said.

He pushed her upstairs, "Go and change before Jerry gets here. That church crypt is not exactly warm."

"Can we not stay here?"

He sputtered, "After what happened to Maruska? Are you serious?"

He sat on the end of the bed whilst she struggled into one of the many boiler suits that Maruska had altered for Porteous' women.

He smiled at her, "Good grief, Nancy, you'd look good in anything..."

Nancy Keeling blushed...

They sat huddled up together on a hard bench in the crypt. Nancy had donned one of Porteous' army greatcoats, although the British military didn't know it had been liberated...She held him tight. The priest looked at her and licked his lips, but he knew better than to tackle a friend of Porteous.

The following evening, as Nancy Keeling was lying alone in Peter Porteous' bed, Helen Shenton was on the lookout for a willing customer at the Volunteer Public House on Baker Street in central London. She had managed to extract two pounds from Nancy's regular client up in Wembley, Reginald Barstow, who, despite his initial reluctance, was pleased with Helen's performance. The additional ten shillings was for 'extras.'

Helen was sitting with a casual acquaintance in a corner when two Royal Air Force servicemen approached them carrying drinks. Helen could feel her leg being squeezed under the little round table; they had scored...

The taller man spoke first, "Hello, ladies. I'm Colin and this here's me mate, Gordon."

Helen's acquaintance smiled, "I'm June and this is Helen." She paused and pointed to the drinks, "Are these for us?"

The man named Gordon nodded, "Are you two looking for business?"

Helen swept up her drink and gulped it back, "We do like a man in uniform, don't we, June."

June giggled, "We certainly do."

Helen looked at these two young men. The taller one was probably better-looking, but either would do, provided they had the requisite fee.

Gordon Cummins smiled, "This place is a bit of a dump. How about we go down the West End; much more action down there?"

Helen and her new friend June were freelancing; no chance of going down there to encounter the likes of Mifty Mitchel or any of Charlie Maitland's crew.

Helen needed two customers that night. She wasn't in the mood for socialising. She banged down her glass; "Two pounds, and you pay the five bob for a room."

Colin Gibson breathed out audibly, "That's a bit steep."

June smiled, "Your choice; take it or leave it."

The barmaid glared at the foursome as she cleared away some empty glasses, "I hope you ladies are not working here. This is a respectable establishment."

Gordon Cummins slipped her two sixpences, "Buy yourself a drink, love, and mind your own business." He didn't look at her.

The barmaid pocketed the coins and sloped off, swearing under her breath.

Fifteen minutes of haggling followed before the ladies agreed on thirty shillings plus the room.

The receptionist in the run-down hotel on the corner of Balcombe Street and Dorset Square was used to renting rooms by the hour. If you were lucky, you might encounter clean sheets, but that would be a stroke of good fortune. She looked at the foursome,

"Five bob a room and no monkey business. There's a copper on the corner."

The men each placed two half-crowns on the scratched desk. She slid over a grubby guest book,

"Sign there and I want you out as soon as the air raid siren goes off; do you understand?"

Helen whispered audibly, "Don't worry, this won't take long."

June burst out laughing.

Colin Gibson pushed the female known as June into the first floor bedroom; the door slammed behind him.

Leading Aircraftman Gordon Cummins led Helen Shenton up to the second floor. The place was cold. Helen could smell the damp. The room was bare, but at least the sheets were not too dirty. Cummins sat on the end of the bed.

"What do I get for my thirty bob?"

Helen smiled at him, "Let's see the money first."

He sighed, dug into the pocket of his navy blue uniform and extracted a one-pound note and a crumpled ten-shilling note. He handed them over. Helen deposited them in her bag. She unbuttoned her coat. He stood up, lit a cigarette and went to the window. She removed her clothes except for her boots and lay on the bed. She beckoned him over, not wanting this encounter to take too much time.

He approached her, unbuttoning his trousers, "Where's your stockings?"

She shook her head, "I haven't got any. There's a war on, you know."

He grunted and climbed on top of her. She pushed him away, "Put on a rubber, if you don't mind."

She didn't see the fist that smashed into her face. He screamed at her,

"Rubber? Fucking rubber? I'll give you a fucking rubber!"

The little stars began to dissipate from Helen's vision. She quickly regained her senses. He was back on top of her. His hands went around her neck. He began to squeeze. Helen's survival instincts kicked in. She brought her knee swiftly up to his groin with a sickening thump. She felt the pressure on her neck release. She sucked in a deep breath as he rolled over and off the bed. He collapsed in a foetal position on the dirty rug on the floor.

She breathed in again, stood over him, and swung a boot into his chest with as much force as she could muster. She heard a rib crack. He cried out in pain. She contemplated levelling another boot to his head but decided this piece of scum wasn't worth it. She quickly gathered her belongings and ran naked down the stairs and banged loudly on the door where June Cook was entertaining Colin Gibson.

"June! June! Open the door. That bastard just tried to strangle me."

The woman gingerly opened the door. Helen pushed past her into the room. Helen pulled on the coat over her naked body. Colin Gibson sat up in bed; he hadn't quite finished.

"What's going on? You're disturbing us."

Helen stared at him, "Listen, you idiot, your mate put his hands around my neck. Is he the fucking Stocking Strangler?"

June began to dress; she already had her money. The copper on the corner could deal with this...

The receptionist banged on the door, "I told you there was to be no monkey business. You are disturbing my other guests."

Helen shouted at the old woman, "Fuck your other guests. You've got a murderer upstairs."

Colin Gibson spoke up quickly, "Now, wait a minute. I'm sure there's a perfectly reasonable explanation for this."

Helen shouted at him, "Are you mad? Look at my face; it's a mess."

Helen's eye was beginning to swell and close, "Your mate did this."

Just then, Gordon Cummins appeared at the door. He looked sheepish.

"Sorry, sorry. I think I've had too much to drink." He was pulling on his uniform.

Helen shouted at him, "Sorry doesn't cut it mate." She turned to the receptionist, "Go and fetch that copper."

Cummins held up his hand, "Hold on! Hold on! I'm sure there's no need for that. Can we work something out?"

"You can work it out when you are swinging from a rope in Wandsworth Prison."

Gibson asked, "Did you hurt her, Gordon?"

"I-I-I may have done by accident, honestly. I was just getting a little carried away, that's all."

Cummins reached into his pocket and took out eight pound notes, "Look, will this suffice?" He dropped them on the bed.

Helen quickly calmed down. With the other money she had earned, this would keep the moneylenders off her boyfriend's back for a week or so.

The receptionist spoke up, "What about my trouble?"

Helen tossed her a crumpled one-pound note. "If he's not out of here in two minutes, fetch that copper."

"On my way, Miss." She bustled out of the room, muttering to herself.

Gordon Cummins hastily dressed. He muttered one more sorry and fled the hotel.

Helen stood by the water basin at the side of the room and dabbed cold water onto her bruised face. She turned to the airman who was still sitting up in bed, hoping that somehow his evening hadn't been ruined.

She growled at him, "I'd be a little more careful in choosing your friends, if I was you."

Colin Gibson lit a cigarette and shook his shoulders, "He's not my mate. Never seen him before this evening. He's from a different unit to mine. I'm from Dorset on a few days leave. I think he said he was in training to be a pilot."

June started to get dressed. He raised his voice, "Hey, what about me?"

The two women turned to him and spoke in unison, "Fuck you!"

The snow was falling as Leading Aircraftman Gordon Cummins stumbled up the fire escape as he attempted to avoid the guards back at the Air Crew Receiving Centre in Regents Park. He was well beyond the curfew, but the men had a suitable arrangement with the security staff that would turn a blind eye for a suitable fee. Besides, it had become a habit of returning personnel to write up the times in their passbooks in pencil, so times could always be altered.

Cummins was breathing hard. He hadn't thought this one out properly. If he had managed to kill the girl, how would he explain that to his friend? What was his name? And what about the other tart? June, was it?

He slipped on the cold, wet steel and swore loudly. The night had cleaned him out of nearly all his money. How would he explain that to his wife, Marjorie? The rent was due at the end of the week and he had promised her a night out. He had his itch and he wasn't able to scratch it...

For Cummins, it wasn't the sex that interested him. It was the cutting after that made him satisfied...Maple Churchyard had been a soft touch; a young girl out on her own looking to make a quick pound or two. She was an easy target. Now he was permanently stationed in London, he didn't have to concern himself with making the trip back to Wiltshire after the itch had been scratched.

Cummins resolved to work only on his own now.

He pushed open the door to the room he shared with three other men. He wrinkled up his nose as the smell of stale beer and cigarettes assailed him. He quietly slipped off his clothes and got into bed, trying his best to put the night's events out of his mind. If anyone asked, he had been in his own bed for most of the night...

By the time Helen Shenton had made her way home, her eye was well and truly closed. She threw off her clothes and clambered into bed. She sobbed quietly to herself. The house was empty; Nancy was probably with Porteous. She should really have reported her encounter with the man called Gordon to the police, but they would ask too many questions. Perhaps it would have been better to have gone back to Charlie Maitland? At least he gave his girls some protection. Freelancing was far too dangerous with the likes of that man out and about. If Nancy came back before she left in the morning, she would tell her.

Helen Shenton slept fitfully. Early the next day, she got up, gave herself a cursory wash, packed a few things into an old carpetbag, together with nearly twenty pounds and the several sixpences that were stacked on the gas meter, and left the house. She pushed her key back through the letterbox. She managed to board a train from Waterloo back down to Hampshire just before ten in the morning. Nancy was still over in Kensal Town with Porteous; she never saw Helen again.

Chapter 4
February 1941
A close encounter

Nancy Keeling looked at Alice Halpin who in turn looked at Peter Porteous. He raised his eyebrows,

"She's in the wind, ladies..." He was referring to one Helen Shenton who had disappeared with a week's supply of sixpences for the gas meter.

Nancy growled, "Bloody girl. I don't mind her buggering off back to Hampshire, but to take those sixpences..."

Alice spoke up. Her Liverpool accent was more pronounced, "Maybe that thug Mitchell got hold of her?"

Nancy shook her head, "Nah, she was freelancing. She wouldn't have gone anywhere near the West End and Charlie's boys. I'll ask on Saturday if anyone has seen her when I go back to work."

Alice sighed and went into the kitchen to make some tea. Porteous searched his pockets and found two sixpences. He slapped them on the table,

"There you go, Nancy, feed the meter with these."

Alice called out, "Don't bother, I'll jemmy it like we do at home. No one ever pays the full price for gas or 'lecckie where I come from!"

Porteous burst out laughing, "Thanks, Alice, but no thanks, all the same..."

Alice shrugged her shoulders and went back to making tea. Nancy looked confused.

The girls were dressed in their boiler suits, with their hair tied under a turban. Porteous had on his Air Raid Precautions uniform even though he wasn't on duty that night. The weather was atrocious. It kept snowing, thawing and then freezing. The wind from the east was as unwelcome as the nightly Luftwaffe raids. They were waiting for the arrival of Jimmy Ryan and his battered Morris van. There was a job on...

Just before six, the three of them were sitting at the kitchen table when the door was rapped loudly. Nancy peered out of the front room window and swore; Mifty Mitchell's Wolseley Hornet was sat on the road with its engine ticking over. She felt Porteous behind her. She leaned back into him.

"What does he want?" he asked.

He felt Nancy shake her head, "Dunno, Porteous, perhaps I'd better find out. Go back into the kitchen and close the door. You know he's got a thing about you."

Porteous put a finger to his lips as he pulled the kitchen door almost closed. He wanted to hear what was going on. Alice nodded and sipped her tea. She wasn't frightened of Mitchell. She had enough contacts back home in Liverpool to take care of thugs like him.

Mitchell leaned on the outside door as it was opened,

"Is yer mate back yet?"

Nancy shook her head. Mitchell leaned into her, "If Ah finds out yer've been lyin' to me, A'll giv' yer what fer as well."

Nancy folded her arms, "Look, I told you, she's not here."

Mitchell grabbed hold of her boiler suit just below the neck with one hand; screwed it into a fist and pushed her up against the hall wall,

"Listen, yer bitch. We picked up a tart called June yesterday freelancin' in Leicester Square. She says she did two RAF blokes wiv another girl called Helen; dark hair, about your height. Does that ring any bells in that pretty little head of yers?"

Nancy swallowed; it sounded like Helen Shenton.

Mitchell went on; "Charlie's sendin' us out to warn the girls. So, Ahm, doin' yer a favour in case yer gets any ideas."

Porteous stood up. Alice reached out an arm and restrained him. She shook her head, reached into a deep pocket of her boiler suit and extracted a long, thin knife. She pressed the metal button and a razor sharp blade sprung open.

Mitchell went on. Nancy could smell his cigarette breath, "Well yer daft mate had a spot of trouble. Seems she may have come across that moron who's bin doin the girls."

Nancy's eyes widened, "What happened?"

"We had the tart slapped a few times, and she said her and this mysterious Helen picked up these two RAF types in a pub in Baker Street, took them back to some doss house in Balcome Street where this geezer tried to strangle her. He gave her a right smack in one eye."

Alice Halpin walked quietly up the hallway; Mitchell relaxed his grip. He could certainly beat up one girl, but he might have difficulty with two, especially the scouse one with the sharp blade.

She spoke quietly, "Take your hands off the lady, Mitchell."

Mitchell smiled, "Ahh, if it isn't the queer one from some shithole called Liverpool. What's up? Are you shagging Nancy as well?"

Alice smiled, "Yeah, Mitchell, you are right. There are parts of Liverpool that are shitholes..." She patted the flick knife in her open palm. "Do you want to make something of it?"

Mitchell let go of Nancy and smiled, "Charlie wants to see yer on Saturday night before you get back to work, okay?"

He turned to Alice who was staring him directly in the face expressionless, "Ahh can get yer a job as well if yer like; plenty of rich women out there who like a bit of the old feminine touch."

Alice pushed the blade back into the knife, "Nah, thanks all the same, I'm spoken for. Now piss off and leave us alone..."

Mitchell's face turned red. He was not used to being spoken to like that, especially by a woman.

Alice nodded at the Hornet, "Go on, you're using up your precious petrol..."

He brushed down Nancy Keeling and straightened her boiler suit with two hands,

"Right oh, Nance, Ah'll pick yer up at six Saturday night. Got a bit of a do over in Kensington. And tell yer freelancing mates not to take any jobs from RAF blokes until we get this bastard sorted."

With that, he was gone. The Hornet belched out thick, blue smoke as it sped off.

Nancy Keeling breathed out loudly and sobbed, "I told the silly girl not to go out on her own."

Alice led her back into the kitchen. Porteous wrapped his strong arms around her, "Look, we know she's okay. She fought him off."

Nancy nodded, "That's why she's buggered off with the gas money..."

Alice asked, "You didn't see her?"

Nancy shook her head, "Only when she returned from Hampshire, and that was for one night only. I gave her my regular up in Wembley. I told her to go and see Mitchell, but she said she didn't want to work for Charlie Maitland any more. She said her boyfriend needed some quick cash to pay off some moneylenders."

Porteous looked at her, "Time to stop, Nancy."

She raised her voice, "I told you, Porteous, I'm nearly there with the money for the house. Just a few more weeks, I think."

Alice looked at Porteous; he nodded. She said, "We'll get the rest of the money for you; okay?"

Nancy pushed Porteous away, "No! I'll do it myself."

Alice Halpin raised her eyebrows; Nancy could be as stubborn as Shira Adelman when she wanted to...

It was approaching seven before Jimmy Ryan's Morris van pulled up. The blackout was in full swing. Porteous locked the front door of the house and pushed the two women into the rear of the van, where they sat on the metal floor with their backs against the van side. He climbed in next to Jimmy Ryan who immediately tossed out his cigarette, conscious of Porteous' asthma condition. Ryan produced a small, silver hip flask and passed it back to Alice. She smiled,

"That's why I like doing the odd job with you, Jimmy." She took a full swig and passed the flask over to Nancy.

He grinned to himself as he expertly manoeuvred the old Post Office van through the darkened streets of London. There was nothing better than having two beautiful women in the back of his van...Well, perhaps, three?

The West End was busy. People were rushing to get home before the early warning sirens began their nightly wailing. From his work as an Air Raid Precautions warden, Porteous knew that from the first siren they would have about one hour to get home or at least to a shelter.

Porteous folded his arms, "Where are we going, Jimmy?"

Ryan stared ahead, "Docks on the Isle of Dogs..."

The van went silent. Alice spoke up, "Jesus, Jimmy. We'll have to be smart and get out before Jerry gets there."

Porteous raised his eyebrows, "I hope it'll be worth it..."

The bombed-out warehouse was on what was left of Heron Quays. There was still the smell of acrid smoke coming from the remains of damaged ships that had been hit previously.

It was-pitch black by the time Ryan pulled up to what was left of the big, wooden gates. He sounded his horn and the gates mysteriously opened.

"Come on, ladies; we've got fifteen minutes to load this stuff."

Porteous hopped out and opened the rear doors. A dim light came on. The large figure of Dennis Elphicke appeared at the door.

"Ahh, Ryan and Porteous. I was wondering when you two reprobates would turn up."

He spotted the two women, "Oh, I see you've brought some decoration with you."

Ryan went up to him, "What have you got for us, Dennis?"

Elphicke jerked his thumb over his shoulder, "A couple of crates of London's finest gin, several boxes of American cigarettes, some clothing and a load of fresh vegetables that came up from Essex this morning."

Porteous stared at the load that was neatly stacked on several pallets; he shook his head. There wouldn't be a lot of room in the Morris van. He sighed,

"Come on, girls, let's get this lot shifted while Jimmy does the paperwork."

Doing the paperwork was a euphemism for Jimmy Ryan handing over a sum of money...

Ryan disappeared with Elphicke.

The three of them formed a chain and loaded the goods into the van as quickly as possible. Alice threw an old blanket over the pile in the back of the van to keep it from prying eyes. Porteous joined Jimmy Ryan in a little back office. Elphicke and Ryan were sipping some malt whisky.

Ryan looked at Porteous, "Charlie Maitland wants to see us."

Porteous nodded, "Yeah, Mitchell told me that some time ago. I've been trying to avoid him." He addressed Dennis Elphicke, "What's he want, Dennis?"

Elphicke lit a cigarette, "He wants a slice of your action."

"I thought the Maltese brothers were only interested in women?"

"Well, he wants to tax you."

Jimmy Ryan smiled, "Does he now? What's he looking for, ten per cent?"

Elphicke smiled, "He wants to tax me to the tune of twenty per cent."

Ryan's mouth opened wide, "Twenty per cent? It wouldn't be worth us doing business at that price."

Elphicke nodded, "Yes, I know. I'm debating whether to fight him or not."

Porteous shook his head, "That might not be a good idea, Dennis. He owns half of the police, and he's not shy of using firearms."

Elphicke reached into a draw and pulled out a Webley Mark 4, "It was my dad's from the First World War and I know how to use it. I've got a dozen or so coming in for my men to use. So if Charlie and his brothers want a scrap, then so be it."

Porteous didn't like the sound of this; buying and selling on the black market was one thing but getting involved in a gang war was not exactly what he had on his agenda. He had spent his life keeping a low profile, which is why he had survived for so long.

The early warning siren began to wail out to the East of London. It meant that the Luftwaffe was somewhere over the English Channel. Ryan slapped down his empty glass, "Come on, Porteous, time for us to make tracks."

Elphicke grabbed Porteous, "Let me know what Maitland wants from you, okay?"

Porteous nodded.

By the time he reached the van, Alice and Nancy were squashed together on the front seat next to Jimmy Ryan.

Porteous sighed, "I suppose I'm in the back, ladies?"

The ladies giggled; Ryan smiled as Porteous clambered into the back and closed the double doors.

"If we're quick, we'll have just enough time to get the stuff into the lock-up in Red Lion Street and then get home and into a shelter."

Porteous pushed his back against a box of gin and sighed.

He felt the van slow down, "What's up, Jimmy?" They were on the East India Dock Road.

"Police up ahead."

"Do you want me to climb into the front? The ARP uniform should see them off."

Ryan shook his head, "Nah, too late. I can't stop or turn around without attracting suspicion. Just lie low; I'll deal with it."

Porteous knew that if the police searched the van, they would all be in trouble.

Ryan slowed down the Morris and wound down the window as a caped policeman approached, steam bellowing out of his mouth in the cold night air. He was in his late fifties and overweight; another retired officer recalled for duty.

He held his lantern into the Jimmy Ryan's face, "Evenin' sir. It's a bit late for you to be out and about."

Ryan smiled at the officer, "Yeah, just taking these two ladies home before the raid."

The policeman held the lamp over at Nancy and Alice, who both smiled coyly at the man, "Evening, officer."

The policeman cleared his throat, "Where have you come from, sir?"

"We've been helping out with a mate who has a small factory in Poplar. He makes shoes for the army."

The policeman shone the light into the back, "What's in the back?"

Porteous made himself even smaller.

"Just my tools and some wood; I'm a carpenter."

"Pass over your identity cards, and we'll check you out. I've got to make a record of them. If all is good, you'll soon be on your way."

Nancy grabbed Alice's and Ryan's cards, "Here you are, officer, I'll bring them out to you."

Alice glared at Nancy...

Porteous could feel his heart thumping in his chest. With that amount of alcohol and cigarettes in the van, they'd all get two years and a bloody good hiding from some sergeant down at the police station.

The policeman held the lamp back at Nancy, who batted her eyelids at him.

He said, "Very well, make it quick, Jerry's on his way..."

Nancy got a dig in her ribs from Alice as she clambered over her. The door slammed shut. Nancy led the policeman over to a darkened shop doorway.

The policeman called out to his fellow officer,

"It's all right, Fred, just recording the identity cards..."

The van's occupants watched as other vehicles went through the checkpoint without being stopped. Jimmy Ryan spoke quietly as he stared ahead,

"Five minutes, tops..."

Alice smiled, "He won't last three..."

Porteous sighed and shook his head in the back.

A few minutes later, Nancy Keeling opened the passenger door, "Come on, Jimmy, he says we can go."

She turned to Porteous, "Pass me a bottle, I need to wash my hands..."

Nancy Keeling rinsed off her hands in some of London's finest gin as Jimmy Ryan sped away.

Having deposited a box of the gin up at the White Horse on Kensal Road, Alice Halpin, Nancy Keeling and Peter Porteous huddled together in the damp crypt in the old Victorian church on Bosworth

Road. The bombing was particularly heavy that night. It seemed as if fat Herman Göring had directed all of his bombers to have target practice on Paddington Station. The surrounding residential areas were taking some huge hits. The booming of the anti-aircraft guns added to the almost unbearable noise. Porteous had his arms around the two women.

There was a lull in the bombing just after one in the morning. Porteous held up his wrist to the dim light of the candles to look at his watch. He shook his head, hoping to hear the all-clear. He and Alice were due on at Smiths for the early morning shift at six. He looked at the sleeping figure of Nancy Keeling. Yes, he was cross with her for 'taking care of that policeman.' If he had been sitting in the front next to Jimmy Ryan, his ARP uniform would have smoothed the way without the need for her to get involved.

His thoughts went back to the story that Mifty Mitchell had related earlier about the so-called Blackout or Stocking Strangler, as he was known in some parts. Freelancing in the West End was definitely something not to be undertaken at the moment. In a way, he hoped that Charlie Maitland would get him first. He would just be chopped up and fed to some pigs out in Essex. If the Metropolitan Police got him, there would be an expensive trial and all the attendant publicity, especially if there was to be a hanging.

Porteous was anxious to get Nancy away from her current life. He recollected how Maruska and Nancy had got on so well despite the obvious contradictions in the way they chose to live their lives. That reminded him; the police and security services indicated that Maruska might have been a German spy. He shook his head. He just couldn't believe it; she hated the Nazis as much as anyone.

A bomb landed close by. The church shook on its foundations. Porteous looked up to see dust scattering from the ceilings. The candles flickered with the vibration. Nancy stirred. Alice snored even louder. He sighed...

The all-clear sounded just gone two in the morning. Porteous half-carried his ladies back to his house on East Row and laid them on his bed, still fully clothed. It was Saturday morning, but the war effort never seemed to cease. He lay down beside them and dozed off for a couple of hours.

Just before six, he dragged a sleepy Alice Halpin out of bed and shoved her onto her bicycle. By the time they rode up to Smiths in Cricklewood, they were both wide-awake and ready for an eight-hour shift making cockpit instruments for Hurricane and Spitfire fighter planes.

Nancy woke up just before twelve, rinsed out her mouth and walked back over the Ha'penny Steps still dressed in her boiler suit, flagged down a taxi and went back to her house in West Hampstead hoping that Porteous would stop by after his shift. She fed the gas meter and soaked in the bath until the water went cold. She climbed into bed and slept for the rest of the day.

Whilst Nancy was sleeping, Inspector Eric Everard of the Metropolitan Police was sitting in his cramped, dusty office on the top floor of Scotland Yard on the Victoria Embankment. After the debacle with Maruska Bergman and the criminal classes of Kensal Town, Everard had been moved to police black market activity in West London. Everard had introduced an identity card checking system. Whenever bobbies on the beat had cause to stop someone, they were required to record the name and number of the person they had checked. At the end of the day, details were entered onto a card by the desk sergeant and a messenger would come by and collect the cards, which would be taken to Scotland Yard for processing.

Outside Everard's office were four female clerks supervised by a sergeant. Their job was to go through the cards and pull up any names that had been flagged and pass them on to the inspector. It was routine and often boring work, but Everard had had some notable successes in bringing these black marketeers to book. His superiors were pleased with his efforts. After all, questions were being asked in Parliament about the actions of these spivs.

The name Jimmy Ryan was on a watch list...

Everard shouted through the open door,

"Beaston! In here, please."

Police Sergeant Derek Beaston got up smartly and presented himself to his inspector, "Sir?"

Everard held up a card, "Jimmy Ryan."

Beaston nodded, "Yes, sir; picked up on the East India Dock Road during a routine traffic check last night just after the early warning had gone off."

Everard looked at the report, "Says here he had two women with him, Alice Halpin and Nancy Keeling. Have you checked these two out?"

"Just about to do it, sir."

Everard looked over his half-moon reading glasses, "Get that bobby up here asap..."

"Sir..."

Beaston left the room, barking orders at his clerks. It took nearly two hours to locate Police Constable Michael Green who was at home in Battersea with his wife and grown-up daughter. He was off duty. He had been since he retired from the force in 1935. Unfortunately, like so many superannuated personnel from all walks of life, he had been dragged back when the war started to backfill those employees who had gone to serve in the armed forces.

He was not amused when the black saloon car appeared outside his terraced house; neither was his wife. Green was rapidly approaching sixty and had far better things to do with his police pension than be out during the Blitz, risking his life for King and country.

Green was puffing and panting by the time he reached Inspector Everard's office on the top floor of New Scotland Yard. Green knew all about Everard and his drive to wipe out all the black marketeers and spivs. Whatever it was, surely it could wait till he was back on duty on Monday? Besides, Green didn't know anyone who wasn't averse to purchasing the odd lamb chop or pound of sausages under the counter. After all, the ration for a healthy male was hardly enough to keep body and soul together. It was all well and good for those posh people in government to set these rules. They usually had enough money not to have to worry about such things as ration coupons.

Beaston pushed Green in front of his Inspector, "Police Constable Michael Green, sir."

Everard looked up from his desk and tossed over the record card containing Jimmy Ryan's name,

"You recorded this name last night; one Jimmy Ryan?"

Green sighed, made a deliberately slow show of extracting his glasses and reading the index card. His heart leaped into his mouth; wasn't that the van he pulled over with two women in the front dressed in boiler suits?

He swallowed loudly; he'd have to think on his feet.

"Looks like it, sir. Is there a problem?"

Everard folded his arms, "What exactly were the circumstances of the check?"

"Sir, we were doing a routine traffic stop just after the early warning had sounded. Ryan and his two companions were in an old Morris van."

"What were they up to?"

Green looked at the inspector quizzically, "Sir?"

Everard sighed, "Did you ask why they were in the van at that time of night?"

"Oh, right, sir. Yes, Ryan said he was taking the ladies home. Apparently, they'd been working in some factory in Poplar; helping out a mate, I think he said, a spot of overtime..."

"Did you search the van?"

Green swallowed again, "Yes, sir, of course," he lied.

"And there was no one else in the vehicle?"

Green shook his head vigorously, "No, sir, I'm positive."

Everard looked at him, "What was in the van?"

"Nothing, as far as I could see, sir. It was full blackout."

"If it was so dark, how did you record the names of the occupants?"

Green's heart was thumping wildly, "I took the cards over to the shop doorway, sir, and used my lamp like I'm supposed to."

Everard dismissed Green with a wave of his hand, "Thank you, constable, that will be all..."

Police Constable Michael Green was sweating profusely by the time he reached the street. He was glad of the cold chill in the air. That was the last time he'd allow a pretty young lady to get the better of him, tug or no tug...

Inspector Everard lit a pipe and stared at the index card, "What was Jimmy Ryan doing out with those two women?" He was speaking to his sergeant.

"Could be quite genuine, sir," replied Beaston.

Everard snorted, "Don't make me laugh, sergeant. He'll have been up to no good; I can guarantee it. I think it's time we paid a visit to Mr Jimmy Ryan. What about the women?"

"Sir, the Ministry of Labour says it will take at least two days to run the checks on them. One of their offices was hit last night."

Everard put his head into his hands, "Jesus Christ..."

Chapter 5
February 1941
Edith Eleanora Humphries

Nancy Keeling stood in front of Charlie Maitland in his office in Greek Street above his seedy and very expensive bar. He sat back in his chair and admired the view. Mifty Mitchell waited at the door.

Maitland spoke up, "Make yourself scarce, Mifty, I want a private chat with our Nance, here."

Mitchell tipped his forehead, "Sure thing, Boss." He disappeared.

Nancy sighed; she'd much rather be on her way to the party in Kensington.

Maitland stood up, "Sit down, Nancy."

He moved over to a drinks cabinet, "Would you like a gin?"

Nancy shook her head as she sat down, "What do you want, Charlie?" She never called him 'Boss.'

Maitland sat down with his drink. He was wearing an expensive three-piece pin-striped suit. His shoes were immaculately polished. A gold chain hung off one wrist and a gold watch was strapped to the other.

Nancy crossed her legs; she was dressed for her appointment later that evening.

"Mifty told you about your mate, Helen?"

Nancy shook her head, "We don't know it was Helen."

Maitland sipped his drink; he could always lay his hand upon a really expensive single malt, war or no war...

"Well then, my dear, let's talk hypothetically, shall we?"

Nancy straightened her dress.

"You see that girl, the one called June, is currently serving drinks downstairs in the club. She can't do much else at the moment, as one of the lads was a little too handy with his fists. When she heals up, I'll put her out on the streets with a minder."

He took another pull at his glass tumbler.

"Well, Nancy, June described your house mate Helen to a tee."

Nancy looked up, "I told Mifty that I haven't seen Helen for ages. She's back home somewhere in Hampshire; that's all I know."

Maitland stood up, "I do hope that's true, Nancy."

Nancy stared at him, not blinking.

Maitland cleared his throat, "Now listen, I'm thinking of bringing you in-house. You'll earn a lot more, and at least you won't be at risk from the Strangler."

Nancy shook her head. The last thing she needed was to go up to the house on the Edgware Road, Maida Vale. The girls up there were like prisoners.

"I'm okay where I am, Charlie."

He smiled, "Sure you are, Nancy, but the clients at the house are much more discerning and much wealthier as well. I can guarantee you at least ten pounds a night and tips. You'll have no rent to pay." He paused and raised his eyebrows, "Where do you live?"

"West Hampstead, Charlie."

He nodded, "Oh yes, that's right. I don't bother myself with these details. I understand you've got a younger sister?"

Nancy's heart leapt into her mouth.

He continued, "Yes, that's right. What's her name, Charlotte, is it? I think she's about nineteen, is that correct? If she's half as good-looking as you, we could make a lot of money."

Nancy stood up, smoothing down her dress, "I'll be late for the appointment, Charlie." She didn't want to engage with the Maltese gangster.

Maitland shouted, "Mifty! Bring up that tart, June."

Nancy could hear the sound of heavy footsteps on the wooden stairs.

Two minutes later, a rather battered looking female appeared at the door. Her face was all bruised and the short, black, flared, cocktail dress she had squeezed into, did nothing to cover the marks on her arms and shoulders. No amount of makeup would conceal the beating that she had been given. Mifty Mitchell smiled at his boys' handiwork.

June stood at the doorway, her head bowed down.

Maitland went over to her and tilted up her chin with his hand, "You see, Nancy, this is what happens if you cross me."

Nancy nodded. Maitland spun June around, patted her on the backside and ushered her out, "Go and smile at a few customers, there's a good girl..."

Maitland looked back at Nancy, "Haven't you somewhere to go?"

When Nancy got down to the Wolseley Hornet, there were three other girls in the car. She recognised the girls. One was in the front passenger seat and two in the rear. Nancy squashed in beside the touchy, feely girl from Kilburn.

The girl leaned over to her. Nancy could smell cheap gin on her breath,

"I've got four pounds already, Nancy..."

Nancy pushed her away and stared out of the window. Working with Peter Porteous and Alice Halpin up at Smiths was certainly becoming a more attractive proposition day by day...

Just as Nancy Keeling was smiling at some rich, minor aristocrat in the private club just off Gloucester Road in South Kensington, Edith Eleanora Humphries was sitting on her own in a quiet pub just opposite Euston Station on Eversholt Street. She had worked this bar before with some success. There were always one or two servicemen looking for a non-too expensive thrill and being forty-eight and a widow, Edith Eleanora Humphries was cheap by most standards.

She was nursing a drink, trying to make it last until she could persuade some young fellow to buy her another and, perhaps, avail himself of whatever goods she had on offer. It was getting late, and the early warning siren would soon be going off. For her age, Humphries was an attractive woman. She'd kept her figure and was a little large on top; always an eye-catching feature for a young serviceman.

She wore a slightly tight pale blue dress. Her cleavage was on show. The old overcoat was draped on the back of her chair. She crossed her legs repeatedly whenever a man looked at her as she pretended to read the early evening newspaper.

She felt the table move as a young man in his mid-twenties plonked a fresh gin and tonic next to her nearly empty glass. She looked up and smiled; he would do.

"Why, thank you, young man. That's very kind of you."

Gordon Cummins smiled, "Can I join you?"

She put down the newspaper, "Of course. It's always a pleasure to have the company of an RAF sergeant."

Cummins put down his pint glass and sat down, "Are you with someone?"

Humphries nodded, "No; I'm sorry to say I'm a widow. My husband died some time ago, leaving me all on my own."

Cummins sipped his beer, "Oh, we can't have that, can we?"

Humphries crossed her legs again; making sure that her suitor got an eye full of her stocking tops.

Cummins licked his lips; this one was going to be easy and none too expensive either. He squashed in next to her. His hand was on her knee after about five minutes; she didn't object.

After three more gin and tonics, she was ready to take him back to her flat just off Albany Road adjacent to Regent's Park; it was one pound for the night...

Humphries was a little unsteady on her feet as they walked up the main road before they turned off into Robert Street. Cummins didn't want to go much further, as his barracks were just at the top of the road. She led him up the stairs to her second floor flat that consisted of two rooms and a kitchen. There was one bathroom on each floor to be shared by the tenants. She unlocked her door and they went inside. She poured two more drinks from a half empty gin bottle and sat next to him on the old, worn-out sofa.

They spoke a little before he felt her nodding off with the alcohol taking its toll. He pulled her up,

"Shall we go in the bedroom?"

She smiled, "Oh, you are such a wicked boy..."

Gordon Cummins mounted a naked Edith Elenora Humphries on the big brass bed that creaked in rhythm to his thrusts. She was past child-bearing age and couldn't care less about wearing a rubber...just the way Cummins liked it.

Try as he may, Cummins could not climax. He looked down at the woman. Her eyes were closed and she appeared to be almost asleep. He stopped. She began to snore. Cummins saw the red mist. He punched her hard into the face; she moaned as he pounded her time and time again until she completely lost consciousness. Her face was a mess. He pulled a pillow over her face and began to have sex with her again. He soon gave up; there was no response from the widow.

He kneeled over her and put his hands around her neck. He began to squeeze. He could hear her gurgling under the pillow. He threw off the pillow and got out of bed. He reached into his RAF issue haversack and extracted a knife. He climbed over her again and slashed her neck. He stood up and watched her bleed. He got bored and plunged the knife into her skull. The blade penetrated her brain.

Gordon Cummins looked at the body as the life began to drain out of her. He calmly walked into the kitchen and rinsed off the knife before drying it and replacing it in his haversack alongside his gas mask. He dressed and then went through the widow's belongings. He stole several pieces of jewellery. Just before he left, he went to the side of the bed where she had disrobed. He picked up one of her stockings; it was still attached to her suspender belt. He slowly unclipped it, held it up to his nose and breathed in her scent. The stocking went in his bag to add to his collection.

He calmly left the flat leaving the door ajar, not bothering if anyone would find the body or not. Gordon Cummins went about his business, not giving the woman a second thought.

Just about the time that Gordon Cummins had his hands around the poor woman's throat, Nancy Keeling was earning her keep over in Gloucester Road. She managed to make nearly fifteen pounds after Mifty Mitchell had taken Charlie Maitland's cut. She was so tired as the Hornet chugged up Kilburn High Road. Her last client had paid her two pounds for her silk French knickers and two stockings. She couldn't be bothered fighting off her female suitor, who seemed to have hands everywhere. Nancy got into bed wearing her pyjamas just as it was getting light on the Sunday morning. She tossed and turned for a little while and came to the conclusion that it would soon be time to change her life...

Edith Eleanora Humphries lived for a further four days lying on her blood-soaked bed before a neighbour, noticing that the door had been open for some time, ventured in to find her mortally injured. The widow died shortly after being admitted to hospital.

Chapter 6
February 1941
Adventures at Smiths in Cricklewood

Alice Halpin was underneath the unreliable pressing machine, again. It was early on the following Monday morning. Peter Porteous was on his haunches next to her, passing her the odd spanner or two. He asked,

"Is it the bearings again?"

The Liverpool accent was thick, "Of course it is; what else could it be?" There was an air of irritation in her voice.

Porteous raised his eyebrows and thought that Phyllis Manley must have gone back to Gosport to complete her training, leaving Alice alone for the next few weeks...

Alice slid out on the battered crawler, "It's fucked, Porteous, not only are the bearings gone again but there's too much play in the housing. It's two hours work, at least if the parts are in the store."

There were specks of oil on her face. Porteous reached over and wiped them off, "I take it Phyllis has gone?"

Alice smiled, "Is it that obvious?"

"Don't take it out on that machine or me..."

She playfully punched him on the arm, "Yeah, sorry..."

The supervisor, Cedric Walker, appeared at the door to the workshop. The girls, who were standing around chatting, scattered to their workbenches.

Walker called out, "What is it, Porteous?"

Porteous looked up, "Have a guess."

Walker shook his head; he straightened up and raised his voice, "Right. Dispersal orders whilst this machine is fixed."

The girls groaned.

He clapped his hands, "Come on! Chop, chop! There's a war on, you know."

Porteous rolled his eyes. The girls hated dispersal orders. They would be sent off to various parts of the factory to cover for absentee colleagues. This was a regular occurrence.

Cedric Walker stood with his hands on his hips as the ladies slowly gathered their belongings and trudged out to distant parts of the factory, muttering to themselves. He looked at Porteous,

"Get it fixed by the end of the shift..."

He strode off.

Porteous looked at Alice Halpin, "Fancy a walk in the fresh air, Alice?"

She smiled at him, "What do you think, Porteous? I'll grab my coat..."

The parts department, or tool shop as it was known by the workers, was situated right at the back of the factory in a dirty, grey building that sat next to a high barbed wire fence. It took the two of them nearly ten minutes to reach their destination as they walked so slowly. They chatted aimlessly until the subject of one Nancy Keeling came up.

Alice looked across at her friend, "You've got to stop her, Porteous."

He quickly glanced at her as they walked on, "I know. What do you think I've been trying to do these last few months? She won't listen to me. She won't take any money to complete the purchase of her mother's house. She's determined to plough her own furrow."

Alice stared ahead, "We've got to do something..."

A bad-tempered and cussed old man named Alfred Dunne ran the parts department at Smiths in Cricklewood. He treated every part and piece of stock as his own personal property and took delight in telling workers that the parts they need to keep this section of the war effort going were not available. And no, he didn't know when or if they would become available...just fill out the appropriate requisition form, and he'd get around to it soon...

They pushed open the creaky and rusty door. Porteous could smell the old man's foul-smelling pipe; it caught his throat immediately.

A bell rang on the door. Alfred Dunne looked up from behind the counter, shot a furrowed brow at Porteous and then went back to his clipboard. The man was slightly overweight at about five feet five inches. He was dressed in an oil-covered, brown lab coat that, like its owner, had seen better days. It was said that Dunne had been wounded at the Battle of the Somme in the First World War as a young soldier but, as he hardly ever spoke to anyone, no one really knew. Most employees at the factory tried to avoid all unnecessary contact with him.

Porteous looked at him as he pretended to ignore him. The man was completely bald except for a circle of grey hair that ran from his ears around the back of his head. There appeared to be more hair coming out of his ears than on his crown. His half-moon reading glasses were perched on the top of his head, with the stub of a pencil stuck behind one ear and a half-smoked cigarette behind the other.

"What do you want, Porteous?" He hadn't bothered to look up.

"Two and a half inch bearings and casings for an Excelsior Mark 2 pressing machine."

"Fill out a requisition form..."

Alice nudged him from behind.

Porteous extracted his pen and completed the form. He pushed it in front of the store man. Dunne had still not looked up. He reached over and took the form, popped his glasses on his face and tutted,

"Sorry, out of stock. Leave it with me and I'll check tomorrow's delivery. Those bearings have been on back order for over a week."

Porteous cleared his throat, "Mr Walker wants the machine fixed today."

Dunne sighed loudly and looked up for the first time, "If I haven't got any, I haven't got any. Don't you understand?"

Then he suddenly saw Alice Halpin who had been hiding behind Porteous.

Alfred Dunne's manner changed completely, "Ah, Miss Halpin. We don't see enough of you down here."

Alice smiled sweetly at him, "That's because we manage to keep our machines running, Mr Dunne."

Alfred Dunne was a lady's man...

Alice Halpin gently tweaked Porteous' leg, "What about a two and half inch bearing for a Mark 3?"

Dunne shrugged his shoulders, "It won't fit. The casings have a different bevel."

Alice tilted her head and flashed her eyes, "But you can make it fit, Mr Dunne."

Alfred Dunne puffed himself with pride. He had learnt his trade as a lathe turner after he came back from the Somme in 1916. The whole factory knew he could do anything that required the turning of a piece of metal.

He opened up the counter, "Well, let's go and check if we've got some in stock, and then I'll see what I can do for you."

He turned to Porteous, "Fill out another requisition for a Mark 3 whilst I see if I can help Miss Halpin."

Alice nudged Porteous as she went past him. Porteous shook his head, sighed and went about filling out a new form. Alice made sure she stayed very close to Alfred Dunne...

Thirty minutes later, Alice appeared back at the counter clutching a cardboard box containing the newly machined parts.

They made a swift exit before Alfred Dunne reappeared to receive his plaudits.

They hurried back to the workshop. Porteous said, "You're as bad as Nancy."

She smiled, "She taught me well, Porteous. I gave him a quick kiss on the cheek as a thank you, and he patted my bottom as I left."

Porteous held up his hand, "Enough! I'd prefer not to know."

They giggled as they walked back into the silent workshop. They sat down and stared at the failed pressing machine in silence. Eventually, he spoke,

"Come on, let's get on with it. I'm on fire-watching duty tonight, and I'd like to get some sleep before I go."

Alice was back under the machine in a flash, "The sodding casings have welded themselves to the housing..."

Porteous shook his head, "Crack them off, Alice." He handed her a ball-peen hammer. "See if you can get them off without doing too much damage."

She swore at him from under the machine...

Nearly four hours later, they sat on a bench and watched as the Excelsior Mark 2 pressing machine with the Mark 3 bearings came back to life and began to spit out cockpit instruments shells. They were both covered in light machine oil.

Alice sighed, "You've got to give it to the old bugger in the tool shed. He certainly can make stuff work with a bit of fettling."

Porteous laughed, "Great word that fettling, but what was the cost?"

She shrugged her shoulders, "Nothing I can't handle. I've dealt with lechers like him, both male and female all my life. If he'd gotten too touchy-feely a swift kick in the balls usually does the trick..."

He stood, reached out his hand and pulled her up, "Come on, time to bugger off. The next shift can crack on with the order"

Nancy Keeling sat on the end of the old iron bath as Peter Porteous attempted to wash off the worst of his day's work at Smiths in Cricklewood. She washed his back with what purported to be soap; it was all she could get in the shop.

She asked him, "What time do you have to be in Chelsea?"

"I'll leave here after six. I need to go over to Kensal Town to pick up some bits and pieces. Harry Harris wants some more things for his lady friend."

Nancy looked at the steamed-up clock on the wall above the door; she had him for a couple of hours at least. She idly waved the water around with one hand.

"Does his wife know he has a mistress?"

Porteous shook his head, "Dunno, Nancy. Not my business. I just sell him stuff when he asks for it."

Nancy put her hand on his head and pushed him under the water, stood up and went to the door, "I'll make you something to eat."

He emerged and flicked water at her, smiling...

Nancy was in the kitchen when she heard the knock at the front door. Instinctively, she glanced at the kitchen clock; it was barely four in the afternoon, with the light beginning to fade. Mifty Mitchell wouldn't be due until nearly eight.

She went to the rarely used front room and peered out behind the heavy blackout curtains that had been pulled to one side to let in the weak winter sun. Her heart skipped a beat; there were two policemen standing on the doorstep. They knocked again.

She went to open the front door, knowing full well that if she didn't answer they would undoubtedly return. She smoothed down her blouse and made sure it was tucked neatly into her beige waist high trousers. She slowly opened the door.

A young policeman, barely out of his teens, blushed when he saw this beautiful, tall woman. The other, in his early sixties, fat and clearly out of any sort of condition for apprehending criminals, cleared his throat as he referred to his clipboard.

"Miss Keeling? Miss Nancy Keeling?"

Nancy nodded sweetly at the young policeman, making him colour up even more.

"What can I do for you, officers?"

The fat one responded, "Nothing to worry about, Miss, just a routine check. I believe you were stopped recently for an identity check on the Mile End Road?"

Nancy's heart raced, "Oh, yes, I was in my friend's van. We were returning from a stint at a factory just after the early warning sounded."

"Have you got your identity card, Miss?"

"Yes-yes, of course. I'll be back in a second."

She skipped up the stairs. Porteous was standing in the bathroom doorway with a towel wrapped around his waist. She put a finger up to her lips as signal for him to remain silent and winked at him...

The fat one perused her card, looked at her picture several times, and then at her. Satisfied it was she; he spoke with a London accent,

"Miss, can you tell me where you are employed?"

Nancy wondered if her heart would leap out of her mouth, "Smiths; Smiths in Cricklewood. I've just started there."

The fat one wrote on his clipboard, "Thanks, Miss Keeling. We won't keep you any longer."

With that, he tipped his hat and sauntered off back down the short path to the road. Nancy winked at the young lad, who turned and rushed after his older colleague. She quietly closed the front door, leaned back against it and breathed out a sigh of relief.

Porteous had pulled on a pair of clean trousers and a shirt; he sat on the bottom of the stairs. She said,

"What was all that about?"

He shook his head, "Dunno, Nancy, but it was because we got stopped the other night."

"Should we tell Alice and Jimmy?"

He smiled, "They'll get short shrift from Alice. She's had years of experience dealing with the police in Liverpool, and as for Jimmy? He lives up in Tottenham. The authorities have no idea he does his business out of that disused shop in Holborn." He paused, "But I can tell you it's a warning to be very careful."

Nancy wasn't so sure, "What if they check up at Smiths? I told them I work there."

Porteous looked at her, "It was always going to be a problem, but I'll go and sweeten the girls in the office first thing tomorrow morning so don't worry."

Five hours later, just before our Germanic cousins arrived to bomb the hell out of London, Peter Porteous was bartering with one Harry Harris over three pairs of good quality stockings and a set of silk lingerie at the top of St Luke's and Christ Church in Chelsea. Detective Inspector Eric Everard sat in his office in New Scotland Yard. Everard had waited patiently for the reports to come back. He was constantly looking at the old clock on the wall of his cramped office. He desperately wanted to return home before the bombing started. If he left it too late, he would end up spending the best part of the night in the dark and dingy basement of New Scotland Yard.

Everard was a complex man. His wife had long since left him to return to the bosom of her family somewhere in Wiltshire. She had taken up with a country doctor but had never bothered to obtain a divorce. Everard was not interested in either the expense or the accompanying publicity. He had a lady friend who would provide him with relief, as and when necessary, for an appropriate fee, of course, but he never saw that other than a financial arrangement. She lived on the other side of London, so he would pay her travelling expenses. Nothing wrong with that, was there?

Everard was wedded to his work. He had a thing about black marketeers, and he wouldn't be satisfied until every single one of them was banged up in some ghastly prison away from honest, hard working members of society. He had Jimmy Ryan and his associates on his radar for some time. He thought he had one of his chief co-conspirators, Peter Porteous, when they lifted him and that part-time prostitute, Edith Bell, when the security services were searching for that suspected spy, what was her name? Oh, yes, Doctor Maruska Bergman.

They couldn't search Porteous' residence on Bosworth Road for evidence because that parachute bomb had obliterated it. Everard stood up. He stuck a pipe into his mouth. He'd had Porteous on a short lead until that stupid magistrate abolished his bail conditions. Whilst he knew that Porteous was still living in Kensal Town, he had no idea exactly where. The address they had on record was the bombed house on Bosworth Road and the local police were distinctly disinclined to cross the steps to make further enquiries, and he didn't fancy a trip over there not without an armed escort...

Everard could hear voices in the outer office. He went over to the door and pulled it open,

"What is it, Derek?"

"The reports are back from West Hampstead and Tottenham, sir."

Everard scared the living daylights out of the messenger, who was a little slip of a girl who should have been in school. She fled quickly.

He clicked his fingers, "Well, what does it say? Come on, man, I haven't got all day."

Detective Sergeant Derek Beaston skimmed the notes, "Nancy Keeling checks out, sir, as does the Alice Halpin girl. The addresses match up to the identity cards."

"What about Jimmy Ryan?"

Beaston flicked over the page, "All in order, sir. He wasn't home, but his landlady said he lived there and was spending most of his time with the Air Raid Precautions service."

Everard shook his head, "Damn!"

He thought for a moment, "What about their employment status? We know that Porteous works up at Smiths."

Beaston perused the notes again, "It says here that both Halpin and Keeling work at Smiths. That ties in with what the Ministry told us." He paused.

"It also says that Ryan is unemployed owing to his past convictions, sir."

Everard struck a match and attempted to light his pipe, "Right, Derek get up to Smiths first thing tomorrow and check out their records. If those girls are lying, we could pull them in for further questioning and make their lives difficult. We might even get enough evidence to convince a magistrate to issue search warrants on all their residences."

Beaston wanted to object, but then held his tongue.

He asked, "What do you want to do about Ryan, sir?"

"Keep sending one of the locals up to his lodgings until he's actually interviewed. That will at least upset the landlady. You never know, she might get a little fed up and ask him to leave. Meanwhile, get one of the girls to chase down his ARP unit and we'll bother them as well."

"And Peter Porteous?"

"Oh, I've got something special in mind for him..."

It was gone nine-thirty the following morning by the time Detective Sergeant Derek Beaston pulled the black Vauxhall 12 saloon onto the tarmac apron in front of the main gates at Smiths in Cricklewood. The car was anonymous. The casual observer could not ascertain that this was indeed a police issue vehicle. It had no blue lights nor was it fitted with warning bells. The security guard stubbed out his cigarette, gathered his clipboard and wandered nonchalantly over to the car. Beaston slowly wound down the window and stuck out his warrant card. The guard stiffened,

"Who would you like to see, sir?"

"Whoever is in charge of Personnel."

The guard ran a pencil down the board, "That'll be Miss Jackson. She's in Building 2. I'll phone ahead to announce your arrival."

He pointed to a dirty grey building, "Park in the front visitor's bay."

With that, he sauntered away. The double gates mysteriously opened. Beaston crunched the gears as he pulled forward; he could never get the hang of these police issue vehicles...

He was met at the foot of the stairs to the suite of offices where management pretended to manage. He looked up as Dorothy Jackson leaned against the rusty, iron railings. She was dressed in a knee-length dark- coloured skirt and some beige knitwear. Her black court shoes elevated her height about three inches. Around her neck a string of pearls clung to her figure fighting for space with the brightly coloured string that held her reading glasses. She must have been in her early fifties, but she had retained much of her youthful good looks, especially her ample bosom to which many male eyes were instantly drawn.

Beaston cleared his throat, "Miss Jackson?" He didn't bother to wait for a reply, "Can you spare me a few minutes of your time?"

"It's Mrs Jackson, constable," came the terse reply.

"And it's Detective Sergeant Derek Beaston, ma'am."

Her eyebrows furrowed, "What can I do for you, Sergeant?"

She showed no inclination of offering to take him inside. He shivered in the cold of the February morning.

"I need to check on a couple of your employees, ma'am."

Dorothy Jackson sighed, "Oh, very well. Perhaps you'd better come inside."

She straightened up, smoothed down her skirt and pushed open the exterior door, "Please come with me."

He followed her past a range of offices and one larger one that he presumed was the typing pool, where about twenty women of varying ages and sizes clacked away at typewriters equally of varying ages and sizes. A few of the ladies glanced up, saw that Beaston was somewhat unremarkable, shook their heads and returned to their mundane tasks, wishing that the morning tea bell would sound sooner rather than later.

Dorothy Jackson pushed open the door to her little glass office, "Take a seat, please, Sergeant, now exactly what can I do for you?"

Beaston pulled out his official pocket book, "I need to check on three of your employees to confirm they are working here, if that's okay with you?"

"Is this an official request, Sergeant?"

He nodded, 'Yes, ma'am. We periodically follow up on those who have been identified at checkpoints."

She sighed, "Oh, very well. Give me their names and I'll check for you. You do know that there are nearly one thousand personnel employed on this vital war work?"

It was a question that did not require an answer.

Jackson reached into her desk and extracted a notepad and a silver fountain pen. She propped her reading glasses on her nose and looked at the detective expectantly.

He coughed, "Alice Halpin, 21B West Heath Drive, Golders Green, Nancy Keeling, 16 Crediton Hill, West Hampstead..." He paused as her pen glided smoothly across the paper in copperplate writing...

"And Peter Porteous, last known address 10, Bosworth Road, Kensal Town."

Dorothy Jackson momentarily froze; Peter Porteous supplied most of the girls in the office with stockings, lingerie and other hard to obtain items without the need for ration coupons. Indeed, she was currently wearing a pair of his hard-to-get hosiery....She wrote down his name as Beaston continued,

"His last known address was completely demolished by a parachute bomb last year, and he hasn't bothered to inform the Ministry of his new abode."

She stood up, "I'll get one of the girls to bring you some hot tea whilst I locate their files. I could be a few minutes."

Beaston nodded and sat back...

Dorothy Jackson hurried into the typing pool and signalled Dawn Fraser to approach her. She clicked her fingers at a mousy girl sitting in a corner, "Nell, make some tea for our visitor."

The girl scuttled off, glad for something to do apart from walking around collecting finished typing from the other ladies and placing it in the in-tray on the elevated desk.

Dawn Fraser whispered, "What's up, Dot?"

Dorothy Jackson led her over to the door and spoke quietly, "Got a copper in my office asking about Porteous, the Halpin girl and someone called Nancy Keeling."

Dawn Fraser swallowed, "Jesus, what's Porteous been up to?"

"Dunno, Dawn, but see if you can dig out their files. Bring them to me here, please."

She handed over the piece of paper upon which she had written the three names. Dawn Fraser disappeared off to the filing room. Meanwhile, the ladies of the typing pool had ceased their clattering. Jackson raised her eyebrows and the clattering recommenced.

Dorothy Jackson grabbed the office junior as she walked past her carrying a pot of tea on a wooden tray. "Chat him up for me, there's a good girl..."

Nell's one major talent was chatting up menfolk...

Dawn Fraser poked her head out of the filing room and beckoned Dorothy Jackson. She pulled her supervisor into the dusty room. She was clutching two Manila files bearing the names, Peter Porteous and Alice Halpin. Jackson quickly flicked through them. They seemed to be in order.

She looked at Dawn Fraser, "The Keeling girl?"

"She doesn't work here, Dot. Remember Porteous came in looking for some headed notepaper?"

Jackson put her head in her hands, "Jesus, that bloody Porteous will be the death of us all." She paused, "Okay, run back to the pool and type out a starter's sheet; that should keep the officer happy."

Dorothy Jackson left Detective Constable Derek Beaston to enjoy his hot tea for about three minutes. She paused at the door, smoothed down her skirt again, and ran her fingers through her hair. She gently pushed open the door.

Beaston had his notebook open. He held his pen expectantly. Jackson dropped the two Manila files on the table and sat down,

"Now, what can I do for you, officer?"

Beaston cleared his throat, "I just need you to confirm some details, that's all."

Jackson placed her reading glasses on her nose, "Is there a problem?"

Beaston sipped his tea, "No, No, of course not. We are just doing some routine enquiries, that's all. Now, I don't want to keep you…"

"Yes, yes of course…"

Dorothy Jackson flicked open a file. The policeman asked,

"Can you confirm that Peter Porteous does work here?"

The office supervisor ran a painted nail down the top sheet, "Yes, certainly. He is a foreman over in one of the pressing and assembly workshops."

Beaston's pen scratched on his notebook, "When did his employment commence here?"

"March 1938. He started not long after he had been medically discharged from the army. His discharge papers indicate that he suffers from asthma."

Beaston looked up, she was telling him nothing that he already knew, "Is he a good attender?"

There was another pause as Jackson turned over some papers, "Yes, attendance is very good. He is allowed some leeway as he is an Air Raid Precautions warden."

"Do you have his current address?"

"Just the Bosworth Road address you gave me earlier; he must have forgotten to update the office. I do remember when his home was bombed. I understand he lost someone close to him?" She sighed, and continued, "It happens all the time, I'm sorry to say. We have numerous workers here and there's always something like this at the moment."

The policeman pushed over a card, "Could you get his new address and let us know?"

Dorothy Jackson nodded. She closed the file, "Alice Halpin?"

"If you wouldn't mind."

"She came to us not long after Porteous in May 1938. She had previously worked in a glove factory in Liverpool. She came with excellent references, and we have her as Porteous' deputy. Her address is 21B West Heath Drive, Golders Green."

There was a knock on the door and Dawn Fraser appeared with a freshly typed starter's sheet; the ink was barely dry...She handed the paper to Jackson, smiled at the policeman and left.

"Ah, here we are. Miss Nancy Keeling; only started here two weeks ago. It appears she's in temporary accommodation, which is why a personnel file has not yet been created."

She passed the sheet over to Beaston who asked, "Is this normal?"

"Is what normal?"

"That it takes a few weeks to create a file?"

Dorothy Jackson folded her arms, sat back and sighed, "Regrettably, yes. There is so much staff turnover at the moment with the evacuation and husbands' deployment. We often get ladies who start one week, leave the next, and then come back to us once their husbands are sent away."

Beaston sighed as he copied down Nancy's details. He gulped down the rest of his tea, stood up and said, "Just get your files up to date and Miss Keeling's details before the Ministry pays you a visit. And don't forget to send me Porteous' new address."

He went to the door, tipped his forehead and said, "I'll bid you good day..."

Dorothy Jackson breathed out loudly and closed her eyes. Dawn Fraser opened the door and peered in, "Everything okay, Dot?"

"Get me Porteous as soon as the bugger clocks in..."

Peter Porteous poked his head around the door of the typing pool. Dawn Fraser jerked her thumb in the general direction of Dorothy Jackson's office,

"Dot wants to see you now..."

Porteous raised his eyebrows. Normally, the reception he received from the girls in the office was much warmer, especially when he had items for sale.

He took a ten-minute ear bashing from the office manager before he managed to placate her with the promise of three more pairs of stockings and one pair for Dawn as she had actually forged the starter sheet.

"Who is this Nancy Keeling anyway?" demanded Jackson.

"Oh, just a friend who needed to satisfy the Ministry of Labour as to her employment status."

"Is she going to come and work for us?"

"Well...not just yet, Dot."

"Bloody hell, Porteous, what do you think this place is? That damn copper threatened us with a visit from the Ministry, and it's not just your ghost lady that I've got to worry about. This place doesn't revolve around you, despite what you might think."

Porteous held up his hands, "All right, Dot, I'll get it sorted."

She leaned into him, "You'd better bloody well make sure you do. I want this lass up here and working within a couple of weeks before the Ministry turns up."

Porteous' mind was going ten to the dozen, "I'll do my best, Dot..."

He left rapidly before she could think of anything else with which to bash him...

Alice Halpin was sitting on a workbench, swinging her legs. She had a smile on her face,

"I told you not to do that letter for Nancy. How are you going to get her to work here in the next couple of weeks?"

He shook his head, "Dunno, Alice, but I'll think of something, don't worry..."

Chapter 7
February 1941
A Change of Heart

Nancy Keeling sighed. She was tired and bored. This party should have finished hours ago. She looked at the old wall clock; it was close to three in the morning. It was so late that even the bombing had stopped, not that that had discouraged the over-indulged youngsters from one of the top universities out for one last fling before their country called them up.

The private rooms above the public house on Fulham Palace Road had been booked for the night and with so much alcohol being sold, the landlord was reluctant to evict his guests, especially when they were paying double.

She looked at Mifty Mitchell who stood with his arms folded by the door and tapped her wrist indicating her watch. He shook his head and mouthed an obscenity at her.

She sipped her drink, which the barman had obligingly watered down for her over the evening. She charged her clients full price for the gin and tonic but shared the spoils with the young man behind the bar. Every penny counted...

Margaret Heywood approached her; she rolled her eyes. Miss Heywood was the lady from Kilburn who had offered her five pounds for a night of unbridled passion... Nancy folded her arms as the petite lass approached,

"What do you want, Margaret?"

Heywood sidled up to her, "You see that tall one over in the corner, the one with the dark hair?"

Nancy looked up, "Yes, so what?"

"Five pounds each for a double."

Nancy shook her head, "Not a chance. If you think I'm going with you and him for a fiver, you must be joking."

Margaret Heywood pouted, "Come on, Nance; it'll be the easiest money we'll earn tonight."

Nancy looked across at the man who was destined for a very short and terminal career in the Royal Air Force as a Hurricane fighter pilot. He smiled at her. She said,

"I doubt he's ever been with a woman before."

Margaret squeezed her arm, "Exactly; we'll have him finished before he's had a chance to get on his rubber."

Nancy sighed again, "Tell him ten pounds each, and then okay it with Mifty for five and we'll pocket the difference."

Margaret Heywood scuttled away to set up the deal, as Nancy mentally calculated how much more of this business she would have to endure before she could go and work at Smiths. She just knew one thing and that was she would rather die than go and work in the house on the Edgware Road in spite of the potential for good money.

She looked over at Mifty Mitchell who was stifling a yawn. He nodded almost imperceptibly.

Margaret Heywood pushed her way back through the maze of wandering hands. The university students were clearly the worse for wear. Most of them couldn't have managed it if they tried, as they had consumed too much alcohol.

Heywood waved two crisp five-pound notes at Nancy, "Half now and half after."

Nancy slid off the end of the table upon which she had been sitting, "Come on then; let's get him done..."

Nancy Keeling pulled her dress back over her head. Margaret Heywood was correct. He had popped even before she had managed to disrobe. The sight of two partially dressed beauties in front of him had been too much for the young man. He lay back on the bed, closed his eyes and began to snore. Heywood straddled him. She half turned him over, reached into his back pocket and extracted his wallet.

"Just take what we are owed, Margaret."

Heywood looked at her, "Look at this, Nance, he's even got three more fivers and a load of singles."

Nancy stared at her, "Go and give Mifty his share and then hold mine for safekeeping."

Margaret Heywood looked at her as she got off the bed, "Where are you going, Nancy?"

Nancy reached for her coat, "I'm going home…"

Heywood licked her lips, "What's the hurry? Look, I've got the five pounds you wanted."

"Tomorrow night at my place. Eight sharp and don't be late. And no funny business, do you hear?"

Margaret Heywood smiled at her, "I'll tell Mifty you're not feeling well."

Nancy shook her head, "Tell that bastard whatever you want…"

Nancy slipped out of the back door and scarpered down the old iron fire escape. The night was cold. She looked up. It was a bright sky; no doubt the bloody Germans would be back for a second bite at the cherry. She reached into her bag as the cold night air caught the back of her throat; she shivered. She had a liberated ARP torch that Porteous had given her. You had to press the button to keep the light on…

The full moon lit up London's darkened streets. The occasional car went past slowly picking out its way amongst the debris. She paused in a shop doorway as two policemen sauntered along on the opposite side of the road. She didn't want to explain herself to anyone.

She walked down Fulham Palace Road and turned into Lille Road. There were still some revellers out enjoying the lull in the bombing. She toyed with the idea of hailing one of the infrequent taxis that were out but dismissed it preferring her own company at least until she had reached St Luke's and Christ Church in Chelsea where Porteous was on duty...It took her over an hour and a half...

Michael Mifty Mitchell went into a rage about the disappearance of one of his highest earning ladies...

Peter Porteous was dozing when the Bakelite telephone rang next to him on the old wooden table; he jumped. He shook his head and glanced over the parapet at the dark vista. He silently cursed the bright moon. He knew the bombers would soon be back. The telephone rang again. He picked it up,

"Hello."

"Porteous; it's me, Nancy. Come down and let me in."

Porteous spluttered, "Nancy? What in God's name are you doing here?"

"Just come down and open the bloody door, would you?"

Nancy had opened the little box that contained the telephone on the wall next to the door.

The receiver went down with a bang. She slammed the box shut. Porteous winced. He struggled to his feet and felt his chest. He took a deep breath and immediately went into a coughing fit. Nancy heard him as he clumped down the stairs. He turned the old brass key and pushed on the wooden door.

Nancy's eyes opened wide, "Jesus, Porteous, you look terrible. Are you having an attack?"

He breathed out, "I hope not; my medication is all at home."

Nancy took his arm, "Breathe slowly. Have you got some water up in the gods?"

He nodded. They went back up to the look-out. He sat down in the old chair and gulped half a bottle of tepid water; his breathing gradually returned to normal.

She said, "You shouldn't be doing this, Porteous. You spend all day in that factory, and then you come here."

He rolled his eyes, "You sound like Maruska."

Nancy looked away; Maruska Bergman had taken his heart, hook, line and sinker, "Never mind about Maruska," she said, irritably, "Try looking after yourself."

Porteous reached out and took her hand, "There's a flask of brandy in my bag."

Nancy rifled through the bag, found the small silver flask, unscrewed the cap and took a hefty swig.

"Hey! Save some for me."

Nancy looked at him whilst the bottle was still at her mouth. She drained the whole lot.

He looked at her, "Thanks for that...What's troubling you tonight?"

She pushed away his arm and plonked herself on his lap. He could feel her sobbing against his greatcoat. Gradually, the tears subsided. He felt her shiver. The night was cold, and she only had on a thin coat.

He gently lifted her off and sat her down on the other chair, "There's a spare coat on the top landing. Stay there until I fetch it."

Nancy looked over the parapet glad that she had some brief solitude. The night was clear with the full moon lighting up the whole panorama in front of her. The Germans didn't need any fancy navigation equipment. The place was lit up as though it was in floodlights. She shook her head.

Porteous pulled her up, wiped away her tears and draped the old coat around her. She wrinkled her nose, "Which dead person was wrapped up in this?"

He smiled as he pulled the coat together and fastened a few of the buttons. He turned up the collar so her face just peaked out. He pushed her back down. Her arms were trapped inside the coat.

"What's up, Nancy?"

"I can't do it any more."

"Do what?"

"Whoring."

Porteous let the word slowly sink in. He had been waiting for this moment for a number of months; he knew it had been coming. She had never described herself as a whore before. She preferred the phrase 'entertainment business' whenever she was asked about her line of work. He didn't push the conversation. A silence descended upon them. He stared out at the night sky knowing that the Luftwaffe would soon be back.

She began to talk, "You know tonight I took ten pounds off a young man. He couldn't have been much older than Charlotte. He had just finished at some posh university, and he's off to fly in those flimsy planes. He's got the whole world in front of him, and yet he'll probably be dead in the next few months."

She paused and shrugged her shoulders, "Never mind, he'll get a hero's funeral and a gong of some description. If he's lucky, he'll have a gravestone somewhere in the country where his grieving parents can visit him on a Sunday afternoon."

Porteous stared at her, "It's the price of war, Nancy. There are plenty of other youngsters out there who will suffer the same fate as him."

She glared at him, "At least he's doing something worthwhile not like me."

Porteous folded his arms and stared at her.

She went on, "What do I do? I lay on my back while some fellow pays to enjoy me."

He was about to say it was her choice but held his tongue knowing that Charlie Maitland would not be so inclined to let her go without a fight.

"You have a job at Smiths."

She nodded, "Do they know what I am?"

He shook his head, "No. They just know that you are a friend of Alice and me, that's all."

"Will they find out about me?"

"Not unless you tell them."

She pursed her lips, "Can we go next week?"

He stood up, "Of course. I'll go and see Dot Jackson first thing tomorrow. She's always looking for copy typists. Otherwise, it will be in the workshop with Alice and me."

He wondered what had changed her mind so suddenly, "Why the change of heart, Nancy?"

She looked out into the night-time sky; "I've got enough money for the house..."

Porteous thought for a minute, "What about Charlie Maitland and that Mitchell fellow? They aren't going to be very pleased."

Nancy looked down, "I'm not thinking about them at the moment."

"Look, Mitchell knows where you live. You can't hide from him forever."

She shrugged her shoulders, "I'll move out. I won't be able to afford the rent anyway on what they pay at Smiths. London is a big city."

Porteous smiled, "There's plenty of room in my house."

Nancy smiled to herself, "I thought you'd never ask..."

The telephone rang again. Porteous picked up the receiver, "St Luke's and Christ Church"

He paused and listened intently, "Okay, thank you."

Nancy looked at him; he raised his eyebrows, "The buggers are on their way back; they are over the Channel now. The early warning will go off in about ten minutes."

She stood up to leave, "Unbutton me, and I'll find a shelter."

He shook his head, "No. You'll be much safer here. Besides, you can help me." He nodded at a pair of binoculars on a small table in the corner.

Just then, they both heard the sound of the heavy wooden door at the bottom of the stairway.

"It'll be Harry Harris. He's got a key. Stay there, he won't mind."

Harry Harris was breathing hard by the time he had climbed the stairs. He pushed open the door to the parapet and sucked in the cool night air.

"Ah, I see you've got a visitor, Porteous."

Nancy was still wrapped up in the old great coat, but Harris could see what a beauty she was. He wasn't going to object to her presence. He leaned over the old stone wall,

"Did Central call?" he asked.

Porteous nodded.

"It's twice as many this time..."

Porteous shook his head, "Looks like you are going nowhere, Nancy."

Harris looked at Nancy Keeling, "Ah, so this is the famous lady that Porteous keeps on about?" He looked her up and down as she turned away to hide her blush.

"You can come and type letters for me any day..." He burst out laughing.

Nancy was intrigued. So, Porteous often talked about her?

Harris addressed her, "You work at Smiths?"

She nodded. He responded quickly, "They must be very lucky..."

Porteous interrupted, "Come on, Harry, leave the poor girl alone."

Nancy closed her eyes; the brandy was beginning to bite.

She lapsed into a deep sleep whilst the two ARP wardens bartered over silk stockings, lingerie and cigarettes... By the time they had finished, the contents of Porteous' bag had all been transferred to the old brown holdall that belonged to Harry Harris. Porteous had five crisp new one pound notes neatly tucked into his breast pocket.

"Jesus, Porteous, you are going to bankrupt me."

Porteous shook his head, "It's not my fault you are providing for two ladies..."

Nancy was lying on a four-poster bed wearing only a white camisole top and a matching pair of French, silk knickers. She looked at the prone body of her lover as he lay on his back with one hand behind his head. She snuggled up to him. She could taste his sweat, intermingled with alcohol and cigarettes; smoking was something she'd have to stop when she moved in with Porteous...Her long, thin fingers carelessly twirled the coarse black hairs on his chest. She thought about climbing on top of him but decided that she would let him sleep so that he could regain his strength.

The sound of the dull booming of the anti-aircraft guns made her look up from her bed. The room was dark; she padded across the thick carpet and opened the blackout curtains so that she could witness the show. The death and destruction of an air raid held a sort of fascination for her. The intermittent flashes were coming from way over in East London. She pulled on her cigarette, carefully cupping the glow so as not to upset any passing ARPs...

She turned to her lover. She couldn't recognise who he was. There had been so many; some casual, some long term. She looked away as she stubbed out the burning ember. Looking again, the face of her lover had changed. She climbed back on the bed and shook the prone man, urging him to get up before the shells came. He snored even louder. The bombs were getting closer and closer...

She opened her mouth to shout at the sleeping man, but no words came out...She tried to scream as the explosions got louder and louder. She felt herself being shaken violently....

Nancy Keeling woke up as a really loud explosion shook the church tower; it seemed to sway this way and that, but she couldn't be sure if it was the brandy. She was slumped on the old deck chair tightly wrapped up in the greatcoat. Porteous had carefully placed an old blanket over her as she snored gently in the cold night air.

Porteous was shaking her as the night was lit up with explosions and a deafening noise. She slowly came to her senses. Harry Harris was shouting down the telephone. A pair of binoculars was glued to his face. She could only just make out his words,

"Looks like Sloane Square!" He was shouting directions to the fire marshals.

She craned her head over the parapet as a blinding flash made her blink rapidly in an attempt to clear her retinas.

"Nancy! Nancy! Get in behind the door!"

She felt herself being pulled up and shoved rudely behind the old, oak door that was at least one hundred years old. She sank down into a corner as Porteous closed the door firmly.

The raid seemed to go on forever. It looked like the bombers were trying to target the moorings on the River Thames between the Battersea and Albert Bridges and not having much success. She sank down into the greatcoat with the blanket between her knees covering up her bare legs. Her hot breath steamed out of her mouth as the tower shook violently again.

Just short of two hours, it all went quiet. The booming of the anti-aircraft guns was no more. She gently pushed on the door. Porteous was shouting instructions at Harry Harris who was still on the telephone trying to direct the Auxiliary Fire Services to the ever-mushrooming fires. Porteous glanced at her as she slowly made her way to the edge of the parapet and peered over to a vista of small fires that seemed to be everywhere. She looked at Porteous in a state of incredulity.

He raised his eyebrows; "They left us a parting shot of incendiary devices just to keep us busy."

She looked across at the Royal Hospital. There must have been at least ten small fires. She could just make out a group of workers attempting to extinguish a blaze in one of the outbuildings.

She watched intently as both Porteous and Harris went about their business with a cold efficiency in the face of such death and destruction. Eventually, they both sat back and sighed; their evening's work was done.

The telephone rang again; Porteous picked it up. He listened intently and replaced the receiver.

"Home time, Miss Keeling. The Germans have retreated back across the channel."

Harris looked at Porteous. Despite the cold, there were beads of sweat on his forehead.

"Bloody Hell, Porteous, that was some show. Where's the brandy?"

Porteous smiled, "Warming Miss Keeling's stomach."

Harris shook the empty flask and swore again.

Nancy looked away.

Harris stood up and lit a cigarette. He offered one to Nancy but she declined. Porteous was writing up the log.

"Harry will take you home as soon as I've finished the paperwork."

Nancy smiled at him, "What time are you on at Smiths?" she asked.

"Late shift today. When can I expect you? I'll get Jimmy to give us a hand with his van."

She shook her head, "Not till the weekend. I have some last minute business to conclude."

Porteous didn't want to enquire. ...Nancy Keeling would do what Nancy Keeling wanted...

The air was thick with acrid smoke when the three of them pushed open the door to the tower. The Vicar stood looking at them with his arms folded. He certainly didn't approve of Nancy.

Harry Harris spoke quickly, "Oh, good morning, Vicar. This is my daughter Nancy; she got caught out by the second raid. It's all in the log."

Nancy smiled at him and held out a hand, "Pleased to meet you, Vicar..."

He held out a limp wrist. Nancy squeezed it; he flushed up...Porteous winked at her.

"Come on, Nance, time to get you home..." Harry Harris strode off purposefully towards his ancient motorcar.

Porteous fell into bed back in East Row; he was exhausted. Harry Harris minded his Ps and Qs as he chatted amiably to his passenger, having been under strict instructions from Porteous not to mess around. He dropped Nancy Keeling at the top of her road and went off to a debriefing at ARP HQ in Tottenham, still clutching the bag with his items of ladies apparel and a few dozen dodgy cigarettes.

Nancy couldn't be bothered to have a bath. She climbed into bed with a warm feeling thinking that all her troubles would soon be over...or so she thought...

Chapter 8
February 1941
Maida Vale

Margaret Heywood was in her small flat just off the Kilburn High Road in Gascony Avenue. She had two rooms on the top floor of a terraced house and if she stood on her tiptoes in the back room, she could just see Kilburn Grange Park. No one bothered her as she slept most of the day, only rising in the early evening to prepare herself for work. She made sure she was in the bathroom on the second floor before her neighbours arrived home from their various places of work. Some were junior clerks; some were factory girls and some, like her, were in the entertainment business.

Mrs Clarkson, the dragon of a housekeeper, who lived on the ground floor, wasn't too bothered about the ladies' occupations just as long as the rent was paid every Friday evening. No male visitors were allowed. Mrs Clarkson guarded her front door against all intruders, male and female alike.

Margaret Heyward sat up in bed and stretched. She had slept well thanks to the half bottle of gin she had persuaded the young barman to liberate for her at the end of the party in Fulham Palace Road. After all, the young men who had booked the room and the ladies, had paid for it...

She reached for the old coat she used as a dressing gown and pulled it over her shoulders. She was quite excited. She had a rendezvous with one Nancy Keeling at eight o'clock just up the road in West Hampstead with no one to bother her. Michael Mifty Mitchell had given her night off whilst he went to see his boss,

Charlie Maitland, to discuss what to do with the errant Nancy. Besides, there were no parties booked for that night. Indeed, bookings were diminishing thanks to the increased intensity of the bombing raids. London was emptying fast. Soon, paying customers of the kind that liked to splash money around, were becoming a rare breed.

She had hinted to Mifty Mitchell that she would quite like to work in the house in Maida Vale, and could he ask Charlie Maitland if this was a possibility? She had been rebuffed. To get to work in the house you had to be under age or extremely beautiful and Margaret was none of those. The clientele of the large Georgian house were rather discerning. At twenty-six, she had crossed that threshold. She envied Nancy Keeling and couldn't understand why she was so averse to entering that establishment. I mean, Charlie Maitland had paid off Scotland Yard so there was no bother from the police and there was no danger of the Blackout Strangler ever setting foot in the place.

Margaret Heywood shook her head and snuggled back under the covers. She decided she couldn't be bothered going down to the cold bathroom and feeding the greedy gas meter just to get some hot water; the old tin bath that hung on the kitchen door would do...after all, it was only Nancy...

She settled back in the warm bed and closed her eyes. Margaret had been in London for about two years. The final argument with her father was the last straw and his constant nagging for her to 'do something with her life' was getting her down. Well, she was doing something with her life, wasn't she? Okay, it wasn't exactly something he would have approved of, but needs must, don't they? And she now had a sizable pot of money tucked away from prying eyes. Well, it was under the sink in an old tin, anyway. The last time she counted there was nearly two hundred pounds in used notes underneath some old letters; enough for her to move away and start a new life somewhere.

Margaret lived a fairly frugal life except she had a fond liking for Mother's Ruin, as her father had labelled it. She rarely got through the day without a few large gins, just to keep out the cold, you know. It helped to have a slightly fuzzy brain when some fellow was pounding away at you...

It was the vicar's fault anyway. If he hadn't stuck his hands up her skirt when she was thirteen perhaps she wouldn't be here right now? The cleric paid her for his pleasures...Thursday night after choir practice became quite lucrative for her. His vices showed her how to make easy money. She had done well at school and a routine job in a local office beckoned her. A couple of the vicar's acquaintances also paid for her services. Margaret Heywood had no need for a regular job and the promise of a husband.

It was all going so well until the vicar decided to lavish his attentions on a much younger girl and then a certain Austrian fellow decided to create a bit of a fuss across in Europe. Her regular clients disappeared into Britain's military machine. Margaret began to drink too much and soon the money ran out. It was then that her father began to ask questions of his only daughter who seemed to spend all day in bed and then go out late in the evening and come home smelling of strong drink and cigarettes. She soon left leafy St Albans to join an old school friend who was in the 'entertainment business' in London. Margaret had never worked the streets nor did she intend to venture down this particular alley if she could help it. Running that seaside boarding house in somewhere like Sussex was her ultimate goal...

Mifty Mitchell had loaned her out to a middle class couple in Acton. The lady of the house continued to employ her when the husband got called up for some war work or other. She was realising that she preferred the fair sex when it came to this game...it was a lot less messy...

Margaret Heywood had a 174. She wasn't bothered about her reputation and the Ministry of Labour wouldn't trouble her again...

She dozed off and then woke with a start as one of the noisy neighbours decided to drop something loud and heavy on the downstairs landing. She glanced over at the clock. She sat up with a jolt; it was after six and pitch black outside; the old coat was still draped around her shoulders. She sprang out of bed and rushed into the small kitchen that consisted of an old white sink that had a cold-water tap and an ancient gas water heater that clanked and groaned when called into service. The small gas stove had two rings but Margaret hardly ever cooked anyway. She quickly filled up the old tin bath with piping hot water, disrobed, stepped into it and gave herself a thorough wash.

Just before eight, Margaret Heywood pushed open the gate to Nancy's house in West Hampstead. Five crisp one-pound notes were tucked into her purse.

Nancy Keeling's head pounded as though there was a little man inside her skull with a jackhammer. It was nearly nine o'clock in the morning. The sun was shining brightly through a crack in the worn blackout curtains. Fortunately, her back bedroom window overlooked the recreation park that contained the air raid shelter so there would have been no trouble from the ARP wardens. She could taste stale gin in her mouth together with the horrible hint of too many cheap cigarettes. She shook her head as the pounding got louder. She opened her eyes to see the prone and probably unconscious figure of Margaret Heywood lying next to her. Her sleeping partner was naked. Nancy rolled her eyes. At least she had on a pair of French knickers. She couldn't remember what had happened after the two of them had virtually consumed a whole bottle of cheap gin and smoked countless cigarettes.

She shook her head again. The pounding was coming from downstairs...

She slowly slid out of bed, reached for the dressing gown on the back of the door and threw it over her shoulders. She went over to the washstand and gulped some water rinsing it around her mouth before spitting it out into the Victorian bowl. She opened the bedroom door; the house was cold. The noise was audibly louder. Someone was banging on the front door.

She slowly padded down the carpeted stairs. She could see the door vibrating as it was banged. Pretty soon the door would give way and the last thing she wanted was a large bill from the landlord, although she hadn't seen him since the heavy bombing had started. She pulled the cord of her robe tightly around her waist.

She called out, "Hello! Who is it?"

"Police! Open up, or we'll kick this door open."

Nancy froze as she sat on a step. Were the police back to do another check? No, they would just have sent that old one and the young lad again.

Now, if Nancy had been clear-headed and not heavily hung over, she would have gone into the front room and peered through the curtains to ascertain the exact status of her caller. Unfortunately, this was not the case.

She stood up, "Okay! Okay! Take it easy. I'm coming."

The banging ceased; she heard a voice, "Get a fuckin' move on. We ain't got all bleedin' day."

Again, if she'd had not been so hung over, she would have noticed that this probably would not have been the way an officer of the law would have spoken to her. Instead, she walked up to the door and slid open the top and bottom bolts before she removed the chain by the lock. She stopped and listened. There was the sound of silence.

She turned the door handle slowly. The door crashed into her face as it burst open. She stumbled backwards. A rough pair of hands around her neck, forced her to the ground, face down. Something sticky, yet warm, began to trickle down from her forehead where the door had clouted her.

A strong hand pushed her face into the tiles of the hallway she couldn't see her assailant. And then she heard a familiar voice,

"All right, Freddie, for Christ's sake, don't kill 'er. Charlie wants 'er in one piece..."

She opened one eye to see the smiling face of Michel Mifty Mitchell peering down at her.

Freddie Fox relaxed his grip, stood up and grabbed hold of the back of her dressing gown.

He pulled her up, "Oops! Sorry about that, old girl. You seem to have cut yer forehead." He pushed her up against the wall, still gripping the collar of her gown tightly.

Nancy tried to look away as Freddie Fox's breath was none too fresh.

A sharp slap stung her face, "Don't yer turn away from me, bitch! Look at me when ah talks to yer."

He pretended to brush her down, but his hands lingered too long on her breasts, "Hey Mifty, she's a bit of all right, ain't she?" He turned his head towards Mitchell.

Nancy brought a knee quickly into Fox's groin. He yelped, as he fell to the tiled floor. It was a big mistake...

She didn't see Mitchell's closed fist as it sunk into her solar plexus and drove all the wind out of her. She collapsed back to the floor, vainly gasping for breath; she curled up into a foetal position. The blood from the cut on her forehead soaked into her hair.

Freddie Fox vomited onto the tiles. He spat viciously, "You fuckin' bitch. You'll pay for that."

He pushed himself up to his feet, leaned against the wall with both hands and began kicking at the prone woman. Mitchell pulled him off,

"Whoa, Freddie, take it easy, Charlie says to give her a bit of a slappin' but don't kill her."

Freddie Fox was breathing heavily as he was pushed back against the stairs. Mitchell told him to check out the house.

Fox swore to himself as he climbed up the carpeted stairs. He shoved open all three of the bedroom doors and glanced inside. He did the same with the bathroom door. He shouted down to his mate, "Nottin' up here, Mifty."

Mitchell had dragged Nancy into the kitchen and shoved her into a chair, "Don't yer fuckin' move."

He quickly searched the front room and the back room. Finding nothing, he pulled up a chair to the kitchen table, sat down and produced a battered tobacco tin and promptly commenced to roll up a thin cigarette. He looked at Nancy and tutted, shaking his head.

"You're a very silly girl, Nancy, leaving me with those posh knobs in the pub in Brompton."

He shook his head, "If you had asked, I would have sent you home; it was getting late, anyway. But no, you have to be difficult, don't you?"

He grabbed Nancy's chin and pulled it towards him. She spat at him...

She got another sharp slap on the side of the face for that one.

Mitchell smiled, "Don't worry, girl, you'll soon get the crap knocked out of you where yer goin'."

The eye below the cut on her forehead was beginning to close, "I'm not going anywhere with you two pigs. I quit so get out and leave me alone."

Mitchell shook his head, "You'll quit when Charlie says so and not before."

Freddie Fox came back through the kitchen door, "All clear, Mifty."

He looked at the dishevelled Nancy Keeling as she slumped in the wooden chair, "Any chance of five minutes with this one?"

Mitchell smiled, "If only, Freddie. Charlie wants her in one piece, and I've seen your lady friends after you've been with 'em. Most of 'em can't walk for a week!"

They both burst out laughing. Fox grabbed at his crotch, "It's not my fault the good Lord blessed me in that department."

Mitchell clicked his fingers, "Bag, Freddie, now."

Fox produced a cut down dirty sack and handed it to Mitchell.

They fixed a handkerchief tightly around her mouth to stifle any shouting. Mitchell threw the sack over her head. Fox then tied her hands behind her back and roughly pulled her to her feet. He ran his hands down her body. Nancy kicked out. She could just see through the weave of the old sack. It tasted of old, rotten potatoes. She began to struggle against her binds, but only got a quick cuff on the back of her head as a reward. She went limp. If they were going to carry her out, she wasn't going to help them.

For his size, Michael Mitchell was as strong as an ox. He leaned into Nancy and threw her over his shoulders, "Get the door, Freddie."

Fox quickly opened the front door and held it open. Mitchell carried the struggling Nancy Keeling to the Wolseley Hornet. Fox opened the rear door and Mitchell tossed her onto the back seat.

He growled, "Don't make a fuss, Nancy, otherwise, Freddie here is gonna show yer what he's got..."

Freddie Fox squashed in beside her and placed a big, strong hand on her head. She doubted she could move even if she wanted to. Tears welled up in her eyes as the car coughed into life and sped off.

Margaret Heywood gingerly pushed open the heavy wooden wardrobe door as she heard the car drive away. She shivered in the cold air of the early morning. She reached behind her and grabbed Nancy's coat; she wrapped it around her naked body.

Out on the landing, she peered over the railings. She could see a pool of vomit on the tiles. The stench assailed her nostrils. Her heart thumped loudly in her chest as she slowly crept down the stairs. She had no idea if both of Charlie Maitland's thugs had vacated the premises.

She nervously called out, "Hello? Is there anyone there?"

She plonked herself down on the last step of the stairs and sucked in deep breaths, deliberately trying to slow down her beating heart.

Silence...

She carefully stepped over the pool of vomit and went into the kitchen. One of the chairs was tipped over. She righted it and pushed it back under the table. She sat down.

Margaret Heywood had an inkling that Nancy would get punished for leaving that private party early, but she didn't expect this. She shook her head, stood up and grabbed the mop and bucket that sat in the corner. She ran the tap over the sink and waited until the water was steaming hot. She found some laundry bleach under the sink, poured in into the hot water and slowly mopped up the mess in the hallway. She hoped this wasn't Nancy's...

She opened the back door and threw out the dirty water.

She made a cup of tea and sat down trying to decide what to do. She still had goose pimples on her skin. Subconsciously, she turned up the collar of Nancy's coat as though it gave her extra protection. What should she do?

She sipped the hot liquid, grasping the cup with both hands. Her mind went ten to the dozen. Was she safe in this house? Would Mitchell come back looking for her? No. Mitchell knew she lived over in Kilburn. Why would he come here? She wasn't due back at work until the weekend; there was plenty of time to find a way out of this.

Should she go to the police? She quickly dispelled that idea...

What was Nancy's friend's name? She shook her head. Nancy didn't talk about him much except that he was very special to her. Was he her boyfriend? What was his name?

She pulled at her hair; a few strands came off in her hands. She always did this when she was nervous. She took a deep breath. Wait a minute. Didn't he live over some place that had a strange name? Ah, the Penny Steps; no, the Ha'penny Steps, wasn't it? Supposed to be a dangerous place or something. She shrugged her shoulders and padded back upstairs. Since there was plenty of hot water she might as well have a bath before she left. No harm in that is there?

Margaret Heywood soaked in the bath until the water began to cool off. She stood up and shook the water from her body. She used her hand to wipe away the steam from the mirror over the sink and stood back as she toweled herself down. It was nice to have a bathroom to herself and not have some waif banging on the door...

She opened the cabinet door and used Nancy's toiletries. She stood at the back bedroom window and gazed out over the recreation ground. It was one of the bright, sunny winter days that the German Luftwaffe loved so well.

Her clothes were sat crumpled up on a chair. She, too, couldn't remember much about the previous evening except that she had finally gotten Miss Nancy Keeling into bed. She smiled at the thought...Where did Nancy keep her money? She opened Nancy's purse; five, crisp one pound notes were still there...

She borrowed some of Nancy's lingerie and stole a pack of good quality stockings from the chest of drawers next to the wardrobe. She dressed and quietly left the house in the Crediton Avenue, West

Hampstead, making sure the outside door was firmly closed behind her...

Nancy Keeling knew exactly where Charlie Maitland's boys were taking her. She lay quietly on the back seat as Freddie Fox's hand gradually released its pressure. It must have taken them about thirty minutes to get down to the large Georgian house in Maida Vale. The Hornet pulled onto the small crescent shaped drive in front of the house. The drive was just large enough for a horse and carriage to deposit the wealthy owners. The mews at the rear of the building would have housed the stable and the grooms man accommodation. The large black door opened as Mifty Mitchell carried a now docile Nancy up the steps, closely followed by Freddie Fox. A refined voice spoke,

"Put her in here, Mifty. We'll take it from here."

Mitchell looked at the supercilious woman and decided she would benefit form a slap as well.

He tossed Nancy onto a chaise longue and roughly pulled off the sacking. Nancy blinked quickly trying to adjust her eyes to the harsh, bright late morning sunlight that flooded in through the open curtains. She looked around at the opulence of the room. A fire crackled in the large hearth. The wallpaper looked like it had been liberated from the Savoy Hotel in the West End of London. The deep red carpet was so thick that it absorbed all the sound of footsteps. There were three matching armchairs opposite the chaise longue.

"Good heavens, Mitchell! Since when did you have permission to beat the girl up?"

Mitchell shrugged his shoulders, "Charlie told us to give her a slap. The cut on her forehead was her own fault. She should have opened the door when we first asked. Anyway, patch her up and use her as a maid like you always do with new girls."

Madame Monique Fontaine spoke with a refined French accent, "I have plenty of ladies' maids. It's girls I need. Monsieur Maitland promised me someone special."

Mitchell shrugged his shoulders, "This is what we got, Monique. Make do with what you are given."

Madame Fontaine lifted Nancy's chin, "Hmm, I suppose she'll do after she is healed up." Nancy shook away her hand.

Fox said, "She's a bit feisty, Miss; watch out for her."

Fontaine walked over to the wall next to the fireplace and pulled the bell chord. She turned to the two men, "What are you still doing here?"

She clapped her hands, "Off you go, quickly. I have clients calling soon."

Mifty Mitchell blew her a kiss; as he walked over to the door, "Take good care of her Madame. She'll be a good earner."

Madame Monique Fontaine waved them away with her hand as two ladies appeared at the door dressed in maid's uniforms. They curtsied to the Madame.

She leaned over Nancy Keeling, extracted a large switchblade and clicked the metal button. The razor sharp blade sprang open. Nancy's eyes widened, in horror.

The Madame's lips came up close to Nancy's face. "Now listen here, Miss Claudine, my ladies respect me, especially for what I have done for them. I treat them well, and they enjoy their lives here. They earn good money and they live rent and board free. You get one week off in every four when, how shall we say, you are indisposed. The rest of the time you work, eat and sleep. We buy you nice clothes, but you won't need them very often." The maids behind her giggled... Madame Fontaine shot them a withering glance...They both bowed their heads in unison.

She went on, "If you play the game nicely, you'll earn good money and then, when I say so, you can leave and enjoy the rest of your life. But, please don't cause me any trouble otherwise Mr. Maitland will send you off to one of the opium dens in the East End and once the girls go in there, they very rarely come out in one piece."

Nancy felt the blade press against her skin as the woman continued, "You'll work as a maid until I know you can be trusted. I'll assign you to a couple of the youngsters. They are very popular with our discerning clients. Oh, by the way, maids don't get any time off..."

Madame Fontaine's blade slipped through the gag that was binding Nancy's mouth. She spat the bitter taste from her mouth,

"My name is Nancy, Nancy Keeling."

Fontaine pulled her up, spun her around and slashed the thin cord that bound her wrists. She grabbed the collars of the robe and pulled the garment open. It fell to Nancy's feet. Her arms instinctively went across her chest.

Fontaine leaned in and wrinkled up her nose; she pulled away in disgust.

"Goodness, she smells like a gin soaked whore from Piccadilly Circus."

She turned to the two maids, "Take Miss Claudine to the top floor, bathe her and give her suitable clothing. I don't want to see her down here again until that face is healed up."

She clicked her fingers; the maids curtsied again. They each took an arm and escorted Nancy out of the room.

They swerved around the big wooden staircase and made their way to the back stairs. They didn't say a word until they reached the top floor and pushed Nancy into a large bathroom with a roll top, Victorian bath. One of them ran steaming water into the tub. The other pulled off Nancy's knickers and tossed the items into a linen basket, saying,

"You can wash them when you do laundry for your ladies."

The water was scalding hot, but they shoved Nancy into the bath whilst the cold water was running.

"What do you think, Elsie? Do you reckon she'll do?"

The maid named Elsie smiled as she lathered Nancy's back with expensive smelling soap, "Oh, she'll do alright. They'll be queuing out the door for this one…"

The other one pouted as she poured water onto her hair from a white enamel jug, "Yeah, I suppose you're right once we can get the smell of gin out of her and those cuts and bruises heal."

She paused her task, "It's not fair, is it? Madame Fontaine won't let us anywhere near the clients. I swear that young lord would have me if she would let him." She stared into space.

Elsie snorted, "Stop dreaming, Martha. The only time you'll get taken is off some back alley in Kings Cross by a worker smelling of cheap beer and cigarettes with his trousers around his ankles."

Martha snorted and splashed her companion, "Bloody cheek. I'll have you know the vicar's son took a shine to me back in Gloucestershire and don't forget that airman, he wanted me to meet his ma and pa."

Nancy opened her mouth to speak, but a firm hand pressed her head under the water and held it there. Nancy struggled, but couldn't get up out of the water. After what seemed an age, the pressure released, and she came up gasping for air.

Elsie shouted at her, "Don't speak unless you are spoken to. Do you understand?"

The hand pushed her underneath the water again.

Nancy came up spluttering and stared ahead, wondering how she had gotten into this mess.

"That's better, Miss Claudine, keep it closed, and you'll do okay."

"My name is Nancy, Nancy Keeling and you'll all regret this."

This time, two sets of hands pushed her back under the water and held her there. Nancy did not struggle but lay there, conserving her breath even when they released their grip. They pulled her up roughly,

"Jesus, Martha, don't kill her, for God's sake."

Martha chuckled, "Nah, she'll live. Watch."

She placed a hand on one of Nancy's nipples and squeezed hard.

Nancy yelped as she tried to push away the offending hand.

Elsie smiled, "That always works…"

A voice shouted at them from the doorway,

"That's enough, take her out, dry her and bring her to my office."

The maids looked down and curtsied, "Yes, Ma'am," they replied, almost in unison.

They rubbed a naked Nancy Keeling dry, wrapped a towel around her head, slipped a robe onto her and took her across the landing. They shoved her into what looked like a doctor's surgery. They curtsied again and left the room.

The woman was in her fifties. She was wearing a plain, dark dress and a pair of raised court shoes. Her legs were bare. Around her neck was a string of pearls. Her hair was tied back in a fierce bun. She wore no makeup except for a little lip-gloss of some indeterminate colour.

She spoke with an Irish accent, "How old are you, Claudine?"

Nancy sighed, "My name is Nancy."

The woman smiled, "No matter. We've all got real names out there, including me but believe me, it's better to use the name they give you so that when you leave you can forget about this sorry place."

Nancy looked at her, "What is your name?"

"They call me Loretta here. That's all you need to know. Well, that and the fact that I used to be a doctor in Dublin until I got sent down for helping young ladies rid themselves of a little problem or two, if you get my meaning?"

Nancy nodded, "I've been there, Miss Loretta."

Loretta stopped, "How old were you?"

Nancy looked away, "Old enough to know better."

A stethoscope appeared, "Take off your gown. Let's have a listen to your chest; we can't have you working here with Consumption."

Nancy complied.

"Do you smoke?"

Nancy nodded.

"Knock that on the head, if I were you."

Nancy nodded again thinking of Porteous.

The stethoscope lifted off her chest, "Good, you have good bi-lateral breath sounds; no rattles of bangs. Let me listen to your heart."

"How old are you, Nancy?"

It was the first time she had been called by her real name.

"Twenty-three, Miss."

"Ever had the clap?"

Nancy shook her head, "I always insist on rubbers, Miss."

The defrocked doctor nodded, "Good, good; but watch out; most of the clients don't like wearing them. They'll pay extra for that privilege but don't be fooled by them. I've seen too many cases of gonorrhea and syphilis."

Nancy looked at her, "Why are you here?"

Loretta shrugged her shoulders, "It's the nearest thing I can do to work as a doctor and Mr. Maitland pays well. I'll be back in Dublin if this bombing doesn't stop soon.." She paused and sighed,

"Okay let's stop talking. I'll see if I can sort out your cuts and bruises."

She examined the cut, "What happened here?"

"Mitchell and Fox shoved a door into my head."

She raised her eyebrows, "I think you might have a little thin scar from this. I'll see what I can do. You know I've patched up gunshot wounds, countless stabbings, broken bones and other assorted ailments since I've been working here."

Nancy looked at her thinking of Doctor Maruska Bergman.

The doctor worked on Nancy's cut for about thirty minutes before pronouncing herself satisfied with the results.

She rang a hand bell on her desk and the two maids came back smelling of cigarettes. She sat down and buried her head in paperwork not bothering to look at Nancy.

An hour later, Nancy was dressed in a short, black maid's uniform. It barely reached her knees and she subconsciously continued to pull it down in vain. She stood in front of a fierce looking housekeeper known as Madame LeStrange and was lectured at for about fifteen minutes. She was informed of her duties and then escorted to a top landing and shown two bedrooms.

LeStrange pointed to the two bright red doors.

"You take care of the two girls in these rooms. You dress them, clean up after them, and change the bed sheets after each client. They are currently sleeping, but they must be up, bathed and dressed in order to receive visitors after noon each day. If they want something, you fetch it for them. If they request something that requires you to go out, you come to me and I will make the arrangements."

She paused and looked at Nancy. She lifted up her chin,

"Hmm, I can see why Mr. Maitland wants you here. Behave yourself and you'll make lots of money. Now, go about your duties..."

With that, she turned on her heels and left Nancy standing in the corridor.

Chapter 9
February 1941
Another victim

Just as the sun was setting on Nancy Keeling's first night in Maida Vale, Leading Aircraftman Gordon Cummins was sitting in the canteen eating what was loosely described as the evening meal in the requisitioned cafeteria in Regent's Park Zoo. He'd had enough of square-bashing for the day. What he desired were a few pints of beer and a good woman to quench his needs. All thoughts about his previous victim, Edith Eleanora Humphries, had long since faded into the past.

He stood up, pushing away the half-eaten food and returned to his quarters. He washed his face and generally tidied himself up, and took some of the money he had obtained from the sale of some of Edith Humphries' jewellery to that slightly dishonest pawnbroker in Lisson Grove. He used to go to that Jewish shop in Star Street, Paddington, but it seemed that his wife had murdered him...It was a pity because the old Jew was none too particular where the items came from and, as for appropriate identity, none was demanded or given. The chap in Lisson Grove asked for his service card, but not to worry, Gordon Cummins had stolen one off a new recruit. He had five one-pound notes and change in his pocket.

Gordon Cummins fancied a decent cup of tea and a cake before he went off to sink a few beers and find a lady, willing or not. He marched into Maison Lyons Corner House in Marble Arch and sat down. A waitress soon brought him his refreshments. He sat there for a while; carelessly glancing at a newspaper he had lifted from the rack in the corner. Gordon Cummins was an intelligent man. He had passed the examination for aircrew without difficulty, and he was glad for the change of posting, especially to London where he could indulge his passions without too much difficulty. He knew that once he had finished his training he would be posted to some far away airfield where there was little to do except drink beer and fraternise with the local females, most of whom were either married or engaged to other service personnel.

He looked up as a mature lady entered and sat down at a vacant table. She was good-looking and well-dressed as though she was a professional and not one of the common factory girls. He observed her as she ordered a glass of white wine. She had rosy cheeks from the cold, and he overheard that she was celebrating her forty-first birthday. He licked his lips as he finished his cake and drank the last of his tea. He stared at her nylon-clad legs and his heart skipped a beat. That feeling was coming over him again.

She looked over at him and smiled at the serviceman. He returned the smile, lifted his teacup and mouthed the words 'Happy Birthday' to her. She nodded a thank-you.

He stood up, dropped a few shillings on the table and went up to her table,

"As I said, Happy Birthday. Perhaps you would like something a little stronger to celebrate?"

Evelyn Hamilton blushed, "Oh, I'm not so sure. I don't often take strong drink."

Cummins bowed slightly, "Well, if you change your mind, I'll be downstairs in the bar having a drink."

With that, he stood up straight and marched confidently down the stairs, where he ordered a pint of beer and a whisky chaser. He looked around him as he stood at the bar. As usual, there were more servicemen than civilians. Many had ladies attached to them. There were no females on their own or with a friend. Since that debacle in

Balcome Street, Leading Aircraftman Gordon Cummins resolved to work entirely solo.

After a few minutes, he felt a female presence at his side. He turned to see a slightly flushed Evelyn Hamilton next to him. She smiled at him,

"I think I will take that drink with you."

He returned her smile and turned to the barman and ordered another whisky for her. He held out his hand as he introduced himself,

"Leading Aircraftman Gordon Cummins."

She gingerly took his hand, "Evelyn Hamilton lately of Upminster in Essex but shortly on my way to a new position in Grimsby."

Cummins grasped her soft hand; this was clearly not a factory girl.

He said, "Well, Miss Hamilton, I am very pleased to meet you."

She blushed again and looked down. Not for a long time had she been in the close presence of such a good-looking young man, who was quite dashing in his Royal Air Force uniform. He looked a little on the young side for her but all she was after was some company to celebrate her birthday.

He pointed to a vacant table and led the lady over and pulled out her chair for her. They chatted superficially for a few minutes, and Cummins learnt that she was not a good-time girl. She was, in fact, a pharmacist on her way to a new job on the East Coast. Despite this, he tried it on by placing his hand upon her knee.

She quickly shoved it off, "Now, now, young man. I'm almost old enough to be your mother."

Cummins tried to put an arm around her, "Come on, wouldn't you like a bit of company?"

She moved away from him, "Sorry, but I'm a respectable woman."

She replaced her half-finished drink on the table with a bang, stood up and straightened her clothes.

"Thank you for the drink, but I'll be on my way home now."

Gordon Cummins raised his eyebrows, gave her a mock salute and returned to his drink. He wasn't bothered; there were plenty of ladies out there in the blackout more than willing to be paid for their company. He shrugged his shoulders.

Evelyn Hamilton pulled up the collars of her coat as the cold February air hit her as she walked out onto the street. It was still busy with people thronging to the bars and public houses before the air raid sirens sounded. She quite fancied another drink, so she walked along the Marylebone Road until she came across a crowded public house.

She pushed her way in and made for the bar. The barmaid smiled at her as she ordered another whisky. She sat down in the corner but was not hassled by any of the servicemen and women who crowded into the place.

The air raid was late that night, but as the early warning sounded she noticed that many were making their way down to the cellars still clutching their drinks. The barmaid grasped her arm,

"Come on; it's much better here than that dreary shelter down the road. You'll be quite safe here. The walls are thicker than the average Jerry."

Evelyn Hamilton smiled as she was swept along a narrow passage and down some rickety stairs. She smelt the damp and stale beer. She found herself pushed into a corner by the barmaid, who produced a small flask of something and offered it to Hamilton.

The bombs began to fall. First, far away over East London and then much closer as one of our German friends decided to attempt to take out that bastion of free broadcasting, the BBC. The place shuddered as bombs rained down on this part of London. The booming of the anti-aircraft guns got louder and louder and seemed to make the place vibrate. She felt the barmaid snuggle up to her and took another swig from the flask. She thought it tasted like cheap gin.

Some plaster flaked down upon her. She brushed off the dust from her clothing, taking great care not to snag her expensive stockings that she had taken from the pharmacy in Upminster as the owner cleared out his remaining stock. She dozed off despite the terrible roar coming from somewhere outside.

The all-clear sounded just after one in the morning. One by one, the evening drinkers gradually moved back upstairs and out onto the street. She whispered a quick thank you to the barmaid who smiled at her, wishing her a safe journey home.

There was chaos out on the road. Auxiliary fire engines were attempting to douse a flaming building on the corner of Baker Street. The fire lit up the scene, and she could see the good ladies from the ambulance services tending to the dead and injured. There were bells ringing everywhere.

She stopped, thankful that she would soon be out of this carnage. So far, the Luftwaffe hadn't targeted Grimsby, but she knew it could be.

She picked her way through the debris, anxious to make her way to her lodgings in Gower Street by the British Museum. She half-wished she had worn slightly lower heels, but it's not everyday you get to celebrate your forty-first birthday. She reckoned it would take her about three-quarters of an hour to reach her temporary home. She was tired and the effects of the alcohol dulled her senses.

She walked along the Marylebone Road, past Regent's Park and on to the Euston Road. She had chosen these lodgings because it was a relatively short walk to King's Cross station the next day from where she could catch a train to Grimsby, provided any trains were running after the night's bombing.

She turned into Gower Street. For some reason, Evelyn Hamilton began to feel uneasy. She stopped in a darkened shop doorway. The street was now quiet. She bent down to retie a shoelace. She stood up, straightened her skirt and that was when her nightmare began.

She tasted the sweat of a hand that clamped against her mouth so tightly that she could hardly breathe. She kicked out and got a firm slap on the side of her face. She was pinned against the glass doorway. She opened her eyes and saw a heavily breathing male figure holding her in a vice-like grip.

It took her a few seconds to realise it was the same man who had earlier purchased a drink for her in the tearooms, Gordon Cummins.

Her brain went into overdrive. He must have followed her and waited for his chance. She brought her knee up to him, but he was expecting it and deflected the blow. He struck her on the side of the head. She saw little flashing lights across her eyes.

She heard his voice, "Turn me down, did you? Are you too high and mighty to reject me? I would have paid you well."

Cummins dragged her out onto the road. He had one arm in hers and the other across her back, supporting her body. It looked to the casual passer-by that he was taking home a lady that had far too much to drink.

He pulled her into a street-level air raid shelter in Montague Place, which, one hour before, would have been packed with Londoners attempting to avoid the bombing. But now, it was empty. Evelyn Hamilton smelled stale air.

Cummins pushed her onto the floor. She fought back ferociously with her fists and legs. She felt her skirt being roughly pulled up over her waist. His weight pressed her firmly to the dirty floor. Two hands pulled at her underwear. She felt her stockings rip as her knickers were shoved below her knees. There was a pause as Gordon Cummins unbuttoned his trousers. And then, it all went quiet.

Cummins gripped her neck with his two hands and slowly squeezed the life out of Evelyn Hamilton. He breathed heavily as he kneeled up. He had a golden opportunity to rape the forty-one-year-old whilst the corpse was still warm. Instead, he took out his knife and inflicted a cut on an exposed breast.

He fastened up his trousers. He often got to this point yet could not manage to perform actual intercourse. He toyed with the idea of mutilating the corpse but apart from making a small cut over one of her eyebrows, he turned his attention to her handbag where he managed to steal eighty pounds. His mood changed when he realised he had obtained so much money. It was enough to keep him happy for some time. As he walked out of the shelter, he tipped some of the contents of the bag onto the pavement.

He left the dead body of Evelyn Hamilton on the damp floor, with her skirt raised up over her waist and her knickers down by her ankles.

With so much cash in his hands, Gordon Cummins wandered back up to the Marylebone Road seeking out a more willing lady...

Chapter 10
February 1941
East End Adventures

Porteous' hands were numb by the time he reached Crediton Hill in West Hampstead. The day was very cold. The east wind seemed to cut through him as he pedalled away from Smiths in Cricklewood. He smiled when he remembered that his father used to call it a lazy wind because it cut right through you instead of going around. He was relieved when he pushed open the front door.

He called out; there was no reply.

He wheeled the bicycle across the tiled floor and leaned it against the wooden staircase.

He called out again, "Nancy! Nancy! Are you still sleeping? It's gone four o'clock."

He waited for a reply; there was none.

He shrugged his shoulders and pulled off his woollen mittens, blowing warm air onto his frozen fingers. He climbed up the stairs and pushed open the back bedroom door, expecting to see Nancy Keeling fast asleep. The unmade bed was empty. He stopped abruptly and glanced around the room. Drawers were pulled open but not closed. Some items of lingerie were hanging over the edge. The dressing table was littered with cosmetics that were strewn across the lace mat. He sat on the end of the bed and looked around. There were two empty gin bottles; one on the night stands either side of the bed. The bottle tops were on the floor.

He picked up one of the two glasses and examined it. There were smears of lipstick on one side. The colour was definitely not Nancy's.

He shook his head; didn't Nancy say she was about to change her life?

He went back downstairs and boiled up some water to make some tea. He leaned against the sink and looked around. The door to the hallway was open. He could see marks where someone had attempted to clean up something. He thought he could smell bleach. He leaned down and opened the little cupboard under the sink. The glass bottle was nearly empty. He knew that Nancy would never let it get that low. He raised his eyebrows and put it back.

The clock chimed four in the afternoon; he was due down in Chelsea by nine, and he needed to grab a few hours sleep before he went. He carried the cup back up the stairs, had a quick wash in cold water, as there appeared to be no gas in the meter and no sixpences in the usual place, and got into bed. He was half-hoping that Nancy would return, having gone out on some errand or other. He soon dozed off...

He woke up just before seven in the evening. It was pitch black outside. He drew the curtains before he switched on the light; Nancy had not returned. He washed his face and went down the stairs. He opened the hall cupboard and was surprised to find Nancy's expensive coat still hanging on the hook. Now Porteous had gone to great lengths to get this coat. She rarely left home in the winter months without it. He quickly rifled through the other cheap coats. He recognised a couple that belonged to Helen Shenton. Nancy's only other presentable coat was still there. He shook his head, sighed, quietly donned his greatcoat and wheeled his bicycle back out through the front door.

The roads were busy with last minute commuters and other assorted flotsam and jetsam of London making their way home before the Luftwaffe returned to rain down their deadly cargo. A truckload of soldiers passed him on West End Lane shouting abuse at him. He waved back to them.

He reached the Ha'penny Steps in about twenty-five minutes and parked his bicycle at the side of the White Horse on Kensal Road, knowing full well that no one would attempt to steal it. That was the thing about residents of Kensal Town. They might steal and plunder from elsewhere but they never took what did not belong to them from their neighbours.

The pub was crowded with early evening drinkers. He nodded at a few as he made his way to the bar, with the dense cigarette smoke catching his throat. The landlady, Edith Bell, was busy serving customers. One of the barmaids sidled up to him with a smile,

"Ah, Porteous, can I get you something to drink?" She opened her eyes wide, almost suggestively.

Before he had time to answer, a harsh voice sounded and she felt herself being yanked backwards,

"Leave Porteous to me. How many times do I have to tell you?"

Edith Bell pulled the barmaid out of the way and sent her packing,

"That bloody girl will be the death of me."

Porteous smiled, "She's just being friendly, that's all."

"Well, there's being friendly and being friendly. Anyway, I wouldn't normally see you in here at this time of night. I thought you were fire-watching later?"

She poured him a small beer and set the glass down in front of him.

He took a sip of the refreshing liquid, "Have you seen Nancy, Edith?"

She shook her head, "Not since you were all here last weekend. Which reminds me, Can Jimmy Ryan get me some more gin?"

Porteous ignored the question, "It's just odd, that's all. I popped around to her house on the way back from work like I usually do. The house was empty."

Edith Bell shook her head, "That sounds like Nancy, I'm afraid, Porteous. There's so much going on in that girl's head God knows what she's up to. I did tell her to steer clear of Charlie Maitland, but she didn't listen."

"I told you she's stopped working for him."

Edith smiled, "I think I've mentioned before that you don't stop working for Charlie Maitland, he stops you. He'll let her go when he's good and ready, and not before."

She reached out and put a hand on Porteous', "Don't worry, she'll turn up. Go and get ready for your shift in Chelsea, and don't forget to tell Jimmy about the gin."

With that, she turned to bark more orders at the errant barmaid, who smiled and winked at Peter Porteous.

The intense bombing that night soon made Porteous forget about the missing Nancy. The Luftwaffe was hell-bent on making a mess of not only the docks in the East End, but also the bridges crossing the Thames in West London. An array of ordnance, including land mines or parachute bombs, and incendiary devices, was deposited upon the good citizens of London. The whole area of Chelsea seemed to vibrate under the constant booming of the anti-air guns that were strategically placed in and around the parks and open spaces of the area. Porteous was constantly on the Bakelite phone calling in the fires that sprang up as the bombers deposited numerous firebombs

It seemed to be the order of every night. First, a so-called pathfinder aeroplane would come in and light up the intended target with firebombs, and then the main bombers would do their best to destroy the objective. The pathfinder planes could be heard coming in low, and the searchlight crews would attempt to pick out the bandit for the ground gunners to aim at. Porteous had a bird's-eye view of the competition.

If there was any ordinance left after the main bombing runs, it was simply deposited anywhere, regardless of what was on the ground. That night there were fires everywhere, with the Auxiliary Fire Brigade struggling to respond to the ARP calls.

The air was thick with acrid smoke that irritated Porteous' asthmatic chest. Harry Harris relieved him just before six in the morning and Porteous picked his way in the darkness on his bicycle through streets of burning buildings and rubble back up to Kensal Town and then after a quick wash-up to Cricklewood for a day's shift in the factory.

He was greeted by Alice Halpin as he wheeled his bike into the yard.

He asked, "Have you seen Nancy, Alice?"

She looked at him, "No, I thought she was with you."

He shook his head, "I called in at the house yesterday, but there was no sign of her. It was a little strange. I know Nancy is not the tidiest of people, but the house was a mess."

As they walked to their workshop, Porteous related what had occurred the previous day. Cedric Walker shouted at them to get the girls started...

Just before four in the afternoon, Peter Porteous and Alice Halpin pushed open the door to Nancy's house in West Hampstead. Porteous called out,

"Nancy! Nancy!"

There was no response.

Alice skipped up the stairs; Porteous leaned on the kitchen sink with his arms folded.

Alice came back through the kitchen door clutching the two glasses that she had lifted from the bedside cabinets. She sniffed a glass and wrinkled up her nose, "Cheap Gin."

Porteous nodded, "I thought so."

Alice held up a glass to the light and examined the lipstick mark, "Hmm. That's definitely not Nancy's. It's too bright for her."

Porteous stared at her, "Could it be Helen's?"

"Let's have a look, shall we?"

Alice put down the glasses on the kitchen table and went back upstairs into the front bedroom that had up till recently been occupied by her housemate, Helen Shenton. She rummaged through the dressing table drawers and scattered a range of cosmetics on to the top, underneath the mirror. Porteous appeared behind her.

"It doesn't belong to her, does it?"

Alice sighed, "Nah, it's too bright for Helen as well. I never saw either of them with this colour."

She paused as Porteous sat down on the bed. He looked around the neat and tidy room, "She's long gone," he said.

Alice sat beside him and put an arm through his, "Look, she's probably travelled back to Norwich or something. You know, that mother of hers is always in some sort of trouble."

He looked at her, "It's possible, but I'm sure there's something wrong. There's obviously been another female in the house, and don't forget she's supposed to be moving in with me at the weekend before she starts at Smiths on Monday. If she doesn't turn up, Dorothy Jackson will eat me alive."

"We'll worry about that at the weekend, okay?"

Porteous wasn't convinced.

She said, "Let's get back to Kensal Town before it gets too dark. What time is Jimmy picking us up?"

"Six o'clock."

"Come on then, I want a hot soak before then and something to eat..."

Alice Halpin and Peter Porteous squashed onto the front seat of Jimmy Ryan's Morris van. The vehicle looked old and worn out from the outside but underneath, it was sound as a pound, as Jimmy liked to say. The battered look of the van dissuaded would-be thieves from attempting to liberate it from its rightful owner. Jimmy Ryan kept the engine and running gear in tip-top order as he reckoned it wouldn't be much use if it broke down with a load of black market goods in the back. His connections gave him access to petrol, but even he had to pay over the odds for it without his ration coupons.

Alice had her arm in Porteous'. He was quiet that evening as Ryan picked his way through the debris of the previous night's bombing.

She asked, "Where are we going, Jimmy?"

"Lock-up in Devas Street, Bromley-By-Bow. Dennis Elphicke is expecting us. Got to be in and out, smartish..."

Porteous looked up, "Has he got some gin for Edith?"

"Dunno, Porteous. I asked him for some. We get what we are given."

Porteous nodded and stared at an Auxiliary Ambulance as they drove past. The ambulance girls had three bodies on stretchers covered in blankets on the ground awaiting transportation to the local mortuary. He closed his eyes as Alice's arm tightened in his. Ryan passed over his little hip flask,

"Some half decent brandy here..."

The old Post Office van pulled up in front of a darkened lock-up at the rear of St Andrew's Hospital, just off Devas Street.

Jimmy Ryan turned off the engine and hopped out, "Wait here until I get the go ahead from Dennis."

Alice took another pull at the brandy. Porteous asked,

"Where's Phyllis?"

"Alice sighed, "Dunno, Porteous. Some Godforsaken barracks in deepest, darkest Hampshire, I think. She won't tell me."

"Is she back at the weekend?"

Alice nodded, "I think so. If she comes back, we're going to stay in bed all weekend..."

Porteous smiled, thinking of Maruska Bergman and the hours they lazed around in bed.

She leaned into him, "Don't worry about Nancy, she'll be back."

Just then the driver's door opened, "Come on you two, no time for kissing and cuddling."

Dennis Elphicke sat on a couple of packing cases, drinking some hot tea. Two of his minders hovered in the background, moving some stock around.

He said, "I had a visit from three of Charlie Maitland's boys yesterday."

Jimmy Ryan looked up, "Oh yeah, what did they want?"

"Well, that's just it, Jimmy, they didn't say. They took half a case of whisky and buggered off. I reckon it was some kind of message."

Porteous glanced at Elphicke; Alice straightened up. "Did they ask about us?"

Elphicke nodded, "Yup, they certainly did. They wanted to know if I had seen either of you two."

Porteous sighed at Ryan, "We are just going to have to see him, Jimmy."

Ryan shook his head, "Not if I can help it."

Elphicke spoke up, "I think you should, Jimmy, even if it's just to find out exactly what he wants." He paused,

"Anyway, that's something for you to think about, but don't leave it too long, okay?"

Ryan nodded, "Perhaps Dennis is right. We need to know what we are dealing with here."

Elphicke stood up, and looked over at Alice, "Where's the pretty one tonight?"

Alice glared at him; Porteous smiled.

"Come on, Jimmy, let's settle up while your two oppos load the van. I hope you've brought plenty of cash?"

Jimmy Ryan disappeared into the back office, whilst one of the minders stood over the pile of cases to make sure that Porteous and Alice only took what was theirs. The other accompanied his boss whilst the paperwork was completed.

The black Vauxhall 12 saloon car sat on the corner of Devas Street and Devons Road. The two occupants had a reasonably good view of the male and female as they loaded the boxes into the old Morris van. It was dark, so they couldn't exactly identify who they were. Police Sergeant Derek Beaston sat in the driving seat. Next to him was the imposing figure of Inspector Eric Everard of Scotland Yard. Beaston was desperate to get out of the car, as Everard had incessantly smoked his pipe; he never could get used to that evil smell. He had contemplated winding down the window, but he knew his boss would sharply tell him off, muttering about the cold weather.

The two policemen had had a stroke of luck. They were watching Dennis Elphicke when the old post office van belonging to Jimmy Ryan had turned up unexpectedly. A tip-off earlier that evening had sent them on this surveillance job. The anonymous telephone call was almost missed by one of the girls in the office; they were always getting calls put through by the switchboard about allegations of black marketeering from disgruntled neighbours, jealous of some hard to obtain item or other that someone seemed to have down the street. Just quite how this caller knew where to send the inspector and his sergeant was a mystery, at the moment.

Beaston sat up and wiped the condensation off the windscreen, "Sir, shall we arrest them?"

Inspector Everard smiled, "Not just yet; let's see where they go. Besides, what they are carrying could be entirely innocent."

Beaston replied, "Not likely, sir, at this time of night."

Everard struck another match and tried to breathe some life into the dying embers of his pipe, "Perhaps not, Derek, but the night is yet young..."

For Derek Beaston the night was not young; he had a wife and two children waiting for him at home...

Eric Everard was content to let the suspects run; you never know where they may lead you. The early warning sirens began to wail. Beaston looked anxiously at his superior; his wife didn't like sitting in the damp Anderson Shelter at the bottom of her garden on her own especially with the two young children.

Everard held out his hand as if he knew his sergeant would be anxious,

"Hold on a little, Derek, we've got a good half an hour before the Jerries come. There's always the shelter back at the Yard."

That was the whole point, thought Beaston, he wanted to get back home and not be cooped up with a load of people he didn't really know or want to know, for that matter.

Everard spoke quietly as he opened the window and knocked out the burnt tobacco from his briar pipe, "Let's go, Derek..."

He reached forward to start the car as Jimmy Ryan's Morris pulled away. The solenoid clicked; there was the sound of silence. The Morris went past them. Everard thought he could see Peter Porteous in the front seat with some girl virtually sitting on his lap, but he couldn't be sure,

"I said, start the car, Sergeant."

Beaston began to panic, "I did, sir, I think the battery has given out."

Inspector Everard swore loudly, "Get the bloody crank handle then."

Beaston tumbled out of the car as the inspector craned his head to see the van disappearing down the road.

Beaston was turning the handle wildly. The car wouldn't start despite his best efforts. Everard leaned over and placed his foot on the accelerator,

"Turn it again, for God's sake!"

The car spluttered and stirred into life. Beaston rapidly got back into the car, performed a swift turn and went as fast as the saloon would allow along Devons Road, all the way to Burdett Road. He screeched to a halt on the corner and both officers peered up and down the main road.

Beaston swallowed noisily, expecting a right old verbal thrashing from his superior.

Everard stared ahead and spoke quietly, "Get this pile of scrap into the garage first thing tomorrow morning, Sergeant. Now let me out. I'll make my own way home..."

The inspector quickly exited the car, slammed the door shut, pulled up his collar and walked away into the dark night. Beaston sat there and watched him disappear.

Jimmy Ryan decided that travelling on the main roads was not a good idea. He had turned up Bow Common Lane and passed the old cemetery, briefly crossing the Mile End Road.

Alice asked, "Where are we going, Jimmy?"

Porteous answered for him, "We are avoiding the road check points, Alice. The police would never set one up on a backstreet. But, don't worry, Jimmy could find his way through this maze of streets blindfolded."

Alice wasn't convinced; "I'd prefer it if he did it with his eyes open in this blackout."

Jimmy Ryan snorted..."Don't worry, I'll get you home all right."

They pulled up in front of Porteous' house on East Row in Kensal Town. The van was soon emptied of two boxes of reasonable quality gin, forty pairs of stockings, one thousand cigarettes, ten pounds of rolling tobacco and three boxes of powdered egg. After a huddled conversation between the two men as Alice watched from the doorway, Jimmy Ryan drove off with several boxes of whisky...

Porteous was in the bathroom on the first floor. He was very tired. He ran the bath until it was almost full and gently lowered himself into the hot water. Alice appeared at the door,

"Do you want something to eat?" She enquired.

He shook his head, "Nah, too late Alice; save it for tomorrow. I'm just going to soak here for a few minutes and then I'm going to bed."

Alice Halpin stared at him, "What about the air raid?"

She could hear the anti-aircraft guns booming out over East London.

He sighed, "I can't be bothered any more."

She walked up to the old roll top bath and waved water over his shoulders,

"We need to go to the crypt."

"Not tonight, Alice. I've had enough. I'm going to sleep in my own bed. If you want to go to the church, then off you go."

Alice Halpin sighed, pulled on a nightdress and snuggled up to Peter Porteous as he slept, oblivious to the heavy bombing that fell all around them...

Inspector Eric Everard stood in front of his superintendent the next morning in Scotland Yard. He related his exploits over in East London.

Chief Inspector Alfred Barrett looked vaguely interested, "So, what you are telling me is that you could have had this fellow Porteous and his mate Jimmy Ryan in a cell if that bloody car had started?"

Everard nodded. Forsythe raised his eyes,

"Ah, well, it happens sometimes. What do you want to do?"

"Raid the lock-up on Devas Street, Sir."

Barrett looked ahead, "I suppose we could, if you think it's worth it?"

"Well, we know it belongs to Dennis Elphicke. If there's stuff in there that he can't account for we could put him away for some time."

Chief Inspector Barrett nodded, "Okay. Just exactly where did this tip-off come from, Eric?"

He shook his head, "Came through the switchboard, Sir."

"Hmm, perhaps a little too convenient, don't you think?"

Barrett sighed, "Okay then, keep me informed."

Later that afternoon, six police officers led by Everard and Beaston smashed open the door to the lock-up on Devas Street. The place was completely empty...

Chapter 11
February 1941
Information

The late afternoon February sun did nothing to warm Peter Porteous' heart as he trudged down Tottenham Court Road towards the bottom end of Greek Street in Soho. Many of the shops were boarded up; some had fire and bomb damage. He wondered when this war would ever end.

He was tired. He had finished his shift at Smiths, quickly called in at Nancy's house in West Hampstead in case she had returned, and then taken the Tube down to the West End. Jimmy Ryan said he would meet him in the pub on the corner of Frith Street, the King's Arms. Porteous knew this pub as a hangout for the criminal classes and, of course, Charlie Maitland's boys. In fact, Porteous figured that the place was actually owned or controlled by the Maltese gangster.

He pushed his way into the public house. Jimmy Ryan was over in the corner engaged in a furtive-like conversation with a couple of half familiar faces. Ryan beckoned over Porteous. As he approached, the conversation died.

Ryan smiled at him, "Porteous, would you like a drink?"

Porteous shook his head and acknowledged the two other men, both of whom had pints of beer in their hands.

Porteous stood there and looked at Jimmy Ryan, who was speaking quietly.

"I'm sure we can accommodate you in some way or other, but as I have said repeatedly, this stuff doesn't come cheap, when and if we can get it." He looked up at Porteous, "Isn't that correct, Porteous?"

Porteous nodded discreetly, not knowing whatever Ryan was talking about.

Ryan continued, "Now, gentlemen, if you'll excuse us, I have some business with Porteous."

The two men took the hint and wandered off into the crowd.

"Who are they?" whispered Porteous.

Ryan sipped his drink and raised his eyebrows, "A couple of chancers after some malt whisky. I don't trust them."

"Let's not take on any more business until we can get this problem with Maitland sorted out, okay?"

Ryan leaned into him, "I received a message from Elphicke this morning. I had to go down to the docks to see him."

Porteous looked up, "What did he want?"

"There was some trouble over in Bromley-By-Bow."

"You mean where we were the other night?"

Ryan nodded, "It seems that some coppers raided the place."

Porteous stared him out, "Did they get anything?"

"No. Fortunately, Dennis Elphicke has a contact in Scotland Yard. It seems that Inspector Everard and one of his merry men have been watching the lock-up for a couple of days. It appears that he also clocked you as we drove off."

Porteous was shocked, having prided himself on being able to keep a low profile for a long time, "Jesus, Jimmy. What's going on? Why didn't they lift us?"

"Something about a problem with the car or other. Anyway, we were bloody lucky."

"But, how did they know about the lock-up?"

"Well, my dear Porteous, that's a very good question. Elphicke's contact says that the switchboard got an anonymous phone call about some black market activity."

Ryan paused, "Elphicke's boys cleared the premises quickly and shut up shop. The leaseholder is apparently off serving in some corner of the Empire, and Elphicke managed to acquire it."

"So, he's somehow 'un-acquired' it now?"

Ryan drained the last of his beer, "Yup. Can't be traced back to him or us."

"You say Everard saw me?"

"He thinks he saw you and maybe Alice, but he doesn't know her. We need to be more careful. But that's not important. What's important is how they got the information. Dennis had spent the last two days clearing his warehouse in the docks in case that place gets the knock as well."

Porteous thought for a minute, "Something dodgy going on here."

Ryan nodded, "Yes, and I think I know who's the dodgy one."

Porteous smiled, "If you are thinking of taking over someone's slightly unauthorised business, the best way to do it is to get the boys in blue to do it for you."

Ryan nodded, "Yup; that's my thinking as well. Nice and clean with no broken heads or dead bodies littering the streets. This has got Charlie Maitland's paws all over it."

Porteous swallowed, "I think I will have that drink after all."

Jimmy Ryan pushed his way to the bar and got Porteous half a pint of warm beer and one for himself. They both stood there sipping their drinks and contemplating.

Ryan spoke first, "What do you reckon?"

"Let's just see what Maitland wants."

"He's going to tax us first and then tell us he's taking us over after he's seen off Dennis Elphicke."

Porteous nodded, "Exactly." He breathed out, "Let's just see how the gangster wants to play this…"

The club in Greek Street was more of a dive than a refined drinking establishment, but it gave the Maltese criminals an air of respectability. The local council had certified the club and, as Maitland paid off the local police handsomely, there was never any real trouble from the authorities. Porteous and Ryan approached the front door with an air of trepidation. They didn't want to be caught up in a gang war, but neither did they want to lose their lucrative sideline.

Two burley bouncers stood either side of the doorway. Ryan spoke to the smaller one,

"Porteous and Ryan to see Mr Maitland."

The doorman jerked his thumb backwards but said nothing. Ryan and Porteous entered the building and immediately went down a set of steps. A hatcheck girl dressed in a tight black, sleeveless cocktail dress with her breasts bursting out of the top asked them for their membership.

This time, Porteous spoke, "We are here to see Mr Maitland."

Hatcheck girl smiled sweetly and picked up a telephone. She wound the handle twice and then paused,

"Two gentleman to see Mr Maitland." She paused again and then asked Porteous, "Who shall I say is calling?"

"Porteous and Ryan."

The girl smiled sweetly again as she replaced the receiver. It pinged as it landed on the cradle,

"Take a seat in the bar and someone will collect you shortly."

Porteous wanted to be in and out swiftly, not sitting in this club drinking expensive fake alcohol.

The hatcheck clicked her fingers and a scantily dressed waitress appeared in front of them,

"Follow me please, gentlemen."

Porteous couldn't help noticing that she had deep bruising to her bare shoulders and back.

She led them to a table and said, "My name is June and I will be pleased to serve you today. What can I get you?"

Ryan spoke up quickly, "Just a couple of beers, please. We are waiting for Mr Maitland."

Her eyes flicked towards the stairs in the corner that were guarded by yet another burly man.

The waitress almost curtsied as she turned. She was wearing a very short black, flared dress with a white make-believe pinafore stitched into the front, a pair of sheer, black tights and some high heels. Her dyed-blonde hair was tied back in two short ponytails.

Porteous leaned into Ryan and almost whispered over the gramophone record that played from a loudspeaker on the stage,

"Did you see the bruising on her shoulders?"

Ryan nodded, "I wonder what she did to deserve that beating?"

Porteous shook his head, "I'd rather not know."

June returned with two bottles of beer and two glasses. She made a performance of opening the bottles with a silver opener and pouring the liquid carefully down the side of the glass.

Ryan reached into his pocket to take out his wallet.

She spoke quickly, No, don't worry, you can pay later."

With that, she turned quickly. Her dress lifted up giving the customers a show of her underwear.

Ryan sipped his beer; at least it was cold, "Hmm; takes practice to do that..."

Porteous snorted as he drank.

He looked around at the half-empty venue. The customers were entirely middle-aged men dressed in suits and ties. Some carried rolled-up umbrellas, no doubt getting a cheap thrill before they took the train home to their nearest and dearest.

Many of the patrons had similarly clad ladies at their tables all drinking what purported to be champagne. Porteous knew how difficult it was to obtain the real stuff at the moment. He wondered where Maitland was getting his supply.

One customer had a lady sitting on his lap. He was clearly the worse for wear and there were two empty champagne bottles on his table. Porteous shook his head...

His thoughts were interrupted by a loud voice from the bottom of the stairs,

"Porteous; Ryan. Mr Maitland will see you now."

The waitress, June, looked up from her position at the bar...

Jimmy Ryan and Peter Porteous stood on the polished wooden floor in front of Charlie Maitland. They were grateful that his brother was not with him. Maitland was dressed pristinely in a grey, three-piece, pinstriped suit, white shirt, red tie and highly polished shoes.

His dark hair was slicked back. He had an open bottle of a single malt whisky in front of him. He shot his cuffs and slowly poured out a measure,

"Well, my good friends, at last you've come to see me." He sipped the golden liquid, "You did keep me waiting, though, didn't you?"

Porteous stared at him; Jimmy Ryan looked at his shoes...

"Well, no matter. You are here now. I'd offer you both a drink, but you're not staying long."

Porteous spoke up, "What can we do for you, Charlie?"

Maitland swung around in his chair and put his feet up on an upturned wastepaper bin.

"It's like this, you see. You cheap pair of grifters are a pain in the ass but..." He paused, "You are actually quite good at what you do. Wouldn't you agree?"

"If you say so, Charlie."

"Oh, I do, Jimmy, I certainly do. You are the only ones who can sell into that shithole, what's it called, Kensal something?"

"Kensal Town, Charlie..."

"Yes, yes, thank you, Jimmy. It's quite lucrative up there, isn't it? I mean, you have a captive audience of crooks and criminals and the local lads from the police dare not enter there except mob handed. Isn't that right, Porteous?"

Porteous nodded.

Maitland was on a roll, "Well, except for that time you had a Kraut spy in your midst. You had half of the security services and the army knocking on your door. Correct me if I'm wrong, Porteous."

Porteous shook his head, "Yes, I suppose that's about right if you believe there actually was a spy on the patch."

Maitland sipped his drink, "Hmm, my mates in the police tell me that you were knocking off a rather nice lady doctor from Czechoslovakia or some such place in Eastern Europe. Is that right?"

Porteous stared at him. He felt Jimmy Ryan's leg brush against his.

"Well, no matter," he repeated, "We all live and learn, don't we?"

He gulped the whisky, "Okay, let's get down to business, shall we?"

He didn't wait for an answer, "Right, you get your goods from Dennis Elphicke."

It was a statement rather than a question.

No answer; Maitland went on,

"You see, my good friend Dennis is thinking of selling me his business, lock, stock and barrel. I'm seriously considering purchasing it. So, you'll be working for me. That's about right, isn't it?"

Porteous spoke up, "Does Mr Elphicke know he's selling his business?"

Maitland stood up, and pointed his finger at Porteous, "That's a very good question, Porteous, but I understand he's having some trouble with the police, if you get my meaning."

Jimmy Ryan swallowed audibly.

"So, I'm happy to let you continue working with him for the moment, subject to the usual taxation, I think, and then when Mr Elphicke finally decides to sell you'll both be working for me full-time. How does that sound?"

Porteous glared at him, "I have a regular job, Charlie, and I do ARP work in the evenings."

Maitland shook his head, "Oh dear. Then they'll just have to recruit your replacements, won't they?" He stared at Porteous.

"Never mind, it'll sort itself out, it usually does. Now, enough of this friendly banter, I want twenty per cent of your gross profits which is not bad since I can provide security and no trouble from the police. You'll be able to carry on selling whatever it is that you do sell, but soon you'll be purchasing exclusively from me. I'll have a down payment for services rendered by the end of the month. Now, off you pop, I've got real stuff to deal with."

They turned and went to the door. Maitland spoke up again,

"One last thing, Porteous, tell that whore Edith Bell, the landlady of the White Horse on Kensal Road, I want her pub..."

He waved them away, "Go on, off you go and don't forget to settle up for your drinks before you leave. This club is not a charity..."

Porteous and Ryan stood about one hundred yards along from the club on Greek Street; the light was beginning to fade. Porteous shivered as the cold, easterly wind blew against his face,

"What was all that about, Jimmy?"

"God knows, but it looks as though we could do with avoiding it."

Ryan turned on his heels, "I'm off to see Dennis and get to the bottom of this. Let's just clear out the stock we have at the moment and lie low for a while until this thing sorts itself out."

Porteous nodded, "Agreed; I'll go and give Edith the good news and maybe work out some extra security for the pub."

Ryan nodded and disappeared off into the early evening revellers, desperate for a cheap thrill before Jerry returned with their nightly bombing.

Porteous wandered down to Shaftsbury Avenue deep in thought when he felt an arm link into his. He turned to see the waitress from Maitland's club,

"Are you Porteous?" she asked.

He stared at her, "Yes, who wants to know?"

She leaned into him, "Look, I need to talk to you. Can we go somewhere quiet?"

Porteous seemed reluctant; he didn't know her, let alone trust her.

She pulled his arm, "Look, I've got some information for you."

He stopped walking, "Is this going to cost me anything?"

She smiled at him, "Only the price of a G&T..."

June Cook led Porteous away from Soho. It took them about twenty minutes to get down to the Embankment. She guided him into a Victorian public house that seemed rather quiet. He went to the bar and ordered a gin and tonic and a small beer for himself. He wasn't in a rush that evening, as he was not fire-watching. He looked at his watch; Alice Halpin would be safely wrapped up in the arms of Phyllis Manley somewhere in Golders Green.

He went back over to the little round table near the blazing fire. He noticed that she still had on her little waitress dress under the long, black coat. When she crossed her legs, the coat opened to show her nylon-clad legs. She blushed when she saw him looking at her legs and quickly pulled the coat over to hide them.

She took a deep pull of her drink,

"Oh, I really needed that; Charlie doesn't let the staff drink on duty."

Porteous looked at her, "Would you like to tell me who you are?"

June Cook looked around at the sparsely occupied pub, "This is where the girls come with their fellows. Charlie's men don't come here; it's out of bounds to them. The landlord is a retired senior officer from the police. He won't have anything to do with them."

Porteous, "Who are you?"

She smiled at him, "I'm June Cook. I was with your friend Helen Shenton the night she was attacked by that bastard in Balcome Street."

June Cook had Porteous' full attention...

"Helen is a friend of a friend," he muttered.

"And is that friend someone called Nancy?"

The coat split open again. This time she made no attempt to cover her legs.

Porteous nodded, "Yes; have you seen her?"

Cook shook her head, "No, but I know where she is..."

There was a pause. Porteous spoke, "Nancy told me you got a beating from one of Charlie's boys?"

She nodded, "I'm sure you've seen the bruises. Charlie likes me to display them as a warning to the other girls to behave themselves; at least my face has almost healed up."

Porteous sipped his warm beer, "Tell me about it..."

She took a deep breath, "I met Helen in the Volunteer pub in Marylebone. We were both out to make a little money. Two RAF chaps picked us up. We took them to a doss house in Balcombe Street. Helen went upstairs with one of them, and I had mine in a room below theirs. Well, after a short while Helen barges in with her face all battered and bruised, claiming that her man had tried to strangle her. He had punched her a few times, but she fought him off.

He came down later, saying he had just got carried away. Anyway, he gave her eight pounds to keep quiet."

Porteous shook his head; thinking about the sort of life Nancy was leading. He sipped his beer.

"I haven't seen Helen since that night. She said she was going back home, or something."

Porteous nodded, "Yes, that's what we think as well. What about Nancy?"

"Well, I'd seen her in the club before. I heard she is one of Charlie's top girls. She only works on call-outs and private parties. After the encounter with the strangler, I was back freelancing just off Oxford Street and I got picked up by one of Charlie's boys. Some thug named Freddie Fox did most of the beating."

Porteous snorted, "Yeah, him and Mifty Mitchell."

She looked at him, "You know of these two?"

"Yes, especially Mitchell; he's Nancy's official minder."

"Well, somebody told Fox that I had been seen with Helen, and then all hell let loose. I got another beating, so I just told them everything about what had happened. I knew Helen had done a runner, so I thought it didn't matter."

He nodded, "Yes, I don't think we'll see her again. She was Nancy's housemate. They were quite close. She's better off where she is now."

He thought for a second or two, "Why didn't you go to the police about the strangler? You could have put him away permanently."

She laughed and banged down her drink, "Why do you think I'm here, Porteous? I skipped bail back home in Leicester. It was the fourth time I had been picked up for soliciting outside that Army barracks. The magistrate told me I was going to get sent down." She paused and stared into the distance, "It's a pity because I was earning good money from those young soldiers."

"If I'd gone to the police, I'd be back in a cell in Leicester before I could put on my coat."

"Yes, but what about the strangler? He's killed at least three already."

"Charlie's going to get him..."

Porteous shook his head, "Yeah, right."

She plonked down an empty glass. He took the hint and went and got another. The barmaid stared at June Cook.

"What about Nancy?" he enquired.

June Cook leaned into him and whispered, "She's in the house in Maida Vale..."

Porteous spluttered his beer, "You know this because...?"

"One of the girls in the club mentioned it. Charlie has been threatening to take her there for some time."

Porteous nodded, "She told me."

"She's a lucky girl. All that money and free food and lodgings."

Porteous stared at her, "She doesn't want to go. She's got a job lined up as a typist."

This time, June Cook spluttered, "Are you serious? What kind of money does that bring in?"

"It's not about the money, June, it's about dignity."

June Cook snorted, "You can't eat dignity, Porteous. Do you want the address of the Maida Vale house or not?"

"I know where it is."

She stood up and swallowed the rest of her drink, "You'll not get her out until Charlie has finished with her."

He stood up, "What about you? Why don't you just run?"

She shook her head, "Why? I have a good job in the club. The customers like me. I get good tips and Charlie lets me keep most of them. I get two nights off in the week and I stay in one of Charlie's hostels. If I go with a customer, I'm allowed to keep half of the money. It's safe and no one bothers me. Where do you think I'm off to now, dressed like this?"

Porteous had no idea...

"One of the regulars is sweet on me, so I go down to his house in Croydon for the night..."

Porteous leaned into her; "Nancy told me that Charlie was going to put you out on the street once your bruises have healed."

That wiped the smile off her face...

She recovered her composure, "Then I'll run..."

She blew him a kiss and disappeared out of the front door...

An hour or so later, Peter Porteous walked slowly up the Edgware Road and onto Maida Vale. He could hear the early warning sirens over to the East of London; he didn't have much time. The road was busy with people desperately trying to get home before the bombing started. He wasn't too bothered. If he couldn't return to Kensal Town, he would ride out the night in one of the many shelters. He knew of a church crypt in Desborough Street. He could make it there.

He came to a large Georgian detached house with a horseshoe drive that was originally built for a carriage to proceed in and out without the need for a turn. There were steps up to the main, highly polished front door. A deep basement ran the whole length of the property. He looked up and counted four floors. The house was in complete darkness. He picked his way carefully along the unlit road. He crossed over, as the traffic seemed to die away suddenly. He observed two Air Raid Precaution wardens walking along the street looking for the slightest chink of light so that they could go and shout at the occupiers. He nodded discreetly to them as they walked past. They returned his nod,

"Time to get to a shelter, mate."

Porteous smiled, "On my way now, Guv."

He ducked into the front garden of the house opposite as the front door opened. Two male callers hurried down the steps and disappeared into the darkness.

The sirens began to wail close to him. He could hear the first booming of the anti-aircraft guns, a long way in the distance. The night was still, and calm; perfect for the pathfinders to lead the way in for the deadly bombers.

He walked up to Hall Road and tuned right. The little road that contained the mews was immediately on his right. He went into it, extracting his ARP torch. He flicked it on and off, just long enough to pick his way in the darkness, although he was helped by the full moon.

He soon found the house. He slipped back into the shadows as a large black car motored out of the old coach house, the doors of which were quickly closed. What light that emanated from there was quickly extinguished.

He stared at the house; Nancy Keeling was somewhere in there...

The church crypt was crowded by the time he pushed his way in. He had tripped once in the darkness on the Harrow Road as he made his way quickly. The pathfinders had lit up Paddington Station with incendiary bombs. The station was on the agenda for that evening...

He found a corner as a cup of tea was thrust into his hands, and sat down. Peter Porteous had a lot on his mind...

Chapter 12
February 1941
Maida Vale

The bell outside Nancy Keeling's attic room was ringing loudly. She peeked out from under the bed covers. Her roommate was snoring loudly. She unstuck her eyes and glanced over to the female, who was on her back with one hand behind her head. Her mouth was open. Nancy reached over to the little bedside table and picked up a box of matches. She casually flicked the half-full box over at the woman. The box hit her full in the face. The woman snorted, turned over and went back to sleep.

Nancy pushed off the blankets. She immediately felt the cold. She looked at the dying embers in the hearth. She walked up to the window that overlooked the rear of the house and pulled back the heavy blackout curtains. She wiped away the condensation and stared down at a couple of the house- minders who were sat on a bench smoking and laughing. It was about ten in the morning. She looked over towards St John's Wood. There was still smoke rising from the bombing of the previous evening. When the sirens started, staff retreated to the basement. There was even a wood and coal store lower than that but most refrained from venturing in there, partially because it was colder than the basement, but mostly the rats didn't like to share their place of safety.

She shook the sleep from her head. She remembered that the all-clear had sounded just before two in the morning and staff were allowed back up to their rooms. In some ways, she didn't mind the nightly raids from the Germans, as it kept the amorous punters away;

bad for business but easier on the domestic staff that didn't have to clean up after them.

Nancy pulled on a dressing gown over her thick, cotton nightdress. She sighed as she sat back on the bed and dragged on a pair of woollen socks that some kind soul had left in her bedside locker. She padded out of the door and went to what had originally been called a water closet by some Georgian designer. It looked as though it hadn't been updated since then.

She closed the door, locked it and sat on the pedestal.

It had been nearly a week since she had been dragged here against her wishes; if only she had gone straight to Porteous' after she had agreed to move in with him. She wondered what he was up to. Had he been and incurred the wrath of the supervisor, Dorothy Jackson? She smiled at the thought but Porteous had a way with women, especially those who were slightly more mature; he'd have her sorted...

The incessant bell in the top floor corridor finally ceased. Nancy heard her bedroom door slam. That meant that her snoring roommate had finally woken. She heard her on the steps as she went down the back stairs. She stood up, yanked the chain. The lavatory flushed noisily. She went up to the sink, pulled the nightdress over her head, and gave herself a thorough wash standing in an old tin bath that hung conveniently on the back of the door. She looked in the mirror and ran her fingers through her auburn hair. She thought it could do with a wash, but no matter, by the time she had fixed that maid's hat on her head, little could be seen.

She brushed her teeth, quickly rinsing out the bitter tasting bicarbonate of soda. Her tummy rumbled; they didn't feed you much here, especially if you were seeing clients on a regular basis. It wouldn't do to put on a little weight, would it?

Back in her room, she dressed carefully, making sure her stockings were straight before she pulled on the maid's uniform. She looked in the mirror and pronounced herself content. She slipped on her shoes and went to wake her 'ladies.'

As she opened the door, Madame LeStrange confronted her, looking at her wristwatch,

"Hurry up, Claudine, get both Faith and Hope up and ready. They've got gentlemen callers just after one today."

Nancy looked down and curtsied. She brushed past Madame LeStrange saying,

"Esther is up already, Ma'am. She's gone downstairs."

LeStrange nodded, "Good, good. We'll get some sense out of that girl in the end..."

Nancy pushed open the first red door. She was hit immediately by the smell of that sweet-smelling tobacco. She went immediately to the fireplace. Fortunately, she had banked up the coal before she went to bed and the fire was still lit. She poked the coals and waited till the fire flared up, and then threw what remained in the scuttle onto it. She quickly brushed the hearth and then went and opened the heavy blackout curtains. She looked down onto Maida Vale. It was busy, with most commercial activities being undertaken in the daylight hours, so as to avoid the attentions of the bombers as soon as darkness returned.

She heard a stirring behind her,

"Claudine! Is it that time already?"

Nancy feigned a curtsey, "It is, Miss Hope. You've got callers soon."

Hope buried her head in the soft, feather pillows, "Can you get me some tea?"

Nancy nodded and scampered downstairs to the landing scullery where one of the maids, Elsie, was busy with some early morning chores,

"Elsie, tea for Miss Hope and Miss Faith, please."

Elsie was one of the ladies, who had roughly greeted Nancy when Mitchell and Fox had deposited her there,

"Fetch it yourself, Miss High and Mighty."

Nancy swore at her and skipped back upstairs, knowing full well that tea would be brought up very quickly and the coalscuttles would be replenished.

Nancy pushed open the bedroom door. The girl was still face down in the pillows, sleeping blissfully. Nancy sat on the bed and gently cajoled her,

"Miss, time to get up."

The girl turned over. She was naked. Nancy reached over and placed a silk dressing gown on her shoulders, "Come on, Miss, let's get you to the bathroom."

Nancy stood her in the bath and poured hot water over her body. She soaped the girl all over.

Hope asked, "Can you wash my hair?"

Nancy shook her head as she looked at the waif who claimed to be eighteen but had the body of a fourteen-year-old, "Later, Miss, I promise."

Hope pouted as Nancy towelled her dry and sat her on a stool in front of the dressing table. She pulled a brush through her hair. Hope took the brush off her and began to work it herself,

"I'll lay some clothes out on the bed for you. Can you manage to dress yourself whilst I go and wake up Miss Faith?"

Hope nodded slowly, "Come back and help me put on my stockings, I can never get them straight."

Nancy nodded and hurried through the door.

She quietly pushed open the adjoining door. Miss Faith was already sat at the dressing table. She glanced up at Nancy as she sipped her tea,

"Is Hope up, Claudine?"

"She is, Miss."

"Good, then come and dress me."

The dress code for the working girls in the house was quite simple; satin lingerie, usually pristine white or black stockings, over which they threw a silk dressing gown. Some clients preferred them to be in children's nightdresses.

Nancy had her dressed in about five minutes. Faith pushed her away,

"Go and see to Hope; I can manage. Just come back and fix the fire."

Nancy curtsied, wondering if the younger girl would soon adopt the same superior attitude, as her neighbour who claimed to be almost seventeen. Nancy reckoned she was jealous of her because Faith knew that soon she would be cast downstairs to work with the other ladies, as a new youngster would be brought in to replace her.

Hope was struggling with her garter belt. Nancy pushed her fingers away and began to sort out the troublesome clips.

"Where are you from, Miss Hope?"

"Not far outside Swindon."

"Do you miss it?"

Hope shook her head, "Not really. At least I get fed here, and I have a nice warm bed to sleep in at night."

"What about your parents? Don't they miss you?"

"I doubt it seeing it was my father who brought me here."

"What about your mother?"

"Went off with the milkman after my dad hit her for the last time."

Nancy could sympathise with that.

"Do you like it here?"

"I suppose so. The work is not hard, and I've got lots of money saved."

Nancy didn't doubt it.

"Don't you think you should be in school?" She was thinking of her sister, Charlotte.

"I used to like school, but I stopped going when my father sent me over to the dairy farm to earn a few pennies." Hope sighed, "I didn't mind the work helping with the milking, but it all went wrong when that farmer wouldn't leave me alone."

Nancy sympathised again. Hope reached down and lifted up her face,

"What did you do to deserve this?"

Nancy pushed her hand away, "I was a bad girl, Miss," She lied…

Nancy stood up. Hope put her arms around her waist and buried her face in Nancy's chest. Nancy hugged her. The girl was just a child. She just couldn't see what men wanted in this youngster. Nancy had a choice; this girl didn't…

The adjoining door opened and Faith walked in,

"Leave us, Nancy, go and make the bed, our gentlemen will be calling soon."

Nancy curtsied again and went past the older girl. She quickly tidied up the room, cleared away the teacups and made sure the small drinks cabinet was full. She heard men's voices on the stairs. She went to the door and opened it. The two girls were lying on the bed as the men entered.

Nancy curtsied again, closed the door and went across the landing to her own room, where one of the scullery maids had left her some bread and butter and a pot of lukewarm tea. She sat on the end of the bed, wishing she were somewhere else.

An hour later, she stuck the younger girl in the roll top bath, and scrubbed her from top to bottom. She could hear Faith singing whilst she was in the bath.

Nancy leaned into Hope, "How was it, Miss?"

Hope looked at her blankly, "It was nothing...Can you wash my hair?"

Nancy wrapped a towel around the girl's head, managed to put her into a nightdress and put her back to bed; she would change the sheets when she woke up before the evening callers. She quietly closed the door and went to her room. She hadn't seen her roommate since the morning bell.

She had just sat down when the scullery maid knocked on the door. Nancy opened it,

The scullery maid, Elsie, glared at her, "Doctor Loretta wants to see you."

The maid turned sharply on her heels and went off, not waiting for an answer.

Nancy Keeling sat on a hard chair as the defrocked doctor stared at her,

"Madame Fontaine wants to know when you will be fit to receive callers for yourself. Take off your clothes."

Nancy removed her dress and stood there in her underwear.

The doctor stood her up and examined Nancy's still bruised body. Loretta pulled off the maid's cap and inspected the healing cut just below the hairline,

"Hmm, not bad, even though I say it myself." She paused, "Get dressed..."

Nancy pulled on her clothes as the doctor wrote on some notes, "You're not ready yet, Nancy. I think at least another couple of weeks for that cut to mend itself, never mind the bruises."

Nancy smiled to herself; this gave her at least some time to engineer her escape.

"Don't worry, I'll sort out Fontaine. She doesn't dare cross me. If they want me to do the necessary for these ladies, they'll keep me sweet."

Nancy fixed her hat in front of the mirror. Loretta asked,

"How are your girls?"

Nancy looked at her, "Faith is old enough to know better, but I worry about Hope. She's only a child."

Loretta snorted, "How old do you think Faith is? Maitland insisted on me passing Hope fit. You know she's the house's biggest earner. They pay a fortune to be with her. She's got a regular Member of Parliament as a client, not forgetting that Bishop from south of the river?"

Nancy nodded, "I've seen these men. At least they are not hurting her."

Loretta stood up and went to the window. She looked out over Maida Vale,

"You know that many of the houses along this road were child brothels in the early Victorian times. Now there's only this one, and Charlie Maitland owns it."

Nancy let her talk, "Those places were frequented by lords and ladies from the aristocracy. I'd never seen anything like it before I came here. Yes, I've sorted out younger girls when they have found themselves in a little trouble, but this is on a commercial scale."

Nancy asked, "How does Maitland get away with it?"

She shrugged her shoulders, "He pays, like they all do, plus he's got a couple of senior police officers as regulars. This place is off limits to the local boys in blue."

She turned from the window, and smiled at Nancy, "You're not going to stay, are you?"

Nancy looked away, "Not if I can help it."

"Good, that's the spirit. Wait for your opportunity and take it. I'm off back to Dublin as soon as I can, and then to America where they have no idea of my background. There's a shortage of doctors in the rural parts, and they won't ask too many questions. I've got an acquaintance in one of the hospitals who is prepared to write a reference for me."

Nancy smiled, thinking of how hard it was for Maruska to get licenced.

Nancy asked, "When do you think they'll let me out?"

Loretta shook her head, "Not for a while but keep your eyes open, an opportunity will present itself."

Loretta waved her away, "Go and sort out your girls and keep this conversation to yourself." She winked at Nancy.

Nancy stared at the plate of cold meat and potatoes, wishing she could sample some of Alice's concoctions. Alice Halpin could make the cheapest cut of scrag end of lamb taste like a delicacy. Nancy hadn't had hot food since she had arrived in the place, neither had she been down further than the doctor's surgery on the second floor. She longed for some real fresh air.

She looked in on Hope, who was sleeping soundly with the towel still wrapped around her head. At least the nightdress was still on her. She tidied up the room and placed some fresh sheets on the bottom of the bed, ready for a change when her charge had awoken. She opened the little silver box on the dressing table. It chimed once. Inside it were five fresh new one-pound notes. She took them out and pulled out a larger casket from under the bed. This box contained some of her personal things.

Nancy picked up some discarded clothes and tucked the cash into a brown purse. It was bulging with money. She sat back and examined the rag doll that Hope had brought with her...She sighed...

The bell sounded again out in the hallway. Time for the evening routine to start again...

Men started arriving about six in the evening. Nancy changed the sheets four times until the early warning sirens started just after nine o'clock. She spent the air raid down in the basement with Hope's head on her lap. They were wrapped in blankets. Faith preferred the company of the older working girls over on the other side of the basement next to the warm ovens...

Nancy retired at about two in the morning, having tucked Hope up into her bed and banked up the coal fire. Her roommate began snoring as soon as her head touched the pillow.

Nancy lay awake contemplating her escape...

The bombing finished early the following night. It had been quiet with only a few customers. Nancy made sure Hope was in bed and then went back to her room where her roommate was sitting on the bed dressed only in her underwear. Nancy nodded at her as she went over to the window and looked out from behind the blackout curtains; she could see virtually nothing except the glow from the fires out in the distance.

Her roommate spoke, "It's nothing special out there, Claudine."

Nancy rolled her eyes, "It's Nancy; I'll never be a Claudine."

Nancy could hear the woman laugh, "That's what they all say when they first arrive. But don't worry, you'll soon be a Claudine."

Nancy turned around, "Who are you, then?"

"My real name? No one here cares. Esther will do; that's close enough."

Nancy went and sat on the bed opposite the woman, "How long have you been here, Esther?"

Esther looked off into space, "A couple of years, I think. You lose the sense of time here, with every day being the same."

"What's your story? They brought me here against my will."

Esther snorted, "Yeah, we all know that. You should have been here weeks ago without the bruises. Monique Fontaine didn't want you. She said you'd be trouble."

Nancy smiled at that, "How does she know?"

"Ask that pig, Maitland."

Nancy went and sat next to her, "What do you do here?"

"Same as you, only for the ladies on the first floor. I clean up after them, and believe me, what you've got across the hall is nothing compared to what I have to do."

Nancy looked at her, "Tell me..."

Esther sighed, "Look, there are about twenty ladies; most live off the premises in one of Maitland's abodes near Marble Arch. They arrive in the late afternoon and get dressed to receive the callers. There are five bedrooms on the first floor and I share the duties with an out-girl who comes in every day. Because of the bombing, the gentlemen arrive shortly after six, and then it's like a merry-go -round of cleaning, changing beds and throwing the dirty linen in the laundry chute. It usually goes quiet about nine before the early warning sirens go off."

Nancy looked at her, "Are you able to leave the house?"

Esther nodded, "I can, but I've nowhere to go now."

"Why are you here?" Nancy asked.

"Doctor Loretta did me a little favour..."

"Where's your fellow?"

"I dunno. When I got pregnant, my dad threw me out. Cecil brought me here before he disappeared off into the army."

Nancy enquired, "Cecil is your man?"

Esther's eyes lit up and she reached behind her pillow. She took out some letters that appeared to have been read multiple times,

"He writes nearly every week. He's a chef somewhere up in Scotland, I believe, but he's not allowed to tell me."

Nancy reached out and took her hand, "That's nice."

Esther stared past her, "When he gets out, we are going to set up a home together." She paused,

"Will you help me write to him? I'm not very good with letters and words."

"Of course, do you want to write one now?"

Esther smiled...

Nancy composed a really lovely letter for Esther, who fell asleep dreaming of her fellow and never once snored throughout the night...

Nancy awoke really early, pulled on a dressing gown and slipped silently down the stairs. The house was quiet; she heard the big hall clock chime four. She went into the scullery and lit the gas under the kettle. She poked her head out into the corridor and looked down towards the back stairs. A young lad was seated on a chair with his arms folded. His head was on his chest and he was fast asleep. Nancy turned off the kettle before the whistling woke him and went silently over towards the youth. He appeared to be guarding the entrance to the back stairs. Nancy remembered that she had been brought up this way when she first arrived.

She crept back to the scullery and quickly made a cup of tea. She walked back up to the sleeping man and coughed...He started up with a panic,

"Sorry, Miss LeStange, I wasn't sleeping honest..."

He blinked away the sleep in his eyes; Nancy smiled at him.

"It's all right, I won't tell her, I promise. Here, drink some tea, this will help you stay awake."

She thrust the steaming cup into his hands as he stood up.

"Thank you, Miss Claudine."

Nancy looked surprised, "How do you know who I am? I've never seen you before."

"Miss, the whole house knows of you. Mr Maitland says we have to take special care of you."

Nancy didn't like the sound of that.

"What's your name?"

"William, Miss." He tipped at an imaginary hat, "I watch the stairs and do some fetching and carrying for Miss LeStrange."

"Does that include going out?"

Oh, yes Miss. I live in the hostel with the girls in Marble Arch. It's my job to escort them here and take them home."

Nancy opened her eyes at him, tilted her head sideways and opened her lips slightly, "Would you take a message for me?"

William backed away, "Oh, I'm not sure about that, Miss." He flushed up.

The young man couldn't have been more than eighteen or nineteen. He turned away, "Miss, you better go back upstairs."

Nancy reached out, "Look, I'm not asking you to do something really bad, it's just that I have a younger sister who will be worrying about me."

He stammered, "I'm-I'm not sure, Miss. Madame LeStrange says you're not even to go downstairs except for the air raids."

Nancy stood back and smiled, "It's okay, William, I was just asking. Don't worry about it."

He blushed again...

Nancy Keeling grabbed her cup and went noisily back up the wooden staircase. She pushed open her bedroom door; a plan of escape was beginning to work its way around her brain...

She got back into bed. Esther began to snore loudly again...

Chapter 13
February 1941
Another war is declared; first shots...

Peter Porteous walked into The White Horse on Kensal Road just before six the day after his meeting with Charlie Maitland. Nancy Keeling had been taken to the house on Maida Vale some time before. He had been up there in the hope that he might catch sight of her, but to no avail. For all he knew, Nancy might be content working in the house but, somehow, he doubted it. The problem was that he didn't know what to do.

The bar was crowded; no wonder the brewery insisted on the establishment staying open despite the bombing. He made his way to the bar to be confronted by his flirtatious barmaid who went by the name of Sinead. She opened her big green eyes and smiled at him,

"Do you want a drink, Porteous?"

He nodded at the Irish woman, who must have been in her early twenties. He knew she was attached to a slightly older fellow who worked on the railways.

He asked, "Where's Edith?"

The woman scowled, "She's upstairs. Now, what would you be wanting with her?"

Porteous smiled, "None of your business, Sinead. Now be a good girl and fetch me a small beer." He slapped a sixpence on the counter saying, "Keep the change..."

She flounced off to pull the drink. As soon as she returned, he lifted the bar flap and went behind the counter. He grabbed the drink off her. She leaned into him and whispered quietly,

"Now that your doctor has gone, would you be looking for a little late night company?"

Porteous snorted, "Perhaps...I'll let you know after I've spoken to your fellow..."

The woman coloured up...

He climbed the stairs and called out, "Edith! Edith!"

Edith Bell appeared at the top of the stairs, she was half-dressed.

"Come on up, Porteous; I'm just fixing myself."

She noticed that he was carrying his beer, "Did that little minx bother you?"

He shook his head, "Nah, but I think she'd like to."

Edith Bell grabbed his arm, "Keep away from her, Porteous, she's nothing but trouble. I'd sack her if I could get an honest and reliable replacement."

Porteous sat on the end of the bed and watched his favourite landlady finish getting dressed. She sat on the stool next to the dressing table, applying some make-up,

"What's on your mind, Porteous?"

"A couple of things, Edith. Jimmy and I had a meeting with Charlie Maitland yesterday."

Edith snorted, "What does that Maltese gangster want with you?"

Porteous looked at her, "He wants to take us over after he's seen off Dennis Elphicke."

Edith shook her head, "Well, good luck to that."

"There's something else, Edith," he paused. Maitland wants the White Horse."

Edith stood up, "He'll be lucky. I'm pretty sure the brewery won't deal with him and if he ever did get a foothold in here, I'd make sure my friendly magistrate revoked the licence. Anyway, who does he think he is? This is my pub and until I say otherwise, he can beggar off."

Porteous smiled, "He can be pretty persuasive, you know."

Edith's nostrils flared; she raised her voice, "Just let him try. He's got to get across the Steps first and to do that he'll need to come mob-handed. This pub belongs to us from Kensal Town not some two-bit shyster, who thinks he can just take over whenever his thugs want. He can keep to his tarts and brothels in the West End."

Porteous held up his hands, "Okay, okay; I'm just passing on the message but in the meantime, make sure you get some muscle on standby. He'll send a couple of his goons first to soften you up."

Edith smiled, "They dare not even come over the Steps in peace, never mind in anger." She paused, "I'll take care of it, Porteous, don't worry."

She turned to finish her make-up, still muttering to herself, "What was the other thing? You said there were a couple."

"Nancy; I know where she is, Edith."

Edith Bell turned around, a lipstick in her right hand,

Porteous sighed, "In a house of ill repute on Maida Vale."

She froze, "Jesus, Maitland's place? That's not good. How did you find out?"

Porteous spent the next ten minutes telling her all about his meeting with the female, June Cook, the one who had been with Helen Skelton the night she was attacked.

"You say you went up there?"

Porteous nodded, "Just a quick look, that's all. It's pretty secure. It's going to be difficult getting in and then out."

Edith raised her eyebrows; "She might like it there."

This time it was Porteous' turn to get angry; he stood up, "Come on, Edith, she's finished with that game. She told me she wouldn't go there. She's supposed to be moving in with me and starting work at Smiths in the typing pool."

There was a silence that was eventually broken by a shout from downstairs,

"Mrs Bell! Mrs Bell! There's someone here asking for you."

Edith Bell rolled her eyes, "All right, Sinead, I'll be down in a moment."

She quickly pulled on her skirt and looked at herself in front of the mirror.

"I'll be back in a minute..."

Porteous sighed and went into the living room. He sat down and picked up a two day old copy of the Evening News and began to flick through it...

Edith Bell walked into the bar to be confronted by a good-looking woman in her mid-twenties. Edith pushed past the barmaid and went up to the woman,

"Before you ask, this is an orderly house, so you can't work here."

Margaret Heywood smiled, "Ah, so it is true what they say, one whore can recognise another..."

Edith stared at her, "What do you want?"

"I don't need any more work; I've got plenty enough already. I'm looking for someone called Porteous."

"And why do you think I would know?"

"Come on, Mrs Bell, this is the White Horse in Kensal Town. There's nothing happening in these parts that you don't know about. Why do you think I'm here? When I started asking for Porteous, everyone told me to come here, to your public house."

Edith softened a little, "What are you drinking?"

"Ohh, I'll have a gin. Could you make it a large one? I've got to be at work in about an hour."

Edith poured her a generous measure, "Do you work for Charlie Maitland?"

Margaret Heywood ignored the question as she sipped her drink, "Look, I need to speak to Porteous about his friend Nancy Keeling."

Edith now had Heywood's full attention, "What about Nancy?"

Heywood plonked down her empty glass, "Ah, so you know Nancy?"

Edith Bell lifted the bar top and said, "You'd better come through…"

Peter Porteous sat on the armchair opposite Margaret Heywood as she related the events of how Nancy had been taken; the Evening News lay half- read on his lap. Edith Bell perched herself on the end of the dining room table.

"So, let me get this straight, you spent the night with Nancy?"

Heywood smiled, "Yes, unfortunately I can't remember too much as we did rather drink a little too much."

Edith spoke up, "Why were you there, Nancy's never mentioned you before, has she, Porteous?"

He shook his head, "Not as far as I know."

Heywood, straightened up, "Look, we sometimes work together. We share the same minder, Mifty Mitchell."

Heywood didn't want to tell either Porteous or Bell the real reason why she was there.

Porteous asked, "Are you sure it was Mitchell who took her?"

Heywood nodded, "Sure, I heard his voice and that of his mate Freddie Fox. It was Fox who clouted her after she kicked him in the balls."

"Was it you who cleaned up in the hallway?"

"Yes, I couldn't leave it like that. It would have stunk the whole place out," she paused, "She's up in the house in Maida Vale."

Porteous nodded, "We know. We spoke to one of Maitland's girls in Soho."

Margaret Heywood stood up, "In which case, I'll take my leave of you. I came to tell you what happened and I've done that."

Edith reached out to her, "Look, you don't have to work for Charlie Maitland, you know. There's plenty of work out there for a bright young lady like you."

Margaret Heywood was at the door, "Yup, you might be right, but I'll be out of here by the end of the year if I survive the bombing. Nancy's not the only one who can save money, you know."

With that, she was gone but not before she had a furtive conversation with Sinead, the barmaid; something about there being good money to be earned working elsewhere...

Porteous looked at Edith Bell, "Looks like Nancy put up a bit of a fight."

Bell nodded, "Yes, and she'll have paid for that severely..."

Over in the East End, Jimmy Ryan sat opposite Dennis Elphicke. They were discussing Charlie Maitland's threats to take over Elphicke's operation. Elphicke had cleared his warehouse in the port and decamped to an alternate venue some two miles away from the docks themselves. This, he was at pains to add, had caused him great inconvenience and someone, or organisation, would be paying a high price for this.

Elphicke was most concerned that probably someone from Maitland's organisation was tipping off the police. It was purely by good fortune that Elphicke had a contact in Scotland Yard who was more than willing to tip him off, for suitable compensation, of course.

Elphicke sipped his tea, "I'd take great care, If I were you, Jimmy."

Ryan nodded, "We're lying low for a few weeks, Dennis. Porteous has enough on his plate anyway with Nancy's disappearance."

"Hmm, no doubt down to Maitland as well?"

"Looks like it. The problem is that bloody brothel is guarded day and night. Some of the regular clients are very powerful people who would be loath to see any direct action by the police." He paused, "Anyway, that's not your problem. We'll leave Porteous and his people up in Kensal Town to sort that one out."

Elphicke smiled, "Yeah, I'm not sure what Maitland's boys think they will get out of the White Horse, especially if they think Edith Bell will just roll over and hand over her pub just like that."

Ryan looked at him and leaned in, "What's the plan, Dennis?"

Elphicke stood up, "Well, I've a few ideas, Jimmy. For the meantime, we'll react to whatever the Maltese gangster throws at us. I've taken on a dozen more boys and doubled the guards on any deliveries, just in case he attempts to steal any of our goods. There are enough traders around the capital to carry on business for the moment. We're going to be dealing a lot more in food as there appear to be growing shortages." He looked at Ryan,

"Can you shift food, Jimmy?"

"Dunno, Boss, our market is primarily nylons, clothes, alcohol and tobacco. But we'll sell anything, I suppose, provided it's either rationed or in short supply."

"My contact in Scotland Yard is trying to find out about that tip the other night. My guess is that it probably came from someone in Maitland's organisation. If I can find out who that was, the boys will sort him out. I'm not going to take this lying down, Jimmy."

Jimmy Ryan looked at him and swallowed; street black marketeers needed peace and quiet to get on with their lives and business...

Elphicke went on, "Leave it with me, Jimmy. Your account is good; you are all up to date. Just knock out what you've got and come back when Porteous' mind is focused on the task in hand..."

Jimmy Ryan drove back to the shop in Holborn, debating whether he should decamp, like Dennis Elphicke...

Just before midnight as Jimmy Ryan was counting the potential cost of vacating the Holborn premises, three of Dennis Elphicke's men bundled an unfortunate Soho pimp from Wardour Street, into the back of an old Bedford HC van with false number plates, drove the hapless man to a partially bombed out warehouse in Limehouse and beat him up. They dumped him outside the back door of Maitland's expensive house in Hampstead during the latest bombing raid...

At eight the following morning, Charlie Maitland was awakened from his slumber by the constant ringing of the telephone that sat on the little ornate table by his bed. He grunted as he picked up the receiver,

"Yeah; what is it?"

"Is that you, Charlie?" the voice demanded.

The naked female lying next to Maitland stirred; he poked her in the ribs.

"Who is it?" asked Maitland.

"Have you got my message?" asked Dennis Elphicke.

"What are you talking about?"

"Look outside your back door, you idiot."

"Hold on," muttered Maitland.

The naked woman sat up, exposing her small breasts; Maitland glared at her. She rolled over and promptly went back to sleep.

Maitland grabbed a silk dressing gown and shuffled down the carpeted grand staircase. He pushed open the door to the kitchen and went across the back door. His eyes opened in horror as he saw the battered and bruised body of one of his street pimps. He quickly opened the door and pulled in the groaning body.

The pimp's eyes opened, "Elphicke's boys, boss…"

Maitland rushed back upstairs and grabbed the telephone; he shouted down it,

"Elphicke! I'll fucking kill you…"

A calm voice answered, "Now you listen, you Maltese crook, you stick to your whores, and I'll stick to trading. If you do that, we'll all rub along nicely. There's no need for this trouble. We're all just trying to earn a living."

Maitland shouted down the phone, "You're a dead man! I'm coming for you!"

The naked female stirred again. She peeked out at her boss from under the sheet.

Elphicke tutted, "Look, I can take you and your pimps anytime I like. You just leave my boys to get on with their jobs especially Ryan and Porteous. If you don't, I'll be coming for you. Oh, one more thing, if I find out who tipped off the police about my establishment in Bromley-by-Bow I'll make a right mess of them. No one likes a grass, Charlie. Now, fuck off and sort out your injured man…"

The phone line went dead.

Maitland hurled the Bakelite receiver onto the little table. The female sat up again, blinking, "What's up, Charlie?"

The accent was refined.

He shouted at her, "Shut up and get dressed; haven't you got a school to go to? I'm not paying those fees for nothing."

She ran into the bathroom clutching a thin robe.

Later in the morning, there was a disturbance in the house in Maida Vale as three of Maitland's boys dragged in the injured man. He urgently required the attention of Doctor Loretta…

Chapter 14
February 1941
A letter and a plan of sorts

Nancy Keeling was dreaming. She was always the one who had such vivid dreams. When she awoke on those frosty winter mornings in Norwich, her younger sister Charlotte would climb into her bed and demand to be regaled with stories of dashing young men coming in to sweep her off her feet. Even if Nancy hadn't had such entertaining dreams, she would make them up so that Charlotte would be pacified.

This dream, however, wasn't so good. When you mix up good times with some of the unpleasant men who have availed themselves of her body, the brain tries to calculate which side has had the upper hand.

And then there was Peter Porteous; he had never tried to take advantage of her. Sometimes she wondered if he was not sufficiently attracted to her? She dismissed that idea; Nancy Keeling could have any man she wanted; or so she thought...

This time, the dream made her hot and covered with sweat despite it being a cold February morning and, as usual, the coal fire had extinguished during the night. Nancy's eyes opened; there seemed to be a bit of a commotion on the floor below hers. She dismissed it, but sat up thinking she should change her nightdress. The one she was wearing clung to her body; she shivered. The noises got louder; it sounded like a shouting match.

She blinked the sleep out of her eyes; what was it? Oh, yes, a very late night. A group of wealthy and privileged men had returned after the all-clear had sounded, demanding to have satisfaction with the ladies of the house including her two very young charges. She looked at the clock; it was barely nine-thirty.

Monique Fontaine, the brothel mistress, had insisted that Nancy prepare her ladies to receive men. Nancy had to wake up the two of them and get them ready. Hope cried; Faith just shrugged her shoulders. No matter. They were both ready within half an hour as the clients sipped expensive brandy on Madame Fontaine's Chesterfield sofa and chairs in the reception room.

Nancy counted six of them. They finished around three in the morning. Nancy bathed Hope but Faith was already sleeping. Hope insisted Nancy read her a bedtime story.

Nancy got up; she shivered and peeled off the damp nightdress. She reached for a robe on the hook behind the door and quickly pulled it on. She tossed the wet nightdress into her linen basket for the scullery maids to wash later.

She opened the door; the shouting got louder. She looked over at the back steps. The door was open. She fastened the cord of her robe and crept up to the door. Voices echoed up the passageway.

She leaned in; she thought she could hear the Irish accent of Doctor Loretta. There was a lot of cursing, especially coming from the men who were huffing and puffing.

She pulled the robe around her even tighter and began to creep down the stairs; the house was beginning to stir. It was unusual for residents to be up and about at this early hour. Gentleman callers were not usually welcomed until well after lunch.

The commotion was coming from the doctor's office. She crept along the hallway and began to peer into the room. Three men were holding down a young man who was writhing in agony. Nancy could see the battered and bruised face; she winced.

One of the men looked up at her; she thought she recognised him. He smiled at her. The doctor looked over, "Nancy! Get in here, quickly."

Nancy went into the room, not knowing what to expect. Loretta spoke to her,

"Look in that top drawer under the sink. You'll find a hypodermic needle and some glass vials. Bring them to me now!"

Nancy scuttled over to the sink and opened the drawer. She took out a needle that was in a little box and three of the vials. By the time she had returned to the struggling patient she had the shirt ripped off, exposing his arm. Loretta signalled Nancy to take her place and hold down the arm. She quickly took out the syringe, broke the top off a vial and stuck in the needle. She expertly lifted the plunger with her thumb and sucked up some of the clear liquid.

She examined the needle up into the light, flicked it a couple of times and squirted out some of the contents before sticking the sharp point into a rapidly swelling vein.

Over the next two minutes or so Nancy felt the tension leave the young man as he gradually relaxed. One of the men leered at Nancy, whose dressing gown had opened slightly at the top. She flushed up, and quickly pulled it together, wishing she had taken the time to put on a fresh nightdress before she had left her room.

Loretta spoke up sharply, "All right, you three idiots, you can leave now. Tell your boss I'll make sure the lad recovers, but he won't be working for a few weeks. Now bugger off...."

They took their leave rapidly, not wishing to upset the doctor. One of them tipped his hat as he pushed past Nancy,

"Nice to see you again, Miss..." He laughed.

Nancy looked at the doctor, "What's going on, Miss Loretta?"

The doctor looked up as she held the now comatose young man. She shook her head,

"One of Maitland's boys has gotten himself into a bit of a mess."

Nancy walked around the prone body; she tilted his face, "He's only a kid, Doctor."

She raised her eyebrows, "Yeah, like his ladies Maitland, likes to get them young and impressionable."

"What happened to him?"

"Not sure, Nancy, but methinks there is a war brewing between Maitland and some black market fellow named Elphicke or something."

Nancy's heart skipped a beat, "Dennis Elphicke, Doctor Loretta."

She looked over at Nancy, "You know him?"

"Sort of. He does business with my good friend."

"Hmm, with friends like that, you don't need enemies."

Nancy shook her head, "No, Porteous is a good friend. He won't let anything happen to me."

The doctor snorted, "Then why are you here, Nancy? To make up the numbers?"

Nancy looked away; she'd never thought of it that way before.

Loretta said, "Come on; help me turn him on his side so he doesn't vomit and asphyxiate himself."

They heaved the young man into a recovery position. Loretta stood back; Nancy asked,

"What did you give him?"

"Morphine, Nancy. Enough to knock him out cold, so I can examine him and make a plan to treat him."

She pulled up a chair next to the patient.

Nancy asked, "What do you think happened to him?"

"Dunno, really. I get young men like him brought in from time to time. He's lucky. It seems they just beat him up. There's no stab or gun shot wounds. Who ever did this knew he'd be in a bad way but knew enough to limit his injuries," she paused,

"I reckon he's got a couple of broken ribs and maybe some crush injuries to his fingers, but he'll live. He'll be peeing red wine for a few weeks, looking at the bruising around his kidneys, and he certainly won't be entertaining the fairer sex for a while."

Nancy looked at the young man, who couldn't have been more than twenty. He looked as if he would have trouble growing a moustache.

She whispered, "It seems that whoever did this left him outside Charlie Maitland's back door..." She smiled, "It's about time Maitland actually saw the results of his actions. I've had too many girls brought in here a lot worse than this fellow for simply disobeying him. It's time someone did something about the thug and his brothers."

A stern voice made Nancy jump,

"Miss Claudine! What are you doing here?"

Nancy turned around to see the glowering face of Madame Monique Fontaine; she blushed and attempted a curtsey.

Doctor Loretta spoke up, "It's okay, Monique, I asked Nancy to assist me; she's finished now."

Fontaine looked at her and clicked her fingers; "Let's have you upstairs. I'm sure your girls will be looking for you."

Nancy nodded again and as she walked past her, Fontaine grabbed her arm,

"Make sure I don't catch you down here again. Go and put on some clothes. This is a respectable house."

Nancy walked slowly back up the stairs. The door boy, William, was sitting on his chair next to the door. She smirked at him, as she brushed past; he blushed and tried to look away.

She said, "Good morning, William."

He nodded at her and tipped another imaginary hat, "Morning, Miss. I got told off because you were down there. You're not supposed to be below this floor."

Nancy batted her eyes, "Oh; I'm so sorry, William. I'll make sure I stay up here in future."

She walked past him and then turned, "Did you think any more about contacting my sister for me. She'll be worried."

William stammered, "I don't know, Miss. Madame Fontaine would not be very happy. I need this job."

Nancy's eyes flared at him, "Job? This is not a job. There's plenty of work out there."

"I know, Miss, but I don't want to be called up."

Nancy smiled, "So you are hiding here?"

William looked away, "I got into a bit of trouble, Miss."

Nancy went back up to him, "What did you do?"

"I got caught with some forged pound notes. I was only trying to buy a drink for me and my mates in the pub. The landlord called the police and I got arrested. The magistrate released me on bail because I had not been in trouble before. I never went back to answer." He shrugged, "So, you see, I don't have anywhere to go."

Nancy spoke quietly, "You know you'll have to answer at some point, unless Scotland Yard has the misfortune to take a direct hit from the Jerries."

William smiled, "That's what I'm hoping. I can't go back home because the police already turned up at my mother's house looking for me."

Nancy nodded, "Look, I just need a short letter to go to my friend who will pass it on to my sister. That's not too much to ask, is it, William?"

"I-I-I don't know, Miss."

Nancy reached out and touched his arm, "It's okay, William, there's no hurry."

He stood in close to her, "Do you want out of here, Miss?"

"I do, William, before they put me to service the gentlemen callers."

There was a slight noise on the steps; William pushed her away, "Off you go, Miss..."

Nancy ran up the stairs. She opened Hope's bedroom door. The girl was still fast asleep. Nancy wondered how these girls could sleep so easily given what they were going through.

Twenty minutes later, Nancy was washed and dressed; her roommate was still snoring. Nancy pushed open the door to Hope's bedroom. The girl didn't appear to have moved. Nancy poked the coal in the fire, wondering if Charlie Maitland had an unlimited supply of the fuel when all others have a meagre ration. Shortages didn't seem to apply to the Maltese brothers.

She gently shook the girl, "Hope, Hope; it's time to get up."

The young girl finally stirred, "I've got tummy pains, Claudine."

Nancy smiled, "You've got your period?"

"I think so; I feel funny."

"Good, that means no visitors for you. I'll send for the doctor, but she's a little busy at the moment."

Hope buried her head in a pillow, "I'd rather work than have these pains."

"Maybe the doctor will give you something for them; come on, I'll draw you a hot bath. That always used to help me."

The girl looked up, "What are yours like, Claudine?"

Nancy looked away, "I don't get them any more..."

The scullery maid came in and glared at Nancy,

"Madame Fontaine says to get Miss Hope ready for an early caller."

Nancy looked at her, "Tell Madame Fontaine that Hope can't work for the next few days; I'll get Miss Faith ready to receive the gentleman."

The scullery maid huffed and puffed and then left the bedroom.

Nancy turned to the girl, "Come on and soak in a hot bath, it will do you good."

The girl yawned and swung her legs out of the bed. She reached for Nancy's hand and allowed herself to be led into the large Victorian bathroom that was rapidly steaming up.

Nancy went across to the other door and opened it into Miss Faith's room. The older girl was sitting up in bed smoking,

"Yes, I heard, Claudine, I'll be up in a minute."

Nancy reached across and removed the burning cigarette,

"Don't you know it's dangerous to smoke in bed?"

She stubbed out the cigarette, reached over and took the girl's arm, "Come on; the bell will sound soon enough."

She disrobed in front of an ornate mirror, tossing her nightclothes onto the floor; she looked at herself, turning this way and that,

"Don't you think I'm pretty, Claudine?"

Nancy didn't look up at her; she was too busy picking up the discarded clothes,

"Why, yes, Miss, I do. That is why you have so many callers. Now come on, Miss Hope's in the bathroom. Let's go to the one down the hall."

She handed her a thick woollen dressing gown and led her into the bathroom. She could hear Miss Hope singing to herself as they passed the open door of the bathroom.

Nancy ran the bath as Faith continued to regard herself in the mirror. Nancy finally looked at her charge; her mouth opened in horror. There were welts across her back together with deep scratches. The bruising was already beginning to show.

She grabbed Faith by the shoulder, "What happened here, Miss Faith?"

The girl shook her head, "Oh, it's nothing."

Nancy shook her again, "What happened?"

"I can't remember; Mr Rawcliffe gave me some funny powder to breathe into my nose. When I woke up, he had gone."

"Did you also smoke that sweet smelling tobacco?"

She nodded as she sank into the hot water. Nancy pushed the girl's head under the water. Faith spluttered as she came back up,

"What was that for?"

"Just washing your hair, Miss, that's all. You wouldn't want the gentlemen complaining that you are none too fresh, would you?"

Nancy stood up, "Now stay there until I come back…"

Twenty minutes later, Miss Faith was lying on her stomach on the doctor's examination table; Madame Monique Fontaine was standing behind the doctor,

"I wondered why Mr Rawcliffe was in such a hurry to leave last night."

Nancy stood back, folded her arms and said nothing; these people would get their payback when the time was right…

Fontaine turned to her, "Did you not check up on her after her last caller?" There was anger in her voice.

Nancy flared at her, "Of course I did. She was sleeping, so I left her to her rest. That man was the third caller she'd had."

Fontaine snapped at her, "Don't you address me in that tone…"

Nancy looked down.

Fontaine turned towards the doctor, "How long?"

"At least a week, I'd say. You've got to stop those girls smoking cannabis; it's making them lose their inhibitions and as for that cocaine, they are far too young for that stuff."

Fontaine shrugged her shoulders, "It helps them relax. Our clients prefer the girls mellow."

Loretta shook her head; "Let me put some astringent on these scratches. I can't do much for the bruises. Mother nature will just have to take her course."

Fontaine raised her voice, "What about Hope? Can she work?"

Loretta didn't look up from her work, "Nope. Definitely not."

Fontaine cursed and turned to Nancy,

"Get them both dressed; they can go down and help the ladies on the first floor. You can go with them."

Nancy had a grin on her face as she turned to the door. Faith was whimpering as the antiseptic stung her body...

Later that afternoon, three of Charlie Maitland's men set upon a gentleman wearing a pin-striped suit and a bowler hat as he left his office in High Holborn. Stephen Rawcliffe was given a sound beating, relieved of his expensive wallet, a gold watch and the tidy sum of forty pounds. He was told never to return to the house in Maida Vale ever again...

About the same time, Edith Bell was tending the bar at the White Horse in Kensal Road. The pub was quiet, with only a few hardened drinkers staring morosely into their beer. Edith was polishing a few glasses. The barmaid, Sinead, was sulking at the other end of the bar having been told off, yet again, by her landlady.

Edith looked up as the door opened. A young man appeared wearing a thick overcoat with an upturned collar and a flat cap. Edith had never seen the fellow before and since Porteous' warning about Maitland, she was constantly on the lookout for trouble.

The young man walked up to the bar; he loosened his coat. Edith smiled at him as the Irish barmaid suddenly found herself looking brighter again.

He spoke with a soft voice; Edith relaxed. He wasn't the sort of bruiser that Maitland would send out to take over an establishment like hers.

"A small beer, please."

Edith pulled on the old wooden hand pump, expertly filled up the glass and placed it down in front of him. He handed over a three-penny piece. Edith tossed it into the open till drawer.

He sipped the beer,

"Can I speak with Mrs Bell, please?"

Edith froze for a minute; two of her customers stirred in their chairs.

"I'm Mrs Bell; what can I do for you?"

As the young man reached into his greatcoat pocket; chairs scraped upon the wooden floors. Two men stood up, half-expecting trouble.

The man produced a brown envelope; "I have a letter for Miss Charlotte Keeling..."

Peter Porteous looked at Alice Halpin and Edith Bell as they sat around his kitchen table in his house in East Row, eating another one of Alice's meals. It's amazing what you can concoct from a few vegetables and some beef dripping enticed out of the butcher on the Harrow Road without a ration card.

There was an open brown envelope on the table.

Dear Charlotte,

I am well and in good spirits, for the moment. I was in a little accident, but I am recovering well. I am working in a large house in Maida Vale. You know, the one I told you about recently? I didn't want to go, but the work is not too bad at the moment. I am looking after a couple of very young girls.

As soon as my injuries heal, I will be put to work with the other ladies in the house. I am trying to avoid this. I am not allowed out presently, but as soon as I am, I will be making my way to see you and mother.

Please say hello to her from me.
Your loving sister,
Nancy

Porteous had read and re-read the letter at least five times. Edith Bell spoke out,

"This is good, Porteous. At least we know she is well and in not any immediate danger."

Porteous didn't answer.

Alice spoke up, "She's a clever girl, that Nancy." She reached for the letter,

"Who was the young man who brought it?"

Edith Bell looked at her, "Says his name is William. He works in the house minding a staircase or other. He was very young to be involved in this unpleasant business."

Alice glanced down at the letter, "It says here she'll be put to work with the other ladies in the house shortly."

Porteous looked up, "She's done with that work; I told you. I think she'd rather hurt herself than go back to it. It doesn't matter how much they are willing to pay her."

Edith stared ahead, "We need to get her out as soon as we can."

Alice looked at her, "Yes, but how? We can't go mob-handed to the place. For all we know, they've got weapons. I know I would if I'd had so much money invested in the place."

Edith went quiet for a moment, "Let's look at this logically. We know we can't use force to get her out. Maitland's boys are much too powerful. We could wait until she slips out, but they know she would only come here for refuge. I'm not sure the good residents of Kensal Town would be prepared to go up against the Maltese brothers."

Porteous finished spooning some of the stew into his mouth, "What we need is the authorities to raid the place and shut it down."

Alice snorted, "Just how do we do that? The brothel is protected."

Edith raised her hand, "Wait a minute; Porteous is right. We get the police or whoever, to raid the place. The girls will be taken into custody, interrogated and then put up before the magistrate; the maids and doormen will be given a slapping and booted out, and then the Madame will be arrested." She paused, "I heard it's some French woman; she'll have to take her chances."

Alice repeated, "As I said, just how do we get the police to raid an establishment that has their protection?"

Edith looked at her, "We embarrass them into action. I mean, for God's sake, there are undcrage girls in there."

"Exactly." The Liverpool accent was harsh, "Who do you think their clientele is? I'm telling you it'll be lords, esteemed Members of Parliament, big city types and of course, the police themselves. We had one in Liverpool. Everyone knew what it was, but it never seemed to get the attention of the police. It would still be there now if Jerry hadn't bombed it."

Porteous reached out and touched her arm, "Hold on, Alice. Edith is correct."

He looked at the pub landlady, "Who do you know in authority, Edith?"

She paused, looked at Porteous quizzically and snorted, "My ever-so friendly magistrate and I know he's not a client there..."

They put their heads together for an hour or so before Alice Halpin went off to the arms of her lover, Phyllis Manley, back in Golders Green and Edith went back to tell off her errant barmaid.

Peter Porteous donned his ARP uniform, went down to Chelsea, watched for a few fires and sold Harry Harris five pairs of slightly substandard stockings...

Chapter 15
February 1941
Trouble

The transport links between Edmonton in North London and Scotland Yard were so badly disrupted by the previous night's bombing that it took Inspector Eric Everard nearly two hours to get to his office. He was not in a particularly good mood. He had left his mistress lying in bed as he closed the door to his two-bedroomed terraced house in Montague Gardens.

Somehow, he had managed to pull rank and got one of those Anderson Shelters at the bottom of his garden, although he'd had to pay seven pounds for it. Two likely lads from the pub down the road knocked it up for him for a couple of quid. He had spent a week or so installing a bed and a small portable gas stove with a double burner so that he could make some tea.

He wondered why the authorities thought that the shelters were such a good idea, since they gave no protection whatsoever if there was a direct hit. The argument was that the shelters protected the occupants from falling masonry...however, it saved him from the tedious walk down the official shelter near the railway station at Silver Street, never mind that he wouldn't have to share it with the great unwashed.

The bombing had been light that evening, so as soon as the all-clear had sounded he retired with the lady from Catford...He was making sure he got his money's worth. He had left her tucked up in his nice warm bed...

He walked into his office to be greeted by his Chief Inspector. The girls were pretending to look busy, as was Detective Sergeant Derek Beaston.

Everard took off his coat, knocked out his pipe and sat down. His superior was finishing his tea; at least the girls in the outer office had remembered their manners.

Chief Inspector Alfred Barrett looked at Everard; there would be no small talk this morning, "Eric, we've gotten word of some trouble brewing."

Everard sighed, "What is it, sir?"

"Charlie bloody Maitland."

Everard regarded his superior quizzically, "Maitland? He belongs to the Vice boys, sir."

"Yes, that's what we all thought. One of his street pimps was picked up yesterday for fighting and being drunk and disorderly. Well, It also appears he failed to answer bail back in Manchester some time ago so he's about to be potted back up there for a stretch or two."

Everard picked up his pipe, still wondering where this was going.

Barrett continued, "He was well and truly drunk, but he kept muttering something about one of his colleagues who had been badly beaten by the Elphicke crew.

Chief Inspector Barrett well and truly had Eric Everard's full attention,

"Why would Elphicke have one of Maitland's boys beaten up?"

"Well, that's what was puzzling us."

Everard sat up, "It doesn't have anything to do with the raid on that property in Bromley-by-Bow, the other night, does it?"

Barrett extracted a cigarette, "Hmm, possibly. You know we never did find out where that tip off came from the other day, never mind that the place was empty when you kicked in the doors."

He lit the cigarette, inhaled deeply and breathed out, "Elphicke's also vacated his main warehouse down by the docks."

Everard nodded, "Yes, my sergeant mentioned that the other day. We're still trying to locate his new place."

Everard packed his pipe with the last of his tobacco and lit the foul-smelling weed,

"Did the pimp say anything after he sobered up?"

Barrett shook his head, "No; I think he realised he'd said too much. It seems that the fellow who got the beating was his mate. He had taken great exception to it and picked a fight with the first person he met. We packed him off in handcuffs back to Manchester as soon as there was an available train. They can have him as far as we are concerned."

Everard said, "Best thing for him, sir, and a lot less paperwork for us to do..."

Barrett smiled, "Agreed, but where does that put us with Maitland and Elphicke? We don't have any firm evidence at the moment. What's happening at your end?"

Everard shook his head, "Nothing at the moment, sir. It's all gone a bit quiet since we raided that place, but we've got our eyes on a couple of Elphicke's boys; one operates out of Kensal Town and one from Tottenham. They're both ARPs; a pair of slippery customers as well. We just haven't managed to catch them red-handed."

The Chief Inspector looked up, "Hmm, Kensal Town, you say?"

Everard nodded, "Remember that flap over a possible spy when MI5 got involved?"

Barrett raised his eyebrows as Everard went on, "Well, we had this fellow Porteous on a tight leash until some stupid magistrate started giving us grief."

Barrett stood up, "Wasn't he connected with the alleged spy? Wasn't she a doctor or something?"

"His lover, sir. Unfortunately for him and the Security Services, she managed to get herself blown up when his house was hit by a parachute bomb."

Barrett looked out of the window, "Pity, I heard she was a bit of all right in the looks department."

Everard cleared his throat...

"You know where this fellow works?"

"He's a supervisor at Smiths in Cricklewood."

Barrett stood up and made his way to the door, "Pick him up and sweat him. I'll go and see what our colleagues in Vice are up to."

Chief Inspector John Lodge's doting parents told him when he was a child that if he worked hard and listened to his superiors, he would always succeed in life. John Lodge was certainly smug about his successes. He had started as a lowly beat bobby over in Shepherd's Bush, where the most dangerous thing he ever did was arrest a few of the barrow boys on the market for selling stolen goods. However, he had acquired a taste for the ladies of the night, especially those who worked at the rear of the market in Lime Grove. It was easy to get a knee-trembler down some back alley when it was dark, as the girls reckoned it was simply paying the 'rent.'

Lodge made sure that none of his fellow officers ever troubled the ladies...

A promotion to sergeant in the West End broadened his horizons. Now he was dealing with the odd murder or two and organised prostitution, the latter pricked his interest and moreover, kept his adult needs satisfied.

Rising through the ranks as a detective, he soon managed a transfer to what was known as the Clubs and Vice Unit based on the third floor of West End Central Police Station in Saville Row. Here, he oversaw the day-to-day running of the unit, whose primary responsibilities were to police the numerous bars and drinking establishments and limit the activities of the street prostitutes. He had a small section dealing with the growing trade in obscene material, but he farmed that out to a group of officers because he couldn't be bothered by all the fuss of a few 'dirty' books and pictures...

Chief Inspector John Lodge was overly protective of his territory. Woe betide any unsuspecting officer who innocently stumbled across his 'clientele.'

At times like these, when there were so many overseas soldiers in London, business with the ladies of the night was particularly thriving. There were a couple of local pimps who were allowed to trade on the peripherals of the West End, for an appropriate fee, of course, but the man he did business with most of all was one Charlie Maitland and his fellow Maltese brother. They paid handsomely for protection.

All things to do with the Maitland brothers were solely in the bailiwick of Chief Inspector John Lodge.

He was sat in his little glass office at the end of the squad room when the little girl who pretended to be his secretary knocked timidly on the door. Lodge was studying the racing form. He didn't bother looking up. He raised his hand to her and beckoned her in.

The girl was pretty; you wouldn't expect Chief Inspector John Lodge to employ any lady who wasn't.

"What is it, Barbara?"

"Chief Inspector Barrett from Scotland Yard to see you, sir."

Lodge finally looked up from his newspaper, "What does he want?"

"He didn't say, sir, but he says it's important."

Lodge folded up his newspaper, straightened his tie and finally said, "Well, you'd better show him in, then."

The girl rapidly disappeared. Officers from Clubs and Vice didn't particularly like those from Scotland Yard, but Lodge thought it better to find out what the officer from Command wanted. In pecking order, officers from Scotland Yard generally had superiority over those from outlying stations.

Lodge stood up as Barrett walked in. Lodge vaguely knew Alfred Barrett from some conference or other he had been required to attend some time before the war kicked off and disrupted everyone's routine. He held out his hand,

"Good afternoon, Alfred."

Barrett stiffened up, "Good afternoon, Chief Inspector."

Lodge indicated him to sit down on the hard wooden chair in front of his untidy desk,

"What can I do for you?"

Barrett took out a silver cigarette case and extracted a cigarette. He lit it without offering his fellow officer one,

"How's business, John?"

"Oh, you know, busy like the rest of us. I'm having trouble hanging on to my officers as many are being called up, and I'm not sure bringing back retired coppers is such a good idea."

Barrett raised his eyes, "Yes, we have the same problem; too much crime and not enough men to deal with it."

There was a pause; Lodge fiddled with some papers on his desk, wondering where this was going. He asked, "What's happening in the black market business?"

"Well, here's the thing. We've got it under some form of control. I mean, isn't everyone partial to the odd half a pound of butter or a few extra ounces of sugar from under the counter from time to time? I know I certainly am. You see, that's not what we are after."

Lodge peered at him, "What are you after, Alfred?"

"The organisers at the top. The ones who are stealing valuable cargo from bombed-out ships in the docks; the ones who are liberating army supplies and then selling them on; the ones who are murdering and chopping up competitors to get what they want..."

He paused to let that sink in...

"Charlie Maitland comes to mind..."

Lodge sat up rather too quickly, "Maitland? He's not in the black market business."

Barrett sat back with a smile on his face. Lodge didn't appear to know as much as his smug impression led others to believe.

"Ever heard of someone called Dennis Elphicke?"

Lodge shook his head slowly.

"Well, he controls what goes in and out of the docks. It's quite a simple operation really, although it took some time to get to where he is now. He begs, steals and borrows from the ships that come in and knocks the stuff out through a network of chancers out to make a few bob on the side."

"You mean spivs."

Barrett nodded.

"What's all this got to do with Charlie Maitland? As far as I know, he doesn't do any trading except for his girls."

"Well, that's the problem, John. We have information that Maitland and his merry band are about to go into the black market business."

Lodge smiled, "I doubt it very much. That stuff is far too insignificant for Maitland."

"Then why did Dennis Elphicke have one of Maitland's boys picked up and given a good hiding the other night?"

Lodge shook his head.

"Well Chief Inspector, We have it on good authority that Maitland wants to make a move on Mr Elphicke and, needless to say, our Dennis is not having it. Now, my superiors back at the Yard don't want another war going on. They've got enough problems with Jerry's nightly raids and the havoc they are causing."

Barrett stood up and looked down at Lodge, "Now, get off your arse and sort this out...my commander wants a written report by close of play tomorrow."

With that, Chief Inspector Alfred Barrett walked out, blew a kiss at the slip of a girl and retraced his steps back into the fresh air, wishing he could wash his hands and get rid of the dirt that one picks up from visiting Clubs and Vice.

John Lodge went almost purple with rage. He stamped to the door of his office and shouted out,

"Sergeant Booth! Get in here now!"

Detective Sergeant David Booth looked up from his desk. He was casting his eyes over a black and white glossy French magazine that contained some rather nice pictures of naked women in a variety of poses.

He stood up and tossed the magazine aside, "Boss? What's up, Boss?"

He didn't even have time to say anything as he walked into the office,

"Grab your coat; we're off to see Charlie Maitland."

The Maltese gangster kept them waiting nearly half an hour. Booth's boss was in such a bad mood that he wouldn't even let him have a bottle of beer served up by that nice new waitress, June, wasn't it?

Maitland sat at his over-large desk, still dressed in his expensive Saville Row pinstriped suit. His brother, Alfredo, remained on the sofa sipping a drink. He was also immaculate, with his polished shoes shining in the light.

"What's the fuss, John?" He lit a cigarette.

"I've just had Scotland Yard in my office wittering about a possible war opening up on a different front to the one we currently are experiencing."

Maitland looked at his brother and then turned to the detective, "And what war would that be, John?"

"The one you're about to start with some hooligan from the East End named Elphicke or something."

Maitland raised his eyebrows and smiled, "That's not a war, Johnny boy. That's a slight skirmish."

Lodge raised his voice, "Well, whatever it is, I want you and your lads out of it."

Maitland poured himself a drink, "It's not your decision, or his." He pointed to the hapless sergeant who was trying to look invisible at the back of the room.

Lodge leaned on the desk, "Now, look here, Charlie. I can keep you sweet with the girls and the dirty books, not to mention the illegal gambling and drinking establishments you have on your patch, but I can't get involved in a gang war over some knock-off stockings and a couple of cases of gin."

Maitland smiled again, "Is that so, Johnny boy? I thought it was me who called the shots in this relationship, not you."

He stood up and leaned into the chief inspector's face, "You listen, you bent copper, I decide what I'm going to do, not you. I've watched that little crook from the East End get rich doing what he does, and I want a piece of the action."

He sat down and sipped his drink, "I've been reasonable with the fellow. I've offered to buy him out and take over his operation but, how shall I say, he's being a little reluctant at the moment."

Lodge shook his head, "Look, Charlie, better to stick with what you are good at. I've got no control over what happens at Scotland Yard. If this all goes south, I can't protect you. You've got a good living with the ladies and your establishments, why would you want to mess it up?"

Maitland began to swivel in his chair, "You see, Johnny boy, that's where you and me differ. I'm an entrepreneur, not like you. I make things happen, whilst you and your lot just react. So, I'm expanding my little business into the buying and selling market. With all this rationing going on, I can make a little extra. Isn't that right, Alfredo?"

His brother smiled and nodded.

Lodge sighed, "I know about one of your lads taking a beating the other day."

Maitland stared at the policeman, "My, word does travel fast. I'll deal with that. You just keep out of it."

Lodge snorted, "Oh, don't you worry, not my business. Scotland Yard are all over that. You'll have a job finding someone as amenable as me there. I'm only going to stick to the terms of our agreement. You run the girls and your clubs. I'll continue to see that you aren't bothered too much. You step out of line and mess with Mr Elphicke, I won't be able to protect you."

Maitland looked over at his brother who nodded discreetly.

Maitland smiled, "Go back and tell your lords and masters that you have delivered their message. Help yourself to a drink before you leave, and I'll discuss the options with my brother. Just hear this, someone has to pay for my lad the other day. I take great exception to having this mess turn up in my own backyard."

Lodge said, "Just do what you have to do, but get it over and done with as soon as possible. There's a bloody war on, don't you know?" He paused on his way out, "Just one last thing, if you are going to tip off the police about something, do try and make it not so obvious where the information came from..."

Maitland coloured up...

Detective Chief Inspector John Lodge and Detective Sergeant David Booth stood at the bar whilst June Cook smiled at the younger policeman. She made sure he had a good eyeful of her charms. They ended up consuming several drinks before they left. June Cook managed to waylay the sergeant on his way back from the toilets and persuade him to meet her for a quiet assignation later in the week...

Later that evening, just before the early warning siren, Charlie Maitland picked up the Bakelite phone on his desk and made several telephone calls.

The following morning, three burly uniformed police officers led by Detective Sergeant Derek Beaston bundled Peter Porteous into the back of an unmarked van to the horror of Alice Halpin and the girls on the early shift at Smiths in Cricklewood.

Chapter 16
February 1941
An interrogation and another murder

Two rather large uniformed policemen lifted Peter Porteous out of the back of the unmarked police van that had driven into the rear yard of Marylebone Police Station in Broadley Terrace, just off Lisson Grove. Porteous hadn't been able to see out of the blacked-out windows, so he had no idea where he was being taken.

He had sat handcuffed between the two policemen on a bench as it slowly picked its way through the debris of the previous night's bombing. Porteous was nervous.

He was taken to an interrogation room similar to the one he had been kept in the morning after his house on Bosworth Road was demolished by that parachute bomb; the night his beloved Maruska was killed. The custody sergeant handcuffed him to a metal bar under the table.

He looked around him; he was tired, having come off a late shift down in Chelsea watching the Germans bomb the hell out of London. He closed his eyes to think about his present circumstances, which were not exactly good.

If he told them where he had moved they would send in a team of officers to go through his home from top to bottom and as there were a few items in the place that clearly shouldn't have been, this might not be good for him...The good residents of Kensal Town wouldn't tackle a mob of policemen...

They kept him waiting for three hours. He was wondering if Alice Halpin had managed to get the girls on the shift to complete the orders for the day, and then he realised that wasn't really very important. What was important was why the police had suddenly decided to pick him up...

The door opened roughly. Detective Inspector Eric Everard and Sergeant Derek Beaston came in followed by a rather demure lady in a pencil skirt clutching a notepad and pen; she looked at Porteous and blushed.

Beaston shouted, "Wake up, Porteous, this is no time for sleeping."

Porteous opened his eyes. He recognised Beaston as the one who had made enquiries about him, Nancy and Alice up at Smiths. His heart skipped a beat when he saw Inspector Everard. He was the one who had been rather unpleasant to him over Maruska's death. A uniformed policeman stood by the door with his arms folded.

Porteous sat up, "Why have I been brought here?"

Beaston shouted again, "Shut up! We ask the questions, not you."

Porteous sighed.

Everard said, "Read him his rights, Derek." The DI didn't want anything to come back and bite him later.

Beaston went through the police caution. The secretary began to scribble in some indecipherable language known only to her. She kept smoothing down her skirt and glancing at the handsome Porteous.

Everard slapped a file on the table and slowly opened it; he reached into his inside pocket and extracted a pair of half-moon reading glasses that he perched on the end of his nose.

"Ah, Mr Porteous; it says here you are employed as a supervisor at Smiths in Cricklewood..." He looked up, "Doing good war work, I do believe."

Porteous shifted on his chair. The handcuffs were overly tight and had begun to chafe his wrists.

"It also says you work as an Air Raid Precautions Warden; why you are indeed a model citizen."

Porteous looked at him disdainfully; sarcasm was never going to get a rise out of him.

Everard closed the file and tossed it to one side, "I hope you've noticed that we have a file on you?"

Porteous spoke for the first time, "They have a file on me at Smiths and so does the War Office for my ARP work, and I'm sure the Ministry of Labour has one as well." He shrugged his shoulders.

Everard smiled, "Yes, but they don't mention the fact that you are a criminal, do they?"

Porteous stared back at him, "What do you mean I'm a criminal? I have never been charged with a crime, let alone convicted of one."

Beaston snorted, "That's because we haven't caught you yet."

"Where do you keep your black market goods, Porteous?" Everard asked.

Porteous shook his head, "Sorry, don't know what you are talking about." He pulled at the handcuffs, "Can you remove these, please?"

"You know, the stuff you get from Elphicke that you and Jimmy Ryan knock out to your nearest and dearest."

For a split second, Porteous flinched; he would have to be careful here,

"Sorry, can't help you."

Everard sighed, "Look, we know you and Ryan work for Elphicke. You have been seen entering and leaving premises in the East End owned by him. Do you deny ever going to visit him?"

Porteous leaned back, "Never been anywhere near the fellow."

Everard opened the Manila folder again, "What about the time Ryan, Nancy Keeling and someone called..." he peered at the file, "Ah, yes, Alice Halpin, were stopped on the East India Dock Road. Were they coming back from visiting Mr Elphicke?"

Porteous shook his head, "You'll have to ask them, I wasn't with them."

"So you know Ryan, Keeling and Halpin?"

There was no point in denying it, "Yes, of course, Alice Halpin is my deputy on the shift at Smiths, Nancy is an old friend and Jimmy Ryan is a fellow ARP."

Beaston asked, "What do you do at Smiths?"

"We make cockpit instruments for fighter planes, but you already know that."

"What about Nancy Keeling?"

Porteous shrugged his shoulders, "She's a typist; works in the office."

Beaston again, "That's interesting because she hasn't been in work for a few days."

Porteous wondered how they knew that...

"I don't know; I'm not her keeper. I do know that her mother up in Norwich is not too well. Perhaps she's gone to visit her."

Everard leaned into Porteous, "What's your current address, Porteous?" He flicked open Porteous' identity card that had been taken off him when he was searched at the main desk; it still recorded the old address on Bosworth Road.

"I'm sort of between houses at the moment since my place was bombed."

Beaston clicked his fingers, "Come on; come on! We haven't got all day."

Porteous gave them Nancy's address in Crediton Hill, West Hampstead, knowing full well that there would be no one there and that there wouldn't be anything there that shouldn't be.

He added, "That's Nancy's house; I stay with her from time to time. Otherwise, I stay with Mrs Bell in the White Horse on Kensal Road."

Beaston turned to the uniformed policeman by the door, "Go and get a warrant and search this house in Crediton Hill and whilst you are at it, one for this disreputable pub."

Porteous smiled to himself; he knew they wouldn't go anywhere near Edith and White Horse.

Everard smirked, "Who is this Nancy Keeling? Has she replaced the doctor from Czechoslovakia in your bed?"

Porteous started up suddenly. Beaston scraped his chair as he stood up,

"Mind yourself, Porteous; remember where you are. There are some rather steep steps leading down to the cells. You wouldn't want to have a nasty accident on them, would you?"

Porteous breathed in slowly; he felt his chest tighten...

A big grin appeared on the detective inspector's face, "Oh, we seem to have touched a raw nerve, Derek, don't we?"

"I wonder if this Nancy is a spy as well?"

"Could be, Sergeant, could be. Perhaps we'll have to let the security services know about this."

"Good idea, Sir..."

Porteous coughed, "Can I have some water, please?"

"Oh, do shut up, Porteous." Everard paused, "Tell us about your ARP work. Where is it that you fire watch?"

Beaston ran his finger down a sheet of paper, "Says here, Chelsea, Sir."

"What exactly do you do, Porteous?"

Porteous had enough and sat back; he really wasn't feeling too well. He stared at the detectives.

"I'll tell you what he does, Derek, he sits in a church tower drinks tea and God knows what else and when he sees a fire he picks up the telephone and guides the Auxiliary Fire Service to the scene. Very demanding work, isn't it Porteous?"

Porteous shook his head.

Everard changed tactics, "What do you know of Charlie Maitland?"

Porteous said nothing; he repeated his request for some water.

Everard turned to Beaston, "Tell him, Derek."

The sergeant went into a long spiel about the evil Charlie Maitland, who appeared to have his eyes on the black market business. Of course, Porteous already knew this. He stared blankly.

Everard spoke sternly, "Now listen here, Porteous, there is some bad blood brewing between Maitland and Elphicke. I wouldn't want to be caught in the middle of it if I were you. If you have information about this rather serious matter, you'd be well advised to share it with us. Do you understand? It's bad enough dealing with one war, never mind tackling another."

Porteous stared at the detective.

Everard sighed and stood up, "Put him in the cells for the rest of the day and keep him in overnight if he hasn't started talking. Perhaps some solitude will loosen his tongue."

Porteous, asked again, "I'm not feeling very well. I think I have an asthma attack coming on, and my medication is at home."

Everard scoffed, "Take him down to custody, Derek, and make sure he doesn't slip on the stairs..."

Peter Porteous spent a rather uncomfortable night on a hard bench in one of the cells. He had managed to calm his breathing and stave off a serious asthma attack. The custody sergeant took pity on this obviously sick man and gave him a cup of tepid water against the instructions of the detective inspector.

Porteous listened to the booming of the anti-aircraft guns throughout the night and the dull thuds of shells landing way over in the East End of London.

About the same time that Porteous was struggling for breath in that damp cell in Lisson Grove, Evelyn Oatley was just finishing her shift at the dingy drinking club in Broadwick Street, Soho. The early warning sirens were about to sound, and her manager had decided to shut up shop early. There weren't many customers in the place anyway. The manager's boss, one Charlie Maitland, wouldn't know he'd closed up early anyway.

Evelyn Oatley had had a sparse night anyway. Few customers meant even fewer tips. Being a nightclub hostess during the Blitz was not exactly a profession with good prospects. There was money to be made if a customer could be persuaded to avail himself of her not inconsiderable charms.

She was in the back dressing room changing out of her hostess clothes. Her friend, Leta Ward, was sat at a battered table smoking a long, thin cigarette she had purloined off a Polish airman. Ward looked at Oatley,

"Are you going to call it a night, Evelyn?"

Oatley glanced over as she pulled on a pair of French knickers, "Not to sure; I could do with a client. The rent's due tomorrow."

Ward smiled, "Well, I'm off home. I've had enough for the evening." She stood up and extinguished her cigarette,

"Where's your husband? Can't you get some money off him?"

Oatley snorted, "Haven't seen him in a while. Last I heard, he was dodging his call-up papers. He's somewhere over in West London."

She posed in front of the full-length mirror, "Are my seams straight?"

Ward nodded, "Good luck then. Make sure you go to the shelter when the Jerries come back."

With that, she skipped up the wooden stairs and out into the cold evening's air.

Oatley pulled on her beige raincoat and followed her work colleague out into the street that was busy with revellers desperately trying to get home. If you couldn't make it before the transport ceased you would be stuck in one of the uncomfortable shelters or, if you were lucky, down in one of London Underground's deep stations fighting for space between others and the rats, of course.

She walked down to Shaftesbury Avenue amid the throngs of people. She smiled discreetly at any single men in the hope of catching their eye. She paused outside a café that was desperately trying to shoo out customers so that they could close up before the bombing commenced. She noticed a man in a Royal Air Force uniform. He smiled at her.

She looked down coyly; he would do. These uniformed types always had money...

The man approached her. She noticed he was quite handsome.

He spoke as he tipped his hat, "Good evening. Are you doing business?"

She looked down, "It depends on what you are looking for."

"Oh, I prefer blondes like you. I usually find they are a little more adventurous."

She leaned into him and whispered, "It's two pounds and no funny business."

He nodded.

She took his arm, "Come on, my flat is just up the road in Wardour Street."

Gordon Cummins smiled to himself; this was far too easy..."

Just before nine o'clock the next morning, two meter readers found the badly mutilated, naked body of Evelyn Oatley sprawled across her bed. She had been beaten and strangled before her throat was cut. She had been excessively slashed, especially around her genitals. The contents of her handbag were strewn around her room.

Gordon Cummins had managed to scratch his itch again....

For the next three nights, you would be hard pushed to find a working girl on the streets of Soho, much to the continued annoyance of Charlie Maitland, who was losing too much business.

Officers from Scotland Yard managed to lift some usable fingerprints from her bag, but there was no matching set on record that could identify the killer. The commander in charge of Soho summoned all his detective chief inspectors to a meeting and informed them in no uncertain terms that this blackout killer should be apprehended at all costs.

It was dawn when Peter Porteous was finally released from Marylebone Police Station. He just wanted to get home, take his medication and get some sleep. Smiths would have to do without him for the day.

He walked to the Edgware Road and caught a bus back up the Harrow Road and crossed the Steps. He opened the door to his house on East Row to be greeted by Alice Halpin in her nightdress. She quickly pulled him in, sat him down and administered his medication just as she had seen Doctor Maruska Bergman do many times in the past.

Alice packed him off to bed for the rest of the day promising to come back after her shift and cycled up to Cricklewood and make Porteous' excuses.

Chapter 17
February 1941
A plan of sorts...

Cyril Cooper was proud of his somewhat modest success. Having been brought up an orphan in the North of England, he had succeeded beyond all expectations. He was born in the late 1880s, the illegitimate son of a housemaid who had unfortunately been impregnated by the master of the house before being thrown out for gross moral turpitude. Cooper's mother died in childbirth. He wouldn't have survived except for the attentions of an experienced and unpaid lady who seemed to help birth all the foundlings in the small rural mining village.

An overly strict and middle-aged couple took him in, educated him and sent him off to a church boarding school where he seemed to spend an inordinate amount of time on his knees in the cold, damp chapel. At the age of sixteen, he was effectively sold off to a merchant in Manchester to learn all about the cotton trade. He got on well and by the age of twenty-five in 1914 at the outbreak of the First World War he was the chief bookkeeper of the firm.

He was wounded in the leg at the Battle of The Somme in 1916 and then spent the rest of the War working in a pay office in Aldershot Barracks. At the age of twenty-nine he was back in the merchant business over in London Docks.

Being an ambitious sort of fellow, he soon found himself managing all the clerks and was answerable only to the chief accountant. He joined the Conservative Party and was soon initiated into the local Masonic Lodge.

Using these connections, he set out on his own and built a thriving business importing and exporting all sorts of goods. One might have presumed that the outbreak of the Second World War in 1939 would have put paid to his business but, on the contrary, he soon discovered that there was much money to be made especially buying and selling goods in short supply. The only difference between him and Peter Porteous was that Cooper was legitimate, and the former was not.

Cyril Cooper lived in a fairly large house in Kilburn, not far from Margaret Heywood, as it happens, in Brondesbury Park. Although he never married, he always seemed to have at least one housekeeper who was pleasantly surprising in the looks department. His last housekeeper only left the warmth of his bed when the bombing became too much for her to tolerate; she went off to stay with her sister somewhere up country. He missed her for a time, especially her cooking, but there were always the little ring of ladies loosely connected to his Masonic Lodge who could satisfy his carnal needs.

And then there was the honour of being a magistrate. It was through this line of work that Cyril Cooper first came across Edith Bell. She was one of many ladies that passed through his hands whom he got to know in all senses of the word.

Edith had first approached him when her husband, the actual licensee of the White Horse on Kensal Road, decided to clear off and join his mistress somewhere south of the river. The pub was profitable, and being the only one in Kensal Town that was still open, the brewery was anxious to maintain the current management. So, one day, Edith made herself up nicely and went off to see her magistrate down at Marylebone Courts.

Having insisted upon a private meeting with him to explain her personal circumstances, it really didn't take her long to persuade him to transfer the pub licence over to her. In fact, there was no good reason not to as Edith was of previous good character despite protestations from the local constabulary who would have given anything to have the White Horse permanently closed.

If you are a good-looking female sitting on a man's lap with his hand up your skirts, it's actually quite easy to get what you want...Edith offered him more favours when it came to the licence renewal, and had been known to visit him in his house in Brondesbury Park. It was Cyril Cooper that got the bail requirements removed from Edith and Porteous that had so upset Detective Inspector Eric Everard after the unfortunate bombing of Porteous' house on Bosworth Road and all that fuss about a supposed enemy spy in Kensal Town...

Edith Bell perched on a chair in Peter Porteous' bedroom on the first floor of his house in East Row. Alice Halpin sat on the end of the bed and watched Porteous gingerly sip some of Alice's homemade soup. The ordeal at Marylebone Police Station, together with the asthma attack, had taken its toll on him. He had been cajoled into taking some time off work at Smiths, much to the annoyance of Cedric Walker, his supervisor, and also Harry Harris had told him to stay away from his ARP duties until he had fully recovered.

Deep down, Porteous was secretly grateful, as it would give him some time to take stock of his current circumstances, especially the slightly dodgy trading that he and Jimmy Ryan had made so lucrative.

Edith Bell was well made up and looking very glamorous. She had even bagged the last pair of good quality stockings from Porteous' stash, unbeknown to him; she'd deal with that little issue later.

Porteous looked at Edith, "You don't have to do this, you know. We'll find another way to get Nancy out of that house."

Edith raised her eyes, "Look, we've been through it. It's the only way I know of apart from going down to Maida Vale mob-handed with half of Kensal Town carrying scythes and pitchforks. We can't just organise a peasants' revolt any more. There's a bloody war on, in case you have forgotten?"

Alice smiled and reached out to Porteous, "Let Edith do her thing. We'll just worry about you for the present."

"Where's Jimmy," Porteous asked.

Alice responded, "He came earlier. He said the police searched his house in Tottenham, but they found nothing. Anyway, the coppers are too busy dealing with that Blackout Strangler after that body was found the other day."

Edith shook her head; "I just hope they catch him soon. How many has he done?"

"At least three that we know of. I heard one of the girls at the factory say that the police think he may have been responsible for a lot more. Apparently they are going over a stack of unsolved murders to see if they can link him."

Porteous shook his head, "Yes, I overheard a couple of policemen at the station talking about the latest victim; apparently one of Charlie Maitland's club hostesses who did a bit of freelancing on the side. The bastard cut her up badly with a tin opener..."

Alice shuddered, "All the more reason to get Nancy away from her chosen profession."

Edith stood up and did a twirl, "Will I do?"

Alice laughed, "The old boy will melt in your arms."

"He's taking me for afternoon tea at Lyon's in Marble Arch and then back to his place for the evening."

Porteous asked, "Will you be okay?"

Edith snorted, leaned over and pecked Porteous on the cheek. She wrinkled her nose and turned to Alice, "Better get him in the bath, he's none too fresh."

Alice laughed, "That's exactly where he's going as soon as he has finished his soup."

Edith Bell could be heard clumping down the wooden staircase and off into the afternoon air.

Alice turned to Porteous, "When Jimmy popped by this morning, whilst you were sleeping, he suggested it might be better if you lay off trading for the time being, especially if that inspector has got eyes on you. Besides, he says Elphicke has gone to ground and there's nothing available at the moment. He says to wait and see what happens after the dust settles on his little dispute with Charlie Maitland."

Porteous nodded, "You might be right, Alice. I haven't got the energy to do much at the moment."

"I rode past Nancy's house after the shift; it's all nice and quiet there. It doesn't look as though the police searched it."

"Yeah, I reckoned it was all talk. No magistrate is going to authorise a search warrant on the say-so of a copper alone. If they had caught me with any illicit goods, that would have been a different matter." He paused, "I don't know how long I can stall them over this address."

Alice looked at him, "There's nothing here, is there?"

"Just a couple of pairs of stockings. That's all that remains."

Alice didn't have the heart to tell him that Edith had just taken the last pair...

She said, "Come on, I'll run the bath for you."

He asked, "What time is Phyllis coming over?"

Alice looked at the clock, "About six, I think, unless they keep her in the office. I said I'd meet her by the Steps."

"Is there enough food?"

Alice slapped him on the arm as she lifted off the tray with his empty bowl, "Of course there is..."

Maison Lyons Corner house in Marble Arch was busy by the time Edith Bell managed to reach there; the buses were somewhat erratic owing to the intensity of the previous evening's bombing. It was going dark as she made her way through the busy ground floor shops that still seemed to have a reasonable selection of cakes and pastries if you had the correct money, of course.

Edith wasn't out of place in this fine establishment. She entered the tearoom on the first floor and looked around at the ladies dressed in their fur wraps; she smiled when that phrase her mother had told years ago 'fur coat and no knickers' came to mind. There did seem to be a lot of middle-aged ladies accompanied by smart looking men from all sections of armed forces, all resplendent in their crisp uniforms.

The waitress approached with a look of disdain, "Do you have a reservation, Madam?"

Just then, she caught the waving arm of her magistrate, Cyril Cooper.

She answered the snooty waitress, "No, but my friend over there does...Now, do me a favour and bring me a fresh pot of tea, there's a good girl."

The waitress coloured up, not helped by Edith patting her on the bottom as she walked past...

Cyril Cooper stood up as Edith walked up to the table. He was pleased to see his guest extremely well presented this evening. He helped her with her coat and pulled out a chair. She sat down with a smile,

"My, my, Cyril, you are looking handsome this evening."

The waitress plonked down the pot of fresh tea, "Will there be anything else, Madam."

Edith waved her away, "You know you just can't get the staff any more, William. I've got the same problem in the pub. Only the good Lord knows what state it will be in when I return."

He smiled at her, "I know what you mean. Any time I get a decent worker, they are whisked off to serve King and country, but let's not talk about such mundane matters."

Edith poured herself a cup of tea and topped up Cooper's, "Shall we have some cakes, William? I do say they look absolutely lovely. I've never seen such a selection since the war started."

He clicked his fingers and the waitress came back sulking, "Can you bring a tray of your best cakes, please?"

The female almost curtsied as she left.

Edith asked him, "Are you not afraid your posh friends will see you here with me?" She glanced around.

"Of course not, I'm single and so are you. What could possibly be the problem."

Edith Bell was not actually single, as she'd never bothered to divorce her errant husband, but no matter. She hadn't laid eyes on him for years.

He continued, "Anyway, I'm a respectable man, and you are a respectable woman enjoying each other's company..."

They enjoyed several cups of tea and an equal number of cakes before they took their leave of the place and grabbed a taxi to take them home. Edith looked up at the house in Maida Vale where Nancy was being kept as the cab drove past.

They spent the evening thrashing around on his large double bed before they decamped to the cellar when Fritz returned with his deadly cargo. Helpfully, Cyril Cooper had installed a bed in the darkened room so, except for the incessant booming of the anti-aircraft guns on Roundwood Park, the pair had a decent night's sleep.

They were back up in his bedroom when Edith finally revealed the main purpose of her visit even though she had thoroughly enjoyed his virile antics throughout the night...

Edith Bell propped herself up on an elbow and looked at Cyril Cooper. For a man in his mid-sixties, he wasn't bad-looking, and he certainly knew how to please his lady friends. He was dozing as dawn was breaking on this late February morning.

"Cyril, I'd like to talk to you."

His eyes opened, "Now you know, Edith, I'm not the marrying kind, so let's not go there."

She smiled and playfully slapped him on his arm,

"No; it's not about that. I want to ask you if you can help me with something."

He sat up, "Do you need some money?"

"No, no, of course not. The pub does very well, and I have a few other irons in the fire. It's a bit delicate."

"Well, go on, then I'm waiting..."

"I have a younger sister; she's about ten years younger than me. She lives over in Richmond. Well, she has three children; two boys and a girl."

Cooper wondered where this was going.

"It's the girl. She was always a little headstrong and was messing about with some unsavoury boys. Well, she disappeared one night and never came back. It turns out that she's working for some criminal named Charlie Maitland. Have you ever heard of him, Cyril?"

Cooper snorted, "Maitland, that Maltese gangster? I don't know why the bloody Home Office hasn't deported him and his wretched family."

He paused, "Wait a minute; does that mean she's whoring for him?"

Edith feigned a tear, "Yes, we believe so, and she's only fourteen."

"What? Fourteen, you say?"

Edith nodded, "We heard she's working in one of his brothels in Maida Vale."

Cooper got out of bed, "Bloody hell, Edith, that's bad. Look, I'll make some tea. We'll talk about it when I come back."

Edith made to get out of bed. He held up his hands,

"No, no. Don't get up; I haven't quite finished with you, yet..."

Edith smiled...

He sat up in bed, sipping the hot drink. Edith put her feet on his legs.

"Now this is what I know; I heard it down at the Lodge. Charlie Maitland controls most of the prostitutes in the West End as well as half of the legal and illegal drinking establishments. That house on Maida Vale has been operating as a brothel since early Victorian times. It just changes hands periodically, and now it's Maitland's time to own it. There were a lot of rumours a few years ago that it specialised in child prostitution but only for the rich and famous. There was a little fuss about it, but it all died down and now, because of the War, the authorities aren't particularly interested in it."

He sipped his tea; Edith reached over and put her head on his chest.

She asked, "Don't you think it's wrong that a place like that can operate in the middle of the twentieth century?"

He nodded, "Of course it's wrong. I'm forever more getting the girls up before me on the bench for soliciting. It's no use fining them as they just pay it and then get back out on the streets, but there's not much we can do, but there is another problem."

"What's that, Cyril?"

"The buggers in Clubs and Vice. They eat from Charlie Maitland's table, and I don't just mean scraps."

Edith pretended to be shocked, "Oh, you mean Maitland's paying them off?"

"He's been doing it for years. I had one of his girls up before me. It was the fifth time she had been picked up for soliciting, so she should have been sent to Holloway for a minimum of three months. Well, would you believe a sergeant from Clubs and Vice pleaded for her to get bail before sentencing? He claimed she was doing some work for him. Three of my softer colleagues released her on her own surety, and guess what? We never saw her again."

"Something should be done about it," said Edith.

"After that particular case, we made representations to the Lord Chief Justice through our presiding judge, but it was a waste of time. I heard that the house on Maida Vale gets a visit from Paddington Police Station from time to time, but when they get there, the place is usually empty. It's as though they have been warned."

Edith raised her eyes, "What can we do?"

"I'll tell you what. There's a Metropolitan Police senior officer in the Lodge. I'll mention it to him this evening and see if we can't get your niece out. She should be home with her parents."

Edith snuggled up to him, "Oh, I'm sure my sister would be ever so grateful..."

He replaced his cup on the saucer on the little table at the side of the bed and turned to her,

"I'd much prefer it if you showed how grateful you were..."

Cyril Cooper sought out Superintendent Reginald Price after the Masonic meeting in the lodge that same evening. Price was an affable man who would much prefer to be tending his roses in the back of his garden in Acton than still pushing paper around his desk at Scotland Yard. He should have retired about three years ago but the threat of a conflict with Germany kept him in his office and now with London in the middle of a bombing Blitz from the Nazis, it would have been churlish for him to have even made an application for retirement.

His wife preferred him to be at work; she'd much rather he was out from under her feet during the day. So, Superintendent Reginald Price spent his time co-ordinating the work of the various departments within the Metropolitan Police, ensuring that in these times of great danger, what limited resources were available were used effectively. He was a stickler for procedure; he liked things completed properly and as he always did things by the book, it was his way that things were done.

Cooper and Price sat at a little table near the open hearth that had a blazing log fire warming the bones of the assembled men. They were sipping a sweet sherry from the well-stocked cellars that had been converted into a makeshift bomb shelter for members who couldn't get home after the early warning siren sounded.

Cooper relayed the story of Edith's missing niece without actually mentioning any names. Price looked interested and then mildly shocked at the suggestion that young girls were working in the establishment. He had two granddaughters of his own about the same age. He asked,

"I've seen the figures of the numbers of women arrested for prostitution. There's been a massive increase. War makes for strange bedfellows." He laughed at his own joke.

Cooper nodded as he sipped his sherry, "There are so many armed forces' personnel on the streets looking to relieve their male tensions, and there'll soon be another influx of overseas soldiers as well. What's Clubs and Vice doing about it, Reginald?"

"On the face of it, very little, so it appears. They run a very strange operation out of West End Central on Saville Row. We had their detective chief inspector up before us recently about this so-called Stocking Strangler who appears to be targeting working girls. This DCI, what's his name? Oh, yes, John Lodge; he claims that by being less harsh on Maitland and his crew, they are managing to contain the problem to a few streets in Soho."

"But that's not true, Reginald, they come up before the bench from all parts of this side of London."

Price finished off his drink, "I know that, you know that, and so does the Commissioner. The problem is this bloody war. There just aren't the resources to chase down these gangsters." He paused,

"I tell you what, Cyril, we'll pop over to the chief superintendent at Paddington Green." He looked at the clock over the mantelpiece, "Let's see what he knows about this nasty little brothel on Maida Vale seeing as it's on his patch."

Chief Superintendent David Stanley was a brusque, no nonsense copper from the valleys of Wales in his late fifties. He was strictly chapel and his religion gave him his code of life, well, that and his affiliation to the Masonic Lodge. He neither drank alcohol nor smoked. A swear word never passed his lips, and he only slept in his wife's bed once per month so as not to be tainted by sins of the flesh.

The three men greeted each other with the usual Masonic handshake. Stanley belonged to a different Lodge than the others. A rather plain looking secretary made them a pot of tea.

Stanley looked disapprovingly at Reginald Price when he took out his pipe; his office was strictly non-smoking...

He looked at Cyril Cooper. It wasn't all that unusual to have a magistrate sitting opposite him, as they were always complaining about levels of crime. But never mind, if one does a favour for a member of the bench then it's not unreasonable to expect one in return, like a very short notice search warrant supplied on some rather thin evidence. So, he listened carefully as Cooper went through the story of his 'acquaintance's' niece.

Stanley stood up and wandered over to the window. He peered around the heavy blackout curtain at the gloom that was once the vibrant and exciting City of London.

He turned, "I know all about that brothel in Maida Vale. We've raided it a few times, but we never seem to find anything out of the ordinary. We've had rumours but never any proof."

Reginald Price looked at him, "That's because Maitland and his boys are always tipped off."

Stanley stared at him and then smiled, "I've been saying that for years. You know that in early Victorian times there were several child brothels on Maida Vale and no one could do anything about them because the madams were protected by the aristocracy who were, by and large, their main clientele."

Cyril Cooper spoke up, "We've now got a report of an underage girl in the place. If you need a warrant, I'll sign one off."

Stanley sighed, "Unfortunately, it's not that simple. As you are probably aware, the Maitlands have influence in Scotland Yard. To do anything about them, you have to go through Clubs and Vice, and that's a complete rat's nest. Every now and then, I get an instruction to enter the premises on Maida Vale, but that's so the Commissioner can keep the politicians quiet. It looks good on his statistics. If I bring this to the attention of the Vice Squad, nothing will get done."

Barrett smiled, "You've got complete control over crime and policing in this area, why should you need to inform them?"

"It's all right for you, Alfred, you are already past retirement age. I've still got a few years to do."

Cyril Cooper couldn't really understand what was going on, "Look, you have possible evidence of criminality on your patch, what's to stop you? Think about the plaudits your station would earn in the press if you managed to shut down a child brothel."

Chief Superintendent David Stanley held up his hands for silence. It was as though he was asking God for guidance. He momentarily closed his eyes.

Cooper looked at Price...

Stanley breathed out and sat back down, "Okay, we'll do it." He looked at Price, "Have you got a decent and honest DCI at the yard, Alfred?"

"I do, Sir, I certainly do. I'll get him up here for a meeting first thing tomorrow, if that's okay with you?"

Stanley banged a push bell on his desk; the mousey secretary came in looking quite scared, he said,

"Cancel My appointments up to Sunday, Miss Morgan; I think we are going to be a little busy..."

He looked at the other two men in the office, "How does Saturday night suit the pair of you? Might as well catch them at their busiest. One never knows who or what one might find in that esteemed establishment..."

Chapter 18

Thursday, 20th February 1941
Meetings

Bright and early the following morning, Superintendent Reginald Price walked down two flights of stairs from his office at Scotland Yard and marched into Detective Chief Inspector Alfred Barrett's office. Barrett made to get up,

Price waved his hands, "Stay seated, Alfred, I've got a little job for you."

Price didn't really need another job: his in-tray was more than full, but what can you do?

Price sat down, "I hear there might be a war about to start between two of London's finest gangsters?"

Barrett smiled, "My, doesn't news travel fast around here?" He picked up a Manila folder that contained the rather brief report that had arrived at his desk sometime in the evening from a certain Detective Chief Inspector over in Clubs and Vice.

"Yes, the DCI over at Vice had a word with Maitland. He says it will get sorted out before the trouble kicks off."

Price asked, "Who is the DCI?"

"Lodge, John Lodge."

Price snorted, "He's as bent as a nine bob note."

"Yes, undoubtedly, but he does manage to keep a lid on Maitland's activities."

Price stood up, "Have you got a good and honest detective inspector?"

Barrett looked at him, "Erm, yes, I think so, Sir. What's this all about?"

"Go and tell him and his sergeant to meet us at Paddington Police Station just before midday. Grab your coat and tell your lass out there you won't be back for a few days."

Barrett stared at him quizzically, "Sir?"

Price was at the door, "We are going to take the lid off Maitland's activities without Clubs and Vice interfering..."

Chief Superintendent David Stanley's little office overlooking the Harrow Road was crowded. Opposite him sat Superintendent Reginald Price, Detective Chief Inspector Alfred Barrett, Detective Inspector Eric Everard and Magistrate Cyril Cooper.

Everard was confused; his job was to stamp out black marketeering, not dealing with grubby brothels. His sergeant, Derek Beaston, was thoroughly enjoying himself outside chatting up the mousey secretary Miss Morgan who, despite her protestations, was more than happy to enjoy the attention.

The assembled guests were drinking tea and indulging in some biscuits the indomitable secretary had manage to rustle up.

Stanley had a map pinned up on the board behind his desk; he pointed to it,

"Right, we need two teams of six officers," He looked at Price, "Can you get some beefy lads from the Yard, Reginald?"

Price nodded, "I've borrowed some beat officers from traffic; they'll do, provided there's not much action. Most of them are retired coppers dragged back in."

Stanley smiled, "We'll make it gentle for them. My lads will do the heavy lifting." He turned back to the map that Miss Morgan had brought up from the archives. "There's a mews at the rear so put three of your lads at the back as I don't want anyone sneaking out. The rest can look threatening when we go in."

There was some mirth at that.

Everard spoke up for the first time, "Sir, I'm not sure what we are doing."

Barrett looked at him, "It's all right, Eric, we are just doing the public a little service."

Everard stood up, "Sir, I know what this place is. It belongs to Charlie Maitland. Shouldn't we be liaising with Clubs and Vice?"

Price stood up, "Not this time, Eric, we have it on good authority that there are under-age girls working in there."

"So, shouldn't Clubs and Vice be doing this?"

Stanley sat back down and steepled his hands, "Ordinarily, Eric, yes, but if we get Vice involved and they raid the place, they'll find exactly nothing, and you know it."

Cyril Cooper spoke to Everard, "Look, Inspector, we have a reliable report that there is a fourteen-year-old girl employed in prostitution on the premises. If we can get her, we may be able to shut down Maitland and his family once and for all."

Everard looked at his boss, Reginald Price, "Does the Commander know about this, Sir?"

Price stared at him, "No. Nobody will tell him until the deed is done. Is that clear?"

Everard coloured up, he looked at Cooper. Was this the interfering magistrate that got Porteous and that Bell woman released from bail conditions?

"Right, I suggest we bring three vans; I'll sort that out at this end. Just get your coppers up here on Saturday night at about six in the evening. I think we'll do the place before the early warning siren goes off, and then leave some men behind to pick up the late-night callers after the all-clear. They won't have committed any offences but it could cause them some embarrassment."

There were nods of approval. Stanley looked at Everard, "You and your sergeant will do the door knock. Once the door is opened the rest will pile in, truncheons at the ready. I want all the occupants secured in those two front rooms downstairs." He pointed to the house plan.

"I've got two female officers redeployed from Juvenile to assist with the working girls. Once they have been frisked, identified and the place searched, everyone will be brought back here for questioning. It's important that we locate and secure any underage females. I'll make sure the station is sufficiently staffed to deal with the expected influx."

He turned to Cyril Cooper, "Have you got the warrant?"

Cooper laid out the document, "Yes, and I even got it countersigned by two of my colleagues. It's rock solid."

Stanley glanced around the room, "Are there any questions?" He paused and then continued, "Good, then we'll reassemble in the briefing room at six sharp on Saturday. It goes without saying that not a word of this should be spoken outside this room. Charlie Maitland's reach goes deep into the force. It's time he was stopped..."

Cyril Cooper couldn't wait to tell Edith Bell all about the plan....

The house on Maida Vale was very busy that evening. Nancy had to deal with a stream of callers, all wishing to avail themselves of both Hope and Faith. Both girls seemed to relish the attention and, of course, the money that was accumulating nicely in their respective little boxes. At one point in the evening, there was actually a queue for the youngsters. Nancy had to ensure both were bathed after each gentleman. The girls downstairs had taken to doubling up to make sure the men were seen off extra quickly.

It all came to a sudden halt when the first sirens sounded much earlier than normal. The callers left the place very quickly, hailing cabs on the road to take them back to their loving wives before the bombing started.

Nancy grabbed her two charges and ushered them down the stairs towards William, whose job it was to see them down to the cellar. Nancy had wrapped a blanket around Hope, who was shivering with the cold. The booming of the anti-aircraft guns began to sound in Hyde Park; it was almost as if the Georgian house was shaking. After one particularly loud explosion, the electric lights flickered and then went out. There were a few panicked shouts before William struck a match and lit a candle. Nancy watched as he quickly went around the cellar, lighting strategically placed nightlights. The crowded place began to settle again.

Hope was snuggled up to Nancy clutching her rag doll. Nancy had not had sufficient time to get her dressed. She looked over at Faith who was engaged in a conversation with one of the day girls. She was smoking one of those funny-smelling cigarettes that Nancy hated. Indeed, since her enforced imprisonment in the house she hadn't smoked one cigarette even though there were always plenty lying around in little silver boxes.

Nancy adjusted the blanket on her charge. Just then, the rear door opened. She felt the blast of cold air around her legs; she was still dressed in the short maid's uniform. She looked over to see one of the doormen come in bundled up in a great coat,

"Jesus, ladies, it's cold out there and the Jerries are making a mess of Paddington Station."

There were grunts of acknowledgement.

She watched as he turned the big, old iron key in the ancient lock and tossed it into a vase that stood on a shelf adjacent to the door. He went and sat down with the girls, extracting a hip flask from a deep pocket in his coat.

Nancy felt Hope's head gradually loll forward as she drifted off to sleep. Nancy could never understand how these two young girls could sleep so easy with what they had to put up with.

She felt her eyes get heavy, but a loud explosion that seemed to shake the house soon awakened her. She looked around; the crowded cellar had gone silent. She noticed Monique Fontaine, Madame LeStrange and Doctor Loretta huddled in a corner. Nancy dozed off again.

She awoke to the sound of silence...

The bombing had ceased. Hope was still stretched out on her lap. Many of the girls had gone back upstairs and were preparing to make a run for home during a lull in the bombing. William had gone with them.

She looked around and gently got up, easing her charge from off her lap. She smoothed down her skirt and walked gingerly up to the back door. She turned the knob; it was locked. She was about to reach into the vase to get at the key when she heard a voice behind her,

"Claudine! Get back to Miss Hope!" It was the voice of Madame LeStrange.

Nancy scuttled back to Hope, who hadn't stirred. She gently picked her up and laid her back on her lap. Nancy's heart beat quickly in her chest. She felt a body snuggle up to her other side. She turned to see a glassy-eyed Miss Faith reach under the blanket and almost climb in.

Nancy put her arm around her. This slightly older girl was just as vulnerable as Hope.

It was nearly two in the morning before the all-clear sounded. Nancy left the two girls cuddling up to each other in Hope's bed. She calmly disrobed, had a perfunctory wash and went to bed. Her room mate was nowhere to be seen.

The German bombers had returned for a second bite at the cherry; that was why they had started so early that evening, well, that and the cloudless sky. The waning crescent moon had given the bombers sufficient light to wreak havoc on London's citizens.

Dennis Elphicke and three heavily built minders walked slowly up Parliament Hill. They could not help but see the burning buildings that lay out before them in the distance, as they looked over London. There was an acrid smell in the air. Although the all-clear had sounded some time ago, one or two searchlights still danced across the sky. The small party looked over to the East of London. Dennis Elphicke wondered if his new warehouse was still intact.

He sat on one of the rusty benches on the top of the hill and looked down. One of his minders started up,

"They're coming, Boss."

Elphicke stubbed out his cigarette and felt for the Webley revolver that was tucked in the breast pocket of his overcoat, with the handle pointing upwards so that he could reach it quickly. He looked over at another group of men who were walking up the pathway from the other side of the Hill from Hampstead. A hand-torch lit their way. Elphicke had approached from Highgate.

He shoved his hands deep into the pockets of his coat and hunkered down. He'd had these sorts of meetings before. The Maltese thug neither worried him nor fazed him. As Maitland's party approached, his men stood off to the side, nervously smoking.

Elphicke felt the bench move as Charlie Maitland sat down,

"Evening, Dennis."

Elphicke half-turned his head towards Maitland, "Charlie," he nodded.

Maitland began, "This is a bit of a shambles, isn't it, Dennis."

Elphicke shrugged his shoulders, "Only because you started it."

Maitland held up his hands, "Okay, okay, let's not get into recriminations, but I have to say making a mess of my lad wasn't exactly right, was it?"

Elphicke raised his eyebrows, "Well you did threaten two of my men, didn't you?"

"Look, Dennis, there's been a little misunderstanding. I don't know what Porteous and Ryan told you but that's not exactly how it went down."

"Well, tell me exactly what happened, then. As far as I know, you told those two that by the end of the month they'd be paying you rent!"

Maitland's minders shifted uncomfortably on their feet.

The Maltese went on, "Look, they came to me offering their services."

Elphicke snorted, knowing full well that was a lie. Ryan and Porteous would never voluntarily get involved with Maitland.

Elphicke finally turned towards Maitland, "Right, let's stop pissing about, shall we? You tell me what you want; I'll tell you what I want, and then we'll all get home to see our nearest and dearest. How about that?"

Maitland shrugged his shoulders, "I just want a little of your action for the West End, that's all."

"I don't supply the West End, as you well know, Charlie; too many bent coppers and your pimps."

Maitland looked surprised, "So you won't mind if I expand my little business, then."

"Suit yourself; nothing to do with me, but I won't be supplying you. I have enough customers already."

Maitland thought about that. He certainly had enough contacts to sort him out with alcohol, but not for other merchandise that was in short supply.

"What about if you let Ryan and Porteous supply me?"

Elphicke smiled, "They won't work for you, Charlie, and you know it. By the time you've taxed them, it wouldn't be worth their while." He leaned into Maitland, "You see that's your problem, you're too greedy. Ryan and Porteous are small fry. They supply that shithole called Kensal Town. That's the limit of their ambitions. If you want to start dealing, check on the Cohen brothers south of the river. They'd sell their grannies if they made them a profit."

Maitland shook his head, "I'd prefer not to be dealing with those Jews. They are rather violent, and I don't particularly like going to South London. I find the locals are a bit backward in their manners."

Elphicke stubbed out a cigarette and lit another one, "Well, it looks to me that you are in a bit of an impasse at the moment."

Maitland stared ahead, "What about if Porteous and Ryan sell me bits of stuff from time to time?"

"You'll have to ask them. Where they sell their stuff is their business, but you won't be getting any discounts so don't ask."

He stood up, "Now, let's not be having any more information supplied to the police shall we?"

Maitland stood up as well, "Not too sure what you are talking about, Dennis."

"If I were you, I'd concentrate upon getting that bastard who is attacking your girls; what do they call him, the Stocking Strangler?"

Maitland snorted, "Blackout Strangler, Blackout Ripper; who cares? We'll get him before the police. We think he's in the RAF, so the word on the street is that none of the girls are to go with any men in the blue uniform."

Elphicke thought about that.

"There's one other thing, Dennis."

"And what would that be, Charlie?"

"Someone has to pay for my man being beaten up."

Elphicke shrugged his shoulders, "So, give Porteous and Ryan a clout if that makes you feel any better. Just keep away from my business. Have a good evening."

He tossed away his cigarette, joined his minders and wandered down the hill towards his waiting car in Highgate...

Chapter 19
Saturday, 22nd February 1941
The Door Knock

Saturday evening came around quickly enough. Chief Superintendent David Stanley of Paddington Police Station was busy, much to the annoyance of the rest of the officers who couldn't help wondering what on earth was going on. One detective chief inspector was temporarily despatched up to Wembley; he had no idea why but Stanley just didn't trust him. The other gathered two detective inspectors around him and they locked themselves into a briefing room whispering furtively. When junior officers casually enquired as to what was going on they were told it was something to do with the war effort.

Beat Bobbies suddenly found themselves deployed to desk duties within the station until Sunday but told to be ready for a briefing late on Saturday afternoon. Three black Morris vans were removed from regular service, cleaned, fuelled and parked up in the garage.

A couple of plain clothed policemen donned street sweeping outfits and constantly swept and brushed the front and back of the house in Maida Vale depositing litter into a wheeled dustbin cart. Indeed, the road had never been kept so clean, although they did get some funny looks from the regular council workers...

Every hour or so, one of them reported back to the station on the comings and goings of the house. Several high profile names were gleaned off the registrations of the cars that deposited them there. Stanley kept a note of these 'model citizens' for use at a later date.

The same could be said of Chief Superintendent Reginald Price over at Scotland Yard. He commandeered a large briefing room in the basement and selected a number of officers with the help of both DCI Alfred Barrett and DI Eric Everard. Three women police officers were sent up to Paddington Green to assist with the probable arrest of either juveniles, women or, more likely, both.

In both briefing rooms, a hand drawn layout of the 'anonymous' house was pinned to a chalkboard. The plans had been requested from the local valuation office on some spurious pretext to do with the rateable value. By the end of Friday, all the officers knew the exact layout of the house; which room was where, but crucially, not the actual address of the house. When an officer enquired, he was informed it was somewhere in Kensington and that they would be told on the day.

The officers also knew exactly what their roles were; who was doing what and where they should be at any given time. This led to three of the more elderly officers complaining that they would be missing out on the action minding the rear of the premises; little did they know...

Over in Kensal Town or to be more precise, in East Row, a similar state of things was occurring between Peter Porteous, Edith Bell, Alice Halpin and Phyllis Manley who had managed to get herself excused from secretarial duties at the Admiralty for the weekend despite the protestations from Alice...

The Edgware Road was busy with Saturday evening revellers trying to get home before the nightly bombing commenced. It was cold and wet, with the easterly wind bringing in more than just cold weather. With low cloud cover, the Luftwaffe pilots had a much better chance of being undetected. The three black unmarked vans cruised slowly along the road; it was only a short distance from the police station.

The lead van turned left into Sutherland Avenue and then immediate left into Lanark Road, where it came to a halt. The vans were parked no more than two hundred yards from the target house.

Price and Stanley were in a Metropolitan Police issue Morris Saloon, in black, of course. Everard and Beaston closely followed them in the Vauxhall 12. Everard got out of the car and casually sauntered up to the first van to check that all was well. One of the street sweepers reported to him that the house was busy. Everard sent him back to continue making a note of all the vehicles that came and went.

Just before seven, Beaston and Everard, accompanied by two of the fitter, uniformed policemen, began to approach the house. The three vans slowly followed them and pulled up in front of the horseshoe drive, blocking both the entrance and the exit.

Exactly at seven, Everard nodded at Derek Beaston whose heart was beating a little quicker than normal...

Beaston pounded on the big, highly polished front door. He tugged at the bell pull. On top of the main staircase, Madame Fontaine looked at one of the doormen,

"Go and see who that is; I'm not expecting any more callers until after the all-clear."

She pushed open one of the bedroom doors; two of her ladies were entertaining a gentleman.

The pounding on the door got louder. She addressed the other doorman,

"Hurry up before they break the bloody door."

The girls sat in the lounge in varying states of undress looked at each other. One of them sauntered up to the large bay window that overlooked the main road. She pulled back the blackout curtain slightly and then gasped,

"Jesus, Madame Fontaine, it's the police."

It took a moment for the house madam to understand what was going on. At first, her brain told her that it was not possible. Didn't Charlie Maitland keep the police sweet? And as for the locals, there hadn't been a tip off, had there? Someone would pay for this…

Beaston leaned heavily on the door. As soon as the locks turned, it crashed open. The doorman was on the pristine tiles, wondering what on earth was going on; this wasn't supposed to happen. Everard stood by as several policemen charged in, blowing whistles. Others were shouting at the top of their heads. Chief Superintendents Price and Stanley casually sauntered into the main hall.

Price looked at the prone man, "Call your boss, there's a good little fellow. I've got some good news for her."

The doorman looked up from the floor. Price clapped his hands, "Come on, we haven't got all day."

Two of the women police officers rushed in just as one of the girls was being manhandled down the grand staircase, shouting and cursing at the Bobby. She was quickly swept up and literally thrown into the front reception room.

A partially dressed man came down the stairs, "What is the meaning of this?"

Everard sighed, reached over, spun him around and had the man's arm so far up his back that he was almost bent double. He got tossed into the other reception room, where a policeman growled at him…

Madame Monique Fontaine appeared at the top of the staircase, she shouted out,

"I'm in charge here. What's going on? I hope you have a warrant."

Stanley smiled, "Oh good…" He turned to Everard, "Do the honours, Eric."

Everard bounded up the steps and grabbed hold of the madam,

"As you're in charge, you are under arrest for keeping a disorderly house and living off immoral earnings."

She snorted, "Don't be silly. Let me call Chief Inspector Lodge at West End Central; he'll soon sort out this mess."

Stanley snorted, "You'll be lucky." He turned to one of the policewomen,

"Cuff this woman and kindly escort her into the reception room with her other ladies."

The brothel madam's feet didn't touch the ground...

Up on the top floor, Nancy Keeling was trying to get rid of Hope's third caller of the evening. The man had had too much to drink and was disinclined to get off the bed never mind dress himself. She grabbed Hope and pulled her into the bathroom, where a bath full of hot water was awaiting the young girl.

Hope was about to protest, but Nancy firmly pulled off the child's nightdress and lifted the waif into the bath. The warm water soothed the girl. Nancy ran next door to chase Faith, but the caller had already departed. Faith was lying naked across the bed. Her eyes were glazed over; she was well and truly out of it; there was white powder on her top lip and nose. Nancy reached over to her and took her arm. The girl shook her off,

"Leave me alone, Claudine, just send in my next client."

Nancy shook her head; there wasn't one, so the girl would just have to sober up and get in the bath, wouldn't she? She heard Hope calling out.

Nancy ran into the bathroom. Hope was standing in the bath waiting for a large, soft towel to be placed around her shoulders. Nancy reached over and draped a clean, white towel around her and lifted her out of the bath, and then she heard the commotion rising up from below.

She had no idea what was going on. She stood Hope on a mat in front of a mirror and tossed another nightdress at her, "Here, put this on quickly..."

It wasn't a request, more like an instruction. The girl didn't object.

Nancy quickly went to the stairs and skipped down. The doorman, William, was nowhere to be seen. She could hear lots of male voices and the shrieks of the ladies on the first floor.

Suddenly, William appeared at the bottom of the stairs,

"Miss! Miss! It's a police raid. You are to stay in your rooms; someone will come for all three of you!"

Nancy had no intention of doing anything she was told...

William shouted again, "Quickly, Miss, otherwise Madame Fontaine will be unhappy."

Nancy smiled at William, "Look after yourself, William, this place is finished..."

She ran back into Hope's bedroom. The inebriated caller was still lying on the bed. She picked up his clothes that were carelessly discarded on a chair and threw them out of the door onto the parquet floor. She took the fellow by his arm and tossed him out after them. He didn't seem to know where he was. All he had on was a loose shirt and nothing else.

The noise from downstairs was getting louder. Nancy quickly went into the bathroom and took hold of Hope, who had managed to put on the nightdress.

"What's happening, Claudine?"

Nancy grabbed her by the arm, "Come on, quickly. Let's get out of here."

The girl pulled back, "Wait! Wait! Let me get something."

Hope shook off Nancy's hand and reached underneath her bed. She opened the box and grabbed her purse, which contained all her savings. She gave the purse to Nancy, who lifted her skirt and shoved it down the top of her knickers into her suspender belt. Hope pushed her feet into a pair of slippers and picked up her rag doll,

"Come on, Claudine, time to go." She paused, "What about Faith? She needs to go as well."

Nancy shook her head, "We'll come back for her; let's get you down the stairs and out of the house."

Nancy led Hope to the back steps, only to be confronted by William; he glared at her,

"I told you to stay in your rooms."

Nancy swore at him, "You can stay if you want to but we are leaving and don't try to stop us."

William began to walk up the narrow stairs slowly towards them. Nancy charged down the stairwell and straight into him. He fell backwards. She still had hold of Hope.

It was then that slow motion kicked in, just like when Nancy had seen those comedy shorts at the cinema. William began to tumble backwards towards the first landing, where the stairs turned ninety degrees. She heard the sickening click, as his head twisted violently to one side and snapped his neck.

Nancy momentarily froze.

She felt Hope pulling on her arm, "Come on, Claudine; he'll wake up in a minute."

Nancy and Hope stepped over the lifeless body of young William, whose only crime was being in the wrong place at the wrong time.

They reached the second floor landing; all was quiet on the back stairs. Nancy gingerly opened the door to the main hallway. She could see several policemen barging in and out of the bedrooms; half carrying and dragging partially dressed women and their clients. She felt the door press against her. One of the ladies of the house dressed only in a flimsy, silk dressing gown pushed past her. Nancy recognised her from her time in the cellar, sheltering from the German bombers.

The woman didn't speak as she shoved her out of the way.

Nancy and Hope followed down to the next floor. The stairwell was still quiet. They reached the ground floor. Nancy peered into the hallway. She could see several officers standing around looking pleased with themselves as men and women were led unceremoniously into the two front reception rooms, Ladies to the right and gentlemen to the left. There was a lot of noise.

Nancy pushed open the door to the cellar. She closed the door behind her and turned the key in the lock. The door wasn't exactly sturdy, but it would present the police with a challenge to open it, if only for a short time. She ran down the rickety wooden steps. She paused to see the woman in the silk dressing gown struggling to open the back door; it was locked.

The place was dark; Nancy hit the light switch and turned it on. The place was suddenly filled with a yellow light. The woman turned around angrily,

"Turn it off, you silly bitch. Do you want them to know we're in here?"

Nancy walked calmly up to her. She could see the woman perspiring heavily from her exertions. Nancy could smell unwashed sex from her.

"Step aside."

"Why the fuck should I?"

"Because the door is locked."

Hope spoke out, "Elaine, step aside. Let Claudine open the door."

Hope knew the woman from her time spent on the second floor.

The woman seemed to relax. She stared at Nancy and then stepped to one side. Nancy reached over to the jar and extracted the key. She pushed into the keyhole and turned the lock. It clicked. Elaine shoved Nancy out of the way, pulled open the door and charged out.

Behind her, Nancy could hear the police banging on the door to the cellar. She knew the door wouldn't hold out for too long.

She pulled Hope through the door and out into the cold February night. She extracted the key from inside the lock and firmly closed the heavy wooden door. She locked the door from the outside and discarded the key into some unkempt bushes. The stair door to the cellar splintered as two large policemen put their shoulders to it.

Nancy could hear shouting. She stopped still and put a finger to her lips, indicating to Hope to be silent. She walked to the double gates and stopped in front of what were once stables that were used by the horses and carriages that belonged to the grand house. One of the gates was partially open. She peered out into the gloom.

About twenty-five yards away, three elderly policemen were struggling to detain the woman Elaine who was thrashing around violently tearing at them with her nails. Her language would have made a sailor blush. Nancy smiled as she pulled Hope through the gate.

"Come on, Hope, it's time for us to leave."

Back in the main hallway, Cyril Cooper stood leaning against the main door with his arms folded. He was disgusted to see so many half naked females cursing and thrashing around as they were detained. He peered into the reception room; there must have been at least a dozen, not counting three mature women, who stood looking stony faced at the two rather large policewomen.

Across the hallway, several men, also in varying states of dress, were sitting silently on the plush armchairs and sofas. Their positions of privilege would soon sort out this mess, or so they thought...

Sergeant Derek Beaston appeared at the top of the stairs, "Sir! I've got what looks like an under-age girl on the top floor. There's another one who is missing!"

Madame Monique Fontaine put her head in her hands. LeStange looked at her, "I told you those girls were a bad idea."

"Oh, do shut up! You didn't seem to complain when you got your share of the money."

Doctor Loretta's heart beat wildly in her chest; how was she going to get out of this one?

One of the policewomen went up the stairs as fast as her not inconsiderable weight would let her. Stanley shouted for officers to find the missing girl.

Beaston led the policewoman to Faith's bedroom. Faith was in exactly the same position as when Nancy had left her, only this time she was convulsing and there were flecks of foam around her mouth. The girl was having a fit.

The policewoman ran up to her and turned her on to her side. She stuck her fingers down Faith's throat to check that her airway was clear. She held the naked girl tight and looked at Beaston,

"Sarge, can you get that doctor up here? There's an injured man on the back stairs and a young girl who appears to be having a fit."

"Doctor? Is there a doctor on the premises?"

The policewoman nodded, "Yes, that's what the Irish woman told me. Says her name is Loretta."

Beaston disappeared.

Two minutes later, Doctor Loretta shoved the fat policewoman aside and began ministering to Faith; she glanced over at Beaston,

"Drugs and alcohol...Can you carry her down to my surgery?"

"What about the young man on the stairs?"

"He's beyond helping..."

Beaston looked at the policewoman and thought; what kind of brothel has a bloody doctor's surgery?

By the time Beaston had carried Faith down to her room, Faith had stopped fitting. The doctor wrapped her in several blankets after placing her in the recovery position. She pulled up a chair and sat down beside her...

Chief Superintendent David Stanley arrived at the door with Cyril Cooper. The policeman asked, "Do you think this is the girl your friend was asking about?"

Cooper shook his head, "I don't know. All I know is that she's fourteen."

Doctor Loretta looked up, "No, this one is a little older. There's a younger one who is fourteen. She has the room next to this one."

Beaston ran back upstairs; he hadn't searched the room thoroughly. After a few minutes, he found a partially naked man shivering behind a rack of dresses in the old wardrobe. Beaston turfed him out and stuck him on the floor. The man was still clutching the clothes that Nancy had thrown out on to the hall parquet.

Beaston asked, "Where's the girl?"

The client shook his head, "Sorry, I don't know." The accent was refined.

Beaston leaned over him, "I'm going to ask you one more time; where is the youngster who occupied this room?"

The man swallowed hard, "I told you, I don't know. She left with the maid; that's all I know."

Beaston pulled him up roughly and tossed him down the stairs and into the surgery,

"This fellow says the young girl left with the maid."

Stanley glared at the sergeant, "What do you mean left with the maid?"

Doctor Loretta smiled broadly...

Nancy pulled Hope across Hall Road and on to Hamilton Terrace. She began to shiver in the cold air. The maid's uniform was more for decoration than practicality. The blackout was more or less complete. She slowed and picked her way carefully, with the young girl hanging on to her hand for dear life. She could hear police whistles blasting out behind her. She just wanted to get as far away from the house as possible. Lights were beginning to come on in the houses behind the blackout blinds as the occupiers began to wonder what on earth was going on down the road.

Nancy stopped and pulled Hope close to her.

Hope asked, "Where are we going, Claudine?"

"Somewhere safe, I promise."

"Will I have to see callers?"

Nancy breathed out, "Not if I can help it..."

They walked on towards Kilburn. Just then, a dark-coloured old Post Office van pulled up in front of them. Nancy turned to run as the rear doors opened. She heard a familiar Liverpool accent,

"For heaven's sake, Nancy, hurry up and get in..."

Chapter 20
Saturday, 22nd February 1941
Paddington Police Station

The custody sergeant looked up from his evening newspaper. The door to the suite had just burst open and there appeared to be a lot of cursing and shouting. He thought he could hear female voices. The suite had been deathly quiet as local villains had been temporarily taken to Willesden Police Station. No one had bothered to tell him why, but he couldn't care less. It gave him a quiet night...

He looked up to see two of his elderly coppers dragging in a hissing and screaming, partially naked female. No sooner than this one was in, another arrived between two other of his Bobbies. And then another; and then another...His newspaper quickly got discarded.

He asked casually, "What's going on?"

The officer was huffing and puffing from his exertions, "Sarge; we've just raided Maitland's brothel on Maida Vale."

The desk sergeant's face went beetroot red with apoplexy, "Who told you to do that, you daft buggers?"

Chief Superintendent David Stanley appeared from behind the mêlée, grasping a well-dressed man by his jacket collar,

"I did, Sergeant, now get off your fat backside, get a load of coppers out of the canteen and process this lot. I want everyone here identified and charged."

The sergeant swallowed loudly, "Charged with what, Sir?"

"The naked ladies with soliciting for the purpose of prostitution, the men with disorderly conduct."

He pointed at the still-cuffed Monique Fontaine, "This one with keeping a brothel and the supply of illegal substances. Oh, and throw in the selling of alcohol without an appropriate licence." He looked at LeStrange, "Do this delightful specimen for aiding and abetting."

Fontaine laughed at him, "You'll be lucky..."

LeStrange looked down nervously.

Stanley shouted out, "I want all the females strip-searched, identified and then locked up until they get shipped off to court on Monday; make sure they all go to Marylebone Magistrates' Court..."

He looked over at the male callers, "Get them bailed to appear later with their solicitors, but make sure you have a clear identification and that someone has been to their address to confirm they actually live there. Probably better to tell their wives why they'll be late home for supper."

He heard voices of protest but he raised his hands to silence them, "Any one of you is welcome to call your solicitors now but we are not doing any formal interviews until Monday. If you want your solicitor present then you'll stay here until then. It's your choice..."

The girls started protesting again; Stanley shook his head...he went up to the sergeant, "Now what was that about informing Clubs and Vice?"

It was three hours before all the prisoners had been booked in and charged. The men were all sat looking rather gloomily at one other in a cold room, muttering to themselves. Not one of them had requested their solicitor. Throughout the night, they gradually disappeared, except when the bombing was at it's highest. The cells were underground, so no need to head for a shelter.

The superintendents sat in Stanley's office with Everard and the magistrate, Cyril Cooper, sipping tea.

Stanley stretched out his laced hands and cracked his knuckles, "Not a bad night's work, when all said and done, even though we didn't get the fourteen-year-old. I've got no idea how she escaped."

"Where's the other minor?" asked Cooper.

Everard spoke up, "Paddington Children's Hospital, Sir. I've got Sergeant Beaston and a WPC with her. She'll probably be okay. We need to identify a place of safety for her."

"How old is she?" asked Price.

"Not entirely sure, sir. One of the other women said she's not even sixteen until July."

Stanley shook his head, "Make sure she's interviewed with a WPC present, inspector."

"Sir, I'll go back up there straight away if that's okay?"

Price waved at him, "Off you go, Eric, and thank you. We'll have a debrief on Monday."

Stanley finished his tea and banged the desk bell. The secretary came in clutching a fresh pot of tea. She was looking a lot more attractive since the last time...

"Can you let me know when Fontaine's brief arrives? I want to be there when she's interviewed. Madame LeStrange, otherwise known by her real name of Doris Smithers, is wanted down in Brighton on theft charges. They can have her."

Price spoke up, "Do you reckon Maitland knows by now?"

Stanley snorted, "Of course he does. He'll have found out as soon as the first girl was brought in. What's the betting that John Lodge and his cronies will be all over this as soon as the all-clear is sounded?"

He looked at Chief Superintendent Alfred Price, "Will you be able to keep control of this, Alfred?"

Price sat back and smiled, "I should think so. My lords and masters can't really complain when there is plenty of evidence of criminality." He sipped a fresh cup of tea and continued. "I wouldn't worry, I've got a good contact in the press. I envisage a nice headline coming, something about underage girls, drugs and prostitution right under our noses possibly being condoned by the authorities..."

Monique Fontaine sat in the cold, damp basement interview room. It was nearly four in the morning. She shivered. As soon as John Lodge found out about the raid he contacted Charlie Maitland who was sleeping peacefully next to his teenage lover in his house in Hampstead. After he had calmed down, he phoned the personal number of his solicitor over in Kensington. Charles Fitch of Fitch, Palmer and Walters, solicitors to the wealthy and not-so-legal citizens of London, was none too pleased. He had better things to do than travel up to Paddington in the middle of an air raid to rescue a brothel madam.

He had just one instruction for Monique Fontaine, "Don't say or admit to anything..."

Chief Superintendent David Stanley bustled into the room, making as much noise as possible. He plonked down his cup of tea, pulled up a chair and sat down. He opened a file and pretended to read it. Next to him was one of his detective inspectors, Robert Doran. Stanley could trust Doran who had been with him for years. The Chief Superintendent didn't normally interview prisoners, but he'd make an exception for this lady...

Robert Doran came from the same stock as his boss; church-going, a stickler for the rules, and a veteran of the Great War.

Stanley passed over the file to his detective, "Right, Miss Fontaine or shall we call you by your real name, that of Angela O'Shaunessy?"

Doran smiled at the woman who immediately flushed up; he continued, "Born in Manchester in 1887. That makes you fifty-four years of age, doesn't it?" He looked at her, "My, you are getting a little on the old side for this game, Angela."

The female looked down. Charles Fitch spoke up, "Look, Detective Inspector, my client will not be saying anything, so either charge her with an offence or release her."

Doran looked at his boss, "I'm sorry, Mr Fitch, your client won't be going anywhere at present."

O'Shaunessy spoke, "I run a private gentlemen's club. Nothing illegal in that."

Fitch reached out to silence her...

"Well there is, especially if you don't have a licence, but never mind, I'll just continue reading." Doran picked up the folder; "It says here you've got three convictions for prostitution some twenty years ago."

O'Shaunessy shrugged her shoulders.

Stanley leaned in, "Whom do you work for, Angela?"

No answer.

Stanley sighed, "Well, I'll tell you. The person who owns your house is one Charlie Maitland, purveyor of alcohol and women in many of his clubs in the West End. It won't actually say he owns the house which is clearly being used as a brothel, because he's got a good firm of lawyers, hasn't he, Mr Fitch?"

Fitch looked down at his notepad; he really didn't want to be here, but Maitland pays his firm such a good retainer he didn't really have any choice.

"Right, Angela, let's stop messing around, shall, we. I'll tell you what we've got, and then let's see how you feel about that." He paused and smiled, "It's a sort of game like the ones we used to play as children, you know, I'll show you mine if you show me yours..."

Doran smiled; he enjoyed working with his superintendent, "Okay, we've found a substantial quantity of white powder in the house which we believe to be cocaine as well as that horrible-smelling tobacco called marijuana. On top of that, there's a small matter of the unlicensed sale of alcohol on the premises."

Fitch spoke up, "There's no proof that any of these items belonged to my client."

Doran looked at his boss, "Shall I tell him, Sir."

"Oh, do go ahead, Robert, I've got a home to go to."

Doran cleared his throat; "We have several statements from your ladies that it is you, Angela, who sells the cocaine to your gentlemen callers as well as the alcohol."

O'Shaunessy laughed, "Who is going to believe the words of a few whores?"

Fitch glared at her, "I told you not to say anything..."

Doran reached over, "So you admit these ladies are prostitutes?"

O'Shaunessy coloured up, sat back and folded her arms.

Doran sighed, "These are petty charges, Angela."

Fitch looked at him nervously as the detective continued, "There's a small matter of child prostitution..." He let that sink in.

Fitch looked at O'Shaunessy who looked at the floor...

Stanley intervened, this was all going nicely, "Yes, we currently have a minor in Paddington Children's Hospital on Praed Street who is recovering from a drug and alcohol-induced fit, although she's not very well. She is only fifteen. She has already made an initial statement, claiming that her mother sold her to a Madame Monique Fontaine for the princely sum of twenty pounds a couple of years ago. Since that time, she has been employed as a child prostitute in the Maida Vale house."

O'Shaunessy swallowed audibly.

Stanley looked at Mr Fitch of Fitch, Palmer and Walters, "Perhaps you would like a few words in private with your client, Mr Fitch?"

An hour later, Angela O'Shaunessy was charged with several offences relating to the supply of prostitutes, including children under the legal age of sixteen and the controlling of a brothel, and other matters contrary to the Offences Against the Person Act of 1861. Chief Superintendent David Stanley didn't think the charges relating to the unlawful supply of illicit substances nor the unlicensed sale of alcohol would stick, but he threw them in any way. She was transported up to the women's prison in Holloway to await an appearance before the magistrates first thing on Monday morning.

Charles Fitch called an urgent meeting of his partners for Monday morning to discuss their on going relationship with one Charles Maitland; dealing with common prostitutes and illegal drinking clubs was one thing, but child prostitution was another...He had the firm's reputation to consider...

Over in Paddington Children's Hospital, the girl named Faith made a full statement to Inspector Eric Everard detailing her exploits at the house, naming several prominent men from public life who were her regular clients. Doctor Loretta had accompanied the girl in the ambulance but somehow seemed to disappear once the child had been given over to the care of the hospital staff.

Eric Everard wanted to know how the other child, Hope, had managed to escape with a maid called Claudine...

Faith fitted again just as he was about to leave.

Chapter 21
Saturday, 22nd February 1941
Consequences

Alice Halpin stepped out of the rear doors of the old Post Office Morris van. She reached up and grabbed Nancy Keeling. The police whistles from back down the road seemed to be getting louder.

"Come on, Nancy, hurry up." She tugged on Nancy's arm.

Phyllis Manley stepped out of the van, "Who is this, Nancy?" She pointed at Hope.

Nancy grabbed the youngster and bundled her into the van. Jimmy Ryan revved the engine, "Come on ladies, come on. Make the introductions later. We've got to circle around and pick up Porteous."

Nancy's heart skipped a beat....

Ryan turned left into Abercorn Place and then stopped at the junction of Maida Vale. The front passenger door opened. Peter Porteous hopped in breathing heavily. The van sped off quickly up Maida Vale towards Kilburn.

Nancy sat with her back pressed against the side of the van. She had an arm around Hope. Porteous turned around with a smile on his face. He reached out to her. She took his hand,

"How-how did you know?" she stammered.

Alice prodded her leg, "Ask Edith..."

There was a large fire burning in the grate in the front room of the house on East Row. Something nice was simmering gently on the stove. Nancy had her arms around Porteous,

"I knew you'd come for me."

He gently pushed her away, "Who is your young friend?"

Hope spoke out quickly, "My name is Elizabeth, Elizabeth Collins, and I'm fourteen years old."

Phyllis looked at Nancy who shook her head discreetly; she said firmly,

"Well, Elizabeth, let's go and find you some proper clothes to wear."

Alice and Nancy took the little girl upstairs and soon sorted her out.

Phyllis Manley looked at Porteous, "What on earth has been going on down in that house?"

Porteous shook his head; "I'm not sure if I'd like to know, but we'll take care of her and try to get her back to her parents."

Porteous heard his name being called from upstairs. By the time he arrived up there, Elizabeth Collins was dressed in one of Maruska's boiler suits. It was a little too big, but the girl was happy to be dressed. Alice took her by the hand and led her downstairs.

Nancy put her arms around Porteous who asked, "What happened back there in Maida Vale?"

Porteous sat on the end of the bed and explained all to Nancy as she peeled off her maid's outfit. She sat on the bed next to him and told him about what she had witnessed during her time away. In the light, he could still see some of her bruises. He put his arm around her and held her tight as she began to sob.

He said, "You have Edith to thank for this and her friendly magistrate."

Nancy had her head in his lap, "Yes, but how did you know I would be able to get out after the police arrived?"

He shook his head, "We didn't really; we just bargained on your ingenuity. If this hadn't worked we'd have tried something else. I hid at the front and Alice and Jimmy were at the back with the van. Phyllis came along for the ride."

She sat up, "All my clothes are at West Hampstead."

"Don't worry, we'll get them. Jimmy's already gone home. The police are watching both of us. Do you want to tell me about Elizabeth?"

Nancy shook her head, "Not now, maybe tomorrow."

He went to the wardrobe and took out another boiler suit, "Here, that's the last one…"

The early warning siren began to wail…

The five of them squashed into the crypt of the church on Bosworth Road. The priest licked his lips when he saw young Elizabeth. Nancy glared at him…

It was four in the morning by the time they climbed into bed in the house on East Row. They had drunk some decent quality gin and eaten well from Alice's stew. Nancy wouldn't let Elizabeth drink any gin, much to her annoyance.

Nancy wanted to sleep next to Porteous, but Elizabeth insisted that she stay with Nancy. He dozed off in the small room on a mattress on the floor.

The following morning just before nine, Nancy Keeling, still in her nightdress, sat opposite Peter Porteous around the kitchen table. Alice had banked up the fire before they had retired; a quick poke soon brought it back to life.

Nancy told Porteous all about her adventure in Maida Vale.

He was shocked, "Just who are these clients, Nancy? Who would want to take advantage of a little girl?"

She sipped her hot tea, "I think many of these men are rich and famous. If you have enough money, then you think you can do anything."

"What's going to happen?"

She shook her head, "I'm not sure."

He took her hand, "Edith has gone up to Brondesbury Park to see her magistrate. She'll find out what really occurred. I just know that Maitland will be mightily annoyed."

Nancy thought for a minute, "He'll probably get away with it; he usually does."

Porteous said, "I'm not too sure this time. These things are cumulative. When the sum of the parts come together, he might just not be in such a good place."

She stood up; there was anger in her voice, "I want Freddie Fox and Mifty Mitchell…"

Later that afternoon, as Alice and Phyllis disappeared back to Golders Green; Edith Bell finally extracted herself from the arms of the magistrate Cyril Cooper and got herself back down to Kensal Town. She was able to inform Porteous and Nancy of the good news about the now closed house on Maida Vale.

It was early evening in the house in East Row. Porteous had gone up to the White Horse on Kensal Road to help Edith Bell with some general maintenance. Nancy Keeling sat at the kitchen table with the girl, Elizabeth Collins, who appeared to be relishing her newfound freedom. Nancy had found some clothes for her and made some slight adjustments. It seemed that all the girl ever wore whilst at Maida Vale were bedroom attire with the occasional lingerie sets, if the customer so requested.

Nancy had made the girl some porridge; that's all she wanted to eat. Nancy looked at her as she spooned the oats into her mouth; the child's rag doll was on the table.

Nancy asked her, "Where are you from, Elizabeth?"

The girl shrugged her shoulders, "I told you, just outside Swindon. I liked it when my mother used to take me to the market on Saturdays, if we had any money."

Nancy smiled, "Do you want to go back?"

The girl paused and thought about this for a second or two, "There's no one to go back to. My father doesn't want me and I have no idea where my mother is."

"Maybe we could find your mother?" Nancy asked optimistically.

The girl stared ahead, "She doesn't love me. If she did, she wouldn't have left me with my father."

Nancy couldn't disagree with that.

Elizabeth asked, "Can I not stay here with you? Everyone has been so nice to me, especially Mr Porteous. And I love Miss Alice and Miss Phyllis; they make me laugh, when I can understand them..."

Nancy was taken aback, "I'm-I'm not sure. Most girls of your age have been evacuated to the country to escape the bombing."

"I'm not going back to the country..." The response was firm; she continued, "If you take me there, I'll only run away. I know how to make money..."

Nancy closed her eyes; she knew that was true.

Elizabeth asked, "Was it Mr Maitland who had you beaten up?"

Nancy didn't answer,

"Are you one of his ladies?" Is that why you were brought to Maida Vale? I had several maids before you, and they all ended up downstairs with the other ladies."

Nancy looked away.

The girl continued to eat, "Then you and I are no different, Nancy."

Nancy breathed in deeply; she leaned into Elizabeth, "Look, Elizabeth, we are no longer those people. I had my reasons for doing what I did. This is the beginning of a new life for you and me."

Elizabeth began to cry, "It's all right for you; you've got Mr Porteous. I've got nobody…"

Nancy swept her up, "Okay, okay. I'll talk to Porteous. I'm sure he'll let you stay with me, but I have to go to work. I have a younger sister and a mother who is not very well. You are too young to work, and I can't leave you here all day on your own."

The girl wiped away a tear, "Can I go back to school?"

Bright and early on Monday morning, Superintendent Reginald Price stood at the back of the Assistant Commissioner's office on the top floor of Scotland Yard. Assistant Commissioner Alexander Braben was not in a good mood, having had his quiet Sunday ruined by several telephone calls from the great and good of London's high society.

Braben snarled at Price, "What on earth were you thinking of raiding that place without authorisation?"

Chief Inspector John Lodge sat looking gloomily on a chair in the corner of the room.

"With respect, Assistant Commissioner, we had a report of underage girls being employed for the purposes of prostitution on the premises and, as it happens, we were proved correct."

"Yes, yes; we know all about that, but you were supposed to go through the correct channel which is Clubs and Vice. That's why we have a designated unit to deal with these issues."

Price looked at Lodge, "If I'd have gone through him, the place would have been empty when we knocked."

Lodge made to get up. Braben shouted at him, "Sit down, Lodge, the Chief Superintendent has a valid point."

Braben sighed, "Look, what are we going to do about these men you arrested? Not forgetting, there's a small matter of a dead man."

"I can't see a problem, Assistant Commissioner, charge them with disorderly conduct. If we can get the fifteen-year-old to identify any of them, we'll do them for abuse of a minor under the Criminal Law Amendment Act of 1885. They should be good for a couple of years in prison. And as for the dead lad, let the coroner deal with it; looks like an accident, anyway." Price shrugged his shoulders.

Braben steepled his hands, "You do know that you picked up two members of Parliament, one official of the Church of England and three sons of the landed gentry?"

Price sighed, "The law applies equally to everyone, sir, even in times of war."

Braben smiled, "I doubt it. Their lawyers will get them off. As far as they are concerned, they were in a private club."

"Yes, sir, a club that has no licence to operate."

"Okay, okay; let's just see how this turns out. In the meantime, get your friendly magistrate to deal with the girls as he would normally. Charge the madam with keeping a disorderly house and living off the earnings of common prostitutes. Drop the drugs and alcohol complaints and for God's sake don't do anything like this again without going through formal channels."

Price smiled; nodded formally and left.

As he closed the door, he could hear the Assistant Commissioner shouting at the corrupt and hapless John Lodge.

Magistrate Cyril Cooper fined the girls twenty-one shillings, regardless of how many previous offences they had on their records. He remanded Angela O' Shaunessy, otherwise known as Monique Fontaine, to Holloway women's prison pending further investigations. He also asked that the police do all they could to locate the unlicensed doctor...

At lunchtime, he met with the leader of the Metropolitan Borough of Paddington to discuss the future of the brothel on Maida Vale...

The coroner opened and adjourned an inquest on young William, the doorman at the house on Maida Vale.

Later that evening, Charlie Maitland and his brother, Alfredo, had a shouting match with Chief Inspector John Lodge of Clubs and Vice. Lodge told him in no uncertain terms never to employ underage girls again.

Chapter 22
Monday, 24nd February 1941
A plan and another murder

Just before five on the Monday morning, Peter Porteous dragged a protesting Nancy Keeling out of bed and made her get washed and dressed. They both had a pressing appointment at Smiths in Cricklewood. Elizabeth Collins spent the previous evening with Edith Bell at the White Horse, where she helped in the bar collecting and washing glasses. A quick shout out to the residents of Kensal Town soon mustered up sufficient clothing appropriate for a teenage girl. They would be enough until Porteous and Nancy could get her to the shops with the right ration coupons, of course. Elizabeth was happy. She slept with Edith in her large bed.

Porteous had borrowed a bicycle from one of the neighbours for Nancy to ride. She complained that this machine was not as nice as Maruska's precious Saxon...

They met Alice Halpin at the entrance. Alice asked,

"How is Elizabeth?"

Nancy smiled, "Up with Edith..."

Porteous escorted Nancy to the general offices. Nancy was dressed formally with some clothes she had borrowed off Phyllis Manley; they fitted quite well and would suffice until she was able, and it was safe, to return to Crediton Hill to retrieve her own apparel.

Nancy was nervous; she was a little out of practice with the typewriter and her speeds were not exactly up to much, but she would have to make do.

The supervisor, Dorothy Jackson looked at Nancy, "Ahh; the elusive Miss Keeling. We were expecting you several weeks ago."

Porteous made to intervene; she held up her hand to silence him, "Don't say another word, Porteous."

He closed his mouth.

She continued, "Have you got nowhere to go, Porteous? And don't forget, you owe me three pairs of nylons or even better silk…"

He shrugged his shoulders, smiled at Nancy and left.

Jackson led Nancy into an empty office and told her to sit down.

She began, "I'm told you've had a bit of a rough time lately."

Nancy looked down.

"Well, many of us have. I've not seen my husband for over six months. I've no idea where the army has sent him. One of my girls had her house bombed the other week. Their children are out in some godforsaken place in the country. So, we've all got our crosses to bear. In short, Nancy, you are no different, so don't expect any favours or sympathy."

She sat down, "Now, we are very busy with the war effort. I'm short of at least three typists. I just want to know that if we train you, you'll stay and not bugger off somewhere else, or worse, get yourself signed up to the services. They are pinching all our best typists at the moment because they pay better. I just want you here every day come rain, wind or shine. You'll work the same shifts as Porteous; sometimes early and sometimes late, and eventually straight days. What do you say, Nancy?"

"I'm staying as long as Porteous is here."

"Good, good. He's a pretty decent fellow, you know, despite his little side-lines."

Nancy smiled for the first time.

Jackson stood up, "Go and sit at that typewriter. I want to see what you can do. Don't worry about your speed, accuracy is more important. I'll send in one of the girls with some work and to complete your personnel file. When you've done that, come on back to the typing pool, and I'll introduce you to everyone. We are all the same; no one has any airs and graces. I'm not going to ask you what you were doing before you came here; that's your business but try and be as honest as you can."

Nancy sat down at the desk as Dorothy Jackson left. She flexed her fingers over the keys. This Olivetti machine was much better than the one she had learnt on back in Crediton Hill.

The door opened, "Hello, Nancy, I'm Dot's assistant, Dawn Fraser." She held out her hand. Nancy took it.

She handed Nancy a handwritten letter, "Just take your time; I'll sit with you as you complete it..."

By lunchtime, Nancy was sitting at a desk in the typing pool, working on some simple tasks until her speed was up to it. The girls made her welcome.

Alice Halpin wouldn't let Porteous pop over to the office and see her during their first break at nine-thirty,

"Leave her alone; Nancy can take care of herself."

Alice sipped her tea, "What are we going to do about young Elizabeth. She can't work in the pub for the rest of her life."

Porteous raised his eyebrows, "Nancy says she wants to go back to school."

"You can't just take in a waif whenever you feel like it, you know. There are official procedures to go through."

"Nancy won't let her go."

Alice smiled and took his hand, "We'll deal with this little problem later, what about Maitland and his boys?"

He shook his head, "I dunno, Alice; Nancy says she will sort it out..."

Just after three in the afternoon, Nancy Keeling pecked both Alice Halpin and Peter Porteous on the cheek and rode off towards Kilburn, promising the pair of them that she wouldn't go back to Crediton Hill on her own.

She pulled her bicycle into the small front garden of the house on Gascony Avenue and tucked it behind the bushes, safe from prying eyes. She went up the steps and rang the doorbell.

Hilda Clarkson appeared at the door. She wore a dirty apron that had seen better days. Her lank, grey hair was tucked carelessly under a headscarf, and she had a cigarette stuck in one corner of her mouth. Nancy stepped back; she hadn't smoked since she was taken to Maida Vale.

Clarkson asked, "Yes? What can I do for you?"

"I'd like to see Margaret on the top floor, if that's okay with you?"

Clarkson snorted and stepped to one side, "Top floor; flat at the rear of the house. No visitors overnight. This is a respectable house."

Where had Nancy heard that before?

Nancy went up the stairs quietly. The place was clean and tidy. The carpet of the wooden stairs was worn but serviceable. She reached the top of the landing and went up to the door at the rear of the hallway.

She leaned against the door; she could hear nothing.

She tried the handle; it turned. She opened the door and peered inside. The flat was small. She entered what appeared to be a living room. Some drying clothes, including three pairs of stockings, were hanging on a clothes maiden next to the fireplace in which was a little gas stove that no doubt gobbled up sixpences. There was a small but functional kitchen at the rear and another room just off the living room.

Nancy tried the door to what she presumed was the bedroom. She gently opened the door that was slightly ajar. She wrinkled her nose as the smell of stale gin assailed her nostrils. She looked in; the place was untidy with discarded lingerie on the floor and on the end of the bed. Margaret Heywood was fast asleep under an eiderdown and several blankets in the bed.

Nancy went and sat on the end of the bed, not caring if she woke up the sleeping female. She picked up a brassiere and a pair of French knickers. They smelled of unwashed female. She tossed them onto the chair.

She reached over to the bedside table and picked up a half-empty bottle of cheap gin. She poured herself a drink and sat quietly, sipping at the bitter tasting liquid.

She prodded the prone body, "Margaret; Margaret, time to wake up. I haven't got all day, and I've got a teenager to look after."

Margaret Heywood stirred, moaning gently; she was in a deep sleep, no doubt caused by the gin.

Nancy poked her a little harder, "Wake up, Margaret."

Margaret Heywood finally stirred, "What? Who is it?"

She sat up. The covers fell off exposing her full breasts,

"What?" she repeated, and then she realised, "Nancy! What are you doing here?"

She tried to cover herself. Nancy gripped the blanket, knowing full well that humans are always much more vulnerable when they are naked.

"Jesus, Nancy, you scared the living daylights out of me. How did you get in?"

Nancy shrugged her shoulders, "You didn't lock the door."

She reached into her bag. Margaret Heywood's eyes opened wide as she saw the four-inch lock knife. Nancy pressed the little silver coloured button and the blade sprang open; it was one of Alice's.

Heywood shrank back.

"It's alright, Margaret, I just want a little chat with you."

Heywood swallowed, still trying to cover her breasts.

"First of all, you owe me five pounds."

"Yes, but we didn't do anything."

"It doesn't matter. The price was five pounds for the night. I'm sure you took it from my purse."

"Okay, okay; I'll get it for you if you'll let me out of the bed."

Nancy moved back a little and released the pressure on the blanket. Heywood threw off the covers and got out of bed. She walked over to the chair and took out her bag. She fiddled with her purse and produced five one-pound notes.

Nancy looked at the naked woman, who now appeared to have little or no shame. She stood in front of Nancy and handed over the notes,

"You know Fox and Mitchell are looking for you. They waited outside Marylebone Magistrate's court all Monday but you were nowhere to be seen. I know all about the raid on the house in Maida Vale. There's hell to pay. One of the girls said that you took the youngster with you." She shook her head, "I heard Mitchell is going to make a mess of your face."

Nancy smiled, "He has to get me first."

Heywood stood over her with her hands on her hips, "If I were you I'd make myself scarce. Maitland is not so much bothered about you, he just wants that girl, Hope, back."

Nancy waved her away, "Her name's not Hope; it's Elizabeth."

"No matter. Now, if you'd excuse me, I'd like to get dressed."

Nancy shouted at her, "Sit down, you cheap bitch. I'll tell you when you can leave. I've got a job for you that's worth twenty pounds."

Margaret Heywood smiled, "Now you are talking..."

At the end of their intense conversation, Nancy stood up and closed the lock knife. She went to the door,

"Put on some clothes, Margaret, and listen carefully, if you mess me around, someone will come here and slit your throat..."

Peggy Campbell smiled at the handsome Royal Air force Sergeant as soon as he entered the Royal Oak public house, just off Baker Street in Central London. She was on the lookout for another client. She had already satisfied the lust of two other men in the dark alleys off the main street and was looking to finish off the evening with a drink and a more relaxed session back in her flat in Gosfield Street in Marylebone.

She had consumed quite a bit of gin earlier in the evening, but at the age of forty-three, she prided herself on being able to hold her drink. The RAF sergeant came and sat beside her. They struck up a conversation. He seemed quite nice. She let him put his hand upon her leg, and then did not object when he moved it higher under her dress. After a few more drinks, during which she told him about her fifteen-year-old daughter, they agreed a price.

She put her arm in his as they walked along Great Portland Street. Just before midnight, she entered the premises where her flat was located. She greeted her neighbour as she passed her on the stairs. Gordon Cummins looked away.

She slowly unlocked her door and led Cummins inside. She told him to pour another drink whilst she got herself ready in the bedroom. He went to the door as she was undressing. He didn't think she was too bad-looking for a forty-something female with a teenage daughter.

He asked her not to remove her stockings, as he quite liked to do that. She smiled; you meet all sorts in this line of business.

She took off her French knickers and lay back on the bed. Cummins licked his lips...She laid on the bed with one hand behind her head with a cigarette in the other. He gently moved her leg so that her knee bent upwards. She smiled at him as he slowly unclipped her stocking. He rolled it down her leg and placed it to his face, breathing in her feminine scent.

He turned his back to her and deftly tied a knot in the garment. He then lay on top of her, gently kissing her face; she closed her eyes to enjoy the sensation even more. He wrapped the silk stocking around her neck and pulled it tight. Peggy Campbell struggled valiantly, but she didn't have the strength to fight him off. She died beneath him, thinking of her daughter...

Just after one in the morning, Gordon Cummins casually walked past the same neighbour on his way out on to the main street and back to his barracks in Regent's Park. The neighbour could hear him whistling as he went up the street.

Fifteen-year-old Barbara Lowe discovered the badly mutilated body of her mother some two days later; Cummins had done his depraved worst.

Peggy Campbell, whose real name was Margaret Florence Lowe, died a terrible death...

Chapter 23
Tuesday, 25nd February 1941
Death...

The day dragged slowly for Nancy Keeling; she found it hard to concentrate on her work. The typing pool was buzzing with gossip about the latest murder of one of Soho's ladies of the night. Nancy kept her head down. During one of the breaks, she scuttled over to Porteous' workshop to confirm with Alice Halpin that all was well for their appointment in the evening; it was, and could Nancy stop worrying? Alice had done this sort of thing before...Porteous left the women to their whisperings and imagined conspiracies.

Just gone three o'clock as the shift finished, Nancy pecked Porteous on the cheek and rode off with Alice along Cricklewood Broadway. When he asked where they were going, he simply got a wave of the hand. Anyway, he had to go and pick up Elizabeth Collins from the White Horse on Kensal Road. Nancy had told him she thought the young girl was spending too much time in there. Besides, Nancy had secured an appointment at the Sisters of Mercy Convent in Lisson Grove for later in the week. The sisters ran a very private girls' school for daughters of the middle classes who had resisted the call to evacuate. There were just two criteria for entry; the girls had to have been baptised a Catholic, and was there enough money to pay the fees? Elizabeth insisted she had been brought up a Catholic...

Nancy opened the door to her house in Crediton Hill, West Hampstead. The house was cold. Alice wheeled her bicycle into the tiled hallway,

"Jesus, Nancy, this place is cold."

Nancy smiled. In a way, she was pleased to be back in her home, but it did bring some difficult memories.

"Go and light the fire in the kitchen; I'll pack some things."

Alice looked at her, "What time is Jimmy coming?"

Nancy looked at the stopped hallway clock; no one had wound it up for weeks.

"I reckon about one hour..."

Alice turned away, "Go on then...I'll make the fire and put on the kettle."

Nancy skipped up the stairs and spent the next forty-five minutes emptying everything out of the two bedrooms. Helen Shenton had left an assortment of clothing in the front bedroom. Nancy stuffed these into a carpetbag she found under the bed. She stripped the beds and tied the sheets into a bundle.

Back in her bedroom, she emptied the dressing table. She could have sworn she had more than one pair of stockings in the drawer...

Jimmy Ryan arrived about half an hour later. Nancy and Alice helped him load up the belongings into the old Morris van. He was a little confused when they told him to leave; he fancied a cup of tea with these two beauties. They pushed him out of the door instructing him not to go to Kensal Town until much later that evening and on no account was he to tell Porteous that they were in Crediton Road; he would probably have a heart attack...

The girls sat at the kitchen table. The fire in the hearth was roaring with the last of the fuel from the outside store. The coalman never did make that last delivery. Nancy had her feet up on the chair. Alice sat reading an old copy of the Evening News.

Nancy asked, "Are you all right with this, Alice?"

Alice didn't look up, "Of course, it's no big deal. We are just cleaning up some vermin, that's all. The police will thank us..." She smiled.

"Not sure about that, Alice..." She paused, "What did you tell Phyllis?"

"Overtime at Smiths."

"What if she checks?"

Alice looked up, "She won't; she's working nights at the Admiralty. What did you tell Porteous?"

"I told him I was going to look at an alternate school for Elizabeth."

Alice smiled, "What if he checks?"

Nancy laughed, "He won't. He's too busy worrying about how he's managed to find a teenager resident in his house along with me."

Alice put down the newspaper, "Is he still pining for Maruska?"

Nancy shook her head, "I don't know. He's affectionate with me. We sleep in the same bed when Elizabeth allows it, but he won't make love to me."

Alice took her hand, "I'm sure he will. Just give him time. It's too soon for both of you. Anyway, looking after Elizabeth will keep him occupied." Alice sipped her tea, "How are you going to work out the legal stuff with her? You can't just take in any old waif and stray."

"Edith asked her magistrate. He told her that with the evacuation, the whole system is in meltdown. No one knows where anyone is and on top of that, quite a few of the children have run away and sneaked back home. It seems that not all were housed in good conditions out in the country. The authorities are just thankful that youngsters are being looked after." She looked out of the window, "If and when this bloody war ever ends, I'll sort it out. Until then, she stays with me and Porteous."

Alice smiled, "I like her...If you don't want her, me and Phyllis will have her..."

Nancy glanced over at her, "Not a chance...Anyway, what's happening with you and Phyllis?"

"Oh, nothing really. As long as we keep ourselves to ourselves, there won't be a problem. Apart from our lot, the only person who knows is our landlady, and she loves Phyllis. I think she quite fancies her herself, especially when she's in her WRNS uniform..." She smiled again.

Nancy asked, "Still no word from your parents?"

Alice shook her head, "They'll come round, eventually; I am their only daughter..."

Nancy wasn't too sure...

Margaret Heywood was nervous. She didn't really like the idea of what she had signed up to do. She sat on the end of the bed. The flat in Gascony Avenue was cold, and she'd run out of sixpences for the meter. She dressed slowly, taking her time to look nice, even though she wouldn't be working for a few days.

She had managed to soak in the bath. It was early afternoon and her fellow residents hadn't returned from work. She stared at herself in the mirror; it was time to leave this profession.

It was six o'clock by the time she pulled on her dress, checked the seams of her stockings and grabbed her coat before she exited the flat. She walked slowly down the stairs. She could hear the wirelesses of some of the other tenants as she walked past their doors on each landing.

She opened the front door and peered out. The Wolseley Hornet was parked across the street with its engine running. She could see two men sat in the car smoking. Mifty Mitchell sat in the driving seat. Freddie Fox was next to him in the passenger seat.

Margaret Heywood walked slowly up to the car. She opened the rear passenger door and slid in behind Freddie Fox. Mitchell glanced over,

"You'd better not be messin' wiv us, Maggie, otherwise it won't just be Nancy bloody Keeling who gets a beatin.'"

Margaret Heywood swallowed loudly. She could still taste the gin from that last drink she had thrown down her throat before she pulled on her dress.

"No, No, honestly. She said she wants to come back in."

Fox turned around, "And you are sure she's back home in West Hampstead?"

Heywood nodded, "Yes. She told me to tell you to pick her up. She wants to see Charlie. She knows where the fourteen-year-old is staying, but she won't tell you if you slap her. Her injuries have only just healed since the last time."

Fox smiled, "Oh, we're not goin to beat her this time. Charlie says I can have ten minutes wiv her on me own..." He laughed, "You can come and watch if yer likes?"

Margaret Heywood turned away as Mitchell tossed out his cigarette end and put the car into gear.

Fox passed over a hip flask, "Here, Maggie, take a drink."

Heywood gulped down the last of the alcohol.

The car pulled into Crediton Hill. Mitchell turned off the lights, placed the car in neutral and cruised up to Nancy's house.

Fox opened the door and got out, "Stay here, Maggie, and don't yer fuckin' move. Mifty will be in for his turn after ten minutes or so. It won't take me long..."

Fox noisily opened the front gate and walked up to the front door of the house. He banged loudly on the doorknocker.

Nancy opened the door and smiled at Freddie Fox. She had dressed really well and had spent some time on her make-up,

"Come in, Freddie, I've been waiting for you."

His hand shot out and gripped her around the neck, "Yer in trouble, Nance; pissing off like that from the house in Maida Vale."

She slowly reached up and removed his hand, "What did you want me to do; stay and get arrested like the other girls in the house?"

He relaxed a little. "Charlie's really cross."

"If Charlie wants the young girl back, then just don't hit me in the face again."

He reached out and grabbed hold of her, "I'll hit yer where I fuckin' like, bitch."

Nancy backed away, "I'll get my coat."

He shook his head, "Not until I've had me fun..."

He grabbed at her; she shouted, "Okay! Okay! Let me go upstairs and take off my dress first. It cost a lot of money."

He looked at the kitchen table, "No need for that, you'll do here...and when we've finished with you, we'll go and get yer boyfriend Porteous. He might not be so lucky as you..."

Nancy backed away; she started to unfasten the buttons on the front of her dress. He pushed her back with one arm and began to loosen the belt on his trousers.

He was too preoccupied with his own desires to notice that Nancy had a long, six-inch blade strapped to her thigh. It was something she had learnt from a certain Czechoslovakian doctor. She had seen it one night when they had been drinking in the flat in Bosworth Road. She had thought it better not to enquire...

Freddie Fox's eyes opened wide as the blade pierced his abdomen and went up under his ribcage, through his lung and straight through the left ventricle of his heart. She pushed him away. He started to gurgle; blood began to ooze from his mouth. He coughed up blood.

She stepped to one side to avoid the blood splatters and forced him down over the table. She pushed hard against his head and leaned into him,

"That's for the beating you gave me last time and for all the women you've raped in your time. Rot in Hell, Freddie!"

Freddie Fox tried to speak, but couldn't get any words out before he died on Nancy Keeling's kitchen table.

She stood back and tried to slow down her breathing and heart rate. She sucked in deep breaths and slowly fastened up her dress. She knew if she attempted to pull out the knife, there would be blood everywhere; she left it in, at least until the body was moved.

She washed her hands in the sink and then went into the front room and very carefully opened the heavy blackout curtain in one corner...

Alice Halpin slipped out from the garden of the house two doors away. She had gone through the gate at the bottom of the garden into the old recreation ground and slipped between the houses at the end of the run of terraced houses and out onto the road. She was glad of the near total darkness of the blackout. It took her eyes a few seconds to adjust.

She saw the curtain twitch in Nancy's front room....

She stood up and boldly walked to the Hornet. She pulled open the door behind Mifty Mitchell and sat down; he began to turn around,

"What do you want, yer scouse queer?"

Alice glared at Margaret Heywood, who was doing her best to shrink as much as she could against the car door.

Alice smiled, "Oh, nothing important, Mifty."

He half-turned, "Well, fuck off then. This ain't no taxi." There was no response. He looked up at the rear view mirror, "Well, what are yer waitin' for?"

Alice Halpin threw the knotted cord around Mifty Mitchell's neck twice. He began to struggle. She raised herself up and pressed her knees into the back of his seat, as she pulled hard on the cord; the knots bit hard into his neck.

His hands came up to try to loosen the cord. He was spluttering. Margaret Heywood began to whimper as she shrank further into the car door.

Alice managed to wrap more of the cord around her hands. She held on for dear life. Mifty Mitchell was a strong man. He was able to get two of his fat fingers under the cord. Alice wasn't sure she could hold him. She sat back and put her feet against the seat and pulled as though her life depended on it.

By this time, Mitchell was almost prone on the driver's seat with his head pulled right back. He'd managed to get the fingers of his other hand under the cord.

Alice closed her eyes; she could see the face of her lover, Phyllis Manley. The grip on her hands was gradually loosening; she wasn't sure how long she could hold him. Perhaps her knife, although messy, would have been deadly and certain.

And then, she felt the pressure release from her left hand. She opened her eyes to see Margaret Heywood pulling for all her might. Heywood was kneeling up on the back seat. This gave Alice the encouragement she needed, and she pulled even harder.

Gradually, she felt Mitchell's body shudder and go limp. The two women held on for dear life, not daring to release their grip. Alice was breathing hard and little beads of sweat appeared on her forehead. She let go with her left hand and began smashing a fist into the pale, blue face of Mitchell. His eyes bulged. She started swearing.

Heywood reached over and stopped her, "He's dead already."

Alice slumped back into the seat, and then slapped the back of Mitchell's bald head once more."

She looked at Margaret Heywood, "Too right; he's fucking dead..."

Nancy opened the rear car door and looked in at the dead body of Mifty Mitchell, "Are we good?"

Margaret Heywood spoke first, "We certainly are, Nancy."

Without speaking, the two women got out of the car and followed Nancy into the house. Freddie Fox was still bleeding out slowly on the kitchen table. Alice grabbed a sheet that Nancy had left and wrapped it around the body as Heywood and Alice lifted him up.

They dragged him back to the car and tossed the body on the back seat. Alice used her feet to push Mitchell onto the passenger side. Nancy ran back to the house and locked the front door. The three women had spent a few minutes wiping away what little blood there was in the kitchen. Nancy had planned to return in a day or so and scrub the place clean.

Nancy climbed onto the back seat next to Fox.

Margaret Heywood stood back and stared at the car as it sped off into the darkness with its gears crunching. Her heart was thumping wildly. She took a deep breath and disappeared into the night...

Alice Halpin had never driven a car before, but what the heck, she had seen her brother drive the car that he had had from outside that posh house in Sefton Park. She reasoned it couldn't be that difficult if he could do it...

By the time they had reached Kentish Town, she was feeling quite confident and was only crashing the gears from time to time.

The car pulled into a bombed-out warehouse just off Rhyl Street. The roof had been burnt clean off, but the walls were still standing. Alice turned off the lights and then removed the key from the ignition. Nancy got out of the car. She leaned in and pulled out the knife. The sucking sound made her shudder. She threw the knife out into the blackness...

She opened up the small boot and took out a battered petrol canister. Mifty Mitchell always carried spare fuel in case there was a supply problem. Alice got out. She opened all the doors as Nancy splashed the petrol throughout the car. She tossed in the canister after it was empty.

Alice asked, "Give us a match then, Nance?"

Nancy shook her head, "I haven't got one?"

Alice glared at her, "What do you mean you haven't got a match? You're the one who smokes."

Nancy reached back into the glove compartment and rummaged around. She found a half-full box of Bryant & May matches. Alice rolled her eyes.

Nancy broke the first match as she tried to strike it. Alice grabbed the box, lit the match and threw it into the car. They stepped back as the whoosh of the igniting petrol startled them.

Alice pulled Nancy away. They ran to the big doors of the warehouse and heaved on them. Slowly, they began to close. The railings were dry and partially warped because of the heat from the original fire. The fire could not be seen from the road until the car, and the bodies contained therein, were well and truly alight.

They secured the place as best they could and calmly walked out onto Malden Road. The early warning sirens could be heard out in the distance over East London.

Alice spoke softly as they walked, "Come on, Nance, do your stuff and get us a lift home."

This time it was Nancy's turn to glare...

Alice Halpin and Nancy Keeling crossed the Ha'penny Steps an hour later. They felt much safer being in Kensal Town. It had taken Nancy ten minutes to persuade a taxi driver to take them up the Harrow Road. He had wanted to go home, but the promise of a good fare and two rather nice ladies in the back with one of them willing to flash her legs at him was too much to resist. He was ultimately disappointed...

Nancy turned the key in the lock of Porteous' house on East Row. Elizabeth Collins bounded down the hallway and wrapped her arms around Nancy. She pulled away,

"You smell funny…"

The youngster could detect petrol on Nancy's clothing; she responded quickly, "Yes, we've been cleaning the house in Crediton Road."

Porteous heard that. He was about to say something when Alice put a finger to his lips and shut him down.

Alice grabbed hold of Elizabeth and hugged her. She guided her back into the kitchen, where the two of them set about preparing something to eat.

Porteous sat on the end of the bed as Nancy peeled off her clothes and changed into her boiler suit.

He asked, "What have you and Alice been up to, Nancy?"

She looked at him, walked to him and threw her arms around his neck; she breathed into his ear, "Nothing important…"

She felt his arms wrap tightly around her waist…

Jimmy Ryan thought it better to stay away and delivered Nancy's belongings the following evening. Elizabeth enjoyed helping Nancy put the clothes away.

It was nearly four hours before the Auxiliary Fire Brigade had the chance to get to the warehouse in Kentish Town. They were too busy with the nightly bombing and rescuing people from half-demolished buildings. There was little left of Mifty Mitchell and Freddie Fox by this time, as the walls of the warehouse finally gave up the ghost and collapsed in on the burning vehicle.

It would be nearly five years before a demolition crew arrived to clear the site in preparation for the building of some urgent post-war social housing. One of the workers found a burnt number plate. He could just about decipher the registration number, but he thought nothing of it and tossed it into the rubbish skip.

Freddie Fox and Michael Mitchell were listed as missing, presumed killed in the Blitz. Charlie Maitland was more concerned about his precious Wolseley Hornet...

Chapter 24
March 1941
Another encounter with a parachute land mine.

At the end of February, Nancy Keeling had taken Elizabeth Collins up to the convent in Lisson Grove for an interview with the Reverend Mother, Sister Angela. The meeting was for the nuns of the Sisters of Mercy to ascertain that young Elizabeth was a suitable candidate to be accepted as a pupil in their exclusive private school that consisted of about fifty girls of the great and good of this part of West London.

An elderly nun ushered them in to a cold reception room that was adorned with saintly pictures and other religious relics.

The Reverend Mother, bustled into the room and after some cursory greetings she sat down and said,

"We don't normally admit pupils midway through the school year."

Nancy smiled, "But, Reverend Mother, these are not normal times."

"Yes, yes. Could you pass over your application form?"

Nancy slid over an envelope. She had spent a good hour extracting the information from Elizabeth.

The nun hummed as she ran her finger down the papers,

"You say your niece hasn't been in school for a few months?"

Nancy nodded, "She has been passed around various relatives since her mother disappeared. I took her in recently."

The nun looked at Elizabeth, "Where is your father, child?"

"I'm sorry, Sister, but I don't know."

The nun tutted and returned to the paperwork, "You say you have been baptised?"

Elizabeth rattled off the name of the church in Swindon that she used to attend from time to time.

"And you have made your first Holy Communion?"

Elizabeth nodded; that at least was true.

The Reverend Mother picked up a small bell from the table and rang it. A young novice meekly came in and almost curtsied.

Sister Angela snapped, "Please take Elizabeth to the chapel and hear her prayers..."

Nancy nodded at Elizabeth, who was led out of the room.

The nun looked at Nancy, "Are you employed, Miss Keeling?"

"Yes, Reverend Mother, I'm a typist up at Smiths in Cricklewood."

The nun furrowed her eyebrows, "Our fees are not cheap, you know."

Nancy smiled and reached into her purse. She extracted a wad of five-pound notes and laid them on the table, "I'm prepared to pay Elizabeth's fees up to the end of the school year as a sign of good faith. From September, we'll pay monthly like all the other parents."

The nun stared at the cash; she licked her lips...

"We envisage all our pupils to attend mass every Sunday. I see you live in Kensal Town? We wouldn't normally expect to receive pupils from that part of London."

Nancy nodded, "In the envelope there is a reference from our Parish Priest at the church on Bosworth Road."

Porteous had pinned the old lecher up against the wall of the crypt until he had agreed to write it...

The nun read it and sighed, "Ah, well, everything seems to be in order."

The door opened and Elizabeth came back in. The novice nodded at her superior.

The nun stood up, "Right, could you bring her back on Wednesday so that we can assess her academic abilities?"

Nancy nodded as the nun continued, "Good. If you'd like to come with me, I'll take you to the school office, and you can complete the formalities and get a uniform list. Completing the formalities was code for making the payments."

Twenty minutes later, Nancy and Elizabeth Collins walked along the Marylebone Road. Elizabeth had her arm in Nancy's.

"What did the nun make you do?"

Elizabeth smiled, "I just had to recite a load of prayers...She says all the girls go to confession every week."

Nancy asked, "What's that? I've never heard of it."

"You go into a little box and tell the priest all the sins you've committed."

Nancy furrowed her brow, "What's the purpose in that?"

Elizabeth said, "Well, the priest pretends to be God so that he can forgive you."

Nancy raised her eyebrows, "What are you going to tell him?"

"Oh, these old men just like to hear what girls do when they are in bed; I'll make up something..."

Nancy shook her head.

Elizabeth asked, "Where are we going?"

"To the shop to get your uniform and then to the bank."

Elizabeth asked, "Why are we going to the bank?"

"To set you up with an account and deposit your money. You've got over three hundred pounds." Nancy paused, "And then I'm going to ask them to act for me so that I can buy a house..."

Elizabeth looked ahead, "Will I not have to receive callers again, Nancy?"

"Over my dead body..."

Later that evening, as Elizabeth was trying on her new and somewhat expensive school uniform under the proud eye of Nancy Keeling, Peter Porteous was drinking tea in the rear of Jimmy Ryan's disused shop on Red Lion Street in Holborn. Several cardboard boxes were stacked in front of them.

"What did Dennis say, Jimmy?"

Ryan shrugged his shoulders, "Said he had a meeting with Maitland. They came to some sort of agreement. He thinks Maitland has lost interest."

Porteous smiled, "Yeah, he's got a lot on his plate at the moment. He's lost his brothel, most of his girls won't work until that Blackout Ripper has been caught, and he can't find Freddie Fox and Mifty Mitchell. He thinks Elphicke has taken care of them."

Ryan nodded, "On top of all that, the police have been cracking down on his unlicensed drinking establishments. It seems that Edith's magistrate has been creating a lot of trouble for him. A couple of senior coppers have been sacked from West End Central, so I've heard."

"Not before time. Dennis says we have to get back to business, but you must stay in Kensal Town whilst I work my patch up in Tottenham. He reckons the next big thing will be provisions. I don't know about you, but I'm finding it's getting much harder to purchase decent food even with coupons."

Porteous went to the boxes, "What do we have here?"

Ryan looked up, "Oh just the usual plus some canned meat from Argentina. God knows how that got across the Atlantic. Dennis said there's a box of actual silk stockings that should fetch a pretty penny."

Porteous raised his eyebrows, "Yeah, tell me about it. I think I owe half of them for favours received..."

Ryan joined Porteous, "There should be six boxes." He counted up, "I must have left the small one in the van; some rolling tobacco."

He left out of the rear door. The van was parked in the service alley behind the shops.

Porteous found the stockings and held up a cellophane packet to the light. He nodded approvingly.

He could see a light outside through a small chink in the boarded-up windows of the shop, as though a torch was being shone at the building. He went up to the window and screwed up his eyes to get a better look. Ryan and he were always conscious of other likely lads who might be entertaining the idea of liberating some of their stock. He couldn't see very much, so he went to the front glass door that had brown paper pasted all over it to deter prying eyes.

No sooner had he reached the door and placed a hand on the knob when the glass shattered. Quite a large piece embedded itself just above his hairline. He fell back as blood began to seep from the cut. The pain was excruciating.

Two male figures leaned over him,

Detective Inspector Eric Everard smiled at Peter Porteous, "Ah, nice to see you again, Porteous. Have you cut yourself perchance?"

Porteous couldn't really think straight; he just knew he was in a lot of trouble.

Everard roughly turned him over, pulled his hands behind his back and handcuffed him,

"Let's start with a charge of handling stolen property, shall we?"

He put his boot on the back of Porteous' head, "Search the place, Derek. No doubt you'll find his mate Jimmy Ryan somewhere."

Beaston ran through to the back.

He pulled up Porteous and leaned him against the dusty shop counter on the floor. He reached into the inside pocket of his overcoat and produced a folded piece of paper; he opened it slowly and held it up to the light,

"You see here, Porteous, this is what is called a search warrant signed by one of your not-so-friendly magistrates. When you've got the blood out of your eyes, I'll let you read it. Stay there!" he growled.

Everard smiled to himself, one more black marketeer potted for the duration, and it would be two, if his sergeant could lay his hands on that Jimmy Ryan.

Everard went into the rear of the shop, examined the boxes and selected one. A large grin appeared on his face. He lifted the heavy box, carried it back to Porteous and dropped it on the floor in front of him,

"Now, what do we have here? Ah, I see it says in bold letters *Property of Ministry of Food.* Now that's interesting. Why would a box of South American corned beef be sitting on the floor of this boarded-up shop in Holborn?"

Porteous turned away; he was looking at a rather long sentence in one of His Majesty's prisons...

Sergeant Beaston came back in breathing heavily as though he'd been running, "Sir! It looks like Ryan has legged it. I watched as his van drove off down the alleyway."

Everard smiled again, "Oh, no matter, we'll pick him up at his digs later. His fingerprints will be all over these cartons, no worry."

Beaston prodded Porteous with his boot, "Gotcha, at last Porteous. I hope you kissed your girlfriend goodbye when you left this evening because you won't be seeing her for such a long time."

Porteous stared at him trying to blink the blood out of his left eye.

Beaston reached into his pocket and took out a clean, white handkerchief. He started dabbing at the blood that was, by now, all over Porteous' face,

"Hmm, that's a nasty cut you've got there, Porteous; it might need a couple of stitches; what do you think, sir?" He turned towards the detective inspector.

"He'll have to wait, Derek. We need to get these boxes into the car. If we leave these premises unsecured, the lot will have disappeared before we return."

Beaston nodded, "I don't think these will fit, Sir, not with the prisoner."

Everard sighed, "Well, just throw him on the back seat. We'll pile the stuff on top of him." He bent down to Porteous, "You won't mind, will you, Peter?"

Everard stood up and opened what was left of the front door. A large van was parked right in front of the shop, "Park the car across the road, Derek and we'll load it from there."

Beaston struggled to manoeuvre the Vauxhall 12 saloon into a tight space across the road from the shop. There was bomb debris piled high on either side of his parking space.

Everard pulled Porteous to his feet, dragged him across the road and threw him face down on the back seat. Beaston arrived with the box of silk stockings and placed them on Porteous' feet, "These for your lady friends, Porteous?" He laughed and went back into the shop.

Everard stood next to the car just as the early warning siren began to sound. He took out his pipe and went about filling and lighting it. After about five minutes Porteous was weighed down with the boxes; he couldn't move if he wanted to, but to be honest, he hadn't even tried. He was deflated, with all the spirit having gone out of him.

He thought about Nancy and the new addition to the household.; Yes, he quite liked having a teenager around the place even though it was an extra mouth to feed. He thought about Alice and how she would be protected now that he wasn't going to be around and last of all, he thought about Doctor Maruska Bergman...

Everard's shout jolted him out of his thoughts, "Come on, Derek, we've got to get back before the bombing starts."

Beaston called, "It's this last box, sir, it's stuck behind the counter, and it's too heavy for me to move."

Everard sighed, tapped out his pipe, slammed all the car doors shut, content that his handcuffed prisoner wasn't going anywhere. He sauntered back over the road and slid in between the box van, making a mental note to get the locals to remove it the following day...

Porteous struggled, but it was no use.

In the shop, the two policemen were stood weighing up how to extract the heavy box; it was well and truly wedged between the floor and the counter. Everard tore open a side,

"Gallon cans of cooking oil. Where the bloody hell does Ryan acquire this stuff?"

He turned to Beaston, "Let's get these out; go and see if there's an empty box in the back." He looked up as the air raid siren began to wail..."Hurry up, man, the buggers are here a little too soon for my liking."

Beaston hurried off, sweating. Everard bent down and began tearing at the cardboard in order to get at the cans.

Somehow, the anti-aircraft batteries on Lincoln's Inn and the searchlights missed the Junkers JU-88 as it swooped down low over the City of London. It flew right up over St Paul's and along Holborn Viaduct. The pilot was looking for the Bank of England but the crew, especially the navigator, were hopelessly lost. They had tossed out some ordnance en route and all that was left was a solitary parachute bomb. The searchlights caught the plane just as the parachute fluttered slowly down through the night sky. The batteries let off a massive barrage of shells at the plane, which was rapidly gaining height as it sought to get away as quickly as possible. Porteous thought he could hear the droning of the plane from under the boxes, and then...it all went silent.

The parachute mine landed about twenty-five yards from Jimmy Ryan's shop in the back alley. It took out nearly all the properties within the close proximity. Inspector Eric Everard and Sergeant Derek Beaston felt the shockwave of the blast from the one thousand kilogram bomb a split second before they disintegrated into small fragments...

The box van parked directly in front of the shop took most of the blast. If Porteous could have seen it, he would have witnessed a spectacular demolition of the metal and wood vehicle. Instead, the police issue Vauxhall 12 saloon was literally picked up and thrown twenty yards down Red Lion Street. Its windows smashed into hundreds of little pieces as the car stopped sliding on its roof before it came to a halt upside down outside a public house.

Porteous couldn't remember much else after that as blackness closed in on him...He thought he was having another asthma attack.

Peter Porteous slowly opened his eyes. Bright winter sunshine streamed across the room. He shook his head; it hurt. He felt a hand on his bandaged arm. The smiling face of Nancy Keeling peered down at him,

"I always said you were a lucky bugger..."

She reached in and hugged him tight.

He asked, "What happened?"

"The auxiliary firemen pulled you out from under an upturned police car at the bottom of Red Lion Street."

"What was I doing there?"

Nancy leaned closer, "Jimmy says that bloody detective arrested you."

It slowly came back to Porteous..."Oh, yes. Is Jimmy all right?"

She nodded. "He said some friendly fireman cut off your handcuffs in return for one of the boxes. The other firemen stole the rest. Jimmy came back for you after the bomb went off."

Porteous sighed, "There were some good silk stockings there."

Nancy rapped him on the arm, "Never mind about that, how are you feeling?"

He made to get up, but Nancy pushed him back down, "Stay there."

He asked, "Where's Elizabeth?"

"In school. She wanted to come and see you, but they won't let in children. I'm not supposed to be here but I charmed my way in with the handsome doctor over there. He asked me if I was a relative; I told him you are my fiancé."

Porteous smiled; some things never change.

Nancy said, "They're not letting you out for a few days, you've got several stitches in your forehead but don't worry it won't spoil your good looks."

"What happened to Everard and his mate?"

Nancy shook her head, "Nothing left of them. It's as though they never existed. The police came and took away the car, not that it's much use to anyone apart from the scrap."

Porteous related the events of the night; Nancy sat there open-mouthed...

Chapter 25
March 1941
The last victims

Margaret Heywood did not leave her flat for three days. She didn't even bother getting dressed. After she had helped kill Michael "Mifty" Mitchell and stood and watched as Nancy Keeling and the funny one, what's her name? Oh yes, Alice Halpin, drive off into the night, with the car gears crunching, Heywood slowly made her way down West End Lane and back to her flat. She had polished off what remained of the bottle of gin, lay under the covers of her bed and went to sleep.

She had woken the following morning still dressed. She got up, and while the kettle was boiling on the little gas ring, she peeled off her clothes and tossed them into the linen basket. She pulled on a dressing gown and retired back to bed. She knew that neither Mitchell nor Fox would be coming for her.

There being no gin left in the flat, Margaret Heywood decided to get dressed. She pulled on some old clothes and went down the stairs and out of the flat. She walked up to Kilburn High Road, where she passed a working men's café. The smell of frying food made her tummy rumble; she hadn't eaten for several days.

She pushed open the door and entered; the place was half-empty. She went up to the counter and ordered some fried bread and eggs. She handed over a ration coupon for the egg...

She sat down at a table and picked up a copy of the previous day's Evening News. Her eyes opened wide as she read about the Blackout Strangler's latest victim.

It had been common knowledge amongst the working girls in the West End about the serial murderer, but the authorities had suppressed the story for fear of frightening the public further at the height of the bombing. Margaret Heywood read about his latest victim, a part-time married prostitute named Doris Jounannet.

Jouannet took her paying customers back to the flat she shared with her husband in Sussex Gardens in Bayswater. The husband, Henri Jouannet, returned home from his night shift in a hotel to find his door locked.

Heywood began to eat the breakfast. She read slowly and carefully.

Not being able to enter his home, Henri summoned the police. His wife had been strangled with a knotted stocking and then extensively mutilated.

Heywood felt the bench move as she read. She looked across at a casual acquaintance from the High Road, Hazel Brennan.

Brennan was another part-time lady of the night; she asked,

"Have you read this?" She pointed to the paper.

Heywood nodded, "When are they going to catch this bastard?"

Brennan asked, "Are you going to eat the piece of fried bread?"

Heywood pushed over her plate, "Help yourself; I've gone off the idea."

Brennan picked up the bread, "That's four of us he's done, Maggie."

"That's why I only work for Charlie Maitland."

Brennan scoffed, "Huh! Charlie Maitland? The police are all over him and his business at the moment. They emptied that brothel on Maida Vale. Word is that he had a couple of under-age girls working there."

Heywood stared ahead; she knew Mitchell wouldn't pick her up any more...She still needed money for her boarding house on the south coast.

Heywood folded the newspaper.

Brennan asked, "What about we go out together this evening? I could do with some money."

Margaret Heywood hesitated, "You mean freelance?"

Brennan sipped at Heywood's tea, "Well, what's to stop you? None of Maitland's pimps are on the streets."

"I'm not sure with this maniac around."

"Look, if we stay together and just do a couple of quickies in a shop doorway or something, we'll be okay if we stick together. There are always a couple of girls in an alley at the back of Regent's Street. It's perfectly safe there."

Heywood still wasn't sure, but she reluctantly agreed, "Oh, go on, Maggie. I'm behind with the rent and I don't want to go on my own."

Later that evening, Margaret Heywood met Hazel Brennan in a crowded teashop in Piccadilly Circus. The place was full of service personnel from all three branches of the British military and some overseas units. They sat and drank some overpriced tea at a small table. They were both dressed for their work. Brennan looked particularly good; she prided herself on being able to finish a man off in less than five minutes after pocketing an appropriate fee, of course. A couple of men approached them, but they turned them away.

They walked up Regent's Street arm in arm. A few swigs from Margaret's hip flask soon smoothed off any fraying edges. They stopped in a darkened shop doorway.

"Here, this will do for a tug or a blow. If they want something else, the alleyway is just at the back."

A soldier dressed in army uniform approached. After two or three minutes, Hazel Brennan, winked at Heywood and led the man by the hand into the alleyway at the rear of the shop.

Heywood stepped out of the shadows of the doorway. A man in a Royal Air Force uniform appeared,

Gordon Cummins asked, "Are you doing business, love?"

Margaret Heywood hesitated, "It all depends on what you want?"

Cummins smiled, "How about we go back to your place? I've got plenty of money." He showed her several one-pound notes.

She shook her head, "No; it's either in here or around in the alley at the back where my friend is."

Cummins looked around, "How about two pounds at your place, or some hotel?"

Heywood shook her head, "No. It's either here, around the back, or not at all."

Cummins saw red mist in front of his eyes. He reached in and grabbed Margaret Heywood by the arm. He attempted to kiss her, but she pushed him away. His hands went to her throat; he began to squeeze. She thrashed out, wildly kicking and punching. Cummins' hands gripped her tightly. Margaret Heywood thought about Mifty Mitchell as she slowly lapsed into unconsciousness. Cummins felt her go limp as she slowly descended to the tiles of the shop doorway. He looked around him; no one appeared to have heard the commotion. He rifled through Heywood's handbag but finding nothing of value, he tossed it to one side. He pulled off his gas mask bag and haversack, kneeled down and began to pick at her clothes, trying to undo the buttons of her dress.

He felt a sharp pain on the side of his head as Hazel Brennan swung her handbag hard against the attacker. He stood up as she flailed at him with her hands, nails and fists. He backed away, not knowing what to do. He had desperately wanted to cut Margaret Heywood, who, by this time, was beginning to come around. She coughed and gasped, trying to suck in much-needed oxygen.

Cummins stood back, realising his evening was ruined. He pushed Brennan out of the way and ran off back down towards the crowds in Piccadilly Circus, leaving behind his personal items.

Brennan helped Heywood to her feet,

"Jesus, Maggie, what was all that about?"

Heywood gasped, "That's the bastard..." She started shouting and screaming, attracting the attention of several passers bye and Police Constable James Skinner.

Skinner picked up Gordon Cummins discarded gas mask and haversack and escorted a somewhat reluctant Margaret Heywood to West End Central

Police Station, where she gave a full statement about her assailant. She finished off the evening having her injuries looked at by a doctor in a nearby hospital.

A few days later, Margaret Heywood picked Gordon Cummins out of an identity parade. The serial numbers on both his RAF issue gas mask and haversack led police to his unit. A search of his belongings turned up a few of the possessions of the murder victims.

Margaret Heywood decided that it was time for her to leave the oldest profession in the world...

The following week, a naked Nancy Keeling slipped quietly and effortlessly into Peter Porteous' bed. He did not push her away when she climbed on top of him...

Chapter 26
April 1958
Cheetham Hill, Manchester
Another story

Nancy Porteous smiled as the little boy ran to her with open arms at the end of the school day. She picked her way through groups of parents congregating at the school gate. She swept him up and squeezed him tight,

"Jack; how was your school day?"

He looked at her, "It was boring, Nanny."

She laughed as his older sister came up chatting to her school friends. Nancy reached out and patted her on the head, "How about you, Hope? How was your day?"

Hope Stevenson smiled, "Same as usual Nanny…"

Nancy took both of them by the hand and led them to her home about one mile away. It was a familiar routine for them ever since she had left Kensal Town all those years before. Her adopted daughter, Elizabeth, had changed her name to Porteous when Nancy had finally managed to get him up the aisle at the church in Bosworth Road. The diocese eventually removed that disgusting parish priest. It seemed that there were too many complaints about his lecherous behaviour for the Catholic Church to ignore. He ended his days closeted in some monastery that seemed to specialise in fallen religious clerics. They managed to keep his offending behaviour away from the police.

The neat little three-bedroomed semi-detached house had a small garden at the rear. Nancy's son-in-law, Francis, had installed a small swing for the children. As soon as Nancy had changed them out of their school uniforms, they ran out of the kitchen door. She smiled at them through the window as they played as though they didn't have a care in the world. She was always thinking of her own childhood back in Norwich where her feckless, alcoholic mother had often left her and her sister, Charlotte, hungry and cold.

Nancy sighed; those days were long gone. Charlotte now had three of her own children. She lived just across the other side of the park where she juggled family life with her responsibilities as chief engineer for some industrial complex on the outskirts of the city. Nancy often had to collect these youngsters from school as well.

They sat at the dinner table, Hope remarked between mouthfuls of fish fingers,

"Nanny, we had a lesson on the Second World War today."

Nancy looked up, "What did you learn?"

"Oh that lots of children were sent away from their parents because of the bombing."

Nancy nodded, "That's true. Times were hard for you children. Everything was in short supply, and you had to have coupons to buy even basic food."

Little Jack spoke up, "Did they have fish fingers in those days, Nanny?"

Nancy smiled, "Certainly not. You had to be lucky to get your hands on any kind of fish."

Hope asked, "What did you do during the war, Nanny?"

Nancy sat back, "Oh, this and that, but mostly I worked as a typist in a factory that made parts for aeroplanes."

"Did you meet Grandpa Porteous during the war?"

"I did. He was a lovely, kind man. I wish you could have known him."

Nancy looked up as she heard the front door open,

"Here you are; that's your mum."

Jack made to get up, but Nancy glared at him, "Finish your dinner...."

He sat back down as Elizabeth Stevenson walked in through the kitchen door. She bent down and kissed her two children on the top of their heads.

Nancy stood up as Elizabeth wrapped her arms around her neck, "Hey Mum! How have the kids been?" Nancy kissed her on both cheeks.

Elizabeth knew full well that the children would never misbehave when they were with their grandma.

"Oh, you know; little hooligans..."

Both children protested with a smile.

Nancy asked, "How was work?"

Elizabeth shook her head, "They keep giving me really boring stuff to do."

Nancy shook her off, "Well, what did you expect? You've only just been qualified. I do believe that, technically, you are a trainee accountant despite your qualifications."

Elizabeth took off her coat and sighed, "Yeah, I suppose we all have to start somewhere." She sat down as Nancy poured her some tea from the pot.

Nancy asked, "Are you hungry?"

Elizabeth nodded, "But Francis has cooked already, so I'll wait until we get home."

"You didn't forget I can't pick them up tomorrow?"

"No, Charlotte said she would get them. Are you staying overnight?"

Nancy smiled, "That all depends upon Alice and Phyllis."

Elizabeth leaned in, "Yes, well don't drink too much. I know what the three of you are like when you get together."

Hope interjected, "Are you going to see Aunty Alice and Aunty Phyllis tomorrow, Nanny? Can we come with you?"

Jack piped up as well, "Yes, please, Nanny. We love Aunty Alice; she makes us laugh so much."

Nancy adopted a stern attitude, "No, of course not. You've got school. Anyway, Aunty Charlotte will pick you up."

Jack looked crestfallen, "But, Nanny, Aunty Charlotte can't cook..."

Elizabeth and Nancy burst out laughing. "Hush, child, don't you say that to her..."

Just before six, Nancy stood at the doorway of her house as Elizabeth put the children into the rear of the car. She closed the door and went back up to her adopted mother; she hugged her,

"Have a nice time tomorrow and say hello to them for us." She kissed Nancy.

"I will see you at the weekend."

"Yes, do come over on Saturday, and we'll do some shopping."

Nancy squeezed her daughter, "Go on, then, and drive safely."

Nancy Porteous opened the front door of the Edwardian detached house in Sefton Park, Liverpool. It had taken her just over three hours to make the journey from her home in Manchester. Elizabeth was always chiding her to learn to drive but somehow, she had never got around to it.

It was just before midday, and her nostrils were filled with the scent of something cooking nicely on the stove in the kitchen. Alice Halpin looked up and smiled at Nancy as she walked in through the kitchen door and wrapped her arms around her long-time friend.

"Hey! How was your journey?" She leaned back and kissed Nancy,

"Slow and tedious," came the reply.

"Well, pass your driving test and acquire a bloody car. I can get you one from the factory with the employees and family discount, like I've told you several times."

Nancy shook her head, recalling the first time that she had seen Alice Halpin drive on the night when Mitchell and Fox came to a sticky end.

"Where's Phyllis?"

Alice turned back to her cooking, "She had to go into the office; some flap or other, but she'll be back later." Alice looked at the kitchen clock,

"Is it too early for an apéritif?"

Nancy smiled, "Oh, go on then, I haven't had a drink since the last time I was here."

Alice wiped her hands on her apron, lowered the gas under the pot and went into the front room. She returned with an unopened bottle of gin, a bottle of tonic and two glasses. She sat down at the table and poured a couple of generous measures.

Nancy looked at Alice; she still had her boyish charm, even though there were now little flecks of grey in her auburn hair that was tied back in a ponytail. She was still a very beautiful woman. The two sat in silence as they sipped the gin. There was an unspoken bond between the two of them that only they would ever know...

Alice pointed to the gin, "Just the one, Nancy. Phyllis wants to talk to you."

"What is it?" Nancy was intrigued.

"She'll tell you when she comes in."

They chatted for some time about family, and then Alice served up lunch. They were clearing away when Nancy heard the door.

"That'll be Phyl; go and say hello."

First Officer Phyllis Manley of the Women's Royal Naval Service stood at the door, shaking off the Liverpool rain. She was dressed in civilian clothes, but Phyllis always looked elegant no matter what she wore.

They hugged, "How are your brats?"

Nancy smiled, "Still brats."

"You are lucky to have them; three from Charlotte and two from Elizabeth. What more could you ask for?"

"I dunno, perhaps some financial help on birthdays and Christmas..."

Phyllis playfully punched her on the arm, "You've got plenty of money, not like us working girls."

"Does the Admiralty not pay you enough?" Nancy laughed.

Phyllis looked down and smiled, "if it wasn't for Alice's salary at Ford's we'd be below the poverty line..."

Nancy looked through the front door window. "How is that I see two rather nice new cars on the driveway?"

Phyllis put her fingers to her lips, "Shhh; we don't want the neighbours to know we stole them..."

Alice called out from the kitchen, "Phyl! There's some lunch for you here. Come and get it before it gets cold."

"I'm just going to change and wash my hands; pour us a gin, will you?"

Later that afternoon, the three of them sat in the front room. The bottle of gin was half empty. They had laughed and cried a lot, reminiscing about their wartime exploits.

Phyllis Manley put down her glass, "Listen, Nancy, I'm going to tell you a story. It's not a complete story, but it's as much as I can say at the moment. You know I'm bound by the Official Secrets Act?"

Nancy sat up, Alice shifted a little uncomfortably on the sofa next to her lover.

"You know in 1943 I was transferred from the Admiralty to HMS Pembroke V?"

"Yes, it upset Alice because she thought you'd be away a lot more."

Phyllis nodded, "Well, it wasn't that bad, as I was stationed in Buckinghamshire."

Nancy agreed, "Yes, you were at home a lot whilst we were still at Smiths"

"In 1946, I was responsible for helping clear out all the files and equipment when HMS Pembroke was being closed down. I can't tell you what went on up there but the war had ended, and its functions were being transferred to a different site."

She paused and sipped her drink, "One of my jobs was to examine the files that the girls brought me, and then I had to decide which ones needed to be kept and which ones could be destroyed. Most of it was routine administrative information about purchasing and equipment. Well, in one box was a pink file. It shouldn't have been there. All pink files were classified Top Secret. It looked as though it had been misplaced there because it was inside a non-classified brown file."

Phyllis stood up, "This wasn't unusual as stuff was always being misfiled. What I would do normally is take anything like this over to Hut 4 where Naval Intelligence was housed. I wasn't cleared for access to these premises. I would just hand it to one of the officers there. Well, as I took it out of its cover I noticed that it was entitled 'Kensal Town.'"

Nancy sat up, "What? Kensal Town?"

Phyllis nodded, "I opened it, and it contained numerous cyphers that had been transcribed from a listening station over in Uxbridge. There were a load of posh girls trained at Collet Court and this one, Cynthia Fleming, was tasked to listen on a certain wavelength for these transmissions. She was helped by a colleague, Henrietta Forbes-Carlton."

Nancy rolled her eyes at the name, "Typical..."

Alice snorted, "They get everywhere...."

Nancy interjected, "Go on, Phyl..."

Phyllis spoke quietly, "Now, I've got to be careful here. The cypher head was called John Porter; his handwritten notes were all over the file. He was some boffin from one of the universities; we lesser mortals didn't have much to do with these people. They kept themselves to themselves. It seems that the high-ups were convinced that these signals were coming from Kensal Town. They were getting much better at intersecting the signals but they never did manage to decipher them. Porter had written one word on one of the pages in bold writing,

Books?"

She paused and said, "I have no idea what that means."

Nancy sat on the end of her armchair, "Maruska?"

Phyllis nodded, "I did a bit of digging at the Admiralty. The files are currently closed, but I'm pretty sure several meetings were held with MI5; they are on the calendar and Porter's written notes are still there. Do you remember the day after that landmine went off destroying Porteous' house, several units arrived in Kensal Town including the police and the Army?"

Nancy nodded, "Yes, that's when Maruska was killed. It caused quite a stir amongst the locals. They detained Edith and Porteous."

"I think they were looking to arrest her..."

"Arrest who?"

"Doctor Maruska Bergman..."

The room went silent, Phyllis stood up, "I've told you too much already. Don't breathe a word of this to Elizabeth, do you understand, Nancy? This is between us only."

Nancy Porteous stared into space.

"Nancy! Nancy! Do you hear me?", Phyllis Manley raised her voice...

Nancy spoke quietly; "Elizabeth never met Maruska."

Phyllis Manley sat back down, "I just thought you should know, that's all. Porteous had a rose-tinted view of his pretty doctor. She could do no wrong for him. Perhaps if he'd known the truth about her, things wouldn't be quite the same."

First Officer Phyllis Manley decided the rest of the story could wait for another time...She looked out of the window, "Come on, you two, it's stopped raining. I fancy a stroll around the park with two beautiful ladies on my arm..."

Nancy Porteous popped into the small downstairs toilet and cried for the loss of her husband...

Author's Notes
The Ha'penny Steps trilogy is a work of fiction.

Research for this series commenced several years ago. Having written books about contemporary London fiction, I had always been fascinated about the area of London in which I lived and worked. I was a young teacher in Kensal Town and I became even more interested in this area that is steeped in working class history.

I went back to Kensal Town in 2021 only to find the original Ha'penny Steps bridge over the canal had been demolished by the local authority and replaced by a modern, easy access crossing. The picture of the original bridge that adorns the covers of all three parts of the trilogy has been taken from a series of photographs on Pinterest. I am also indebted to local librarians and historians who have been helpful in finding pictures of the area pre-demolition and the original Steps.

It was whilst watching the black and white film "The Blue Lamp" of 1950 that my imagination was finally stirred into life. The film has a few shots of the original buildings and tenements on Kensal Road and Bosworth Road. There are little, if any of these buildings left. The Roman Catholic Church on the corner of Hazelwood Crescent and Bosworth Road, The Church of Our Lady of the Holy Souls, remains in all its glory. I do not know if the crypt was actually used as an air-raid shelter during the height of the Blitz, but please allow me some artistic licence.

The Catholic primary school at the bottom of East Row still exists. It was opposite this school that Porteous moved after his home on Bosworth Road was demolished by the parachute land mine in

Part 1 of the series. Again, I do not know if there were ever any houses there, as I can find no existing pictures of the road. Much of the original estate was demolished as part of The Royal Borough of Kensington and Chelsea's slum clearance programme post-war. Many of the houses suffered bomb damage owing to their proximity to the major railway lines that ran into Paddington Station.

The 1951, Ordinance Survey map number 51/28 SW, which I acquired from the National Library of Scotland, is the closest I could find to an actual representation of the complete area, but even this shows some of the bomb damage that was noticeable on The Blue Lamp. The area between Bosworth Road and East Row is now completely taken up by the open recreational space, the delightfully named Emslie Horniman's Pleasance. Mr Horniman, a wealthy politician, donated the land and funds upon which the park was created in 1911. The park was extensively renovated in the 1990s.

Kensal Town is sometimes referred to as Kensal New Town and should not be confused with Kensal Rise which is about two or three kilometres to the north, up Kilburn Lane and into Chamberlayne Road. Kensal Rise was formerly in the Borough of Willesden, now Brent.

From the earliest records, it can be seen that Kensal Town was unique in its own way. Bordered by the Grand Union Canal and the Harrow Road on the North Eastern side (over which the Ha'penny Steps crossed) and the major railways lines into Paddington Station to the South West, it is easy to see how the area became isolated, even more so before the Steps were constructed. It was an essentially working class area, often occupied by the Irish labourers who helped construct both the railway line and before that, the canal. Sanitary conditions were poor with several families sharing one toilet. Criminality was rife throughout, facilitated by the abundance of public houses, some of which still exist to this day. The construction of a public washhouse in Wedlake Street points to the complete absence of bathing facilities in most of the houses. Victorian newspapers often record the prevalence of dog fighting, upon which there was a thriving betting industry.

What is known is that the police rarely crossed the Ha'penny Steps except in pairs and preferably mob handed.

Wartime Prostitution

The West End of London, Soho and around parts of Mayfair and Piccadilly Circus, were literally crawling with prostitutes, both during the Second World War and immediately afterwards. The sudden influx of military personnel, both local and foreign, created a massive demand for the service of sex workers, many of whom were part-time. There is evidence to show that some women turned to prostitution when their husbands were away on active duty to supplement the family income. Some of these workers were freelance, but many were controlled by what are usually referred to as pimps. These people were usually attached to organised gangs. What is known is that areas were carefully protected and woe betides any women caught freelancing.

The situation did not improve post-war as battered Britain embarked on reconstruction. It was not until the Street Offences Act of 1959 that open blatant soliciting was outlawed. This had the immediate impact of removing the working girls off the streets. The Act also applied to the hundreds of night cafés that were used by sex workers and their clients as regular meeting places. The term 'common prostitute' was not removed from the statute books until 2009.

It is sad to say that child prostitution was common until the law began to crack down upon it in the middle of the 19th Century. The 1861 Offences Against the Person Act made it a felony for a male to have intercourse with a girl under the age of twelve (it had previously been ten.) It was not until 1885 that the law was changed to sixteen as the minimum age for consent. Up to that point, carnal knowledge of an under age girl was considered merely as a misdemeanour. Following the passage of the 1885 Act, the numbers of convictions rose dramatically as girls were encouraged to come forward.

It was common knowledge that some of the large Georgian and Victorian houses at the top end of the Edgware Road (the old Roman Road, Watling Street) that runs directly north of Marble Arch and onto the road known as Maida Vale, were child brothels. These establishments were frequented by the wealthy and famous. Girls as young as twelve were often picked up during police raids on the houses. Pressure from improved policing, and from society in general, brought about a rapid decline of this business in these houses. Local newspapers of the early 19th Century often refer to these as disorderly houses. Newspaper articles casually report the ages of the women and girls picked up by the police. Of course, the law only rarely applied to members of the upper classes and the aristocracy.

In some parts of the world, the age of consent still remains below 16. In the Comoros in Africa, it is 13. In Brazil and China, it is still 14. What should also be noted is that increased prostitution led to a corresponding increase in the incidence of venereal disease amongst serving personnel despite many prevention campaigns, and these were the days before the wide use of penicillin.

The Messina Brothers

The five Messina brothers were the sons of Giuseppe Messina, who was a notorious brothel keeper of Maltese origin. Giuseppe and his sons were expelled from Cairo in 1932 for prostitution and the running of brothels. They were returned to Malta, where they had citizenship. The third son, Eugenio, moved to London in 1934, along with his French wife. They set up a thriving prostitution business in and around Central London but concentrating on the Soho area. The other brothers soon followed and anglicised their names. Carmelo became Charlie Maitland, one of the villains of this story. Soon, they had taken over the business from their rivals, and at one point were reckoned to own and run at least thirty brothels.

Initially, they imported women from Belgium, France and Spain. This would now be considered human trafficking. They operated with impunity because of good protection from the Metropolitan Police. At one point, Attillio Messina or Raymond Maynard to give him his English name, stated to the press,

"We Messina are more powerful than the British Government. We do as we like in England."

Following an exposé in a tabloid newspaper and the subsequent public pressure, Scotland Yard was embarrassed into action and set up a task force to investigate the brothers. It should be noted that the Vice Squad (see below) was not asked to undertake this work. By the end of the 1950s, the Messina brothers had been forced to leave the United Kingdom.

Two of the brothers resurfaced in Belgium back in the brothel business but were apprehended, jailed and eventually deported. With the family broken up, Carmello (Charlie Maitland) attempted to re-enter Britain but was arrested and given a six-months prison sentence, after which he was deported to Italy where he died in 1970.

The Messina brothers were at the forefront of organised crime in the 20th Century in London, where they operated under the protective eye of units of the Metropolitan Police. Many infamous gangs followed them, including the Kray twins in the East End and the Richardson family south of the river.

The Clubs and Vice Squad

More commonly known as the Vice Squad, this branch of the Metropolitan Police was originally established in1932 and eventually ended up on the third floor of West End Central Police Station in Saville Row. Its primary focus was to deal with prostitution, nightclubs, licenced or otherwise, gaming and casinos. Its proximity to Soho made it ideal for monitoring the vast prostitution that was rampant in the area.

Many of the illegal nightclubs were in the control of organised crime gangs, which frequently ran prostitution from the premises. The Vice Squad seems to have operated under its own special rules. Its officers jealously guarded their positions, and outsiders were actively discouraged from interfering with what they considered to be internal matters.

The problem was there existed a far too cosy relationship with the purveyors of vice who appeared to operate with impunity. In short, gang members like the Messina brothers simply bribed their way out of any legal difficulties. It is said that brothel owners and pimps paid the Vice Squad for protection. The street girls also paid off the police, in one way or another, for a quiet life.

The Obscene Publications Act brought extra responsibilities to the Squad, which was tasked to enforce the Act in many of the Soho bookshops. What actually happened was that the policing of these premises afforded Vice Squad officers with yet another lucrative income stream. However, this eventually led to the downfall of the unit.

Another exposé in the press highlighted the rampant corruption of one major pornographer and the huge amounts of money he was paying to officers of the Squad. Again, stirred into action by public pressure, an investigation led to the exposure of some very senior corrupt officers including a detective chief inspector, a superintendent and a commander. The investigation led to the dismissal of over twenty detectives. One superintendent was given a twelve-year prison sentence.

The Squad never really recovered from this. To prohibit officers becoming too cosy with the gangs, they were rotated after a maximum of twelve months. This made the posting much less attractive to recruits.

Changes in licensing laws and the relaxation of gaming regulations removed some of their responsibilities. The unit was eventually axed completely in 2014. Incidentally, its base, West End Central Police Station, was finally closed in 2017. It was from this station that officers were despatched to shut down the Beatles roof top concert in January 1969. This turned out to be the last time the Beatles performed live.

The Blackout Killer, Gordon Frederick Cummins

The crimes committed by Cummins are detailed in the story, although I did move the dates of his crimes to one year earlier in 1941 to fit in with the narrative. He was invariably known as the Blackout Ripper, and the Wartime Ripper. I have seen reports where he was called the Stocking Strangler, owing to his preferred method of despatching his victims before he mutilated them.

He was finally apprehended after his run-in with Margaret Heywood in the shop doorway. He was eventually identified through the serial numbers on his discarded service-issued gas mask and haversack.

He was arrested on 14 February 1942, and charged with the murders of Oatley, Lowe and Jouanet on 16 February. He was tried and convicted at the Old Bailey in April 1942. The jury took just thirty-five minutes to find him guilty, owing to the overwhelming evidence against him despite his pleas of innocence. The Executioner, Albert Pierrepoint, hanged him on 25 June 1942.

Cummins is thought to have killed at least six women and attempted to murder another two. All of these vulnerable women, apart from Evelyn Hamilton, were engaged in the sex trade. He saw them as easy pickings. As he went to the gallows still pleading his innocence, it will never be known what motives he had for his crimes.

Acknowledgements

I read widely around the subject of the London Blitz, including some good fiction, that highlighted the work of the Auxiliary Fire Brigade and the Auxiliary Ambulance Service. I have nothing but praise and gratitude for the men and women who regularly risked their lives for their fellow men.

No Cake, No Jam: Hardship and Happiness in Wartime London by Constantine Fitzgibbon gives a detailed picture of life at the time for the less well off.

Ambulance Girls: A Gritty Wartime Saga set in the London Blitz by Deborah Burrows gives the reader a no holds barred account of life as an ambulance girl.

The Blitz: The Story of the Blitz in London by Constantine Fitzgibbon, gives a thorough and very comprehensive account of the bombing and its impact upon London's residents.

The staff at RAF Burtonwood Heritage Centre in Warrington, including John Cotterill, who patiently answered my questions.

Of course, I greatly acknowledge the part played in *Wikipedia* in my writing. The on-line encyclopaedia is my go-to place not only for facts but also to check references. I contribute regularly to the cause.

Most importantly, I would like to thank my old college buddy, Ken Nevitt, who willingly reads my early drafts and then corrects my historical inaccuracies. His attention to detail is breath-taking...He picks up even the most insignificant factual errors. Thank you, Ken! My work colleague, Chris Hotham, reads the drafts and makes very helpful suggestions. Thanks to him as well.

It goes without saying I couldn't undertake these works without the lovely Anaclette who is not only my biggest critic but also my biggest supporter. She tells me in no uncertain terms where I have gone wrong...

We have tried very hard to eliminate any errors. If you find any, whether factual or typographical please email;

Phoneme52@yahoo.com

CR Spencer. July 2024

Other books by CR Spencer

The Penance Trilogy Penance: Disruption
    Penance: Keeping Busy
    Penance: Absolution
    An Unlikely Killer
    The Opener
    The Closer

All available from Amazon worldwide and Smashwords for Kindle, iBooks, Kobo and Barnes and Noble in all formats.

For a preview of the final part of the trilogy, The Ha'penny Steps Part 3; Alice's Story, read on...

The Ha'penny Steps Part 3; Alice's Story

Prologue Part 1

December 1933

Liverpool

A sudden death

Alice Halpin looked out over the dark and foreboding Mersey River. The currents were fast. The tide pulled the water and anything else that was in it, out into the Irish Sea. She sighed and slowly climbed off the crumbling wall that was all that prevented the river from flooding into the streets that surrounded the old Hornby Dock.

Alice knew these docks better than most. She had played in them since she could ever remember. She knew every nook and cranny; every little hidey-hole where she had first allowed a boy and then, much to her preference, a girl to touch her up or, as the locals would say, 'cop a feel' when she was a little older.

Her heart was still thumping in her chest. At the ripe old age of seventeen, Alice Halpin was physically underdeveloped. She was thin, flat-chested and barely five feet four inches but she had a certain beauty about her. Her boyish looks generated the unwelcome attentions of older boys, who would openly boast that they "would soon sort her out..." Alice Halpin had no problem in attracting members of the female sex. Indeed, she used this talent to her best advantage.

She craned her neck over the dock wall one last time to make sure the body had long slipped into the cold and murky depths of the river. The winter tides would soon pull the lifeless man out into the open sea, where crabs and other sea creatures would have an unexpected feast. The cold Mersey River had claimed many a drunken seaman, dockworker, scallywag and assorted villain over the years. If they were not dead before they entered the cold waters, they certainly would be after ten minutes or so.

Alice spat on her hands and rubbed them vigorously as if to cleanse herself of the man. She extracted a worn handkerchief from the pocket of her coat and dried her fingers one by one. She reached under her skirt and tugged at her knickers for the tenth time, making sure they were firmly attached to her body. She smoothed down her skirt and buttoned up her blouse. The bastard had almost ripped the clothes off her before she had the chance to push him off the dock wall. Drunken men are so much easier to kill...

She breathed out audibly as she placed her back to the wall and allowed herself to slide slowly down into a sitting position; she pulled her knees up to her chest and wrapped her arms around them. She would wait there for some time at least until the numerous pubs in the area closed and emptied out inebriated dockworkers. Friday night was always the busiest. Having finished work for the day, the workers would quickly slip home, hand the missus the pay packet and then go out to the backyard for a cursory swill in cold water before they headed off to some smoke-filled hostelry to drink watered-down ale and boast to their mates. At closing time, Alice could mingle with the revellers as they weaved their drunken way home.

Alice had agreed to meet the bastard at ten, knowing full well that he would have had a skin full by then. As a married man in his thirties, there was no way he would have boasted to his mates that he was about to give a young seventeen-year-old lady "a good seeing to." He was out of his area; he knew no one around these parts. Indeed, it would not have been his preference to meet the Halpin girl at the docks. These places, especially where she lived in Dundas Street and all the way up to the main road into Liverpool city centre, had a reputation for violence.

She wondered how she had arrived at this situation. Here she was a sweet little Catholic girl whose family insisted that she attend church twice on a Sunday, and could she please make sure she didn't go out with any boy of the Protestant faith? Alice shrugged her shoulders. She had no intention of going near any boy, Protestant or not. The bastard whose body was now floating out into the Irish Sea was her factory supervisor. Roger Curlew fancied himself with the ladies, and working in the glove factory out at Litherland, gave him access to many of the fair sex.

Alice had started work there at the tender age of fourteen, much to her consternation. She had wanted to go on to the secondary school, indeed, she had passed the entrance examination, but her father would not hear of it. She needed to join her four older brothers in the world of work to bring money into the family home. The eldest brother, Frederick, was now on the docks. He had a wife and a child. The second eldest, Martin, worked in a warehouse in the city. John was the villain. He didn't really have a job, but he always seemed to have lots of spare cash that he lavishly bestowed upon their mother, Hilda. She wouldn't hear a bad word against her beloved son, despite the fact that the house on Dundas Street had been visited several times by members of the Liverpool Constabulary. The last time was when John liberated a car from outside a large house in Sefton Park. The only problem was that Alice was with him...

The last brother, Peter, was a little simple, or so everyone said. One of her neighbours on Dundas Street claimed that Hilda had dropped baby Peter on his head not long after he was born. Anyway, Peter had a job sweeping up and making tea for his fellow workers in a wine merchant's down by the Pier Head. He dutifully got up for work every morning, took his packed lunch and sat on the top deck of the number 17 tram, did a day's work and went home. He spent his time drawing pictures that he painstakingly coloured in using some watercolours John had found for him. Alice shared a room with him.

The supervisor, Roger Curlew, had used his position to take advantage of Alice Halpin. Indeed, he had raped her in a disused storeroom in the factory when she had just turned seventeen. Roger Curlew paid for this indiscretion with his life.

A distant shout awakened Alice from her thoughts. The church clock began to chime eleven. She shivered as she slowly pushed herself back up to her feet. She adjusted her clothes one last time and began to walk to the source of the noise. A fine rain began to fall. Alice pulled her coat even more tightly around her body. She cursed as the rain fell onto her bare legs. The numerous pubs were tossing out the Friday drinkers. She slowly picked her way through the crowds to The Fleece where she knew her mother and father would be. She stood in the doorway as drinkers pushed their way out. She could hear the ever more bad-tempered landlord, Mr Stepway, shouting at those who were not quick enough to drain the dregs of their beer. Harold and Hilda Halpin appeared at the door. Harold Halpin was very rarely drunk and incapable, just sufficiently mellowed and merry. Hilda had consumed several gins purchased for her by the entourage of friends and acquaintances who only met in the pub or the Catholic Community Club, where the beer was strictly rationed on the orders of the parish priest, Father McDermott.

Alice pushed them apart as they walked and linked her arms between the two of them. Harold Halpin smiled,

"Ah; my precious daughter. I hope you've been a good girl this evening?"

Hilda glanced over at her, "Where have you been, Alice?"

Alice stared ahead, "Over with Esther from the factory. She's teaching me to play Whist."

"Who else was there?" Hilda knew that four people were needed to play that card game.

"Just two other girls for the shift. I don't know them too well."

"You'll have to invite this Esther so that I can meet her."

"Yes, Mum, I will..."

The conversation drifted away. Hilda Halpin never mentioned Esther from the glove factory anymore that evening.

Harold Halpin fiddled with his keys at the doorway to the house on Dundas Street. He couldn't quite fit the key into the lock. Alice took it from him. He smiled as his only daughter opened the door.

Hilda asked, "Do you want some tea, love?"

Alice shook her head, "No, Mum. I think I'll just go to bed."

She went into the kitchen, or what passed for it, opened the back door and ran down to the outside toilet where she vomited violently into the bowl. She spat copiously and then squatted over the wooden seat and urinated. She didn't like using the chamber pot in the small bedroom. Outside on the small paved yard, she pushed on the hand pump and washed her face and hands. She would have preferred a warm bath, but the old tin tub only appeared on a Sunday evening and even then she was last in, as the youngest. Occasionally, her mother let her bathe alone and only when it was her time of the month.

By the time she reached the parlour, she could hear her brother John laughing with his parents. He had acquired a couple of bottles of beer and was busy pouring out the liquid into three glasses. She peered in. He smiled at her,

"Ah, my little sister, would you like a drink?"

She shook her head, "I'm going to bed."

Her father looked at her, "Off you go, kiddo, I'll see you in the morning. Are you coming to the match with me?"

She nodded, "Of course Dad."

Harold Halpin would never miss a game at Goodison Park where his beloved Everton played. The Prods could have their wretched Liverpool across Stanley Park at Anfield. Besides, it was an excuse for a pre-match drink in one of the hostelries surrounding the ground, and it would give Alice a chance to flirt with one of the barmaids and get a free drink whilst her dad wasn't looking.

She climbed the stairs and turned into the small box room that was over an entry to the back garden. The room was bitterly cold in the winter. She would often awake to find frost on the inside of the window. Sleeping attire was definitely more practical than glamorous.

Peter Halpin was hard at work at the small desk under the window. John had rigged up a small table lamp so that he had sufficient light from which to draw and paint.

Alice went up behind him and put her hands on his shoulders,

"Wow, Peter, this is excellent."

She gazed at a picture of a number 17 tram. Peter always seemed to draw trams and the occasional bus.

He looked up at her, "Hello, Alice. Is it time for bed?"

She nodded as she peeled off her coat and dress. She laid the coat on the bed.

"Come, Peter. You can sleep with me tonight. It's too cold to be alone. Go and use the privy and don't forget to wash your hands."

"The water's cold, Alice."

She smiled at him, "Go, quickly, otherwise you can sleep on your own."

Peter Halpin scuttled down the stairs, anxious not to upset his little sister. By the time he returned, Alice was pressed up against the wall on the bottom bunk dressed in a thick cotton, long nightdress buttoned up to the neck and wearing a pair of her dad's woollen socks. She felt him climb in beside her. She reached behind her and pulled him closer. He was soon sleeping.

Alice had a disturbed night; there were too many thoughts going through her head. It's not every day that you kill someone...

Alice Halpin clocked in for the early shift at seven first thing on Monday morning. The glove factory was awash with rumours about the missing supervisor, Roger Curlew. Alice smiled to herself and went over to nurse the ancient stitching machine into life.

www.ingramcontent.com/pod-product-compliance
Lightning Source LLC
Chambersburg PA
CBHW070744160726
48004CB00001B/33